# The
# Real World

Kathleen Jowitt

2020

Published by Kathleen Jowitt

Copyright © 2020 Kathleen Jowitt

All rights reserved. This book or any portion thereof may not be reproduced or used in any manner whatsoever without the express written permission of the author, except for the use of brief quotations in a book review or scholarly journal.

This book is a work of fiction and any resemblance to any person living or dead is entirely coincidental. Stancester and its institutions are fictitious.

Cover photograph: detail of a window at All Saints' Church, Luddington, Warwickshire

Cover design by Kathleen Jowitt

First printing: 2020

Printed in 9- and 11-point Palatino Linotype

ISBN: 978-0-9935339-4-5

www.kathleenjowitt.com

# The Real World

## Acknowledgements

As ever, my grateful thanks go to those who have patiently and expertly read my drafts, caught my mistakes, and answered my questions, including Grey Collier, Fiona Erskine, Tony Evershed, A. J. Hall, Sam Hill, Nicola Janke, Mthr Jo Kershaw, Cosmo Matthies, Kieran Pearson, and Maggie Tate-Druiff. Any remaining errors are my own fault.

Thanks also to the friends who helped me work through matters arising from one of the themes of this book coming rather closer to home than I'd anticipated. You know who you are.

## *December*

*Merry Christmas to all our friends! Yes, it's the inevitable Russell Christmas letter! Well, 2016 has been another busy year for us. Maybe that's why Angela and I are both thinking about retirement... but not too seriously. Chris and his wife Hannah moved house this year, and they and the children are settling in well. Colette is still living in Stancester with her girlfriend Lydia and working on her PhD. Richie is now back at home with us and is saving up to go travelling the world in the new year. Might as well get the use out of those maroon passports while we've got them!*

'So,' Colette's mother said, 'are you and Lydia going to get married?'

Colette dried three bone-handled knives and added them to the pile on the table before she answered. 'I don't know.'

'Mm?' The raised eyebrows and neutral, interrogative sound came from Dr Russell's diagnostic toolkit; the mug of sweet tea now cooling on the side was all Mum. Colette was fooled by neither.

'It depends.'

'What does it depend on? Money? Because you know we'd help.'

Colette tried not to squirm. 'I know. It isn't really money.' That was not quite accurate. She tried again. 'We're not nearly at the point where that's what it depends on.'

'You've been together a while now.'

'Four years,' Colette agreed. She hesitated. Lydia's plans were young and nebulous and private, and the whole question was not something that her mother would necessarily understand. She compromised by saying, 'At the moment, we're holding out for a church wedding.'

Her mother touched her gently on the shoulder. 'Oh, darling.'

'I know.' The sympathy hurt.

'And is that realistic?'

'Probably not.'

'Would it matter which church?'

Colette finished drying the cutlery and hoisted herself up to sit on the edge of the worktop. 'We don't talk about it much, because yes, it would matter, and until one or other of the Methodist Church and the Church of England sorts itself out, it can't be either of ours.' She looked at her mother from this unaccustomed viewpoint, noting her angular frame, her neat bob of grey hair, her pale skin sallow from too much time indoors, her black-rimmed spectacles. Was she was seeing her own future? It felt unlikely. It was possible, of course, that she would remember to wear her own glasses more, that her fine brown hair would become better behaved as it greyed, but she could not see her own life settling into the tidy boxes of her parents'. 'You'd want us to, then?'

'Of course I would.' She passed the neglected mug of tea to Colette. 'I'd like to see you settled.'

Colette scowled at the Power Ranger on the side of the mug. 'We're twenty-four. Well, I am. Lydia isn't even that.'

'I know, darling, but perhaps when you've finished your PhD...'

With more force than she'd meant, Colette asked, 'Don't three grandchildren keep you occupied without wedding planning as well?'

'They all adore Lydia,' Dr Russell said serenely.

'As do I. That wasn't what I meant.' With her thumb, she picked at the frayed edge of the cuff of her hoodie.

'We're all very fond of her.' A little hesitation. 'I don't want to nag. It's just that you should know that we do think of her as one of the family, and if you wanted to make that official, we'd be delighted.'

With a slight feeling of guilt, Colette played the Get Out Of Jail Free card. 'Lydia's parents wouldn't feel that way, of course.'

Her mother looked dismayed. 'Oh. No. I suppose they wouldn't.'

There was probably no need to rub it in, but she did anyway. 'They wouldn't come.'

'Really?'

'I'm afraid so.' It was not a lie. Colette slid down from the side to hug her mother. 'I do appreciate you letting me know you'd be happy about it. Just... give it a year or so, OK? Things might change.' She did not specify which particular things those might be. 'Does anything else need doing?'

Together they looked around the kitchen, at the broad pine table with the children's paintings drying on sheets from the *Bromsgrove Standard* at the far end, at the latest batch of Christmas cards stacked unopened on the side, at the rain spattering the window.

'No,' her mother said, 'I don't think there's anything that can't wait.'

Colette rinsed both their empty mugs under the tap, running a cloth around the rims, and left them in the draining rack. 'I'll go and see if Lydia's escaped from the babies.'

'Do. I want to talk to Hannah about... well, things.'

Beyond the kitchen, the house was quiet enough that Colette noticed the creak of the stairs, a sound that had once been as familiar and unremarkable as her own breath. Now she found herself picking her way, mindful of the possibility of sleeping toddlers behind the door at the top of the stairs. She turned the corner onto the landing, and pushed open the door of her own room.

There was a mattress on the floor, but Lydia was on the bed at the moment, flat on her stomach, reading, with her chin propped on one hand and her feet in the air, crossed at the ankle. The light from the bedside lamp turned her tawny hair into a tangle of gold, and her skin to honey. When Colette shut the door she closed the book and placed it on the windowsill, then rolled onto her back. 'Everything OK?'

Colette smiled down at her. 'Fine. Mum's gone looking for Hannah, I assume to talk gruesome gynaecological details over gin and tonic.' She kicked her slippers off and came to lie on the bed alongside Lydia. 'I had a text earlier.'

'Mm?' Lydia pulled her closer.

Colette buried her face in the softness where the collar of Lydia's rugby shirt met the warm skin of her neck. She stayed there for a few moments before asking, cautiously, 'How would you feel about meeting Jess?'

'As in, your ex-girlfriend?' So far as Colette could tell, there was nothing more than curiosity in Lydia's voice.

'As in, my ex-girlfriend. And her current girlfriend, whose name is Izzy. I know nothing more than that.' She added, 'We can be busy if you don't want to.'

Lydia thought about it and then shrugged her shoulders, so far as was possible. 'Yeah, why not? Unless *you* don't want to.'

'I really don't mind either way,' Colette said, and then adjusted that to, 'I think it would be nice to see her, but it's been a while. It might be horrifically awkward.'

'Well, let's find out,' Lydia said cheerfully. 'When?'

'She suggested the twenty-seventh.'

'Oh, we've got all of Christmas to get through, then. What happens next today?'

'Dinner, I suppose. Mum seemed to think that Dad was going to make punch. Be careful of it. He doesn't stint on the booze, Methodist or no Methodist.'

'Noted.' Lydia turned onto her side, pulling Colette towards her, so that they lay thigh to thigh, face to face. 'What I really meant was, does that mean we've got the rest of the afternoon to ourselves?'

*27/12 works for us. Royal oak? Have a lovely xmas x*

When she and Chris and Richie were children, there had been a rule that one present per person (plus, of course, stockings) could be opened first thing on Christmas morning, and that everything else waited until after church. This rule had been relaxed somewhat now there were grandchildren to be considered, but there was such a huge stack of parcels under the tree that it had made very little difference to the timetable: at half past eleven there were still plenty to get through.

Her father had brought a dining chair through from the kitchen and set it next the tree, so that he could distribute presents with minimal exertion. 'And now we have...' He examined the label. His voice barely changed. 'Lydia. From your mum and dad.'

'Thank you,' she said, reaching up from the floor where she was sitting.

Colette glanced downwards to see. It was a smallish, flattish, oblong. Probably a book. Lydia unwrapped the parcel with the same care she had shown with every one so far, lifting the corner of the sellotape with her fingernail, easing the creases out of the paper.

Looking around the room, staring at the bookcase opposite so as not to draw attention to Lydia, Colette tried to tell herself that it was going to be something harmless. *Silas Marner*. Something like that. But she saw Lydia wince. She caught her father's eye and shook her head; he nodded, and went deliberately for a very large, cuboid present. 'And what's *this*? Oh, look! It's for Olivia!'

Olivia attacked the parcel with panache. Lydia took advantage of the distraction to shuffle up closer to Colette's chair. Silently, she handed the book up to her, its wrapping paper still trailing from the cover.

*Following the Straight Path: faithful living*. Colette turned it over and over, reluctant to look inside. Back in the flat they rented in

11

Stancester, in the little sliver of a room that served variously as guest quarters, storeroom, and study, there was a box of books like this. Lydia refused to give them to any church or charity shop, for fear of their finding people who might believe them, but could not bring herself to throw them away.

Hannah was saying, with frayed enthusiasm, 'There, Olivia! Isn't that lovely? Say thank you to Granny and Grandpa!'

Colette handed the book back again and squeezed Lydia's shoulder.

'And here's one for Ben!'

Lydia wrapped the paper loosely back around the book and slid it under Colette's chair.

'And look, here's one for Maisie...'

While the children were distracted, another parcel found its way silently out of the pile and into Colette's hand. She glanced at the label, nodded, and handed it down to Lydia, who dipped her head and applied herself to the task of untying the tightly knotted plastic ribbon.

Colette thought that she could just have slipped it off; then she thought that perhaps she might have her own reasons for not doing so. And certainly, when Lydia had at last unknotted the ribbon and peeled off the sellotape and unfolded the paper and extracted a copy of *The Taste of the West Country* ('with love from Abby, Paul, Jeremy and Katie') there was nothing to suggest that anything might have spoiled her morning at all.

The next two days drifted by in a traditional fug of woodsmoke and blue cheese, with children underfoot and a communal, unsuccessful, attempt at a jigsaw. Richie disappeared to visit his girlfriend at her parents' house. Dr Russell was called out to something that looked like a heart attack but wasn't. And Colette managed not to worry too much about what Lydia and Jess would make of each other.

They took the car to the pub. It was the kind of distance that they would have thought nothing of walking in summer, but the road was not well lit, and Colette found that she wanted a solid excuse not to drink. If this was going to be awkward, she did not want to run the risk of making it any more so. She had reserved a table, which probably hadn't been necessary: there was a quiet bustle about the place, but nobody was having to fight over seats. They'd been assigned a corner next to the fireplace. It was the scene of many a Sunday pub lunch in Colette's childhood, but she hadn't ever met Jess here, even after they had both been old enough to be served.

Jess hadn't changed much. The hairstyle was sleeker and sharper, the make-up more expertly applied and considerably more subtle than it had been when they were sixteen – but the restless green eyes, the low, resonant tone of her voice, those were the same.

'Colette!' Jess presented her cheek to be kissed, which threw her a little. 'And you must be Lydia. Lovely to meet you. This is Izzy.'

Izzy had a distinct physical resemblance to Jess, with her small stature and dark hair, but she had not the same vitality. She smiled shyly and said, 'Nice to meet you,' as if she didn't quite believe it but was prepared to go along with the experiment for Jess' sake; which was more or less how Colette felt about it herself.

Lydia was the one who went to the bar and bought the drinks. Colette rather regretted letting her. It meant that, until such time as she returned, she was outnumbered two to one. She sat down; it made her feel less self-conscious about her height, but nullified any advantage she might have gained by it. Still, she would have felt outnumbered by Jess alone.

Jess was asking, 'When are you going back down to the West Country?'

'Thursday. Lydia doesn't get much leave, and I've got a lot to do in the lab.'

'The lab,' Jess echoed. Her admiration seemed to be genuine. She added, 'That's a pity. We're here for New Year. Mum's doing her famous party.'

Colette remembered Jess's mum's famous New Year parties with some fondness, but on the whole felt content to leave them to Jess – and to Izzy. Izzy seemed unfazed by the prospect. Colette smiled at her. Izzy returned the smile, lazily, and extended it to a spot just past Colette's left shoulder, which turned out to be Lydia coming back with the drinks.

'Well,' Colette said.

'Here we are,' Jess agreed.

It was drifting into awkwardness, with no good reason. Colette searched desperately for something to say, and managed, 'Did you have a good Christmas?'

'Yes, thank you, it was good. I was at my dad's. I came back up here this morning.'

She tried vainly to remember where Jess's dad lived these days. Basingstoke? Biggleswade? 'Oh, so you couldn't have met up any earlier than this.'

'Yeah: it sounds like we only just overlap. Of course Izzy's been up here all the time.'

'How did you two meet?' Lydia asked. 'Or should I know?'

Colette shook her head quickly. Jess said, 'A friend set us up.'

'One of my colleagues,' Izzy added unexpectedly, 'whose mum is Jess's mum's next door neighbour.'

'Ah, right,' Colette said, not following.

'What about you two?' Jess asked.

'University.' Colette hesitated. 'Christian stuff.' When she and Jess had been seeing each other, the question of faith had been a chasm that they'd never attempted to cross; she had felt guilty about it at the time, and felt uncomfortable about it now.

Jess smiled kindly. 'That's really nice.'

'It is,' Lydia agreed.

Colette, not wanting to get into details, changed the subject. 'How are your parents, Jess?'

'They're both very well, thank you.'

'Still talking to each other?'

Her smile was just about tolerant. 'Yes, but less than they used to now that Flynn and I have both left home. Homes.'

Colette nodded. 'Well, say hi to both of them for me.'

'I will!'

Colette suspected that the assent was as meaningless as her own request had been. Jess's parents had paid very little attention to the pair of them and their unexpected relationship, having been absorbed in the collapse of the marriage. In retrospect, it seemed surprising that she and Jess had stayed together long enough to break up to leave for different universities: Jess had herself been preoccupied with the divorce, a raging, spitting ball of thwarted willpower, refusing to accept that she was powerless to dictate the terms of anyone else's relationship. Colette retained vivid but unplaceable memories of trailing behind Jess through the aftermath of screaming arguments; of evenings spent bringing her down from high dudgeons; and yet more vivid, more uncomfortable ones of Jess making weapons of both of them and of what they were to each other. She wondered, now, why she had put up with it; it was, she supposed, partly something to do with the sense of being able to help, and partly the undying awe at the idea that bold, brilliant Jess had seen her, looked at her, liked her, chosen her, let the mask slip in front of her.

It was a long time ago.

Jess turned to Lydia. 'And what do you do?'

Colette felt an incongruous moment of alarm, but Lydia said easily enough, 'I'm working for the city council, doing admin for the team that looks after all the parks and sports and leisure facilities.'

'And how's that?'

'It's OK. Nothing wildly fascinating. It's... It's not what I'm expecting to be doing forever, but it's fine for the moment.'

Colette said, 'What she hasn't said is that she's supporting me in my studies. The funding I get is carefully calculated to be not quite enough to live on. At least, not if you want to have any fun, ever.'

'Right,' Jess said. She turned back to Lydia. 'So if you didn't have Colette to worry about, what would you be doing?'

Lydia looked blank, which, Colette knew, had less to do with not knowing the answer, and more with not knowing which of several possible answers would be safest to disclose: to Jess, to Colette, to herself. After a moment, she said, 'Well, I certainly wouldn't be doing a PhD myself. I couldn't afford it, and there's no funding for arts subjects.'

Jess leaned forward as if scenting blood. 'And if I waved a magic wand and gave you the money?'

Lydia laughed. 'I'd have to think of a topic. Maybe one of the Metaphysical poets. Or one of the less obnoxious Beat ones.' She pursed her lips, thinking. 'I'd quite like to do something around the connection between religious experience and physical experience.'

'I think I understood about twenty per cent of that,' Jess said.

Lydia looked rather flustered and self-conscious, but she kept talking. 'Something about *Howl*, maybe. To be honest, though, I'm not really missing university. Except for the lie-ins, of course.'

It was a cue for Colette to make a dig about the gulf between the arts and the sciences, but she was not quite on top of the conversation, and could only manage, 'The lie-ins are great.'

Jess turned back to her. 'So how long do you have left?'

'It really depends on how much longer it takes to get some useful results. I'm not meant to take more than another year over that, and then I've got one more year to write up. But the funding's going to run out sooner or later.'

'And will I understand if you tell me what you're studying?'

'That depends on how good I am at explaining it.' Colette thought it best not to remind Jess how much help she'd given her during AS-level Chemistry; from this distance, she suspected that Jess hadn't needed as much help as all that. 'Do you know what nuclear magnetic resonance is?'

Jess looked blank. Lydia looked amused.

Colette tried, 'How about superconductors?'

'Yes,' Izzy said, rather to Colette's surprise. 'I mean, I guess. As in conducting electricity, right? So more so?'

'That's right. Basically, I'm, er, that is, the project I'm working on, is trying to make spectrometers work *without* having to use superconductors, by using hyperpolarisation.'

Lydia said, 'Do you ever watch those BBC4 documentaries? You might have seen her supervisor. Barry Parnell?'

Izzy shook her head, but said, 'Go on.'

'He's mostly talking about his pet theory,' Colette said.

'Should I have heard of that?'

Colette rather wished that Lydia had not brought Barry into it. 'So the thing with superconductors,' she said, 'is that they only work at really extreme temperatures. Which means that ever since people worked out what they were and that they were a good thing, they've been trying to find a room temperature superconductor. And by "room temperature" I mean the freezing point of water, but that's a lot more manageable than what they currently need.'

'Ha. Ha.'

'Eh? Oh. Right. *Currently*. Pun not intended.' She sighed. Barry's theory made beautiful, persuasive, sense in her head, but fell down the moment she put it into words. 'So my supervisor has a theory – what he calls the Knot Theory, which has caught on, but doesn't help to explain it any better – that what might do it is a sort of matrix, or lattice, inside which hydrogen could be dense enough to bring the temperature up.'

Jess asked, 'So has anybody ever tried? Could *you* try?'

'People have, and... I don't want to say it hasn't worked, because it might have done, but if it did it wasn't for very long. But that might be because it's really complicated, not necessarily because the theory's wrong. And no, I couldn't try it because that's not what my subject is and therefore I have no access to the equipment I'd need.'

'Pity,' Izzy said. 'You could be famous!'

'Unlikely,' Colette said. 'It would still be Barry's theory.'

'You're so clever,' Jess said happily. 'So, Lydia, what's the weirdest thing that's ever happened to you at work?'

The rest of the evening passed in harmless small talk, and Colette wondered both why she had been worrying, and why she'd bothered.

## *January*

*Happy New Year, and a particular 'Welcome back!' to our student congregation.*
*This Sunday is our Covenant Service, when we renew our commitment to God for the coming year. We entrust our whole lives to God, praying that we may be empty or full, set to work or laid aside, that we may receive all things or have things taken away from us, according to God's will.*
*Weekly News*, Wardle Street Methodist Church, Stancester, Sunday 8 January 2017

Colette excused herself politely ('No, I'm not staying for coffee; I'll see you soon...'), pulled the heavy door shut behind her, and stood for a moment on the church steps. A sharp January breeze whirled around her; impulsively, she stretched her arms out into it, imagined it blowing straight through her. Then someone walked past the gateway, and she dropped her hands again.

She always came out of the Covenant Service feeling slightly flattened. This year was no different: as always, she'd found herself not quite equal to the magnitude of the great vow, yet making it anyway, carried along by the rhythm, the way that everybody around her was saying it. Actually, she thought, it had not been everybody: there had been a few faces missing from the congregation, more than could be explained by over-long Christmas breaks. Some people must have remembered what day it was.

It wasn't that she'd forgotten; just that she'd thought that she could cope with it.

It wasn't that she hadn't coped with it; just that it was harder than she'd remembered it being.

*Let me be set to work for you, let me be laid aside for you.*

There was an element of hoping earnestly that it wouldn't come to that, and there was something more, something worthier, that trusted that grace would fill the gaps, that divinity would make possible what humanity couldn't manage. There was, too, a sense that surely lightning couldn't strike twice, that she'd made it through the worst; and, coupled with it, the knowledge that this sense was not to be relied upon.

She was struck, as happened every year now, with a memory of another Sunday in another January, coming home to their student house from another Covenant Service, and finding Lydia, an unexpected guest, deep in conversation with Peter at the kitchen table, two pairs of startled dark eyes turned on her, while the Covenant Prayer still buzzed in her head.

*Let me have all things, let me have nothing.* She had thought it was going to be nothing, and that year she had been given all things.

She had been given Lydia. (Or had Lydia been pushed into her arms, having been given nowhere else to go?)

Peter was as much hers as he always had been, perhaps even more so now that they'd closed the door on other possibilities and settled on friendship.

She had lost Becky, lost her best friend, lost her all in an instant one awful morning.

Colette thought now that she hadn't dealt particularly well with any of it.

And today she'd gone to the Covenant Service and proclaimed her willingness to be given more of the same. She always did. And she always came out of it feeling like this, having stepped forward to the challenge, and then having been unable to keep from flinching when the moment came.

Sighing, she set off down the steps and across the tiny car park. Now that it was past eleven o'clock Wardle Street was beginning to accumulate a gaggle of shoppers; Colette threaded her way between them with a sense of benign disinterest. The sun glinted on plate glass, on the forks and rakes outside Noakes Homes & Gardens, on the spokes of a burst umbrella stuffed handle upwards into a litter bin. Her open coat flapped back against her arms as she walked; the chill was pleasant.

She checked her phone: nothing, yet. Lydia had been on the coffee rota at St John the Evangelist this morning. She made some swift, half-conscious calculations. St John's was about as far from home as Wardle Street, but out to the north of the city rather than the centre. The service there had started half an hour earlier. It was possible for Lydia to get straight home without crossing Colette's path, if she went a little way to the north and crossed the railway at Sutton Road, but she had said something about getting nice bread for lunch, which meant the city centre, really. She shook the consideration off. They would still probably miss each other.

In fact, she caught sight of Lydia as she approached the point where Church Street became Lower Church Street. She paused a moment, thrown by the sight of two people together where she had expected only one. Lydia's shoulders were slightly hunched, as if she had her hands in her pockets; Colette wondered if she had forgotten her gloves. The other person, about Lydia's height, moved with a self-conscious stride that was almost a swagger.

Colette moved off again, waving as she did so. Both of them waved back. A few steps closer, and Colette recognised Rowan Hurst, who was a second-year theology student. She had not seen this tight-waisted, full-skirted coat before, but she thought that perhaps she should not have let it mislead her: it was very much in character for Rowan. She waited at the corner. The pair of them came closer; now Colette could see Rowan's dark hair cropped short at the back and flopping into their eyes at the front.

She said, as they came into earshot, 'Hello, Rowan. Nice to see you. Is it happy Christmas?' Rowan was the sole Eastern Orthodox representation on Stancester University Anglican, Methodist and United Reformed Church Society, of which Colette was by far the longest-standing member.

Rowan grinned back, setting a new nose stud glinting. 'Yesterday. Thank you.'

The three of them set off across the railway bridge together. 'I was just telling Rowan,' Lydia said, 'that they're invited to my birthday party.'

'And I was just telling Lydia that I'm fairly sure that Folksoc have a Burns Night ceilidh that evening.'

Colette said, 'I think they do; but I was going to prioritise Lydia's party, either way. Are you off back to Station Road?'

'Eventually. I could do with a cup of coffee first, though.'

'Do you know,' Lydia said, 'I must have poured thirty cups of coffee this morning, and didn't drink any of them myself.'

'I didn't stay for coffee at Wardle Street,' Colette admitted.

'Ours got bumped because of some kind of shenanigans in the Anglican parish,' Rowan said. 'Shall we find some?'

Lydia glared at an overcrowded Starbucks. 'The cathedral refectory won't be open yet, will it?'

'No,' said Colette, 'but Aunt Nancy's will be.'

Rowan nodded and turned right onto Southview. 'How was your Christmas?'

'Lovely, thank you. It feels like a while ago now.'

'You must be on Epiphany by now.'

'My lot are.' Lydia dodged a pair of teenage girls with big paper bags from the sales. '*Was* it the Covenant Service this morning, Colette?'

'It was,' Colette said. She turned to Rowan to explain. 'This is a Methodist thing. It's the annual *happy new year, God, and, whatever trials you've got lined up for us in 2017, bring it on* service. It's quite intense. I nearly didn't go.'

'Same as every year,' Lydia said. 'Look, let's go round the back of Debenham's.'

There was something that Lydia wasn't saying, a sort of

suppressed excitement incongruously combined with serenity. Colette wanted to comment, but she suspected that if it was something that Lydia felt comfortable saying in front of Rowan, she would already have said it. She decided to leave it for the moment and followed Lydia down the alley towards the Broadway.

'I saw Rosie Piretti before the break,' Rowan said when they could walk three abreast again. 'She wants Cathsoc to do more stuff with AngthMURC this term.'

Lydia led them towards the river. 'Oh, right? Does she mean another joint social, or is she talking about something more in-depth?'

Rowan said, 'Apparently there used to be some kind of ecumenical prayer vigil?'

Lydia and Colette looked at each other and laughed.

'What? What's so funny?'

'Didn't there just,' said Colette. 'Oh, I feel old.'

Rowan was still looking puzzled.

Apparently finding her own pace too energetic for comfort, Lydia unfastened her coat, though she put her gloveless hands straight back in her pockets when she had done so. 'It was how we met,' she explained. 'If you ever wondered how a mild-mannered Methodist happened to come across an earnest Evangelical... well, it was the Vigil that did it.'

'Who are you calling mild-mannered?' Colette objected, still laughing.

Rowan was delighted. 'No! Tell me more! I knew that Lydia was the lesbian that the Evangelical Christian Fellowship couldn't get rid of, but this is new to me.'

'There isn't much to tell, really. Just, well, that was how we met.'

Lydia chuckled. 'Well, the Fellowship President warned me – this was back when I was a very virtuous hall officer – against getting involved in the Vigil, on the grounds that fraternising with the

Catholics and Anglicans might lead me astray from the doctrinal teachings – which I have to admit he was right about, even though we were only doing the catering.'

'I was absolutely furious with Peter for landing me with the token Evangelical.' Colette glanced left and right and crossed over onto the Old Bridge. They had to walk single file again; Rowan ended up in the middle.

'I was deep in the closet,' Lydia explained.

Colette looked back over her shoulder. 'We cooked forty baked potatoes, and shifted maybe two thirds of them.'

'About six months later, I decided to grow up and deal with what was staring me in the face. Not before time.'

Colette glanced back again. Lydia's tone had been self-deprecatingly humorous; her expression was unreadable.

Rowan said, deadpan, 'So you'd say that the Vigil was generally a good idea?'

'It worked out well for us. I'm not sure I could say the same for, er, any wider ecumenical relationships.' Colette quickened her pace a little to attack the steep slope of Bridge Street, shivering as they passed into the shadows that lay across the width of the roadway.

'The Vigil itself was great!' Lydia protested. 'It was just all the politics.'

'I'm sure there's a guide somewhere. Peter used to write everything down for posterity. I think the main point to take away is: when Fellowship decline to get involved, which they will, for goodness' sake don't write to the *STANdard* denouncing them for it.'

Rowan whistled. 'No! Who did that?'

'One of the Cathsoc committee. By that point he'd been around for about as long as I have now, and I can only assume he was very bored. Because anybody could have told you how that was going to work out.'

'I think Peter wrote all *that* down, too,' Lydia said. 'Colette, you've just walked straight past.'

Colette turned back, and saw that Lydia was right. She was also holding the door open. They filed in.

'Did you ever read it?' Rowan asked.

Lydia closed the door after them. 'I don't need to. I was there.'

'It's somewhere in the AngthMURC paperwork,' Colette said.

'Tell me anyway?'

'Let's get coffee first.'

It took, between them, a latte, a double macchiato, a pot of Earl Grey tea, two flapjacks, and a slice of carrot cake, to explain the ins and outs of it, and it felt more petty the more detail they recalled. Rowan was amused and fascinated, as they might have been by a particularly good historical documentary, but clearly felt entirely detached from the whole messy question.

But then, Colette reflected, a whole cohort of freshers had arrived and graduated and gone since then. It was all a very long time ago.

'So,' Lydia said when Rowan had left and they were standing out on the pavement, 'since you brought up the subject of *whatever God has lined up for us in 2017, bring it on*, I thought I should let you know. I've decided.'

Colette had been expecting this, but it still landed hard. She took a breath in. 'You're going to do it. You're going to do the whole "become a vicar" thing.'

Lydia smiled, and then tamed the smile. 'I'm going to see how far I get, at least.'

'OK,' Colette said, very carefully. 'So tell me what happens next.'

'I talk to Marcus.'

Colette tucked her hand into Lydia's elbow, with an obscure sense of having yielded ground. 'Haven't you been talking to him for the last year?'

Lydia nodded, smiling once again. 'Yes. I mean, I follow up on that conversation we had before Christmas. I tell him that he's right, it's time to go for it.'

That seemed logical enough. 'And then what does Marcus do about it?'

'He passes me on to the DDO, who'll probably give me another very long reading list.'

They turned right at the bottom of the hill to walk north-east along the riverbank. The water glittered in the thin sunlight. There was nothing between them and the breeze now. 'Remind me who the DDO is?'

'Diocesan Director of Ordinands. And then, if I've successfully jumped through all the hoops in between, they send me on a BAP.'

'That's the residential thing with all the interviews,' Colette said triumphantly. 'I remember Peter doing it.' Twice. She added, 'I don't remember what it stands for, though.'

'Bishop's Advisory Panel.'

'Nothing to do with bread products, then.'

'In one sense.' Lydia's voice was brittle. 'In another, it has everything to do with them.'

'I suppose it does.'

They walked on in silence for a little while. Colette allowed herself to think that if it all went to plan and Lydia ended up in a vicarage then at least that would solve the problem of rent. Underneath that she was aware of mingled exhilaration and apprehension, and was not sure whether they belonged to herself or to Lydia.

'If I get through that, then there's three years of theological college, then there's a curacy.' Colette knew all this, but she let Lydia run through it once again. 'One year as a deacon, then two as a priest. On the ground, serving people, loving people.'

'Six years, then.' It felt like a lifetime.

'The next few months will be like what I've just done, but more so, going deeper. Talking more. Then I get to the BAP and it's going to be hell.'

Colette nodded. 'I told you the same thing when I started my PhD.' She meant it as a warning, and she suspected that Lydia knew this. It was all very well to talk about following your passion (she had never used those words herself, but plenty of other people had used them on her behalf), but the cost had been more than she had anticipated; more, perhaps, than she had had at her disposal.

Lydia said, 'And you were right.' Her tone was gracefully neutral.

Colette considered how best to put it into words. 'I said that, and I didn't know what hell was like. Now I do.'

Lydia elaborated: 'It might or might not be hell, and I have to do it either way.'

'I know.' She bit her lip. 'I wish you didn't.'

'I think that's how I would have felt about your PhD, if I'd known what it was going to be like for you.'

Colette tried not to let her surprise show. Lydia had never been anything other than supportive, up until now. 'Fair's fair, then?' She raised her eyebrows.

'I've been enjoying it up to now. I still am. It's just... all got real. And the further I get into it, the more of myself I invest. And what if I'm wrong? What if they don't want me? What if I'm *not* wrong and they still don't want me?'

'What indeed?' It was probably not the most helpful response.

Lydia answered her own question. 'I suppose I just keep on at the council until I work out what else to do.'

She found herself wishing that they had talked about it before. It was not really Lydia's fault that they had not: Colette had, out of a combination of delicacy and cowardice, evaded the subject except insofar as it affected their lives on an immediate and practical level. 'And what about me? Doesn't my presence in your life throw a very large spanner into the works before you've even started?'

'Marcus says no.' Lydia did not sound convinced. 'They'll see past you.'

Colette said, with all the sarcasm that she could muster, 'How gracious of them. I can hear Peter singing *Like a mighty tortoise moves the Church of God* at this very minute. Have you talked to him about it?'

'Kind of. Bits of it.' Lydia frowned. 'He sort of gets it, and he sort of doesn't.'

Colette wished that she had been more specific. 'Because he's already got through the process? Or because you're gay, and he's not?'

'Yes. He gets the deep-down existential worry about, you know, *who are you*, if it turns out that you aren't who you thought you were.'

'Well, I would hope so,' Colette said, remembering the fallout from the first time Peter had gone for selection, and been turned down.

Lydia nodded. 'Yes. More than I hope I ever will, though I think he might be beginning to forget what that feels like. Because of course that *is* who he is. But... OK, he *knows* that I might be turned down for the wrong reasons, and he's very ready to get angry about it on my behalf, but I don't think he quite understands how much it's been weighing me down even up to this point. How often I've said to myself that I won't do it after all because of that.'

'Well, yes, but the whole process...?'

'Oh, yes, that.' Lydia laughed. 'He knows about that.'

'And the... wanting to do it at all?' Which was, Colette thought, the hardest thing of all to understand. She took her hand back, suddenly needing space.

Lydia nodded. 'He wouldn't have gone through the whole thing twice if he didn't, would he?'

Children's shrieks and laughter drifted across the river from the public gardens. 'Where did it start?' Colette asked, hurrying to get the words out before she lost her nerve. 'When did you know?'

Lydia met Colette's eye, and glanced away again. 'The answer to that one changes every time I talk to Marcus.'

'As far back as your church in Hastings?'

A self-deprecating smile. 'Looking back that far, I can see it coming. Well, there was Sunday school, and holiday club, and the band. But no, *that* obviously wasn't going to go anywhere. I was a bit too female.'

'What about when you were a hall officer for Fellowship? Same thing?'

'Yes, same thing. Still too female. And too gay.' Lydia hesitated. 'I think that I really began to understand when Becky died.'

Colette was silent: shocked, and impatient with herself for being shocked.

After a little while, Lydia said quietly, 'There was nothing I could do. Nothing that anybody could do. Nothing that I could say to make anything better. Nothing that I could say that wouldn't have been offensively trite. And yet there we all were, having to live in that house where she wasn't any more. You and Will and Georgia, all devastated in your own different ways. And all I could do was to be there. Which in itself sounds offensively trite, now.'

'You *were* there,' Colette said, low, not entirely trusting herself.

Lydia glanced at her, judging, Colette supposed, how much further it was safe to go. 'I think that up until that point I'd always thought, you know, it wasn't as bad as all that, you could pray harder and things would look better. That God would give you strength. But when Becky... well, that was when I realised that no, it was exactly as awful as it looked, and I was still called to be there. At the foot of the cross, you know? I was more use to you than I was to Will or Georgia, I expect, but at least I was some use to somebody.'

Colette was not sure that she could bear much more of this line of thinking. She returned to the present. 'What does it *feel* like?' she asked.

'Sometimes it feels like restlessness, like I know I'm not doing what I'm meant to be doing.' She broke into a smile. 'And sometimes it's like this certainty at the back of my mind that this is what I'm going to do next, and when I'm not thinking about it then that's what I think I'm going to do. Like, if I get asked the *where-do-you-see-yourself-in-five-years* question, then the answer that first comes to mind is *well of course I'll be a minister.*'

'The way your parents assume that of course you're going to university, and so you do, too?'

'*Your* parents, maybe. But yes, a bit like that. But more –' She broke off, thought for a moment, and continued: 'Did you ever have a moment of revelation, when it occurred to you that no straight person would worry as much as you were worrying about whether they might be queer?'

'*Oh.* Yes. About three weeks after I started going out with Jess, actually.' After two terms' worth of a miserable crush on the Head Boy followed by the world-expanding experience of that unlikely relationship, it had been a liberating realisation for her. Judging by Lydia's face, her feelings were more mixed. 'So is that what it's like?'

'I think that's what's going on. Like, if God wasn't calling me – to *something*,' she added hastily – 'then I wouldn't spend so much time thinking about whether or not I was being called. Unless it's, what's it called when you think so much about something that you keep seeing it everywhere?'

'Confirmation bias.'

'Yes. That. But it doesn't feel... I mean, it *does* feel...' She shook her head. 'Well, I did turn out to be gay. And so I think there probably is something going on, and it feels just as huge and important and impossible.' Her face changed. 'And then I think about it and I remember all the reasons why it might not be going to happen, and there's this immense sadness about the whole thing. And – this is going to sound weird –'

'Go on.'

'It doesn't feel like it's all *my* sadness. Because I'm not sad at all, really. I like my job and I love you and I have a church where I feel like myself, and things are honestly really good. It's like someone's sad on my behalf, and sometimes I can hardly bear it.'

Colette looked behind them, then ahead, and put her right hand into Lydia's pocket to take her left one. 'And yet you keep going with it.'

Lydia's expression was heartbreakingly earnest. 'Of course I do. Because it's an active kind of sadness; it's quite close to anger; it keeps bubbling up through the cracks, and I know that if the answer *is* no then it'll find something else to do, but I've got to follow it as far as it's... navigable, I suppose.' She laughed. 'Good grief. What a tortured metaphor.'

'I think I get the idea.'

'And then, sometimes, when I think, *yes, this is going to happen*, I just get this amazing sense of peace, of rightness. The first time I spoke to Benjy about it. The time I admitted to Felicity that yes, she was onto something.' She paused for a moment. 'And today.'

*From: m.dewitt@stan.ac.uk*
*To: [undisclosed recipients]*
*Monday 9 January 2017, 10:19am*

*Welcome back! Hope everyone had a great Christmas. AngthMURC meetings begin again this Wednesday at 8pm in the Chaplaincy Centre when we welcome speaker Stevie Symonds from Stancester Fair Trade Link.*
*Hope to see you there!*
*Megan*
*Vice-President, Stancester University Anglican, Methodist, and United Reformed Church Society*

Lydia was already dressed for work when Colette came out of the shower. 'I'll be late home tonight,' she said. 'I'm meeting the DDO.'

She wanted to say, *So soon?* She settled for, 'Oh, right?'

'She's the vicar of St Andrew's, so I'm going to meet her at Curzon's, if we can dodge all the students.' St Andrew's was the closest church to the university campus, and its congregation had a significant crossover with that of the university chapel.

Colette adjusted the collar of her dressing gown: she had towelled and combed her hair, but there was still some water dripping down her neck. 'Would I know who she is?'

'Maybe. Reverend Tina Audley?'

The name seemed vaguely familiar, but Colette was unable to attach it to any real person. 'Does Peter know her?'

'No idea.' Lydia made a face. 'I'd assume so; he knows everybody. I mean, St Andrew's isn't nearly as High as All Saints, but it's definitely the same kind of atmosphere. On the other hand, I think she's quite new. Only been here the last couple of years or so.'

Colette abandoned the question. 'So are you going to eat out?'

Lydia glanced in the direction of the kitchen. 'I'll probably have a sandwich, either in town or when I get back here. I don't know how long this is going to take.'

'In which case I'll go straight to AngthMURC.'

'Oh, yes. I'd forgotten it was Wednesday. Well, if there are any of them there who know who I am, you can invite them to my birthday party.'

'I'll do that.'

'Thanks.'

'So,' Colette said, as Lydia gulped her coffee, 'is this the point where I tell Mum to lay off the whole marriage thing because you're going for ordination?'

Lydia blinked a couple of times. 'Is that OK with you?'

'It's fine with me. I've been feeling... not guilty, exactly, but a bit odd, about not telling her what the real reason is.'

'I'm sorry.'

'Don't be. I'm sorry *she's* been pushy about this.'

Lydia said, 'I like your mum.'

Colette laughed. 'So do I. It's just that she doesn't know when to leave well alone.'

'Well, you can tell me later what she makes of it.' Lydia looked at the clock on the oven. 'I'd better go. Love you. Say hi to AngthMURC for me.'

Colette caught her in a swift hug. 'Love you, too. Good luck tonight.'

She dressed at a leisurely pace. Officially, she was due to meet her supervisor at ten o'clock that morning; unofficially, she suspected that this meeting would fare no better than its predecessors of recent weeks. She had been meant to meet Barry since before Christmas; his filming schedule had put paid to their December meeting. She looked at his Twitter feed: other than retweeting someone enthusing about his knot theory, he had posted nothing that might indicate which continent he happened to be on and whether he might be around to attend to the needs of his students. If she was irritated and a little worried by the number of meetings that Lydia seemed to be having with various officials of the Church of England, she was bound to admit that part of it was pure jealousy. Perhaps, she thought, it was just that Lydia was better at chasing people than she was...

She walked up to campus and found when she got there that she had the office to herself. It seemed to be an ideal opportunity to call her mother.

Her call was answered after a couple of rings. 'Colette! Hello, love.'

'Is this a good moment?'

'Yes, until it isn't.'

Colette chuckled. 'Well, let me know when it stops being one, and I'll hang up. How are things?'

'Oh, ticking over.' A précis of the family news followed. Hannah had started a new job, which meant that Chris was doing slightly fewer hours in order to make childcare possible. Richie seemed to be enjoying working at the pub, but had broken up with Jenny. '… And your dad is already counting the days until half term. How are you?'

'Also ticking over. I'm on campus at the moment.' She drew a breath, and used it to say, 'You know how you were talking at Christmas about me and Lydia getting married?'

'I do.' Warmth seemed to permeate her mother's voice.

'Don't get excited. I was calling to tell you why we can't.'

'Oh?'

'Lydia's thinking of –' she hesitated, giving herself time to pick the most neutral way of putting it – 'training for ministry.'

Her mother was silent for long enough for Colette to think that perhaps she should have told her father first. Then she said, 'I suppose that's not really a surprise, is it?'

'Not really, no.'

'And it means you can't get married because...?'

'Because Church of England clergy aren't supposed to. Not unless their partner is the opposite sex, I mean.'

'I don't like your having to dance to the Church of England tune.'

'Nor do I, much, but at the moment it's part of the package.'

Gentle probing: 'And, for all you know, it might always be?'

'Yes. And even if she does get turned down this time round, she might want to try again in a couple of years. Getting married would be shutting the door on the possibility and throwing away the key.'

'No, I see,' her mother said, and added, with abrupt heat, 'Oh, it's all such a mess, isn't it?'

'It is,' Colette agreed fervently. She added, 'You never know, they might change the rules before Lydia actually gets to that point. But I'm not holding my breath.'

'That's fair enough. And I'll stop nagging.'

'*Mum*. You weren't nagging.' It had felt like that, but Colette thought that was probably her own guilty conscience.

'Do you want me to tell Dad?'

'If you like.' Colette had suspected, without having really articulated her suspicion to herself, that her father would be quicker to see both the reality of Lydia's vocation and the snares associated with it. Either way, she was grateful not to have to have the conversation twice.

'I'm happy to,' her mother said. 'So, how are your studies?'

'Oh, OK. I'm meant to be meeting my supervisor, but he hasn't turned up yet...' She felt an entirely irrational reluctance to admit to Barry's shortcomings, as if his flakiness reflected on her to her shame. And she was relieved when she succeeded in steering the conversation round to the technical, and more so when her mother had to ring off.

James, the research assistant, breezed in at around eleven thirty, bearing a steaming cup of coffee and his usual blank A4 pad. Colette had never seen him write anything on any of his A4 pads, but she had never seen him without one. He smiled and simultaneously raised his eyebrows, a trick that looked mocking but which Colette had learned long ago to dismiss as one of his quirks. He had a wide mouth that curved naturally upwards, and dark, slightly pointed, eyebrows over pale blue eyes: it all combined to make him look rather puckish. Had Colette been standing, she would have been very slightly taller than him, but they spent most of their time in the office seated, and had never thought to compare. 'Morning, Colette. Any sign of our lord and master?'

'Not this morning.'

He waggled the mouse of his computer. 'I thought you had a meeting with him?'

'I did.'

'Ah, well, since when was that any guarantee of his actually turning up? Was it important?'

'Yes, but it's nothing that won't keep.' Colette spun her chair around to face him. 'How was your wedding fair?' Because James was engaged, and the saga of the preparations had kept the whole lab group entertained for weeks.

James rolled his eyes. 'I think I now know what it's like to be a woman.'

'Oh?'

He moved a stack of printed pages from his chair to the desk and sat down. 'I was ignored and gawped at in equal parts. Every time I expressed an opinion, the person looked at Giselle to make sure that she approved of it.'

'And did she?'

'She found the whole thing hilarious.'

Colette smiled. She liked Giselle. 'That sounds like her.'

'It doesn't help that she hates making decisions at the best of times. The trouble is, if she doesn't, her mum will.'

'Would that bother you?'

'Obviously.' He shrugged his shoulders. 'I said afterwards that we could just go down the registry office and then get fish and chips.'

'That sounds good to me.'

James laughed. 'Giselle said we might as well not do it at all in that case. I *think* she was joking.'

'I've always thought this whole marriage lark sounded a bit overrated,' Colette said. She did not feel like explaining to anyone else this morning why, for her, it was not only overrated but impossible. 'I wanted to ask you, actually. About the parahydrogen...'

Lydia was in bed when Colette got in after AngthMURC. She was sitting up with a book open and the lights on, but in bed nonetheless. Well, Colette supposed, it was a work night, after all.

'How was the DDO?' she asked.

Lydia frowned. 'A bit weird. No. I mean, she was very nice, and encouraging, but the meeting was a bit weird. Most of the time we got on fine, like when I was talking about being Pip's confirmation sponsor, but every so often we'd touch on something that just didn't go anywhere. Like hitting a brick wall. And it was frustrating, because it was stuff that felt important to talk about, and yet we weren't.'

Colette took her glasses off and placed them on top of the bookcase, then pulled off her hoodie and T-shirt together. 'Was it the sexuality stuff?'

'Partly. I couldn't work out how much Marcus had told her, so I think I gave her more than she actually needed to know. But it wasn't just that. I mean, it *was*: but it was more the way things went with Fellowship after I came out.'

'What, the collective shunning?' She thought about leaving her clothes on the floor, but decided that dealing with them in the morning would probably be more annoying; so she separated the two tops and dropped the T-shirt into the laundry basket.

'It wasn't really a shunning.' Lydia lifted up the pillows on Colette's side of the bed, extracted her pyjamas, and tossed them across to her.

'Thanks.' Colette unhooked her bra and pulled her pyjama top on; then replaced her jeans and pants with pyjama trousers. 'Well, whatever it was.' At the time, Lydia had been insistent about remaining a member of the Evangelical Christian Fellowship, on the grounds that she was still an Evangelical Christian. *Shunning* was perhaps too strong a word, but nobody had really seemed to know what to do with her.

'There just didn't seem to be the space to talk about a Christian community not necessarily being perfect, which I would have thought would be a really important thing to acknowledge. Actually, we talked quite a lot about you.'

'I thought you weren't meant to tell them about me.' Colette had never been entirely comfortable with the idea: it was too much like the early days, when, even after the painful suppression of her feelings had been lifted in the joyous discovery that Lydia felt the same way, their relationship had been constantly distorted by the threat of exposure, the fear of what would happen if the Christian Fellowship found out. And, if it had felt like a relief when that happened, the aftermath had indeed been devastating.

Lydia assumed an expression of comical despair. 'That's not quite fair. As best as I can make out it's important that my important relationships are supportive, and also important that I'm having the right kind of sex with the right kind of people. Or, since I'm not married, not. Anyway, that's the *don't ask, don't tell* bit. It's not your whole existence; it's just what we do in bed.' Apparently prompted by the association of ideas, she patted the pillow next to her.

Colette climbed in. 'Well, let's be thankful for small mercies. It's none of their business anyway.'

*So the Church of England's Shared Conversations have resulted in... an insultingly superficial report. Such a waste of everyone's time. They've made people talk for years, opening themselves up to misunderstanding and abuse 1/2*
@Flissdemeanour, 21:32, 27 January 2017

*… and we're back where we started, except this time we're going to pretend it works for everyone. No same-sex marriage in church. No same-sex marriage for clergy. Nothing about bi or trans folk. 2/2*
@Flissdemeanour, 21:34, 27 January 2017

*\*hugs\* It hurts, doesn't it?*
@LydiaHawkins, 08:14, 28 January 2017

*It does that. I'll try to bring you a better birthday present. Gin, maybe.*
@Flissdemeanour, 08:30, 28 January 2017

*Haha, presence is more important than presents! Either way, I refuse to let it spoil my party. See you later x*
@LydiaHawkins, 10:02, 28 January 2017

The oven had been on all morning for birthday cake and then sausage rolls, and by midday the flat was too warm. Colette opened a window to try to get the air moving, knocking over an orchid as she jiggled the catch to make it stay open. A harsh, appetising smell of fried onions drifted in from one of the other flats. She pulled the chairs out from around the table, extended the leaves, and pushed it back against the wall. It made the room look very slightly longer. Putting the chairs against the opposite wall helped, too. The futon was heavy; she moved it in jolts, shifting it first from one corner and then from the other. She looked at it sideways. Unfolded, it would easily be big enough for two; but they couldn't exactly expect Peter and Natalie to share it when they'd only been going out a couple of months (this time round, at least) and she suspected that ordinands weren't meant to be sleeping in the same beds as their partners even in extremis. So Georgia could have the whole thing to herself, and

Peter and Natalie would have to make the best of roll mats in the little room. Colette sighed, caught herself thinking that with all of them under the same roof it would almost be like old times (except Will wasn't coming, and Lydia hadn't invited Olly) and pushed the thought away before the absence of Becky could land too heavily.

The daylight hours passed in a flurry of vacuuming and making salad and running to the Spar for forgotten ingredients. Lydia started several tasks in succession and left most of them unfinished, distracted each time by something else that needed doing. Some, she returned to; others, Colette took over; and several days later they found one sad bowl of boiled potatoes at the back of the fridge, awaiting spring onions and mayonnaise that never came.

Peter sent a text at about half past four to say that he was in Stancester.

'But not to worry,' Colette read off, 'because he's going to take Natalie up to campus and show her around.'

'She won't see much of it,' Lydia said dubiously. 'It's nearly dark.'

'Maybe that's the point,' Colette said, and waggled her eyebrows when Lydia looked scandalised.

* * *

Two hours later, they turned up, flustering Colette, who still had odd socks on her feet and her hair tied back with a rubber band. Peter introduced Natalie with a proud hesitancy that Colette found rather touching. They looked good as a couple: Natalie was perhaps a head shorter than Peter: short enough to get away with quite staggeringly high heels, tall enough that she would not have looked incongruous next to him without them. She had a glossy sweep of black hair, a complexion like a peach, and the kind of startling red lipstick that Colette wouldn't have known where to start with. Peter was looking better than he had when Colette had seen him last summer, his dark skin glowing under the hall light. Perhaps college food agreed with him, or perhaps spring was coming earlier in Cambridge. He was wearing a scarlet shirt and no tie; well, she thought, in about eighteen months' time he would be restricted to black shirts and clerical collars. Or he would consider himself to be so restricted, which came to the same thing.

Lydia, who was already dressed in black jeans and a fuchsia-pink silk shirt, took their bags and then set them to putting crisps in bowls. Colette escaped to get changed. By the time she emerged, brushed and neatened, the AngthMURC contingent had arrived, and Kaz was asking Peter about getting lipstick stains out of purificators. Lydia's friends from Christian Fellowship days, Mel and Rory, and Rose, had found the chairs next to the window, but none of them were sitting in them. Colette decided that they could look after each other.

*\*\**

Georgia arrived uncharacteristically and apologetically late.

'I should have remembered,' she said, lining up an improbable number of bottles on the kitchen worktop while Colette sliced up a quiche, 'that it was a wedding, and that therefore it couldn't possibly start on time, and that therefore it wouldn't finish on time, and with Isle of Wight roads in the mix there was never any hope of my making that ferry.'

Colette scraped the residue of the quiche from the flat of the knife with her little finger. 'The bride was late, then?'

'The bride was very late. And the sermon was far too long for a wedding, and I've heard it at least twice before.'

'Have a drink,' Colette suggested.

'I will.' Georgia frowned at the selection that she had just produced and chose a hipsterish foreign lager. 'Cheers,' she said when Colette passed her the bottle opener, and then, 'Cheers!'

Colette clinked her own wine glass against Georgia's bottle. 'Cheers. Well, it's very nice to see you, anyway.'

'You too.' Georgia took a swig.

Lydia had fought her way through into the kitchen, her arms full of chrysanthemums.

'Georgia!'

She put the flowers down to hug Georgia, and Colette repurposed a jug that had been got out to put tap water in, but had never got as far as the drinks table.

Georgia returned the hug enthusiastically. 'Lydia! Happy birthday! Did you have a lovely day?'

'I did. Thank you. And for the card.'

'You're welcome.'

'How was the journey?' Lydia asked. 'Oh, I expect you two have done all that.'

'We have,' Georgia said. 'It was annoying, but I'm here now.' She was looking between the two of them, as if there was something she wasn't saying, as if there was something she wanted to say, but wasn't sure how it would be received. 'So.'

'Spit it out,' Colette said.

Georgia was blushing. 'So,' she said, 'that plus one I didn't bring.'

Lydia exclaimed, 'Yes! I didn't know you had one! Tell me!'

'He's actually on your list anyway.'

Colette tried to visualise the names that were *Not Attending*. She hadn't paid much attention. Lydia was looking equally lost. 'No. No idea.'

'It's Will.' Georgia was still looking sheepish, but also very pleased with herself.

'No! How long has that been going on?' Colette asked, to give herself time to work out how she felt about it. Of all the people she had ever shared a house with, privileged, Evangelical, Will had been the one with whom she had least in common; but he had been one of Becky's best friends. He had treated Lydia horribly; but going by her exclamation of excited surprise that was all forgiven.

'It depends what you call *going on*. You could say it goes all the way back to... after Becky died. But I don't think I would; it's just that we started spending more time together after that.'

Colette found herself unable to speak, and was furious with herself for it. Lydia said, a little awkwardly, 'It was a weird time, wasn't it? I mean...'

Georgia smiled sadly, fondly. 'I know. You two had each other, and Stuart didn't know her like we did, and Peter and Olly weren't in the house any more and didn't have to deal with her just *not being there* all the time, and nobody else really got it.'

That, Colette supposed, made a certain amount of sense. Becky's death had thrown the whole world off its axis; if it had thrown Georgia and Will together, too, it was not so surprising. 'Oh, wow. A long time, then.'

'Yes. No. Nothing really *happened* until last year. But he was really upset, you know, because of the heresy thing, and we talked a lot about that, and eventually about other things, too.' Her colour heightened a little more.

'Oh,' Colette said. 'I didn't realise...'

'No, well, you had a lot to think about too, didn't you? Are you horrified?'

'No, of course not. It's just a surprise.' Although she was, a little.

Lydia said, 'I suppose it's one of those things that makes perfect sense on paper, but would never have occurred to me.'

Colette added, 'And I don't think I'm going to believe it until I see the two of you together.'

'Yes,' Lydia said. 'Why didn't you bring him?'

'What he said on Facebook. He's got a church commitment.'

'You'll have to drag him back to Stancester some time,' Lydia said.

Colette was not so sure about that. 'So you must be doing it long-distance. How's it working, with you being on the Isle of Wight, and him...?'

'Not? Yeah, it's a bit frustrating. At the moment, he really likes his job, and I really feel that the Island is where I'm meant to be. But there are weekends. And, in theory, school holidays. Maybe one of us will feel differently in a year or so.'

'Maybe,' Colette echoed, and, finding the kitchen a little hot, said, 'Anyway, I'd better...' and picked up the quiche and took it out to the table.

\* \* \*

The futon had been commandeered by a group of women who Colette recognised from Lydia's church. She summoned their names: the red-haired woman who had achieved a state of balance somewhere between perching on the arm of the futon and spilling on the lap of the blonde wedged into the corner was Eve; the blonde was Felicity, her wife. Pip, in her late forties, with short hennaed hair and a striped Breton top, was a member of Lydia's Bible study group. The other two, Colette was almost sure, were called Claire and Stephanie.

She added a plate of cheese and onion pastry rolls to the quiche, and took the lot over to them.

There were some thank-yous, and some polite dithering, and eventually some people took some snacks. Then Felicity said, 'You should tell Lydia that she looks really good in that pinky-purple.'

'She used to wear it all the time,' said Colette. 'You're right. I will.' She nodded in what she hoped was an equally polite manner, and moved on.

For something to do, she assessed the state of the buffet table once more, combined two plates of sausage rolls into one, and replenished a bowl of crisps from the bag. Her path back to the kitchen took her back past Lydia, who was talking to Peter about theological college.

'So there we are, out in the garden, all ready to begin the time of silent prayer,' Peter was saying, 'and suddenly we get this huge blast of Tony Christie.'

Lydia laughed. 'Oh, dear.'

'And really, what do you *do* with that? What is the theological significance? What has the way to Amarillo to do with the Way of the Cross? The best I could do in the moment was talk about how God is full of surprises.'

'It's about the Resurrection,' Lydia glanced coolly at Colette. 'Obviously. *Very early, on the first day of the week...* Sweet Marie is Mary Magdalene.'

Peter laughed out loud. 'You're a genius.'

Colette smiled and left them to it. It occurred to her that if Peter was talking to Lydia, then Natalie must be somewhere else, and she supposed that she should probably make sure that she was OK.

\* \* \*

She was relieved to discover that Georgia had found her and was talking matters choral. They seemed to have worked out each other's pedigree as choral scholars and were comparing notes.

'So presumably St Mark's is all auditioned, not just the scholars?' Georgia was asking.

'It's *just* scholars,' Natalie said. Had Colette been the other party in the conversation, she would have suspected a snub, but Georgia was ploughing on regardless.

'Oh, OK. And – forgive me, I should know this – is it all adults?'

47

'Yes,' Natalie said, 'or I wouldn't be in it.'
'Ah – I'd assumed you were an alto.'
She shook her head. 'Mezzo. I sing second soprano, mostly. You?'
'Soprano.'
Natalie looked half-envious, half-sympathetic. 'So you don't really have a choice, then. I suppose I *could* get in somewhere that had a treble top line but couldn't find a countertenor, but I really can't be arsed with all this bullshit about vocal purity.'
'Oh my goodness, I know!' Georgia exclaimed. 'It's like, why is there such a reluctance to admit that women exist after the age of fourteen?'
'*Yes!* And are members of the Church!'
'And sing!'
They were smiling at each other, pleased to have found kindred spirits. Colette judged it a good moment to approach with a bottle of red wine and replenish Natalie's glass.
'Thanks, babe.'
Colette moved on to the next group, but heard Georgia say, 'I do miss it. I mean, goodness knows the chapel choir at Stancester was never the same kind of standard as the ones in the Oxbridge colleges, but it was streets above the one I'm singing with now. But I can't spend all my evenings driving halfway across the Island *and* get my marking done.'
'Of course.'
Georgia had seen Lydia over Colette's shoulder. 'Lydia! Are you having a nice party? You need to tell us what's going on in *your* life.'
'Nothing very interesting,' Lydia said.
'Oh, there must be,' said Natalie.
Colette emptied the bottle of wine into Lydia's glass and went to open another one, leaving her to divulge as much of her affairs as she deemed appropriate. She opened another bottle of wine and began another circuit of the party.

\* \* \*

Over in the corner, someone was fiddling with the radio: the strains of *Scotland the Brave* split the air.

'Turn that off!' Kaz called, and Georgia shouted back, 'No, don't!'

Rowan appeared from nowhere and made Colette a magnificent bow. 'We get our ceilidh after all!'

Colette laughed and returned the bow. 'Are you leading, or am I?' She put the wine bottle down on the windowsill.

Rowan shrugged. 'It doesn't make much odds in this. I think I did last time. And you're taller.'

'OK.' She put her right arm across Rowan's shoulders, right hand to right hand, and brought her left hand across in front. They waited for the end of the first sixteen bars, and set off: forwards for four steps – Georgia and Natalie scuttled out of the way – turning on the spot, not loosing hands, keeping going in the same direction, but backwards – back the way they'd come – holding her right hand up and twirling Rowan under it – and then polkaing for the final four bars.

Then she lost Rowan, which wasn't meant to happen. Lydia had cut in. Colette grabbed Peter, who laughed and tried to catch up with her and they hurried through the first few bars of *The Barnyards of Delgaty* in an undignified jostle for the lead. Rowan and Lydia were doing slightly better. Everyone else had, sensibly, retreated as far into the edges of the room as they could get: the St John's women on the futon looked, from Colette's rotating view, like a shipwrecked crew on a life raft. The room was not really big enough for one couple to dance in; two was definitely pushing it, and, when she and Peter collided backwards with a stray chair, knocking a glass of white wine off the seat, they gave up and left the floor to Rowan and Lydia. Shaking with laughter, Colette went to find a damp cloth.

* * *

Somebody more sensible had taken charge and switched off the radio while the band was still leaning on the final chord. Someone else was clapping. Colette looked over: it was Mel, who had at last sat down on one of the chairs. Rory had a hand on her shoulder. Rose was leaning against the wall and surveying the rest of the party with somewhat aloof interest.

She smiled warily at all of them. Mel and Rose had been Lydia's best friends once upon a time, and Colette suspected them of blaming her for the fact that they weren't any more. Still, they were here, and that was to be applauded, even if it set her teeth on edge.

No, she was going to have to speak to them. She sauntered over, rather self-consciously. 'Hello, you three. How's it going?'

'Hello, Colette,' said Mel.

'I hope you're enjoying yourselves.' She knew that she sounded appallingly hearty, but she couldn't seem to help it. 'Rory. No T-shirt today?' He had a vast collection of T-shirts emblazoned with cheesy evangelistic messages, and so far as she could remember he had been wearing one of them on every occasion she'd ever met him, apart from at his wedding.

'I thought he should make a bit of an effort for Lydia's birthday,' Mel explained. 'So I made him put a real shirt on.'

'Lydia wouldn't mind.' This was an understatement. Lydia made a point of enjoying the slogans on Rory's T-shirts. 'Well, it's a very nice shirt, anyway.'

He nodded earnestly; he did everything earnestly. 'Thank you.'

'And are you all still going to Centrepoint?'

'Oh, yes,' Mel said. 'Rory's leading worship there tomorrow evening, in fact.'

'We've got a speaker from West African Mission Group,' he told her.

'Well,' Colette said, 'that sounds very interesting.' She paused, catching Lydia's eye across the room. 'Can I get any of you a drink?'

\* \* \*

'… And so there we all were,' Georgia was saying, 'soaked to the skin, singing from memory because God help you if you got those scores wet, to an audience of three men and a dog… It was fun, though.'

Colette shifted her position, hitting something on the oven with her shoulder blade as she did so. The oven emitted a scandalised *bleep*.

'Mm. So what happened to the kids?'

Georgia opened another bottle of beer. The cap pinged free from her fingers and rolled across the floor. She glared at it. 'Oh, they'd all disappeared to the arcade, of course... Speaking of which – it's gone very quiet all of a sudden.'

Colette peered around the kitchen door. Both the St John's group and the AngthMURC group had thinned, and it couldn't just be because half of them were out in the courtyard smoking. This was the phase of a party that Colette liked the best, when she could tell that people were only there because they wanted to be, when the gloss had worn off and the conversation was uninhibited, and somehow there were still twice as many unopened bottles of wine as there had been at the beginning of the evening.

Georgia never seemed to get tired, which was, Colette thought, just as well, since she was going to have to be the last one to bed. And they were going to have to *make* her bed, which meant getting everybody off it and remembering how to unfold it. At the moment it was occupied by Peter and Natalie: she was dozing with her head against his shoulder and one knee drawn up onto the seat; he was reminiscing with Lydia about university days. He had his arm around Natalie, and her hair spilled over his elbow. She suits him, Colette thought, and was ashamed to note that she was surprised.

*　*　*

Natalie was fast asleep by the time the last stragglers, Felicity, Eve, and Kaz, departed.

'I'm sorry,' Peter said fondly; 'it's been a long day.'

'I don't mind,' Lydia said. 'I could do the same thing myself.'

He looked apologetic. 'And here we are clogging up the room.' He shook Natalie gently. 'Sweetie? Wake up.'

She murmured protestingly.

'Honestly,' Georgia said, 'You two stay here.'

Lydia squinted at the scene. 'I don't think we can unfold that without you two getting off it.'

'I'm sure we could. Let's try,' said Georgia.

'Let's not,' said Peter. 'Where are you putting us, Lydia?'

'In the room we laughingly call "the study". There's just about room for two people in there. Mind the nativity star when you open the door.'

'Why do you have a nativity star?' Georgia asked.

'I often ask myself the same question,' said Colette.

'I took it home to mend,' Lydia said, 'and am probably going to put it off until December. Unless I bribe Colette to do it sooner.'

'Right,' said Peter. He grasped the arm of the futon and attempted to stand up without dislodging Natalie. Startled awake, she exclaimed, 'What? Oh, no, sorry!' and blinked in confusion. Colette couldn't blame her.

'There's a general move towards bed,' Peter explained.

'I was quite happy there,' Natalie said.

'Tell me what I need to do,' Georgia said in the kind of voice that got things done.

They told her, and together, they did it.

\* \* \*

'Happy birthday,' Colette said quietly, when she and Lydia were in bed, and the lights were off. 'Happy official birthday, I mean.'
'Thank you.'
'Good party?'
'Very. Thank you.' She thought that Lydia was smiling.
'You're welcome.'
'So,' Lydia said after a little while, 'Georgia and Will. I didn't see that one coming.'
'Nor did I, though it makes sense now that I think about it.'
'Do you think it'll last?'
Colette considered the question. 'It might do. I think maybe he needs someone to boss him around now that Becky isn't around to do it for him.'
'Did he and Becky ever...?'
Colette found the idea faintly shocking. 'No, she was always with Adam. And frankly I think she had better taste. Though Adam turned out to be a bit of an arse, too...'
After a brief silence, Lydia asked, 'What did Georgia mean, about heresy?'
She rolled over to face Lydia. 'What?'
It was just possible to make out the curve of Lydia's cheek and the soft gleam in her eyes. 'She said that Will was particularly upset after Becky died, because of something about heresy.'
Colette shook her head. 'No idea. No. Wait. Becky didn't believe that Jesus was the Son of God. Of *course* Will would have fretted about that.'
'Oh.' Lydia was quiet for a little while, absorbing that, and Colette wondered if she, too, was fretting about it. Then she said in a

different tone, 'What I'm really surprised by is Natalie's being so much like Georgia.'

Colette was surprised. 'Is she?'

'I thought so. I picked up a bit of that same steamrollery vibe from her.'

'Well, let's hope she uses her powers for good.'

Lydia laughed. 'Oh, I don't know, maybe she isn't. Maybe it's just that they were getting on well with each other. Did you like her? Never mind whether or not she's like Georgia?'

'I didn't really get to talk to her. She seemed OK. And then she fell asleep.'

'I guess it must have been a bit overwhelming for her, all Peter's friends.' Lydia's voice was sleepy, but there was something of an edge to it.

'She didn't seem too bothered by that. Like I say, she was chatting away with Georgia.'

'Well, that's good,' Lydia murmured.

'Yes,' Colette agreed, and closed her eyes.

Lydia was awake and about the next morning far earlier than seemed reasonable to Colette. She was trying to be quiet, but, being effectively confined to the bedroom, could not help being irritating.

'What's up?' Colette asked at last, without opening her eyes.

'What?'

'You're prowling.'

'Oh.' The mattress sank a little as Lydia sat down on the edge of the bed. 'Yes, I am, I guess.'

'What's up?' Colette asked again, her eyes open this time.

Lydia was exaggeratedly still, now, the tension visible in the straitened line of her back and shoulders. She said, without turning, 'Peter says, and I quote, *You should probably talk to Colette about that, though perhaps she's changed her mind, or, I don't know, maybe it was just her way of letting me down gently...* Would you like to talk to me about that?'

Colette groaned and pulled herself up to sit with her back against the headboard. 'Talk to you about *what?*' she asked.

Lydia was twisting her hands, 'I'm sorry to do this before breakfast, but the flat is full of people and I don't think I can wait until everyone's gone.'

Colette took a mouthful of water from the glass on her bedside table. 'But what are we doing?'

'I was talking to Peter last night. He says you had a thing about not wanting to be a vicar's wife.' Lydia shifted slightly so that she was looking at Colette side on.

'Oh. Yes. That.' She realised that she sounded guilty; which, she told herself, was ridiculous.

'That. So. *Was* that a letting-Peter-down-gently thing, or was it a vicars-in-general thing?'

'I don't think I've ever let Peter down gently in my life. Once I threw myself at him violently.' She drank some more water. 'But it is a specific-to-Peter thing. Or, at least, it comes into play with Peter in a way that it doesn't with you.' She reached for her spectacles. It was too early in the morning for this sort of thing. 'I'm working from a limited sample, you realise.'

'Go on.' Lydia uncurled her fingers and placed one hand on the duvet next to Colette's.

'I think it's the gender roles thing,' Colette explained. She glanced at Lydia, and continued, 'I have this horrific vision of life with Peter being one unending stream of cucumber sandwiches and sherry parties after Mass and probably the whole congregation assuming that I was his beard when actually the reverse would be true. Whereas with you – I don't know what it would look like, but I feel as if there would some wiggle room, because people wouldn't have the same expectations of the female vicar's female partner that they

55

would of the male vicar's female wife.'

Lydia laughed, with some irony. 'I see. I should have extrapolated from *wife*.' But her hand moved to cover Colette's.

'I really dislike the word,' Colette admitted. 'I wouldn't use it even if we did get married. In the alternative universe where that was actually possible.'

Lydia nodded, apparently satisfied with that. She sat back against the headboard and stretched her legs out. 'So,' she said in an obvious attempt to lighten the tone, 'tell me about all the times you didn't let Peter down gently.'

Colette groaned again. 'You want dates, times, and locations?'

'No, just a general outline.' She picked up her own water glass and, finding it empty, put it down again. 'Of course, I could always ask him.'

She laughed, defeated. 'He's far too much of a gentleman to tell you, particularly with Natalie in the house.'

Lydia raised her eyebrows as if to say, *you want a bet?*

'But fine, I will. The first time was my first year. First term. Probably about a month in, and it was just after an AngthMURC meeting, because of course it was. He asked me out; I said no, because I'd just broken up with somebody and didn't want to get into anything new.'

'That can't have been what he meant.'

'He must have been talking about the second time, which was a bit less than a year later. He was clearly about to ask me again, and I got Becky to head him off at the pass.'

'Why? And don't tell me you've never thought of him that way, because you clearly have, at least at some point.'

Colette saw no point in denying it. 'It was the vocations stuff. So this was the beginning of his final year, and everything was coming together, he was just beginning to have those meetings that you've been having, and he was applying for pastoral assistant jobs all over the place. It was taking over his life, and I could see that it would take over mine, too, if I got involved with him.' She turned her face slightly away from Lydia, hiding behind a loose strand of hair. 'Call me a wuss if you like.'

'I will, if you don't tell me the bit where you threw yourself at him. When was that?'

'Spring term, second year.'

'Ah,' said Lydia, with the stricken look of one who has just lost the moral high ground.

'Yes.' Colette let the monosyllable die in the flat acoustic of the bedroom.

She frowned at the memory. 'When the trauma of the vocations machine suddenly seemed infinitely preferable to an Evangelical in the closet?'

'When I was letting vodka do my thinking for me.'

Lydia asked, with unsubtle irony, 'How did that go?'

'He was the perfect gentleman.' She could feel the heat rising in her face.

'Of course he was. I needn't have asked, need I? Were you sick?'

'As it happens,' Colette said, 'no, I wasn't.'

'Well,' Lydia said cheerfully, 'that's something. Do you think Georgia will kill me if I wake her up putting the kettle on?'

*I love my husband, and nothing changes that fact, and that fact doesn't change anything. For me, calling myself bisexual means recognising the fact that my life could have taken a different path and, all else being equal, one as godly as the one I'm now following.*
Invisible, Bisexual, Bloggable
29 January 2017

But Georgia had already boiled the kettle, brewed tea in the pot that they never bothered with usually, and stood the empty bottles in neat rows next to the bin. Colette took the dishcloth from her before she could wash up all the dirty glasses. 'You don't have to.'

'I know.' Georgia picked up a tea towel.

Colette did not argue further. While they tackled the washing up, Peter and Natalie emerged one at a time. Each of them headed straight for the bathroom, and emerged clad almost identically in jeans and hoodies. Colette recognised Peter's as dating from his AngthMURC days; she owned a very similar one herself. Natalie's, she saw, was the St Mark's College Chapel Choir edition.

'Did you sleep OK in there?' Lydia asked each of them. Peter said, 'Yes, fine.' Natalie, 'Very well, thank you.' Colette suspected both of them of lying, but they seemed cheerful enough.

'What time are you two heading off?' Georgia asked. 'Peter, I feel like I've hardly talked to you.'

'Stop drying up, then,' Lydia said, 'and go and talk to him. I'm going to put breakfast stuff on the table, and you can help yourselves, OK?'

In fact it was already pushing lunchtime, and by the time everybody had helped themselves it was unarguably the afternoon. Natalie plucked at Peter's sleeve and reminded him that they had advance tickets and needed to be at the station in the next hour if they weren't to pay a fortune for new ones. Georgia looked at her watch and said that she thought she might make the ferry before the one she'd booked, if the A303 wasn't too ridiculous. Then they all wasted ten minutes debating whether it would be quicker for Peter and Natalie to walk to the station or for Georgia to give them a lift before everything came suddenly together and they all three bundled themselves into the car, leaving Colette and Lydia waving from the shelter of the stairwell.

'Let's go for a walk,' Lydia said when there were only the two of them left.

'It's raining.'

'Well, yes. This is Somerset.'

It was difficult, Colette reflected, to keep Lydia indoors in anything short of a Force 10 gale. 'We'd better get on with it, then. We only have a couple of hours of daylight left.'

'We won't go far,' Lydia promised.

So they went upstairs again to put on boots and waterproofs, and tramped down the three flights of grey-carpeted stairs out into the drizzle. The roads and pavements glistened; the air was soft and damp, and Colette's glasses fogged up. She took them off, and the moisture thrummed at her eyelashes. She let Lydia lead the way out of the cul-de-sac, past the little parade of shops and the Dolphin, down to the footbridge across the river. They struck left off the main road. Then they started climbing: along the Victorian terraces, past the big brick houses, and the gardens hidden behind hedges of holly or yew, or despondent copper beech, until at last they reached the top of the hill, and the scrubby open ground. They had it almost to themselves: one lone dog walker was the only other person who had braved the weather.

And from the top of Thorn Hill they looked across the valley to the university, its concrete lines softened by the mist, and then down at the prongs and ridges of the cathedral roof, and saw what might have been Peter and Natalie's train crossing the viaduct and snaking eastwards towards Wiltshire.

Lydia sighed.

'What's up?' Colette asked.

'They've all gone.'

'That's what happens,' Colette said, but she was feeling flat, too, and they walked back down the hill in silence.

'Dinner at seven?' Lydia asked when they got in.

'Fine,' Colette said. 'You're not going to Centrepoint to hear about the West African Mission, then?'

'You what?'

'Tonight's service. Rory was quite enthusiastic about it,' she explained.

'Oh. No. I need to phone Mum.'

It had become a ritual: every Sunday afternoon Lydia would take a breath, square her shoulders, and call her parents.

Sometimes there would be a pause, which would be her father picking up and summoning her mother; sometimes Lydia would start talking straight away, which would mean that her mother had been the one to answer. There would always be a summary of the week's events at work and at church, followed by inquiries about the well-being of various family members.

Usually Lydia would also mention Colette. More rarely, it was something like Pride, or West Country LGBTX. Either way, this would be a sure sign that the call was about to end, and, probably, end abruptly.

'What does she *say*?' Colette had asked once. 'When you tell her about me?'

'Today it was, "Well, you know what your father and I think about that, not to mention what the Bible teaches, so I'm not going to go into it again, talk to you later, bye."'

That was more or less what Colette had expected. 'So why do you keep telling her?'

With a flash of anger: 'Because I'm doing all the work, and if they get to think that everything's OK between us then I'm going to make sure they remember who I actually am.'

The next question was obvious. 'And why do they get to think everything's OK?'

Lydia had sighed. 'Because I can keep praying that one day it will be.'

Colette had left it there.

Lydia's parents never phoned her, perhaps afraid that it would be Colette who picked up. Lydia said that she preferred it that way, that it gave her a chance to prepare. Colette was inclined to believe that.

This week was different, and not only because Lydia had left it later than usual. She was pacing the cramped length of the sitting room, close to bursting with her news, and giving only the briefest answers to whatever it was that her mother was saying.

'Mum,' she said. 'There's something I need to tell you.'

A brief silence. Colette wondered what was filling it, in Lydia's ear. Was it, *If it's about that woman you live with I don't want to hear it*? Or, *So you've finally decided to repent*? She had never met either of Lydia's parents, had only Lydia's own gentle, defiant voice to extrapolate from. She imagined it higher, more querulous.

Perhaps there was only silence.

'I'm thinking about becoming a minister.'

That, Colette thought, was putting it mildly.

A longer silence, marking the edges of an unguessable response.

'Yes, I'm telling them... I'm telling them what they need to know.'

Colette suppressed an angry smile.

'I don't know. I'll find out.' She came round the back of the futon and put a hand on Colette's shoulder, gripping a little harder than was comfortable. Colette reached her own hand up to find it.

'Thanks, Mum. I do appreciate that.' The pressure vanished, and

Lydia was off again, over the other side of the room before she spoke again.

'No, well. Same time next week?... OK, bye then.'

And then there was silence.

'So?' Colette swung her legs off the futon.

Lydia was still pacing. 'Stunned silence. Then a lot of sentences that began with *But...* and didn't finish.'

'Was that what you were expecting?'

Lydia shrugged her shoulders. 'I suppose so. I wasn't expecting it to be good.'

'What was it that you appreciated?'

'She's going to pray for me.'

That should have been something to rejoice in, but Colette knew better than to hope. 'In a good way?'

She rolled her eyes. 'In her normal way.'

'Oh, well. I expect God will act on it to your benefit.' Because, Colette thought, you ought to be able to trust an omniscient Deity to know what you actually needed, and give you that, regardless of anyone else's ideas.

'And hers, I hope.'

'That was exceptionally charitable,' Colette observed.

Lydia snorted. 'Well, I am meant to be practising.'

## *February*

*Well, wasn't that a waste of time? Such a lot of heartache to get to the point where we're grateful for nothing having happened at all.*

*For anyone who hasn't been following this depressing saga (and I can't say I blame you), the Church of England has spent the last three years chasing its own tail to produce a report that was so offensive that its own authors apologised for it, and has now voted not to take any notice of it. I wish the rest of us had had that luxury.*

*(And, writing that, I'm uncomfortably aware that perhaps I do have that luxury...)*
Invisible, Bisexual, Bloggable
16 February 2017

'Well,' Lydia said at last, 'there it is. No notice taken.'

She had stopped at St John's on the way home to pick up some resources for house group, and had, she said, dropped in at Felicity and Eve's for a cup of tea, and got sidetracked into ranting with them about the whole recursive snafu. Upon arriving home, she had cooked a vague approximation of spaghetti bolognese and shovelled her portion down without saying much.

Colette laid her knife and fork side by side and asked, 'And what happens now?'

'Back to square one. Or maybe someone picks up the board and chucks it across the room, and someone else gets out Monopoly instead.' Lydia had a resigned note in her tone. It seemed to surprise her: she added, 'I know I should be glad.'

'Should you?'

She ran her fingers through her hair. 'Well, yes. It is good news. Except it's not really news, is it?'

Colette said, 'No news is good news,' to see how it would sound, and had to admit that it did not sound very convincing.

'Yes, but I want *real* good news, not just this grovelling sense of relief.'

Colette raised her eyebrows. 'That sounds reasonable.'

Lydia took Colette's plate and stacked it on her own. 'Does it? I keep second-guessing myself. I think, shouldn't I be happy with the crumbs that fall from the table? But I'm not.'

'The labourer is worthy of his hire,' Colette countered. 'No. That's not the one I mean. I mean, I think it's reasonable of you not to be satisfied with less than whatever other people get.'

'You're thinking of the labourers in the vineyard.'

'Yes, probably. One flat rate, no matter where you rank in the hierarchy or when you turned up.'

'That's the one. Which reminds me,' Lydia said, in an entirely different tone. 'Two of my colleagues from the council are getting married in May. I'm invited to the evening do. You too, if you want.'

The obvious objection occurred to Colette. 'Do they know I'm, you know...?'

For the first time that evening, Lydia smiled. 'A woman? These two do. I'll have to make sure everyone else does before then.'

'Do you want to go, then?'

'I think so. It sounds as if it will be quite fun.'

'*You* don't sound like you believe that.'

'Don't I?' Lydia looked startled. 'I think it will be a good party. He's Dutch.'

'And she?'

'Is British.' She sighed. 'It's because of Brexit. They've been together for about twenty years.'

'Honestly,' Colette said. 'Why mess with something that's working perfectly well as it is?'

Lydia sighed again. 'I think it's great that they're finally recognising their commitment to each other.'

Colette didn't say the words that first came to mind. 'Where's it happening?' she asked.

'The wedding is at City Hall. The party's at the White Hart. Or at least, it was, the last thing I heard. It's all being done in a bit of a rush, and from what Maddie says Jorick's in charge, and from what Jorick says the children – well, teenagers – are.'

'Lucky for some.'

Lydia was singing a song about the city hall under her breath all the while she did the washing up. Colette dried the plates and cutlery, and then went to turn the TV on. Struck by a thought, she asked, 'Do you need to watch the news?'

'And see all the commentators fail to understand that this is actually a step forward? I'd rather not.'

'Fair enough.' Colette hesitated. 'In that case, there's a documentary on BBC4. Barry's in it.'

'Does that mean you want to watch it?'

'It means I probably should. Get my schmooze points in, maybe learn something. You never know.'

'You can explain it all to me. I won't know any of it.'

In fact, the first ten minutes taught neither of them anything new, and it was not until the presenter walked across a paddling pool full of custard and started talking about non-Newtonian fluids that Colette had to explain anything.

'Hang on,' Lydia said, 'isn't that the Sciences Block?'

Colette, who had been trying to draw molecular diagrams on the back of an envelope, looked up at the screen. 'Yes.'

The presenter intoned, *'I'm at the University of Stancester to find out about some of the extraordinary properties of some everyday materials...'*

A cut to an interior. Colette recognised the backdrop as the newest and best equipped laboratory, which was usually occupied by the Structural Chemistry team.

The camera focussed in on Barry, who had one arm extended languidly along the edge of a desk. He was wearing an open-necked blue shirt, no doubt artfully chosen to bring out his blue eyes and his tan, and looked undeniably striking against the muted off-whites of the lab.

'How old is he?' Lydia frowned at the screen.

'Late forties? Maybe early fifties. It's weird, isn't it, how much more solid people look on telly than they do in real life.'

'What does he look like in real life, then?'

'Oh, you know,' Colette said, feeling foolish. 'Like that, but less shiny. Less high-definition.'

'Does his hair always do that curly thing at the front?'

'He'd had it cut, last time I saw him.'

'Which was surely before Christmas, so a while ago...'

'Yes, but not as long ago as when they filmed this.' Which must have been some time in the spring, going by the look of the cherry trees in the courtyard.

The programme had cut away from Barry, and back to the presenter, who was taking various metal objects out of a plastic crate, apparently at random.

'Sorry,' Lydia said, 'we've missed everything he was saying, and it was my fault.'

The presenter demonstrated the fact that the various different objects could all be used to complete a simple circuit. *'We all know how electricity works,'* he said. *'We all know that metal is a conductor. But not all conductors are created equal.'*

'Oh,' Colette said, disappointed.

'Oh?'

'I was hoping it would be something other than the knot theory. Why don't we get Barry trying to walk on custard?'

'You should suggest it to him. And I still don't get it.'

'Well, it's because the liquid becomes solid under pressure, and then liquefies when the pressure's released again.'

'But *why*?' Lydia demanded, and then laughed. 'Not to sound like a four year-old, or anything.'

Colette reached for the envelope again. 'I always think it would make a great sermon illustration. You could demonstrate a miracle.'

Lydia sniggered. 'And I noticed they weren't using actual custard. Does actual custard not work? Or is it too expensive to make a whole paddling pool full?'

Colette thought about it. 'Do you know, I'm not sure. The egg might do something weird...' She frowned at her diagram: she'd missed a bond somewhere. When she next looked at the screen, an Asian woman was talking enthusiastically about the properties of wood. Barry did not appear again.

'Are you up to anything interesting today?' Colette asked the next morning.

'Not at work. But I'm going to have lunch with Felicity, and bring her up to date with all the discernment stuff.'

'Ah.' Colette felt faintly put out. It wasn't really fair, she knew: Felicity had as much right as anybody to know what was going on in Lydia's life, and more than most. Felicity had been the one who had started all this, had been the one to say to Lydia, 'So have you ever thought about ordination?'

'Is that OK? I did mention it a few days ago.'

Colette remembered, and quashed an irrational surge of resentment. Why shouldn't Lydia talk to Felicity? Why shouldn't she let off steam? Why shouldn't she complain to Felicity about the arcane processes of their Church, and the fact that she wouldn't be getting married any time soon? 'You did. It's fine. Are you still going to want dinner when you get home?'

Lydia stretched up to kiss her cheek. 'If you're cooking.'

It was her turn. 'I'll sort something out.'

It was a grey day, and colder outside than it looked. Colette regretted walking up to campus, but told herself that waiting for the bus on Southview would be even colder. She buttoned her coat up to the neck and quickened her pace.

Campus was quiet: nobody was spending much time outside if they could help it. Outside the Sciences Block, the branches of the cherry trees were bare and dark against the pale grey facade. The windows were dark, too. As she approached the main doors, she saw why: a notice, fluttering in the breeze, explained that some urgent work was being carried out on the electrical supply. She went inside to get out of the cold while she considered her next move.

'Give it an hour,' the porter said, without much optimism.

Colette retreated to the Coffee House in the Students' Union building, and gave it an hour and a half.

She walked back up to the lab with no particular sense of urgency. Whatever the work was, it seemed to have been completed; the apologetic notices had all been torn down again. Colette headed back to her corner of the building with renewed hope. Still, it was out of habit, not expectation, that she looked at Barry's door, and it was with surprise that she saw it was open, and that he was seated at his desk.

He looked up and saw her.

'Colette! This is all a bloody pain, isn't it?'

'Barry!' She stopped herself saying, *What a lovely surprise!* 'I saw you in that *Extraordinary Powers* documentary last night.'

'Ah, yes, that,' he said modestly.

'I thought it was good,' Colette said, not exactly lying.

'Oh, well. I do think it's always a bit strange, when the person who's interviewing you is an expert in their own right, and is pretending they don't know just as much as you do.' He laughed. 'Well... How are things going?'

She twisted her hands. 'Oh, you know. Not too bad.'

'Any progress?'

'I think possibly, yes. There are a few things I'd like you to have a look at, when you have a moment?' She heard the supplication in her own voice and despised herself for it. 'Some results that I'm not quite sure about.' She added, 'James isn't sure about them, either.'

'Oh, yes, of course,' Barry said airily. 'Unfortunately I don't have time today, though. I'm just in and out before I meet Annick. Tuesday?'

Colette suppressed a sigh. She had no idea who Annick was, and didn't much care. 'Tuesday.'

And Barry was gone.

The day was saved, however, by the fact that not only had the spectrometer become unexpectedly available, but the person who had originally booked it had also remembered to email interested parties to say so. Which gave her just enough time to set things going, and meanwhile... She found a notepad and settled into the kind of absorption that she had once assumed would always drive her PhD.

James appeared at about half past three, looking frazzled.

'Cheer up.' She thought she should share her good mood. 'It's Friday.'

'That is certainly true.' He dumped his rucksack on his chair. 'The trouble is, I'm not sure that it helps. In fact, I'm fairly sure that it doesn't help at all.'

'What's wrong with Friday, then?'

'It's the day before Saturday. And Saturday is when Giselle's mother, sisters and cousins are coming down to go out shopping for bridesmaids' dresses.'

Colette did some rudimentary arithmetic in her head. 'Wow. How many of each?'

'One mother. Three sisters. Two cousins.'

'Do you have to go with them?'

He shuddered theatrically. 'No, thank goodness. But Giselle does, so I have to hold her hand and feed her gin when they've all gone.'

'Why do you think it's going to be as bad as all that?'

He spread his hands wide. 'Because they're all different sizes and have wildly different tastes, and the chances of pleasing everybody are approximately zero.'

'I'm told that way back before any of us were born there was a golden age when all bridesmaids had to wear peach satin, by law, and nobody was allowed to complain.'

'Yes, but that was when the bride's mother organised everything, and it hasn't yet got to the stage where we're willing to sacrifice our autonomy for the sake of peace.'

Colette laughed. 'Well, maybe you should still make a stand for peach satin.'

'Trust me,' he said, 'it's more than my life's worth.'

Someone knocked at the door, and they both looked up. 'Come in!' James called.

It was Mariam, who was both the most competent and the most approachable of the departmental administrators. 'Is Barry around?'

'You've missed him,' Colette said. 'He said he'll be back on Tuesday.'

'Ah,' said Mariam. She glanced down at a paper in her hand. 'Not to worry. Unless – James, would you know anything about someone called Tori Luciano? Because nobody else seems to, and Tori Luciano is arriving on Monday, apparently.'

James said, helplessly, 'That rings a vague bell, but...' He shook his head. 'Give me half an hour, and I'll look up what I think I'm thinking of, and come down and see you.'

'Thanks,' Mariam said, 'and when you do see Barry, tell him... Oh, never mind.'

When the door closed after her, James said, 'Tell him what a lot of work he makes for other people?'

Colette smiled sympathetically, and turned her attention to her work. James, muttering darkly about whether he *looked* like Barry's

PA, was out well within his estimated half hour, leaving Colette with the peace of the office and a set of results that were turning into an unusually satisfying graph.

She was roused by the discreet *ping* of her phone. Horrified, she saw that it was already after seven. She grabbed her bag, tapping out, *Sorry – on my way now* as she clattered down the stairs, and sending the message as the automatic doors swished shut behind her. Halfway down the hill, she remembered about dinner, and wasted time dithering over where to buy food. She doubled back to go to the Students' Union shop, and then wasted time dithering over what to buy. What would Lydia have eaten for lunch? Felicity would probably have suggested the vegetarian restaurant on Broadway, because it was close to the council offices, and Lydia would probably have gone along with that. Colette told herself that Lydia would probably not mind what dinner was so long as she did not have to organise it, and selected a large frozen pizza and a four-pack of chocolate mousses.

Lydia did not seem to be at all put out by Colette's late appearance, or disappointed by her unimaginative catering efforts.

'Good day?' she asked absently.

'Yes,' Colette said, a little surprised to discover that this was in fact the truth. 'I got some sense out of Barry, and some more sense out of my results.'

Lydia nodded. 'Good.'

Colette put the oven on to preheat, and, when there had been nothing but silence for a little while, said, 'You're quiet tonight.'

Lydia laughed. 'You know what Felicity's like,' she said. 'She doesn't just persuade you to come out of your shell; she drags you out by force and leaves you feeling like you've been eaten with garlic butter.'

Colette had never had that sort of conversation with Felicity, but she could well believe it. 'What did you talk about?'

'Vocations. And the vote not to take notice. And, apart from that, ancient history.' She seemed to take Colette's raised eyebrows as encouragement. 'How St John's came to be the church it is. Felicity said that there was a really long interregnum, and, because there's a whole load of lay leadership anyway, nobody was too worried. And, because if you want something done you ask a lesbian, by the time Benjy was appointed Ida was churchwarden, and Felicity and Steph were all that stood between the worship and complete chaos, and Claire was single-handedly keeping the children's ministry going.'

'What about Eve?' Colette asked wryly.

'Music group co-ordinator. I should have said, lesbians and bi women. Felicity wouldn't let me forget about Eve. Anyway, it seems that Benjy didn't have to pray too hard before God revealed to him that all these queer women were a divine gift and he should be very thankful for them.'

'So when was this interregnum?'

'Five years ago or so? Felicity said it started about three years after she and Eve moved to their current house.' She added, thoughtfully, 'And of course they must have had a lot going on themselves at that point.'

'I dare say all the church stuff was a welcome distraction.'

'Maybe. They had to do that ridiculous thing, didn't they, where they had to get divorced and then civil partnershipped and then converted back to marriage again when that became legal. Felicity was telling me at my party how horrible it all was.'

'At least they got a couple more parties out of it.'

Lydia grinned. 'Apparently Eve was really pleased that she still fitted into her dress. But they couldn't have the second one blessed, and I think Felicity's still quite upset about that.'

'That's fair enough.'

'Yes,' Lydia said, seriously. 'I would have been, if it had been me.'

*Knot so simple after all: is this the end of the line for Parnell's influential 'knot' theory?*
For the last decade and a half, Barry Parnell's 'knot theory' of superconductivity has exercised a fascination over physics, chemistry, and the liminal space between the two. It's a beautiful theory, whose very elegance is persuasive. Building on the 'lattice' or 'matrix' models of other scientists, it argues that increasing the density of hydrogen can drag superconductivity up towards the El Dorado: so-called 'room temperature'.
Studies by Parnell himself and by other scientists have been taken to support the knot theory, but few would argue that it's anywhere close to being conclusively proven. And findings published last week suggest that it might just be wrong.
Science Today, 22 February 2017

'Colette. Have you seen this one?'

There was an urgency in James' voice, with an incongruous edge of glee, that made her look up immediately. 'What is it?'

'Look.' He beckoned her over with a jerk of his chin. 'Someone's decided to stick a knife into Barry.' He scooted his chair over to make room for her in front of his screen.

She leaned forwards, resting both hands on the edge of the desk, to read the article. 'I don't think they've got it in for Barry, exactly,' she said when she had got to the end.

'Well, not personally,' said James, who had been watching her face as she read it. 'But it's demolishing the knot theory, and considering how closely he identifies with it, they might as well have.'

Colette glanced out of the window and saw Barry stalking across the plaza in front of the building, his shoulders rigid. She felt an unexpected pang of sympathy. 'Heads up.'

'What?' He followed her gaze. 'Oh.'

'Did Giselle's bridesmaids ever decide on their dresses?' she asked, to change the subject.

He raised his eyebrows. 'No – well, they did, but they couldn't get it in the right size for one of them because it's last year's model or something, so the whole idea gets written off and we have to start all over again from square one.'

She tried to look sympathetic; it was difficult when James clearly didn't care either. 'I suppose you couldn't get away with having one of them in something different and calling it a contrast?'

'I think that's the point of the bride,' he said drily.

Colette shrugged her shoulders. 'Well, you're the expert. I still say the answer's peach satin.'

He grimaced. '*Of course*, the other problem is that they then have to get the flowers matched up with the dresses, and Giselle really wants irises, because it was her grandma's name.'

'That's a lovely idea.'

'In theory, yes, it is. In practice, it's yet another thing that we have to work around. Apparently it rules out a whole slice of the colour palette.'

'Oh,' said Colette, who had never considered the question.

The lab door opened with a gentle swish. Just in time, James closed the window on his computer with the *Science Today* story and maximised the one in which he was writing his own paper.

'Good morning,' Barry said, in a good approximation of his usual suave manner.

'Morning, Barry,' James said.

'Morning,' Colette mumbled.

He glanced at her. 'Colette, you told me last week that you wanted to ask about something?'

'Yes,' Colette agreed, her mind blank. 'I – I can't remember what it was now.'

He looked distinctly unimpressed. 'Hmm. Well, if you remember before about three o'clock, give me a shout.' He disappeared into his office. James and Colette glanced at each other.

'What *did* you want to ask him about?' James asked. 'Or can you really not remember?'

Colette wriggled uncomfortably. 'I couldn't, in that particular gap of three seconds. It was that weird spike that I asked you about the other day.'

'Oh, was that all?'

She affected nonchalance. *All?* It was hugely intimidating. 'Yeah.' He looked meaningfully at the door. 'Well, go on.'

'I – I can't. He'll tell me I've been stupid.' Except it wouldn't be in so many words. 'I mean, he'll make me feel stupid.'

James, miraculously, understood. 'I could ask about it. Obviously I'd pretend that it was something that I wanted to know.'

'Would you?' She felt utterly pathetic, but she would feel utterly pathetic either way, and at least if James asked her question she might find out an answer to it.

'Of course.' His expression was kind.

'Please. Yes. Thank you.'

James paused, a step away from Barry's door. He mouthed, 'He's on the phone.'

'Oh,' Colette said, shamefully relieved. 'I guess that's a sign that I should do my own dirty work.'

James came back over and sat down, and opened up his internet browser again.

'Tweeting at the same time, too,' he observed. 'Never let it be said that the man can't multitask.'

Colette looked (*I'd be more impressed if this had come from a more impressive source*) and couldn't look away. She kept Barry's Twitter feed open all afternoon, and watched it with fascinated, horrified, admiration as he got mired ever deeper in self-justification and defensiveness.

At last, having cringed at *I see why someone who's not an expert in this field might think that, but I fully expect to be vindicated*, she said, 'Do you think one of us should, you know, say something?'

James looked dubious. 'Do you seriously think there's any point?'

'He wouldn't listen to me,' Colette admitted.

'He doesn't listen to me much, either, which is why I wasn't volunteering.'

'Oh. Fine. So I suppose there isn't, really.'

Barry left at about half past five, without saying goodbye. Colette did not think it was a good moment to try and talk about the spike in her figures. She slouched home as the sun set sulkily behind her, wondering whether she would be any braver tomorrow.

The building glowed with lights: in the stairwell, all along the top floor, and in some of the flats. Colette counted up from the bottom, three floors, and along the windows, to the right. Yes. Lydia was home.

She climbed the stairs, found her key, and opened the door.

Inside, she could hear the mumble of voices. Lydia was talking to someone. Colette glanced at the coat rack: the only unfamiliar item was a navy-blue corduroy jacket with a long woolly scarf tucked inside the armhole. It wasn't one that she had seen before. She held her breath and listened.

'So that's what you want, then, is it?' Lydia's voice was neutral, careful. Colette froze.

'Of course it is! I've always wanted kids! And I thought *he* did...'

She could not identify the other voice, though she knew she recognised it. She listened; it had subsided into sniffling.

Colette made sure to bang the door loudly, to call 'Hello!' equally loudly, and to apply rather more time and attention than usual to the operation of removing her coat and shoes. When she came into the sitting room, Lydia had an arm around the shoulders of her friend Mel, and was saying, 'There. Let it out.'

'Hi, Mel,' Colette said, pretending not to see the red eyes and the pile of soggy tissues. 'I'll just go and get changed.'

She touched Lydia on the arm as she walked past them into the bedroom, where she turned the radio on and made some noise opening and closing drawers. Then she picked up Lydia's Lent book and read several days' worth of premature reflections, until sobbing had given way to reassurance, and reassurance to goodbyes, and at last the front door closed.

Lydia called, 'Colette? It's safe now!'

She turned the radio off and came out of the bedroom. 'I wasn't hiding.'

'I didn't think you were. Just being tactful. Nor did I really think you'd actually be getting changed.'

'No, but Mel didn't need to know that.' Colette paused. She wanted, and did not want, to ask, *Is she OK?*, which would have been redundant, or *What's up with her?*, which would have been intrusive.

'True. Thanks. She really ought to talk to Rory, not me.'

Trying to be helpful, Colette said, 'Maybe having talked to you will help her talk to Rory. Maybe she'll have said all the stuff to you that she doesn't trust herself to say to him, and now they can have a proper conversation.'

Lydia looked doubtful. 'Well, so long as she *does* talk to him.'

She said it. 'What's up? If you can tell me, I mean.'

A brusque laugh. 'Going by what Mel says, all of Centrepoint knows. He thinks God's calling him to be a missionary. She doesn't.'

'She doesn't think God's calling him?'

Lydia said, delicately, 'She doesn't think God's calling *her* to be a missionary's wife.'

'Ah.'

'Do you know, I'm not sure they should have got married.' She said it with hushed voice, like the heresy it was.

'Well, they could certainly have been less obnoxious on the question of how far they wanted us involved in it.'

Lydia cringed. 'Don't remind me. I couldn't *not* go, though: Mel was the one Christian Fellowship person who was even halfway OK about you and me, in the beginning.'

'Which by definition excludes Rory,' Colette pointed out.

'Didn't we have this argument at the time?'

'Yes. We did. Sorry. And we went to the wedding and it was quite fun, really.' Which was essentially true, although she had known none of the songs and the minister's thoughts on how the man is the head of the woman had been difficult to listen to. 'Why do you think they shouldn't have got married? Too young?'

Lydia hesitated. 'Too *quick*, I think. If they'd left it even six months longer than they did then they might not have done it.'

'Randy Christian syndrome?' She laughed at Lydia's expression of disapproval.

'I wish you wouldn't call it that.'

'So yes, then.'

A sigh. 'Yeah. Anyway, how was *your* day?'

'Well.' Colette took a breath. 'Have you seen the news today?'

'Only the headlines. Why, were you on it?'

'I wasn't. Barry was.'

'Barry your supervisor?'

'The very same.'

Lydia looked concerned. 'What's he done?'

Colette hastened to reassure her. 'Oh, nothing like that. At least, as far as I know. Actually, "the news" is a bit of an exaggeration. If he keeps making a spectacle of himself it might hit the science page of the BBC website.'

'So what's happened?'

'Oh, nothing much. It's just that the whole of his life's work is falling down in ruins, and goodness only knows – she says, selfishly – what that means for my PhD.'

'Falling down in ruins?'

'Well. James said, "demolished". I think it's a bit of an exaggeration.'

'So what does a ruin look like?'

Colette brought up the news story on her phone and handed it to Lydia.

'So he's wrong. His pet theory's been disproved?'

Colette, for whom science, like faith, was a continuous process of casting out lines and having them fall short, of classifying and summarising what she did know in order to move past it to what she did not, knowing that the whole of it could never be known, said, 'It's a bit more complicated than that.'

'*Probably* disproved.'

'Yes, that's closer.' She laughed. 'The thing is, he then spent the afternoon on Twitter explaining how everybody is wrong and the scientific community is out to get him.'

'Is it?'

'No, of course not. And even if it was he'd still have a flourishing career on telly.'

'So what *does* it mean for your PhD?'

'I very much hope,' Colette said, 'that it means nothing at all. It shouldn't, because I'm measuring stuff that can be measured and drawing tiny, tentative conclusions, and either I find something that works or I don't, and anyway I've nearly finished. He's only there to stop me doing anything stupid.'

'So, no need to worry, then?'

'No.'

An hour later, Colette said, 'Give me something else to think about.'

'How would you feel about taking a look at that star?'

She had to think for a moment before she worked out what Lydia was talking about. 'What, your church star? See what's wrong with it?'

'I know what's wrong with it. It needs the plug rewiring.'

'Oh, is that all? I could have done that months ago.'

'Wait a minute.' Lydia went off to the study and came back with the star clutched to her chest, the lead trailing in a loop behind her. It was an awkward contraption of wire coat hangers and tinsel, with fairy lights twined through. She put it down on the table. 'Yes. Look. Some *helpful person* put a biscuit tin or something down on top of it, something with an edge on the bottom, anyway.'

Colette looked, and was quietly horrified. 'It must have been one hell of a biscuit tin. That's gone all the way through the insulation.'

'Well, maybe they stood on it afterwards. Anyway, can you do anything with it?'

'If we have a wire cutter and a screwdriver and a spare plug, and I happen to know that we do, then yes.' She went to rummage for tools in the cupboard in the hall.

Lydia followed her. 'I really should know how to do this. Dad never taught me.'

'You just have to remember which wire goes where. It's not difficult at all.'

## *March*

*The problem is, people make assumptions. They see the husband and the children, and they jump to a conclusion without even knowing their feet have left the ground.*

*No: the problem is, they don't do it out loud. If they made a specific statement, I could contradict that. I tell myself that I would. But they never do, because it never occurs to them. And it feels awkward to raise the subject out of nowhere, so I'm left wondering what is the way of integrity.*

*Is it my business to correct an assumption that someone shouldn't have made in the first place when I've got no proof that they've made it?*

*How far am I failing to tell the truth when I've never lied?*

Invisible, Bisexual, Bloggable
5 March 2017


The church of St John the Evangelist always reminded Colette of her primary school: it had the same greyish bricks, the same white-painted metal window frames, the same golden-brown varnished wood inside. She rather liked it that way. Sometimes it came as a slight surprise to her that the board outside showed service times and contact details for the Rev. Benjy Munroe, rather than those of the headteacher and caretaker.

The service was reassuringly familiar, too. Colette had been here often enough with Lydia that she was able to trace the underlying routine beneath the surface chaos, and now she was beginning to enjoy the services at St John's. They were still more demonstrative than she was comfortable with, and the preaching was not exactly challenging, but she had come to terms with the idea that she could sit out the bits that bothered her, and that probably nobody would worry about it all that much. She was even getting to know the songs well enough that she could keep singing when the person in charge of the PowerPoint got thrown by verses being repeated.

In short, it was beginning to feel like home.

Afterwards, they queued up at the hatch and Lydia took two mugs, one of coffee and one of tea. She handed the tea to Colette.

'How are things?' Felicity asked. She wielded the huge steel teapot with an elegant delicacy to stop the spout dripping between the cups, but she had to concentrate to do it, her fair hair falling forwards into her face.

Lydia said, 'Pretty good, thanks. How was the pancake party? Sorry I couldn't make it.'

Felicity put the teapot down, met Lydia's eye, and grinned. 'Good fun! We only lost a couple of them to the floor.'

Lydia nudged Colette. 'We forgot the star.'

'So we did. Oh well, next week.'

'We'll be at Wardle Street next week,' Lydia pointed out. 'I suppose it's not as if there's any hurry, nobody's going to want it in Lent...'

'It would be good to get it out of the flat now we've fixed it.'

'Now *you've* fixed it.'

'You helped.' A thought struck her. 'Maybe I could come down with it some time during the week?'

Felicity said, 'That would work. I'll be around on Wednesday morning.'

'What time?'

'Anywhere between half nine and half eleven.'

'I'll bring it down around ten, in that case.'

Lydia looked grateful. 'Are you sure?'

'Of course,' Colette said. 'Like I said. Get it out of the flat.'

James was already in the office when Colette arrived on Monday morning, windblown but cheerful.

'Hello,' she said.

'Morning.' He sounded remote but not hostile, and did not turn around. Colette recognised the signs of intense concentration and refrained from causing any further disturbance. Instead, she booted up her computer and loaded the data she had been looking at the previous week. She had left it on Friday morning with some threads hanging loose. That might have been a mistake, but in actual fact the act of re-reading her notes prompted a couple of other possibilities to rise to the surface of her mind. She added them as hasty bullet points:

- *temperature???*
- *but what if current?*
- *changing behaviour*

They would not mean much to anyone else; she knew that if she left them too long they would not mean anything to her, either. That wasn't the point. Pinning down one corner of an idea meant that she could move past it and consider the question as a whole. Although of course even this was only a tiny part of the topic, and the topic as a whole would be a miniscule contribution to the field, even if she did find anything new, even if she had time to investigate it properly and write it up... She didn't care. It was not about being a footnote to a footnote; it was this privilege of looking at something that nobody had looked at before, and having the audacity to try to make sense of it...

After a while, James said, 'Coffee?', and Colette said, 'Yes, please, if you're going,' and fumbled for her purse.

James said, 'Ah, don't worry,' and left before she could argue.

She skimmed her notes, decided that this would probably still be useful tomorrow, and saved the file. She was, she realised, actually quite thirsty.

A short time later, James reappeared with two cappuccinos.

'Thank you.'

'You're welcome.' He sat down and swung around on his chair so that he faced her.

'Any news from Planet Wedding?' she asked.

'Ha. Yes.'

'Not good news?' she guessed.

'There's good news, and there's bad news. The good news is, the bridesmaids finally reached a compromise.'

Colette sucked at the froth of her coffee. 'Well, hurrah. What's the bad news?'

'Don't you want to hear about the cobalt blue taffeta? I can't say I blame you. The bad news is, my uncle had a massive argument with my godfather – who's his second cousin, I think – and we're going to have to redo the whole table plan. Again.'

'Eurgh. What was the argument about?'

James lifted his shoulders skywards. 'Officially, I'm not meant to know. Unofficially, his wife…'

'Whose wife?'

'Well, quite.' He rolled his eyes. 'My godfather's. My mum said she didn't believe a word of it, but she had quite a lot to say about it all the same.'

'So who's going to sit where, then?'

'*I'm* not going to make that call. Not until somebody tells me officially. But we need to get the final document off to the printer this week.'

'So soon?'

'Giselle got this really good deal – they'll do the programmes and the labels and the table cards and all the rest of it, but they need the whole lot by Friday, because they're too busy afterwards.'

'Couldn't you just get Mariam to run the table plan off for you on the big colour printer downstairs?'

'Left to myself, I'd do it in biro – no, pencil – on a lined A4 pad. On the back of somebody else's notes. But Giselle says it's got to match the rest.' He shook his head. 'Let's talk about something else. Did you get anywhere with that anomaly?'

'Yes,' she said. 'Yes, I think I have. Look.'

He came and looked over her shoulder. She pointed. 'Look. This little spike *here*... it matches this over here. I don't know why I didn't think to compare them before.'

'So it does. Well, there we go. Who needs Barry?'

'I came out today,' Lydia said, while Colette was making the dinner. Her tone was almost conversational.

Colette laid the wooden spoon down carefully on the chopping board. 'How did that go?'

Lydia shook coffee granules straight from the jar into a mug. 'Not too badly, I think. We'll have to see what happens.'

'So, why? How?'

'We were doing equality and diversity training, and it got onto sexual orientation versus religion and belief, and there was this one woman from Planning who was dreadfully worried about upsetting people who have *sincerely held beliefs*.'

'Did she have any herself?' Colette asked.

'I don't know. But I got about halfway into hashtag Not All Christians and got so tied up in knots that I thought it would just be easier to admit to being a gay Christian, and ask people not to make assumptions about my sexual orientation or about my beliefs.'

'And how did that go down?' The courgettes were starting to burn; Colette scraped at them with the edge of the wooden spoon.

Lydia assumed a world-weary expression. 'Oh, then we had a guy who said, no, Christians are all homophobic, and the ones who aren't are wrong about Christianity. But Trevor said that under the Equality Act, even if I was the only Christian in the world who thought it was OK to be gay, my interpretation was as valid as anyone else's. And then during the break he said did I want to join the union.'

'Probably a good idea.' Colette watched Lydia's face carefully for any sign of the control faltering.

87

'Yes. So I did. There's an LGBT group, too, apparently.' The kettle boiled and clicked itself off, and Lydia turned away to make her coffee. 'It's just weird,' she said, once she had added milk. 'Every church in the city, it feels like, knows I'm both. Or knows I call myself both,' she amended, bitterly. 'I'm still The Girl Who Came Out To The Christian Fellowship and it's coming up three years since I graduated. And OK, maybe I'm just projecting because news travels fast on campus and *of course* everyone at St John's has a very well-tuned gaydar. But nobody at the council seems to register anything unless I tell them, and OK, maybe I've been playing the pronoun game a bit, and of course they do all know I'm Christian, which is just as well...'

'Why?'

'Because I have to get a reference from somebody at work.'

'A reference?'

'For the bishop's form.'

'Oh,' Colette said, shaken. There had been plenty of forms, but the mention of the bishop made things seem abruptly serious.

'It asks some really searching questions, too.'

'You'll have made some people think today. That's a good thing.'

Lydia nodded. 'One woman said she hadn't realised it was possible to be both, and now she had. So. I don't know: perhaps it was worth it.'

'Well done.' Colette was not sure whether she meant it sincerely.

'Thanks.' It was hard to tell whether Lydia had taken it as being sincere. 'At least it'll give me something to talk about with Tina tomorrow.'

'Coming out?'

'In the context of being a Christian, in the context of work.' She frowned. 'I get the impression she'd rather avoid the topic.'

Colette might have pounced on that, but she wasn't in the mood. 'Maybe stick to the subject of work, then. Presumably she'll be quite pleased about you having some experience in the real world?'

'Peter says,' Lydia said, and then repeated it, with a self-consciously childish inflection, '*Peter says,* that they used to send you off to the real world to get some experience, if you were younger than about thirty, but they've given up on doing that because too many people were finding out that they preferred the real world and not coming back again. So now they're more likely to put you straight through.'

'Well, it didn't work like that for him. Did his parish job count as the *real world,* or not?'

'Who knows? I don't know what he did or said at the BAP, and they're meant to go on that.'

Colette shook her head. 'Either way. Not that it stopped him.'

Peter had picked himself up, gritted his teeth, done two more years as a pastoral assistant, this time in a London parish, and responded to most well-meaning enquiries with a mild, 'Well, they know what they're looking for, and you have to trust them, don't you?' Only with very close friends – Colette and Lydia, Georgia, perhaps some others they didn't know – had he let the hurt and frustration show.

'It's horrible,' he had told them. 'You have to let them see who you really are, and then they don't want you.'

Nevertheless, he had gone back, almost as soon as he was allowed to do so, and done it all over again.

'I don't think it will be like that for me,' Lydia said. 'I sort of imagine it all blowing up so spectacularly that nobody will ever dream of having me back to try again. I'll burn all the bridges, go out all guns blazing, screw you all.' Her expression changed. 'At least, unless it's because they genuinely don't think I have that sort of call.'

She looked lost, humbled. Colette ached for her. 'So what happens in that case?'

She shrugged. 'I suppose I'll have to pray for grace to see it that way and accept the decision. But then it comes to the same thing, doesn't it, because if I accept that their decision is right if that's what it is, then I'm accepting that I don't have a calling – to ordained ministry,' she added hurriedly; 'I know that everybody has a calling of some sort, obviously.'

Colette was beginning to lose the thread of Lydia's argument. 'So you're saying it's now or never? You get one shot at this?'

'Well, whenever or never. I don't know when they'd put me forward for it, if they even do.' She added, looking bleak, 'I just can't see myself doing what Peter's done. I don't think I could put myself through it again.'

Lydia was no less edgy after the meeting with Tina. She summed it up to Colette in one angry monologue.

'… So I have to cross my fingers – *she* didn't say that, though – and say that yes, I'm submitting to *Issues in Human Sexuality*. Is the word "submit"? I can't remember. It might as well be.' She gave an abrupt laugh.

'And does that work?'

Lydia shrugged her shoulders. 'People get through, so it must.'

'So what happens when someone asks you about your relationship?'

'Peter says they don't ask. Not in that way, anyway.'

'Wasn't he single when he went for selection?'

'Yes. Both times. I think they must have assumed that he was the sort of nice young man who'd have no trouble finding some obliging nice young lady to support him in his ministry.' She chuckled darkly and added, 'He'll have to ask for permission from the Bishop if he and Natalie want to get married while he's still at college.'

'Weird.'

'I know.' Lydia made a what-can-you-do sort of face.

'Would the Bishop object to Natalie?' Colette asked.

'I wouldn't have thought so. Imagine what she'd do to the quality of the music in any parish they ended up in!'

'She'd definitely be an asset.'

'As would you,' Lydia said, shortly. 'Oh, I know you wouldn't want to do the tea-and-sympathy thing. Quite rightly: it would be my job. But you would keep me going, and I don't think I could do it without you.'

Colette was touched. 'I think I get more support from you than you do from me.'

'That's not true,' Lydia said. She sighed. 'And we can't get married. I mean, you know that; we've talked about it before. It just... hit home today. If we get married, I won't be selected.'

'It's as black-and-white as that?'

'Yeah. Basically.'

'What would happen if we were to get married after you get ordained?'

'Depends who you ask. Either they find a way to sack you, or they just never give you another job.'

Colette tried to see the bright side. It was not easy. She ventured, 'Would it be easier... if you were single?'

'*No.*'

'Really?'

Lydia was furious. 'In this one case, maybe it would. In every other way, no. I'm not doing this without you. Having you in my life has made me who I am.'

'Right,' Colette said, rather embarrassed. 'But I don't want you to paint yourself into a corner. I want you to be able to make a choice, if it comes to it.'

'They shouldn't be asking me to make that choice.'

'But since they are...'

'It's *not bloody fair*!' Lydia burst out. 'When I think of the thousands and thousands of Christians who are being pushed to marry, and I don't want anything different from any of them...'

Somewhere in the back of Colette's mind, something said, *But I do*. She ignored it and said, 'Oh, come now. Weddings must represent a significant proportion of most churches' income. You can't blame them for trying to increase demand.'

Lydia looked rather shocked for a moment, and then, seeing that it was a joke, replied in the same tone: 'Then why not open it up to same-sex couples and increase the pool of potential customers by another ten per cent or so?'

Colette laughed. 'Don't you think it's interesting,' she said off-handedly, 'that it's the churches that are most keen on the *do not be conformed to the world* thing that are also the most likely to push conformity on their members? Like, if you're not married with two point four kids, don't bother stepping through the door if you don't want to be treated like a second-class citizen.'

'Oh, yes,' Lydia agreed, distracted. 'I always think that someone – not me – should write a book for the single Christian woman. *How to survive in a church full of couples*.'

'Leave the church full of couples and find one that treats you as a human being in your own right?'

'Well, that might be the answer. Maybe it should include a chapter on *Finding somewhere that treats you as a human being without being accused of church shopping*.'

'I see you've thought this through,' Colette said, keeping her face straight.

'Not really, but there are certain parallels...' She added, 'Rose is popping round later.'

'Later meaning when?'

Lydia glanced at the clock. 'Oh dear. In about twenty minutes. I'm sorry.' She went to the sink and drew herself a glass of water. 'I'd better not rant to *her* about not being able to get married.'

'Why? Will she not be sympathetic?'

'I've no idea. But I have a feeling that it wouldn't be very sympathetic of me.'

Colette, being tactful again, took herself off to the study before Rose turned up, and read all the news that she could find on the internet about the collapse of Barry's knot theory. Her laptop threatened to run out of battery, and she had to move the St John's nativity star once again to get at the single pair of sockets. At least, she consoled herself, she would be getting rid of that tomorrow.

The weather alternated between sun and rain as if it couldn't make its mind up. Colette, walking down to St John's, found herself too hot with her jacket, and too cold without it, and, with the star in her arms, the operation of doing anything to correct it too tiresome to bother with.

It occurred to her halfway down the hill that it would have been easier to drive. The star was not heavy, but it was awkward to carry, and the lead had an irritating tendency to unwind itself from around the body and hang down over her elbow, knocking against her thigh. It would have helped just to have put the whole thing in a bag, if only they'd had a bag that was large enough. It occurred to her halfway up the next hill that in fact they did have a bag that was large enough. But it really was not worth turning back now. Grumbling quietly, she continued to the church, the plug knocking her leg all the way.

The main door was unlocked. She pushed it open and stepped inside. She could see through the glass doors that the church itself was empty. Tentatively, she called, 'Hello!'

'Colette! I'm in here!'

She followed the L-shaped corridor around to the kitchen. Felicity was kneeling on the floor, doing something inside one of the cupboards. She looked round as Colette came in. 'Sorry about this.

You couldn't pass me the bin, could you? Yes. That one. And would you mind taking the lid off... Thanks.' She took it from Colette and with a rubber-gloved hand brushed a mess of shredded paper and tea leaves into it.

'What happened there?' Colette asked.

Felicity made a face. 'I *think* it was a mouse.'

'Yuck,' Colette said, because it seemed to be expected.

'I don't know when was the last time anyone opened that cupboard, so goodness knows when it got in there. On the bright side, there wasn't anything in there except a few flower vases and that box of teabags which we should have chucked years ago anyway. I'll have to go through everything else some time. Not today. Anyway, you came to bring the star back, didn't you?'

'Here it is.' Colette stood it on the worktop on two of its points, propping it against the tiled wall.

'You – I was going to say, star. I'll say it anyway. You star.' She sat back on her heels and smiled sunnily up at Colette.

'You're assuming it's fixed.'

'Well, go on, show me. Plug it in next to the kettle.' She put a hand on the worktop to raise herself up to stand.

Colette plugged it in. The LEDs glowed feebly against the daylight. 'There. Good as new.'

'It *is*. Well done. Thank you. That's brilliant.'

She flushed. 'It wasn't anything, really.'

'Rubbish. Time, skill, and effort, at the very least. I'll put it away.' Felicity peeled off the rubber gloves and dropped them into the bin.

Colette unplugged the star again and the lights blinked out. She followed Felicity to a cupboard in the lobby.

Felicity pulled out several cardboard boxes before she found the one she was looking for. She held her hands out for the star and laid it gently on top of a wad of red felt, then closed and replaced the box.

'I hate to ask,' she said, 'but you're here, and you're tall, so: would you mind helping me with the banner up at the front? I've tried doing it by myself, but it won't stay while I get the other end up.'

'Of course,' Colette said, glad to continue favouring practicality over small talk. And for the next ten minutes their conversation consisted entirely of things like, 'Left a bit!', 'Try the big hammer?', 'OK, hold it there!', and 'This nail's bent,' until the banner was correctly placed.

'And now,' said Felicity, 'would you like a cup of tea? Guaranteed mouse-free – I've only just bought this box.'

Colette thought about saying that it was time she was going, but did not wish to appear rude. 'That would be lovely.'

They went back through to the kitchen. Felicity lifted the kettle to assess the quantity of water in it, put it down on its base again, and switched it on. 'Take a pew.'

Colette removed a plastic-seated chair from a stack in the corner and sat down on it. 'Do you come down here every day?'

'Two or three times a week, maybe.' Felicity took a tin down from the shelf. 'Biscuit?'

'Thanks.' Colette took a custard cream.

Felicity explained, 'I work from home, and I only live around the corner, so it's easy for me.'

'Oh, so you actually live in the parish? I didn't realise...'

'Yup. It's not just that I'm one of the congregation of Stancester queer women, though I have to say it worked out very well.'

'Worked out?'

'Well, I don't see how any of us – me, Eve, *or* the church – could have known when we moved in. I bet God's laughing about it.'

'I suppose God has the sense of perspective that makes it easy to laugh about things,' Colette said drily.

'Well, of course. How do you take your tea?'

'Very milky, please. No sugar.'

'Here you go.' Felicity handed her a mug and then fetched a chair for herself. 'So,' she said as she sat down, 'how are things?'

'Oh, they're OK. Nothing very exciting going on. You know.'

Felicity's eyes were quite remarkably blue when she looked you full in the face. 'I think you're doing yourself down. From what Lydia tells me, your studies are really interesting.'

Colette hunched over her tea. 'Oh, well, interesting, yes. But I said they weren't *exciting*.'

'Maybe they are if you take the long view.'

'Maybe,' Colette agreed. 'As it is, most of the excitement comes from the postdoc's wedding planning.' She launched into a summary, more involved than she'd intended it to be, of James's saga.

'So,' Felicity said when she'd finished, as if she'd been waiting for an advert break, 'does that make things difficult for you?'

Colette was surprised. 'For me? Why should it?'

'Well, if he's constantly got his mind on other things...?'

'Oh, I see. No. The worst person for that is my supervisor, who... has a very busy media schedule.' Colette wondered why she was bothering to mince her words. Some sort of misguided scientific solidarity, perhaps.

'That must be difficult.'

Again, she found herself defending Barry. 'It's very good for the university's reputation, and the department's. And, you know, the project might not even exist if it wasn't for his being a big name in this field, so we try to be understanding.'

'It sounds to me like you're being *very* understanding,' Felicity said tartly.

'It's just one of those things,' Colette said, embarrassed.

'And then of course you have Lydia going through the discernment process,' Felicity mused. 'I'd imagine that takes some getting used to.'

'You could say that.' Colette remembered Lydia coming back from house group about eighteen months before, and her face, taut with disbelief, when she said, *Felicity thinks I should think about ordained ministry.*

'How do *you* feel about it?'

Colette felt that it was a bit rich of Felicity to be asking that, and wondered what the reaction would be if she said *I think it's a terrible idea.* Instead, she settled for, 'Well, it wasn't such a surprise, once I'd thought about it a bit.'

'No?'

'Not really. I mean, even when I met her she was a Christian Fellowship hall officer. Before that she'd been really involved in her church at home, in the music group and the children's ministry. And then coming here –' she pointed at the kitchen door, meaning the church beyond it – 'where nobody's going to be difficult about her being a woman or gay, and doing about three hundred per cent more stuff... Well, it was obvious, really, wasn't it?'

Felicity laughed. 'I thought so. But you knew that.'

'Yes,' Colette agreed.

'And I think you're doing yourself down again.'

'Me?'

'From what Lydia says, it wasn't until she met *you* that she started to think of herself as someone with something to offer.'

'Well, that's ridiculous. Like I said, she was doing loads of stuff. If anything, she did *less* after we got together.'

'What makes you say that?'

Surely it wasn't necessary to spell it out? 'Well, because Fellowship stopped giving her things to do once they'd worked it out. They made her resign from everything.'

'And perhaps that was what made her realise how much she'd been doing, without necessarily being thanked for it. Perhaps it stopped her taking herself and her ministry for granted. And perhaps your valuing her for who she was had a lot to do with that as well.'

Colette rather resented Felicity's attempt to frame that as something special, as opposed to simple common decency, and the whole question as being somehow her fault. She said, 'I can't believe that I was the first person.'

'Even if you were only the first person she knew about, the first person she felt sure about, that's quite important.'

'Oh, well...'

Felicity looked sympathetic. 'I can imagine it's a huge thing to come to terms with. The whole identity thing...'

This felt too personal for both of them. Colette said, as repressively as she could manage, 'We're getting there.'

'I'm glad to hear that.'

They were both silent. Colette drained her mug. 'Anyway. Thank you for the tea. I'd better get up to campus.'

When she arrived, she found James seated at his desk, his jacket still on. He was staring at a blank screen. She said, 'Hello.'

He grunted.

'Are you OK?' Colette asked, and chided herself inwardly for asking such a pointless question.

James tried to smile. 'Yeah, sorry.'

'Are you sure?' *Don't push it*, she told herself.

'Yeah.' He paused for a moment. 'I had a stupid argument with Giselle, that's all.'

'What about?'

'Wedding photos.'

'Oh?'

'Well. I said, no way are we spending twelve hundred quid, that's ridiculous, when my Uncle Simon could do it for us for free.'

'Wow,' Colette said, genuinely shocked. 'Is that really what it costs?'

'It's what the one *she* wants costs.'

'Is your Uncle Simon any good?'

'He isn't bad. Like, he'd get some decent shots, I'm sure.' He did not sound convinced. 'And does it really matter? So long as we get married and the important people are there and they have a good time, right?'

'That sounds reasonable to me,' Colette said, warily.

'Right. But according to Giselle, everybody says you don't remember much of the actual day, so we need to make sure we have really good photos so we can remember it later.'

'What, like recreate it, in your minds?'

'Yeah. So she says it needs to be a pro. So apparently we've got to cough up *and* offend Uncle Simon.'

'Bummer. Did you make up?'

'Yeah, kind of.' He shook himself. 'Anyway. I don't suppose *you've* heard from Barry today?'

Colette was just beginning, 'No, he...' when one of the porters knocked at the door.

'Barry Parnell?'

'Not here, I'm afraid,' said James.

'Hmph. This needs a signature.' He glared at the two of them as if they'd arranged for Barry's absence deliberately.

James looked apologetic, but also as if he was getting tired of being apologetic. 'Does it have to be him who signs for it?'

'Well, ideally, yes, but if he's not here then someone else will have to do. Because I'm not taking it downstairs again.'

Colette looked past him at the offending package. It was tall, bulky, and said *This Way Up* and *Handle With Care* all over it.

James said, 'I'll do it if someone's got to.'

While he signed, Colette wheeled their chairs out of the way and watched the man bring the box in. It looked even larger inside the office.

'There,' said the porter.

'Thank you,' said Colette, with a smile she didn't mean.

The porter nodded at her, and left.

The box loomed in the corner. Colette looked at it. 'Could we put it in his office?' she asked.

James tried the door handle. 'Locked.'

'I thought they had a little room to keep parcels in.'

'It may be that Barry's used up his share of good will downstairs.'

'I wish they wouldn't take it out on us.'

She was more glad than she would have admitted to anyone else, particularly James, that there was nobody at the porters' desk when she left the building that evening. She tried to make the incident sound amusing when she told Lydia about it over dinner, but was relieved when the subject drifted round to St John's, the star, and Felicity.

Then her phone buzzed. She looked down:

*Hi Colette, just to let you know before the rest of social, Izzy and I are getting married!! July 2018. Save the date!*

'Holy fuck,' she said.

'What is it?' Lydia asked.

Colette told her.

'Jess?' Lydia sounded puzzled. 'Oh, Jess your ex-girlfriend?'

'The very same,' Colette said. She tapped out, *Wow, that's great news! Congratulations!*

'I assume she's marrying Izzy?'

'She is indeed. Do you want to come?'

Lydia shrugged her shoulders. 'I really don't mind, if you want to.' She narrowed her eyes. 'You seem a bit... upset?'

'Do I?' Colette thought about it. 'I'm surprised, mostly. She's always been really anti-marriage. Her parents split up when we were going out.'

'Did it have anything to do with that?' Lydia's tone was cautious, almost guilty-sounding.

'No...' Colette hesitated, looked at Jess' reply and continued, 'She did try asking them if it did, but I knew she didn't believe that.' She scowled at the memory of Jess's histrionic whine: *is it because of me and Colette?* 'It was a cynical guilt trip, and it didn't work. They split up, and they stayed split up. And ever since then she's been absolutely insistent that she was wrong, that they were much better apart than they'd ever been together, and that marriage was a terrible thing that did terrible things to people.' In the case of Jess's parents, Colette thought, she was inclined to agree.

'And now...?'

She rolled her eyes. 'Now she's apparently forgotten about that. It seems that she and Izzy have got something totally different going on. I haven't asked for the details, obviously.'

'Maybe it's true love.'

'Maybe it's a brain transplant.' That sounded harsh. 'My best guess is that when we were a couple it wasn't a possibility, and now that it is she's realised how much she wants it.'

'That does seem possible. Little foxes in the vineyard? The opposite of sour grapes?'

'Yes, something like that. Not to mention, of course, the fact that we were seventeen and it would have been a really stupid idea.'

'Plenty of people do.'

Colette wondered if she was thinking of Rory and Mel. She said, cautiously, 'I wonder if we'll ever do it. I wonder if it will become possible for us.'

'It *is* possible. That's the really infuriating thing. Just, not in a way that meshes with all the other things that I want to do. If it wasn't for me then you could get married any time you like.'

'You're forgetting that you're the only person I would want to marry, and I don't want to do it if it ruins the rest of your life.'

Lydia blazed, 'It wouldn't.'

'I wonder,' Colette said, still cautious, 'if, by the time it does become possible, we'll actually want to do it, or if we'll be so used to being with each other the way we are now, we'll decide to stick with what we know.'

'I would want to. I'm sure I would.'

'It seems like such a remote possibility that I'm not sure I can even imagine it.'

Lydia said, 'I was reading back through Abby's blog earlier. She was talking about how a bisexual partner just becomes invisible in a heterosexual relationship. And also about making jam tarts with the children.'

'Was she the one making the jam tarts?' Colette asked, not sure where this was going.

'She was. Well, with Rachel as well. But that's not my point.' Lydia waved her hands in the air, frustrated. 'Look. She's queer. She knows she's queer, Paul knows she's queer. She'd tell anybody who bothered to ask, but they never do. And yet she gets to be married. What's the difference between her and Paul and you and me?'

'Not much. Apart from the children, I suppose.'

'Right.' Lydia brought her right hand down on the table with a thump. 'But if they'd never had children and were never going to, then they'd still be just as married as they are now.'

'It's not fair,' Colette said. 'But then we always knew that, didn't we?'

## *April*

9 April – Palm Sunday
St J's/L reading

10 April
Tina? check!!!

11 April
Rose 7pm ish

12 April
Rowan???

13 April – Maundy Thursday
St J's/L talk

14 April – Good Friday
Wdl St

15 April
Peter/Natalie/Georgia/Will – Curzon's!!
Easter Vigil/Pip confirmation – 8pm cathedral

16 April – Easter Day

**Palm Sunday**

Lydia had said all along that she wasn't sure the donkey was a brilliant idea. Still, the children loved it. Ida, standing by with a shovel at the back of the church, muttered to Colette that, with any luck, the palm branches (actually pampas grass, courtesy of some parishioner who'd got fed up with the stuff and dug out the whole clump) would have kept the worst of it off the parquet. Lydia, reading the Evangelist's part in the Passion narrative, kept herself from giggling with what Colette knew must have been a heroic effort.

'It was Benjy's face,' she said afterwards. 'He'd been so sure that it wasn't going to...'

And they laughed all the way through coffee and all the way home.

## Monday of Holy Week

Colette went into the lab because she thought she might as well: Lydia was working these next two days, and the place would be quiet, and she could get ahead on her report. Outside the Sciences Block, the cherry trees were papered with blossom, and the building looked grubby by contrast.

James was there, which wasn't surprising; so was Giselle, which was.

'We're going on into town,' James explained. 'We've got to pick up the table decorations.'

'But James had to finish something off for Barry,' Giselle added, with a conspiratorial glance at Colette, 'so I thought it would be easier if I drove us both up here and then we went straight on to the garden centre afterwards.'

'Garden centre?' Colette repeated. 'Isn't it a bit early to get flowers?'

Giselle shook her head. 'They sell all sorts of things. What we're getting is a load of glass fishbowl things with pebbles and floating candles.'

'Then you've got your make-up trial,' James said.

Giselle, who Colette had never thought of as being a particularly make-uppy sort of person, made a face. Today she was wearing dungarees over a long-sleeved tie-dye T-shirt, with her frizzy hair held back in a thick plait; it made it more than usually difficult to imagine her lipsticked and eyelinered and caked with foundation.

'But before that we need to go and see the photographer, remember.'

Colette pretended that she did not know of any reason why the question of a photographer might have been a point of contention. 'Oh, right?'

'And we need to email the caterers back.'

James said, 'I'll do that now,' and opened a Gmail window.

'And,' Giselle said, 'if we have time, I want to pop into Hobbycraft in case they have any of those little organza bags.'

'Wow.' Colette thought again that it all sounded like a lot more trouble than it was worth.

'Blue, if possible.' Giselle added, presumably for Colette's benefit, 'These are for the favours for the guests.'

'Good luck,' said Colette.

'Thank you,' James said abstractedly. 'Giselle, are you happy with what I've written?'

Colette pulled her chair closer to her desk so Giselle could come past her to see James' screen.

'Perfect. Send it.'

James did so, then put his jacket on while his computer shut down. 'OK. Let's go. Colette, have a lovely break.'

'You too. See you after Easter. Giselle, see you at the wedding if not before. Have fun!'

Although, she thought, as the door closed after them and the office subsided into quiet, that really sounded rather optimistic.

**Tuesday of Holy Week**

Lydia had invited Rose over for dinner several weeks before; but, between church commitments on both sides and some confusion that Colette hadn't followed about Rose's work pattern, it was only happening now.

Lydia cooked, which was fair in some ways but not in others (she arrived home late, having had skeins full of loose ends to tie up before leaving the office for the Easter break, and then had to shop for food), while Colette did her best to tidy up the end of term clutter. Rose arrived precisely on time, looking neat in a turquoise blouse and grey pencil skirt. This impression lasted about five minutes, until she volunteered to help Lydia in the kitchen.

'*Rose*,' Lydia said fondly. 'How do you do it?'

'I don't know. I'm such a disaster.'

'At least it's only milk. It could have been tomato. Or oil.'

Rose, however, seemed to be very attached to the idea that she was a disaster. 'I did exactly the same thing with bolognese sauce once. I ruined one of Liam's shirts.'

'Now, if we're talking about disasters,' Lydia said, 'that *man*...'

Rose chuckled. 'Yes, fine, you've said it before, he's a waste of space and I'm better off without him! I'm just not enjoying being single, OK?' She glared at the two of them.

'OK,' Lydia said meekly. 'Are those potatoes ready?' She gave the stew a final stir and chivvied Rose towards the (now tidy) dining table. Colette dodged round the two of them to collect cutlery and plates and back again to lay the table.

Rose sat down. 'He's going out with Anna,' she said. 'Did you know?'

'No,' Colette said, with perfect honesty, never having met either of them. Lydia didn't say anything, just spooned out the stew.

'I mean, even if it wasn't her, it would be someone else, he's got a queue a mile long.' She glanced from one to the other as if daring either of them to rebuke her for gossiping.

'Yes, but there's nothing special about him,' Lydia said. 'There's a notorious shortage of Christian men.' Colette thought this a bit tactless.

'Particularly at Centrepoint,' said Rose.

Lydia said, 'Is it, though? Or is it just that Centrepoint puts more weight on being part of a couple?'

Rose frowned. 'Does it?'

'I'll never forget,' Lydia said. 'The one week I went there: cake for somebody's wedding anniversary, prayers for somebody else's wedding, prayers for Rory and Mel's engagement, joint talk by the pastor and his wife, news about the children and grandchildren of what seemed to be the entire congregation...'

Her tone was mild, but Colette remembered how much it had hurt her at the time.

Rose laughed, unwillingly. Lydia mused, 'That was one thing that St Mark's never did. It was much more about not getting distracted.'

Colette, whose mind was half on their plans for Saturday, took a moment to disentangle St Mark's college, where Natalie sang, from St Mark's church, which Lydia used to attend.

Rose said, 'That's because it's much more of a student church, I guess.'

'Nothing wrong with that,' Lydia said.

Rose opened her mouth, shut it again, and said, 'You never did tell me how you ended up going to St John's.'

Lydia smiled, as if accepting a peace offering. 'Someone from Fellowship recommended it. Said it's where all the lesbians go.'

**Wednesday of Holy Week**

The next day, Rowan, who was staying in Stancester over the Easter holidays, dropped round for tea, but declined a chocolate biscuit.

'How are things?' Colette asked them.

'Not bad. I mean, I guess you must know this already, but campus is so *weird* without anyone around.'

'What are you doing up there?' Lydia asked.

'Essay, mostly. And spying on postgrads, seeing if I want to be one some day.'

'I wouldn't recommend it,' said Colette. 'Maybe do a Masters, if you're really keen, but then get out.'

Rowan raised an eyebrow. 'That good, huh?'

'It's probably fine if your supervisor isn't unhealthily attached to a theory that might be on the way out, and your postdoc isn't stressing about his wedding twenty-four-seven.'

'Well, actually,' Rowan said, with a sly grin, 'the AngthMURC committee was wondering if you'd be prepared to speak about being a PhD student.'

'It's not really that interesting.'

'And being a scientist and a Christian.' The smile became mischievous. 'Cathsoc have got some big-name Jesuit astronomer coming to talk to them next term.'

'I don't think I'm as exciting as any kind of Jesuit.' A thought struck her. 'If it's science and religion you want, you should get Gordon. Professor Summers.'

'Ooh, that's a good thought. Would he do it? Would you mind asking him?'

'Of course,' said Colette, relieved to have got out of having to be guest speaker herself. 'I'm sure he would. He's lovely.'

'Aren't you leaving things a bit late?' Lydia asked.

'This is for autumn.'

'Ah, right. How have you got press-ganged into organising the programme, anyway? I thought you weren't on the committee.'

'They aren't,' Colette said, 'any more than I am.'

'Oh,' Rowan said, 'it's only because I was going to see you. I said I'd ask. Also, are you going to the next West Country LGBTX?'

'No,' Lydia said, 'because it clashes with Colette's postdoc's wedding.' She glanced at Colette. 'Plus I still need to persuade Colette that she actually wants to come.'

Rowan looked sympathetic. 'Oh, I know, it's not exactly my thing either, but sometimes it's better than nothing.'

'Well, there's that,' Colette said, 'and also it's in Truro, which is a pig to get to from here on any weekend. If we had been going, I'd have offered you a lift.'

'I appreciate the thought. Not to worry. I might or might not go myself. But it's nice to be in a space where people are generally happy to meet you as you are, rather than as they think you should be. *Generally.*'

**Maundy Thursday**

Lydia did the weekly phone call three days early. Colette was not sure if this was something to do with love and being reconciled with one's kin before taking communion, or if she expected it to go badly and so wanted to get it out of the way. If her aim had been the latter, it had certainly succeeded; if the former, it seemed doubtful. Lydia did not seem to want to talk about how it went, and shut herself in the study.

After an hour Colette tapped on the door.

Lydia's 'Hello?' was muffled, and, if not encouraging, not actively hostile.

'Tea?' Colette offered.

'Yes, please.'

She made tea, and opened another packet of biscuits, and brought them into the study. Lydia lifted her head from where it had been cradled in her folded arms; she had been crying. Colette moved *Silence and Honey Cakes* and *End of Term*, put the mug and the plate down on the desk, and, without speaking, put her arms around Lydia's shoulders, and stroked her hair.

'Everything's the same as it ever was down there,' Lydia said, though Colette had not asked.

'Yeah?'

'Mum's busy. Dad's stressed. Mum's stressed too. She's *too* busy. Rae hasn't rung them since Christmas and I'm not surprised.' Her voice shook. 'I said that I was doing the talk this evening and Mum said, "Oh, so they let you...?" Just like that. So I said that Benjy's rationale was that it was an important service but there wouldn't be all that many people there, but it didn't really make any difference. I don't know, maybe I should have mentioned it before, so they would have had a chance to get their heads round it, and maybe even...' She did not finish the sentence.

'*I'll* be there,' Colette said, and hugged Lydia tighter. She saw the draft of the talk where it lay on the desk, double-spaced, the important words marked in highlighter. She had read it through herself, last week, had made a few minor suggestions, but had been impressed. What Lydia had written was concise, but thoughtful; heartfelt without being mawkish. It talked of community and betrayal, fellowship and abandonment. Lydia had known all of those things, but she had not made it about her. Nor, Colette knew, would she do so tonight. She would regain her composure, dry her eyes, and deliver the talk with calm assurance and compassion. 'And,' Colette said inadequately, 'it will be good.'

**Good Friday**

'We could make hot cross buns,' Lydia said, so they tried it, but they hadn't accounted for the time it would take for the dough to rise, and they were late for church. They joined the Walk of Witness mid-way along Wardle Street, and followed the cross and the crowd into the Methodist church. Colette felt flustered and unsettled although, as Lydia pointed out later, there was enough coming and going that it was unlikely that anyone would have noticed.

The mob organised itself variously into the pews or back out of the door, and those who remained settled down for the simple service of readings and music.

Wardle Street Methodist Church was a generous, red-brick building too big for its regular congregation, with soaring windows of clear glass capped with trefoil tracery. It was better resourced than St John's, and, consequently, less chaotic. There was far less likelihood of their turning up on a Sunday morning to find that either of them had been volunteered to do something. Colette almost always knew all the hymns. The preaching asked questions that would never have been asked at St John's, and often left them unanswered, but also left the listeners enriched by engaging with them. St John's told her that she was loved; Wardle Street told her how.

The congregation was considerably older, which always seemed to throw Lydia, but Colette didn't mind. More worrying was the fact that she was never quite sure which of them had chosen to notice that she and Lydia were together.

There were a few people who had made it clear that they knew: the minister and her husband; Gordon, who had been Professor of Physics until his retirement, and who she had been used to seeing occasionally around the Sciences Block; Jean, who always made a point of saying, 'and you *will* bring your Lydia, won't you?' when inviting Colette to summer fêtes or open gardens or tea parties. There were a few who had made it clear that they knew and that they were choosing not to acknowledge the fact that they knew. But when it came to the rest – the majority – of the congregation, Colette did not know, and did not care to guess.

Occasionally she and Lydia came in hand in hand, but she was well aware that wilful ignorance could see that and ignore it. And she felt uncomfortable doing it to make a point. She did not see why she *should* make a point. Wardle Street had been her church for as long as she had been in Stancester; she had been bringing Lydia there for the last three years; they had never hidden their relationship after Lydia had come out. If other people chose not to see it, that was up to them.

Before Lydia it had never mattered. The idea of taking Jess to church was unthinkable, and if anything ever had happened with Peter then *that*, at least, would not have been a problem. (It would never have worked with Peter. If St John's was outside her comfort zone, All Saints was a different planet.) But faith was as much a part of Lydia's life as it was of her own, more so, embarrassingly so sometimes, and she was keen to share it with Colette, and Colette wished that she could share it fully. And she was glad that this meant going to Wardle Street together and sorry that Wardle Street was ambivalent about their togetherness. And sometimes she was conscious of an argument that said she should shake the dust of Wardle Street off her sandals if they were not going to be, as the jargon had it, *fully affirming*, and sometimes she didn't see why she should have to. Lydia had found St John's – but she had kept on going to St Mark's until it was made clear that she wasn't welcome as an out lesbian. Colette was confident that that was something that would never happen at Wardle Street, as much as she feared that nobody would ever assure them of that in so many words.

And it was home, and today was not the day to let any of that get in the way. She drew in a long breath, and released it, once, twice, and felt the sense of bustle and urgency ebb gradually away. She was conscious of, but not distracted by, Lydia's presence next to her. In the long silences she watched the patches of light from the long windows creep ragged-edged over the floor, and felt tears prickle in her eyes.

**Holy Saturday**

'Don't be ridiculous,' Georgia said, her voice indistinct against the roar of traffic noise in the background. 'I'm sure you've both got far too much going on at church to worry about cooking. And Will is dying to go back to Curzon's.'

Peter, consulted by text, agreed. *That sounds great! Natalie has never been there!*

'That sounds like Natalie's typing,' Lydia observed. 'Peter wouldn't use two exclamation marks in two sentences. Still, it's better than texting and driving.'

Colette agreed on both counts.

'And I know you'll say I'm being paranoid, but I think we should leave now.'

The Curzon Arms was busier than Colette had expected it to be; she supposed that the bank holiday weekend tourism must be balancing out the absence of the student body. Herself, of course, excepted. She thought for a moment of inviting Rowan to join them; but it would have felt a bit strange; they didn't know any of the alumni, and probably had things to be doing at church, come to that.

The pub had been refurbished in recent weeks, and a faint scent of new paint still mingled with the gravy and beer. They secured their usual table and held on to it with difficulty. The sash window was open, and from time to time, when there was a lull in the traffic, the gentle buzzing of insects could be heard.

Peter and Natalie were the next to arrive. While Natalie got the drinks, Peter glanced around with ostentatious disapproval.

'They *changed* things.'

'They do,' Colette said. 'You should see what they're doing with the Students' Union.'

'The Union building doesn't count. They're always doing things to that.' His eyes flickered over the place. 'I have to admit, I'm glad to see that back-to-front Routemaster poster's gone. And at least they couldn't get rid of our window.'

'We got here early to get it, and we've been fighting off all comers,' Lydia said. 'You wouldn't believe how many people didn't think we had another four coming to join us.'

Peter sat down in a distinctly proprietorial manner. Natalie, coming back with a tray, laughed at him. 'So this is where it all began.'

'Yes,' said Colette. 'You've seen campus. I guess you might have walked past our old house on Alma Road. But until you've seen Curzon's, you don't really know Peter's university years.'

Natalie looked quizzical, and Colette felt immediately as if she had made a misstep. She added, 'Not that you're necessarily missing much, of course.'

'Oh, I don't know,' Natalie said.

Lydia was waving enthusiastically. Colette turned around, and saw with relief that Georgia and Will had arrived. And yes, it was always lovely to see Georgia, but she'd never expected to couple the words *Will* and *relief*. She waved too.

Of all of them, Colette thought, Will had changed the least. Perhaps she would think differently if she saw him in his weekday suit (surely he must wear a suit), but here, in his university uniform of rugby shirt and flip-flops, his golden-brown hair gelled up away from his forehead, he looked exactly the same as he always had.

It was odd, though, to see him hand in hand with Georgia; odd to see her look up at him with a fond, intimate glance, checking in with each other as a couple before greeting a group they'd surely always known as individuals. Will did the round of the table, kissing Lydia on the cheek, then Colette, then Natalie, before exchanging a manly handshake with Peter; Georgia hugged everybody, including Natalie.

'So here we are,' she said. She beamed around, not quite taking credit for the coincidence, but clearly feeling that everybody else should be as pleased with it as she was. Colette caught herself thinking, *I must tell Becky about this*, and almost side-stepped the pang that came with the knowledge that she couldn't, not properly.

'So how did this work out?' Will asked.

'We're going to Natalie's folks in Paignton,' Peter explained.

'Having been with Peter's family the last few days,' Natalie added.

Lydia said, deadpan, 'We live here.'

'And we're having a mini break in Exeter.' Georgia put a heavy, ironical stress on the words *mini break*.

Will flushed a little under his tan, and Colette tried not to wonder whether it was separate beds. Surely not separate rooms. He said, 'Can I get anyone a drink?'

'If you're happy to drive the rest of the way,' Georgia said, 'I'll have a gin and tonic. That rhubarb one, if they've got it.'

The others smiled and declined, and Will strode off towards the bar.

'So everybody's travelling westwards?' Lydia said.

Peter nodded. 'When my soul's form bends towards the east, yes.'

Natalie looked embarrassed. 'Sweetie.'

'Jerusalem,' Lydia explained. 'John Donne. But Good Friday was yesterday.'

Colette decided to ask for clarification later. 'If it comes to that,' she said, 'Jerusalem isn't where it was yesterday.'

Peter said, with the glint in his eye that said that he'd noticed she was picking an argument, and was up for it, 'Isn't it?'

'No, because the whole Earth's moved on since then.' It was pedantic, but that was the joy of it.

'I suppose it has. But...'

She pressed her advantage, such as it was. 'And so has the sun, and so has the galaxy...'

'But relatively speaking, Jerusalem is still where it was, and I've moved.'

'Relatively speaking, yes,' she conceded.

He tilted his head to one side. 'So does that actually make a difference?'

'I think,' she said, 'that if you're going to say that *your* physical location makes a difference, then yes, it does. Personally, I'm not bothered, but...'

'But you're a Methodist,' Peter said, amiably.

'Anyway,' Natalie said, 'here we all are, going west.'

Will put two drinks down on the table, one in front of Georgia, one in his own place, next to her, and sat down.

'Can your choir cope without you, Georgia?' Peter asked.

'I did feel a bit bad,' Georgia said, 'but they've got a couple of people back from uni, and everyone else makes more of an effort for major festivals, so I think they'll be fine.'

'They could always do *Blessed be the God and Father*,' Will said, unexpectedly raking up his cathedral chorister past. 'What was it, six trebles and Wesley's butler?' He added, 'Not your Wesley, Colette.'

'Neither of them,' Peter said before Colette could decide whether or not to feel put down. 'But you're assuming they've got an organist who can cope.'

Georgia did not answer that, but sang, very low down and growly in her chest voice, '*To an inheritance, incorruptible...*'

Natalie joined in, sounding slightly more comfortable with the range, '*and undefiled, which fadeth not away, reserved in heaven for you...*'

'Aren't you a bit early?' Peter asked.

'I won't be singing it tomorrow,' Georgia said. 'I left it to Will to pick a church for Easter, and somehow I don't think it's going to involve Samuel Sebastian Wesley in any capacity.'

He smiled gleefully, shaking his head. '*In Christ alone*, more like.' Peter shuddered.

Will went back to the Wesley, climbing up the scale in his fruity baritone. '*Who are kept by the power of God by faith unto salvation...*'

Georgia and Natalie joined in again, '*Ready to be revealed in the last time.*' Then Georgia leapt an octave and continued, '*But as he which hath called you is holy, so be ye holy...*'

'It used to be like this all the time, when we were at Alma Road,' Colette said to Lydia. 'Do you remember?'

'I remember doing *Great is the Lord* with chapel choir,' Georgia said, 'and Jeff let everybody who could physically reach the notes sing along in the opening. It was great. Well, OK, it probably wasn't, but he wanted a big sound and he got it.'

'Meanwhile,' Natalie said, 'I had the equal and opposite frustration the other week, of not being allowed to sing something I can manage perfectly well, just because I'm on the alto row this term.'

'Oh, that *is* annoying,' Georgia said, in the sympathetic tone of somebody to whom that never happened any more.

Natalie's brow crinkled in irritation. 'And I can sing it; I think almost all the women can; it only goes up to a top G; and he lets the countertenors go down to join the tenors and basses; but *no*, we're not allowed to, so there are six of us bored out of our tiny minds for eighty-five per cent of the piece and we just join in to add a bit of texture halfway through and then again at the end.'

'Why on earth not?' Colette asked.

'Something about *blending* and *what the composer envisaged*. What he means is, he doesn't like women's voices sounding like women's voices. He wants a choir with a boys-only top line, that's his trouble.'

'It's the trouble with the choral tradition in general, I think.' Georgia inclined her head to one side. 'I don't mean wanting trebles specifically. Like, I've had to sing alto much more often than I'd like, just because the others weren't confident on the harmony. And I can't emphasise enough how much of an alto I'm not.'

'Right,' said Natalie. 'I know what you mean. It's the fact that the repertoire, or at least the repertoire that actually gets sung, is written for the choir that the director would like to have, rather than the choir they actually have.'

'Like so much of the Church of England,' Peter said. 'And meanwhile the people who are already there get...' He let the sentence trail off, and took a swig of lemonade.

Colette caught Lydia's eye. 'Shall we order food?' she suggested.

'Drive safely,' Colette said, as they all gathered up jackets and bags afterwards.

'Of course,' Will said. 'Do you two have any plans for the rest of the day?'

'We're going to the cathedral,' Colette said. 'Lydia is being someone's godmother at the confirmation.'

'Sponsor,' Lydia clarified. 'It's one of my house group members.'

'Well, enjoy it,' said Peter. 'That's one thing I never did, Easter in Stancester.'

Natalie was looking sceptical.

Colette said, mischievously, 'I thought we established that it doesn't matter where you are.'

He laughed. Natalie handed him the car keys. 'Your turn,' she said.

Another round of hugs and handshakes, and the visitors headed off two by two along the pavement.

'Let's go home,' Lydia said, 'and, if I were you, I'd get a nap in before this evening.'

Lydia had a seat reserved at the front of the cathedral, with Pip and the rest of the confirmation candidates and their sponsors, but everything began outside, on the wide steps along the west front. Colette could not remember having seen the vast main door opened before; beyond it, the interior of the building was velvety dark. A verger came around with service sheets and small, unlit candles.

Night was just beginning to fall, and the orange glow of the street lights dominated the sky. Faces were strange, shadowy. Silence fell. Somebody in a black cassock brought out a brazier, and somebody in white robes held the huge Paschal candle, a pale shaft in the gloom. A faint smell of ethanol drifted across the air.

The opening prayer.

A match flared and disappeared into the dark bulk of the brazier, and then a flame shot upwards. The fuel caught, crackling, sending tiny scraps of ash into the air.

Another prayer.

The fiddly business of getting nails into the candle. Some reverent laughter.

The candle, lit from the new fire: a lone bright flame, shielded from the wind by a careful pair of hands. 'The light of Christ.'

The clergy and choir and confirmation candidates and sponsors began processing tidily into the cathedral. Lydia walked next to Pip, who seemed suddenly much younger than Colette remembered. The rest of the congregation followed, less tidily, filling up rows of chairs and clogging up the aisles as everyone gestured for everyone else to go first. At the front, the light was spreading from candle to candle. Colette ended up in the middle of a row, between two strangers. It didn't matter. The man next to her smiled with a serene excitement as he turned to her with his lighted candle, to light her unlit one. The flame was passed from person to person, from east to west, until it was as if they swam in a sea of tiny, glowing, lights, and above them was a great cavernous darkness.

And already someone was singing a long, lovely chant, which felt more familiar than it possibly could be, until Colette realised that she must have learned it from Peter singing it around the house, years ago.

And then, the waiting.

Huge spaces of silence, dark, gold-edged, and, between them, the stories.

The creation.

The burning bush.

The crossing of the Red Sea.

The faithfulness of Ruth.

The valley of dry bones.

Jonah in the big fish.

And then: 'Alleluia! Christ is risen!'
'He is risen indeed! Alleluia!'
The organ crashed out, impossible chords filling the building; high above them, the bells roared. The lights went on all at once. People yelled and whooped; Colette blew out her candle and clapped, and could not hear the sound of her hands.
A final loop-the-loop from the organ, and they were into the Gloria, and it was all familiar again. Collect; Epistle; Gospel; sermon. Colette did her best to pay attention, but she was already weary, and was nervous on Lydia's behalf. It was not long to go now until the

confirmation. Not that there was anything to be nervous about. All that Lydia had to do was say a couple of words; it ought to be far less intimidating than giving the talk on Maundy Thursday, which she had done without faltering...

Another procession? Yes, they had to get back to the west end, to the font. Colette made sure not to catch Lydia's eye as they passed. Pip looked wide-eyed, awestruck; Lydia, careful, concentrating. She was wearing her bright magenta silk shirt again, open over a black vest, and at her throat a silver wire cross that Colette had made for her once upon a time.

The congregation turned to see what was happening at the font. The affirmations, the vows, the water poured out, the Creed, the cross marked in oil upon each candidate's forehead, the baptisms; and then the return to the east end; the congregation turned back as the procession passed. The confirmation candidates lined up along the altar rail, their sponsors behind them.

Colette looked at the Bishop in his robes and thought how very small he looked from here. At some point, she knew, Lydia would have to go and talk to him, and he would have to give his approval for her to be interviewed. In this moment, that seemed a very long way off. He, she, they, were all very small, single dancers in this vast, wonderful, cosmic ballet. She thought suddenly of Rowan, down the road at the Orthodox service, and was glad that this year Easter was the same day for all of them.

The Bishop made his way along the line of candidates, speaking to them, laying his hands upon their heads. The sound was deflected and distorted on its way down the nave. Lydia was more audible than most of the other sponsors, her voice confident if not, from this distance, clear.

'Bishop, I present Philippa to be confirmed.'

The Bishop's voice boomed through the PA system, speaking the words of confirmation. Colette could just see his hands laid on Pip's sleek head.

There, she thought, that's done.

And once again the service rejoined its familiar lines. Colette read the small print about who was allowed to take communion (*those in good standing with their own Churches*) through twice, just in case, and then took her service booklet up to the rail with her by mistake and had to shove it into her pocket lest the minister think she didn't want to receive. It shouldn't have felt any different from taking communion at St John's, she thought, but it did.

Afterwards, though, it didn't matter, and the last hymn was *Thine be the glory*, and she knew where she was with that.

**Easter Day**

Colette woke, and lay watching the sunlight on the ceiling, until she remembered that she wanted to have a shower before church. She prodded Lydia. 'Happy Easter.'

'Hallelujah,' Lydia said sleepily. She rolled over onto her front. 'What's the time?'

'Quarter past eight.'

'You getting up?'

Colette stretched. 'I think so.' She kissed Lydia where the line of her hair swooped behind her ear, and then sat up. 'Want me to wake you up in an hour?'

'S'please. Mmm. Glad I'm not doing the dawn service and bacon sandwiches at St John's.'

'Bit late for that,' Colette said, happily, not expecting Lydia to reply; and then she went through to the living room and opened the window, letting in the new day.

*A knotty problem gets even knottier*

    Professor Barry Parnell's knot theory, already on shaky ground, was dealt another blow this week as one of Parnell's former students emerged with the claim that a discovery made in the course of her research over a decade ago disproves a central assumption of his argument.

    In a post that has been shared widely within the superconductivity community, Tessa Carhart-Johnson publishes her notes and part of the draft of her thesis, claiming that her results – which she says were dismissed by Parnell at the time – demonstrate that the hydrogen atoms inside the 'lattice' cannot possibly behave in the way Parnell's theory requires.

    Parnell said on Twitter, 'Impressive that someone who didn't have the stamina to finish her doctorate still seems to have the capacity to hold an unjustified grudge.'

    The University of Stancester has been approached for comment.

Science Today, Friday 21 April 2017

'Well,' James said, 'this just gets better and better, doesn't it?'

'Has Barry been in today?' Colette stood her wet umbrella in a corner.

'No. He's lying low, I think.'

She snorted. 'Not on Twitter, he isn't.'

'Oh dear. Do I want to look?'

'How's your faith in humanity today?'

James had Twitter open before she had finished the sentence. 'Oh *dear*. Ouch.'

'It isn't really a good look, is it?'

'One hundred and thirty-six retweets.'

'That's gone up since the last time I looked. How many replies?'

'Thirty-four.' He scrolled down. 'They're about equally divided between the defensive replies from the starry-eyed disciples, and the ones calling sexism and wondering whether there's some fire going on under that smokescreen he's putting out. And then they start replying to each other...' He shuddered and turned away. 'I think I'll stop looking at that.'

'Good plan.' Colette nudged the mouse of her computer to wake it up.

'And to think I came to work for a break.'

'Oh, dear. What's up? Wedding stuff again?'

He sighed. 'No, my brother's run off to the Gobi desert in a Volkswagen camper van to found a polygamous cult.'

Colette laughed. 'Isn't he your best man?'

James also laughed, but there was a distinct edge of desperation in there. 'Other brother. Just kidding. Yes, it's the wedding again.'

'Do I want to know?'

'Our caterer's folded. The one you get a huge discount with if you use our venue.'

'Shit.'

'Yeah.'

'So what happens?'

He rolled his eyes and lifted his shoulders. 'Fucked if I know. The insurance is meant to cover stuff like this, but that's a whole load of hassle in itself.'

'Shouldn't the venue sort this out, if they put you onto these clowns in the first place?'

'Well, yes, they should, and maybe they will, but I think it's going to take one of us standing over them with a big stick, and frankly I'm not sure I have the energy.'

'Oh, James.'

He shook his head. 'Giselle was just crying and crying, and I said to her, well, let's just not do it.'

'Did that help?' Colette asked, failing to entirely hide her scepticism.

'Not really. I mean, I think she kind of liked the idea for a moment, and, you know, if it was as easy as all that then maybe...'

'Did she stop crying?'

'No.' His mouth twisted with disgust, or guilt. 'To be honest, I think she heard it as, let's just break up.'

'Ah,' Colette said helplessly. Lydia would have had something more constructive to say.

James slammed his empty coffee mug down onto the desk. 'I hate this. I hate what it's making both of us into. But it's got to the point where it's going to be less hassle just to go through with it. Everything's paid for, now...' Before she could reply, he went on: 'I know, I know. Sunk costs fallacy. But we'd have to offer to pay everyone back and there's no way we could afford it.'

'Wouldn't they rather you were happy?'

He shook his head. 'I'd like to think so, but... Anyway, we'd have to *tell* them. Not just them. Everybody. The entire hundred and fifty strong guest list.'

'Yeah. I see.'

He said, defensively, 'It's not like we're breaking up. Like, I still want to spend the rest of my life with her, you know? It's just that if I'd known the actual getting married bit was going to be this much grief then I wouldn't have suggested it.'

Colette nodded. 'It sounds to me,' she said, hoping that she didn't sound too much like she was pointing out the glaringly obvious, 'like it doesn't matter what I say, you're just going to push on through and do it, at this point.'

'Yeah.' James chewed at his thumbnail. 'I just can't help feeling like it's meant to be easier. Like it really *could* be easier. But it's refusing to be easier.'

'That's what happens when you get humans involved.' It sounded a bit pat, she thought.

'Well, I know *that*. Why do you think I went into chemistry? None of those squishy bits.' He glanced back at his computer screen. 'In theory, at least.'

Colette saw as she approached the building that the lights were on in their flat: Lydia had beaten her home once again. Perhaps,

Colette thought, she would have had more useful thoughts about dinner than she had managed herself. Or perhaps she wouldn't. That had possibilities of its own. She quickened her step.

A man, not one of the other residents, was coming down the stairs, and to her surprise, stopped to greet her. Rory. 'Hello,' she said.

'Hi. I've just been talking to Lydia.'

'Oh, er, right.'

His T-shirt said *Basic Instructions Before Leaving Earth*, with the capitalised initials in red to make the acrostic obvious: not one of his best, Colette thought.

'And now I'm off home.'

Colette, whose thoughts had crystallised into a vision of a Friday night bottle of wine and Chinese takeaway, let a guilty sense of relief settle in her mind, and then dismissed it. 'Well,' she said, 'I'm sorry I missed you. Say hi to Mel for me.'

His expression darkened, but his tone was amiable enough when he said, 'Of course.'

'Is Rory OK?' she asked Lydia, half a minute later.

Lydia wrinkled her nose. 'Ish. He and Mel have had a big row about the whole missionary thing. Apparently it all blew up over Easter.'

'But it's been building for a while, right?'

She nodded. 'I have a horrible feeling that all this going to end up with him going out to Africa on his own, and Mel somehow having managed to get pregnant, and he'll come back without the slightest idea of what to do with a baby, which she'll have managed to get her head around in his absence, and it'll all fall apart, and it'll be my fault.'

Colette didn't see how the last part of it could be true. She grabbed the most plausible thread of the scenario. 'Where in Africa does he want to go?'

'I should know. I don't. Next time – if there is one – I'm going to have to ask about what the organisation actually does.'

Colette was mildly shocked. 'You haven't already?'

Lydia's generous mouth thinned a little. 'It's possible that my subconscious thinks I won't like the answer.'

'What do you mean?'

'I mean, is it American Evangelicals exporting homophobia, or is it something I could actually approve of?'

'Surely Rory wouldn't have the nerve to enlist you in his campaign if it was?'

'He wouldn't necessarily know. And it's not a campaign,' Lydia said quickly. 'He knows that Mel's been talking to me too.'

Colette shrugged her shoulders. 'Fair enough.'

The colour was rising in Lydia's cheeks. 'I'm going to pray about it.'

'Now? Go for it.' She added, 'I'm going to order Chinese, unless you have any better ideas.'

'None as good as that.'

'Set meal B?'

'Is that the one with prawn toast? Yes please.'

'It is indeed.' She found the menu and called to place the order, conscious all the time that Lydia was perched on the edge of the sofa, watching her, and not obviously praying. Which probably meant that she was waiting for her.

Colette did not much feel like praying, particularly not for Rory and Mel, and she was aware of another layer of resentment adhering to the idea that she ought to. But explaining any of that to Lydia was going to take longer and be more wearing than just getting it over and done with.

She put her phone away, sat down on one of the dining chairs, looked at Lydia, and raised her eyebrows. Lydia smiled slightly, shifted a little way backwards, placed her hands palm upwards in her lap, and closed her eyes. Colette kept hers open, fixing them on a point on the opposite wall, and tried to dislodge the festering clump of negativity from her mind.

Lydia was speaking, quietly and clearly. 'Lord, I pray for Mel and for Rory and for their situation they're facing at the moment.'

*Amen,* Colette thought, grudgingly.

'And I pray that you would give both of them your wisdom and your grace to make the right decision.'

*Amen.*

(Yes, that was reasonable.)

'And the love and the patience to listen to each other.'

*Amen.*

(It was surprisingly, gracefully, easy, when Lydia put it like that.)

'In Jesus' name.'

'Amen.'

It was a relief to talk to Peter, who phoned later that evening to see whether what had been reported on the news bore any relationship to reality.

'Peter,' she said. 'Someone sane. That's good.'

'I do hope so. So, what's going on with your supervisor?'

'Ha. Good question.'

'Explain to me, in words of one syllable, what happened. He used someone else's work...?'

She had feared that it was going to end up sounding like that. 'No! In fact, it was probably the opposite, knowing Barry.'

'So go on, tell me. I know the first bit: he has this theory...'

'He has this theory, and he's very attached to it, and at one point it was going to be the next big thing. I mean everybody thought so, not just Barry. He wrote a book.' She glanced at it, up on the shelf next to Lydia's Jane Austens.

'I'm guessing it's not worth my while reading it, now?'

'Probably not. It's not like your reading list isn't long enough already.' She shook her head as if he could see her. 'No, what's come out in the last few days is this idea that Barry's knot theory is effectively discredited by something that came up in this woman's research nine years ago.'

Peter said, slowly, 'You don't believe it *is* discredited?'

'Well. That's the question. It isn't exactly a smoking gun.' She thought for a moment, and added, 'It isn't even a bullet casing. Or, if it is, it's one bullet casing on a battlefield. It's one tiny piece of evidence that either joins up with hundreds of other pieces of evidence to prop up a theory, or is basically meaningless. The only thing that makes this special is that it looks like it's flipped from one to the other.'

'So why is it all only kicking off now? Did nobody notice at the time?'

'That's the thing. This person was one of Barry's own PhD students and, for whatever reason, she's only just come forward now.'

Peter whistled. 'So what, did he suppress it?'

'Actually, *that's* the question. As one of Barry's *current* PhD students –' Colette permitted herself a small measure of bitterness – 'what I think most probably happened is that he just wasn't paying enough attention to her work to notice that it had the potential to explode everything he'd built his career on, if you squinted a bit. But of course everyone's assuming that he kept it quiet deliberately, and to be honest I don't have much sympathy for him.'

'I can understand why you might feel that way,' Peter said carefully. 'Nine years, though.'

That had been playing on Colette's mind, too. 'I know. But she never finished her PhD, and I think maybe it's just taken her that long to get back on her feet and stop second-guessing herself and realise that yes, actually she was onto something big. And then maybe seeing all the stuff about the knot theory on the news, and thinking that if Barry is wrong about this then perhaps she was right.'

'It seems a bit tenuous.'

'I know. I don't know that I'd come forwards, if it were me. I'd have to be really angry.' More angry than she could imagine.

'Hmm.'

'The thing about Barry, is that he's not horrible – thank God – in the way that a lot of men have been, in the news recently.' She hoped that Peter understood what she meant. 'You know. He's never said anything to make me feel uncomfortable. He just... forgets about me. I'm not important. I'm furniture. Somewhere between his desk light and his spider plant. Far, far less important than his phone. I could walk out tomorrow and he wouldn't notice for three years.'

He made a sympathetic noise. 'That doesn't sound like it's very good for your work. Or for you.'

'No, but it's always been that way.' She was not trying to justify him, or make excuses for him. She was just tired of sympathy, of feeling as if it was somehow her fault that Barry was never there.

'So what does all this mean for you now?'

She thought of Tessa Carhart-Johnson's unfinished thesis, of Barry's fury sprayed across the internet, of the mountain of work that still remained to be done on her own project, and felt a shiver of fear. But she said, 'Nothing. I hope. I mean, I've just got to keep plugging away. If it means that Barry actually shows up in Stancester a bit more often than he has been recently, then it'll be all to the good. On the other hand, if he develops a complex about his female PhD students being out to get him, then I should probably start thinking about my other options.'

Peter chuckled, then asked, seriously, 'What would those be?'

'Asking for an alternative supervisor.' She paused. 'Maybe I should have done that anyway, ages ago. I didn't want to rock the boat, but maybe it was a boat that needed rocking.'

# *May*

Mr and Mrs Philip K. Powell
request the pleasure of the company of
Nicolette Russell and Lydia Hawkins
at the wedding of their daughter
Giselle Rowena
to
Dr James Templeton
on Saturday 20 May at 2pm
at Cleobury Park, Stancester

Lydia was excited, regardless of the fact that she knew James only slightly and Giselle not at all. 'Oh, you know,' she said, when Colette pointed this out, 'I just like weddings.'

Colette thought this very generous of her.

Lydia said, 'Do you think this dress will do?'

It was sleeveless, with a flared skirt and a print of purple flowers on a white background. Colette remembered it fondly from one of their early dates, but could not deny that it was looking a little tired. 'You might want to dress it up a bit,' she said.

Lydia frowned at the tangle of beads and chains in her jewellery box. 'What with?'

'I'll have a look. What if you were to starch the dress?'

'Do we even have starch?'

'Under the sink.'

Lydia nodded, took the dress, and went off to the sitting room with it. Colette sat down on the edge of the bed and started untying the knots the necklaces had got themselves into, unhooking earring wires from the chains they had caught in, and putting them into pairs.

Lydia came back a quarter of an hour later and laughed. 'That's very sweet of you,' she said, 'but you were going to have a shower.'

Colette looked at the time.. 'True. I was.'

'Do it quick, and I'll put your hair up for you.'

She obeyed. *Well*, she caught herself thinking in the shower, *it had better be worth it after all that*. She did not think she meant either the necklaces or the starch.

They took a taxi out to Cleobury Park, which was a Victorian Gothic excrescence, bristling with turrets and dripping with barge boarding, at the end of a long, rutted, muddy drive. Inside, it was more tasteful. The hall was dark, with red and black tiles underfoot and oak panelled walls. The room where the ceremony was to take place was decorated in restrained whites and greens, with only the occasional gilt curlicue. Afternoon light streamed in at the tall windows. The people – Colette could not help thinking of them as *congregation*, which she supposed they were, really, in a literal, secular sense – took their places, murmuring excitedly.

James stood at the front with his brother, who looked like a 110% scale copy of himself. Nervousness rolled off him. She recognised his mother, who had visited the lab once or twice, and deduced that the elderly man next her must be James' grandfather.

Barry was there. Colette supposed that she would have to speak to him, would have to introduce Lydia to him. She glanced at her watch, muttered a word of warning and led her over.

'Barry.'

He turned, his TV smile already installed. To his credit, he kept it there as he said, 'Colette. Isn't this a happy occasion?'

'Isn't it?' She drew Lydia forward. 'This is my partner, Lydia. Lydia, this is Barry, my supervisor.'

His eyebrows lifted very slightly. Colette was annoyed: he could have recognised Lydia from the photograph on her desk. He said, 'What a pleasure. I do hope you look after her.'

Lydia said, pleasantly, 'It's nice to meet you. I could say the same thing.'

Colette asked Barry, 'Have you spoken to James? I didn't want to bother him so close to kick-off.'

'Oh, I just wished him luck.' He smiled.

'We should find seats,' Lydia said.

'We should,' Colette agreed.

'Yes,' Barry said. 'Well, lovely to meet you, Lydia; I'm sure I'll see you both later.'

There was a spare pair of seats at the other side of the room, at the edge of a row. Lydia headed resolutely towards them, and, sitting down, struck up a conversation with someone who turned out to be one of James' cousins.

The encounter with Barry had left Colette feeling ruffled. There was not quite enough room for her legs between the rows of chairs, and the label of her dress was scratching her neck. She felt awkward about Lydia talking to people they didn't know, though they seemed pleasant enough. And it felt like church, but was not church; which reminded her that this sense of dissonance would haunt her wedding to Lydia, if such a thing could even be made to happen. Lydia had mentioned the Affirming Baptists recently as a denomination that would celebrate same-sex marriages; perhaps that would do, Colette thought; perhaps it would be enough if it felt vaguely like home for one of them. But that implied an end to Lydia's connection with the Church of England, either before the event or after it, which would make a tangle that would take years to undo. Any marriage, for them, would end Lydia's hopes of ordination, fast and painfully. Colette resented the entire institution.

The hum of conversation continued, gently. Roving individuals were summoned back to their seats, and then other people got up to wander around in their turn. The string quartet reached the end of its set and began again. The tone of the voices around them grew gradually sharper, more concerned.

Lydia flipped her wrist towards her to glance at her watch; Colette caught her hand so that she could look, too. Fifteen minutes late, already. And, because she was more nervous than she would have like to admit, she kept hold of Lydia's hand. Lydia squeezed hers comfortingly.

She can't have got cold feet, Colette thought. Not after all that stress.

Someone behind them was wondering the same thing, out loud. Lydia looked inquiringly at Colette.

'If anyone was going to have second thoughts,' Colette said, 'it would have been James. And he's here.'

She glanced towards the front of the room, to see what James was making of all this, and saw his face contorted with worry, his shoulders drawn up. Someone plucked at his sleeve, and he sat down; but he was up again within a minute, peering anxiously over all their heads towards the door at the back.

The registrar went over to him and whispered in his ear, looking as worried as he was. He said something in reply. She nodded, stepped out into the centre of the aisle, and cleared her throat.

'Ladies and gentlemen, we apologise for the delay to the start of this ceremony. We hope the bride will be with us shortly.'

But she wasn't.

Colette wondered what happened if the bride just didn't arrive. How long would they wait before they gave up on her? When would the registrar have to leave for the next ceremony? Would the food still be served, that troublesome three course meal renegotiated at the last moment with a new caterer? How much of the sale-or-return wine would they get through?

And who would stay with James?

The string quartet played the *Liebesträume* for the third time. Lydia, who had found an ancient tube of Extra Strong Mints in her bag, offered one to Colette. She held her hand out for it, dropped it, had to scrabble on the floor. Lydia looked amused, and gave her another one.

But something seemed to be happening: there was a scraping of chairs and a collective indrawn breath. Then the string quartet struck up the wedding march, and everyone turned to see what was going on at the back of the room.

When Giselle lifted the hem of her skirt to walk down the three steps from the door, they all saw that she was barefoot. One of the bridesmaids carried, along with the bouquet, a pair of very muddy ivory satin sandals.

'She must have walked all the way up the drive,' Lydia breathed.
'Why didn't somebody phone?'
'No battery, I guess. Or no reception. Or no phone. Or all three. You couldn't fit much in those little Dorothy bags.'
'So did the car break down? The car was the one thing that didn't go wrong when they were planning...'
'Shh!'
Colette turned back to face the front, and was struck by the expression on James' face as he watched Giselle's arrival. Relief, certainly, but there was more than that: a tenderness, a delight, that she'd never seen on him before. She glanced away, feeling that she was intruding upon a private moment: nobody ought to look that happy, she thought, with so many other people there; it simply wasn't safe to let them see.

It was as if for a moment the world had slipped into focus, as if she had grasped the point of it, that if it meant that she would be able to look at Lydia like that in public then –

But she would not.

The excitement subsided. The registrar introduced herself, James and Giselle, and James' brother and Giselle's best friend, who were to be the witnesses. Then she said, 'Marriage, according to the law of this country, is the union of two people, voluntarily entered into for life, to the exclusion of all others,' and Colette thought that she could almost hear Lydia's wince.

James and Giselle had written their own vows. Colette had heard plenty about this process over the preceding months, but found herself more moved than she had expected in the moment. James' were surprisingly elegant. (Colette resolved to tease him later about his not having used the passive voice.) Giselle's were clumsier, but came from the heart.

The rest of the ceremony felt like something of an anticlimax: particularly when Giselle's sister, one of the cobalt blue bridesmaids, got up and read, in a mumble:

*What is love? It's you and me.*
*There's nowhere that I'd rather be.*
*What is love? It's me and you*
*Here and saying we'll be true.*
*What is love? It's hand in hand*
*Looking out from where we stand.*
*What is love? It's now and always,*
*Loving you through all our days.*

When it was over, they followed the rest of the gathering through the French windows and out onto the terrace.

'Well,' Colette said. 'There we go. Oh, thank you.' She took a glass of fizzy wine from a waiter, passed it to Lydia, and received another one for herself.

'That was a truly awful poem,' Lydia said under her breath. She glanced around, as if worried that the poet might be somewhere within earshot. 'There should be a quota on rhyming couplets.'

Colette suspected that the poem would not have come in for such censure had the registrar not been required to include the point about the law of the land, so she did not say that it was not as bad as all that. 'Mm.'

'What happens now?'

Colette found the invitation and consulted it. 'Now we hang around while they take the photos, and the reception proper starts at five thirty.'

They sat on a bench under a shady tree while they waited for their turn to be photographed, and chatted with other members of the lab group and with an uncle of Giselle's who turned out to be very interested in the nuclear magnetic resonance project.

At length one of James' brothers called, 'Stancester uni friends!' ('Yes, you too,' Colette said, when Lydia tried to retreat) and they all came forward to be arranged into a group and smile, smile, say *cheese*, smile, move up a little, smile, say *cheese*, and, at length, be dismissed.

'So where are we meant to be sitting?'

Lydia took her hand and led her to the table plan. 'Let's find out.'

They surveyed the diagram, which Colette had to admit was very pretty, with swags of blue flowers adorning each table list.

'That's us,' Lydia said.

Colette was looking at the plan for the top table. *Dr James Templeton-Powell. Mrs Giselle Templeton-Powell.*

'You've got that face,' Lydia said under her breath.

'What face?' Colette hissed.

Lydia lowered her voice further still. 'The one that you get when you think something's tacky as hell but you're far too polite to say so. Last seen when Mel was showing us her birthday card for Rory.'

Colette said, at a normal volume, 'I'm allergic to diamanté and bondieuserie. Sue me.'

Lydia glanced around. Abandoning the whisper, she said, 'That's fine, but why are you looking like it now?'

Colette was surprised. 'I didn't think I was. I was just trying to get my head around the idea of addressing James as Doctor Templeton-Powell. And Giselle as Mrs anything.'

'When would you ever do that, though? You'd call them James and Giselle, same as always.'

'I wouldn't, I suppose,' Colette allowed. 'Unless I was sending them a letter.'

Lydia said thoughtfully, 'Were you thinking about us being Russell-Hawkins?'

Colette frowned. 'Not my style.'

She laughed. 'It wouldn't half annoy my parents.'

That was unusual in itself: Lydia usually tried not to care about her parents' opinions one way or another, or at least tried to look as if she didn't care. Colette said, conscious of uncertain ground underfoot, 'It's still a bit of a mouthful. Too many esses. I don't think it's worth it.'

'Fair enough.' Lydia looked relieved, as if she were uncomfortable with her own joke.

'No. I don't think we'd work double-barrelled.'

'What you could do is to take my surname and keep yours as a middle name – no, wait, listen – because then you would be able to be N. R. R. Hawkins, and you could publish an epic fantasy series.'

Colette turned to see Lydia's teasing grin. 'Let's wait until I've *written* an epic fantasy series, shall we?' Belatedly mortified, she asked, 'Did I look like I thought it was tacky, then?'

Lydia laughed. 'I thought so. I don't think anyone else noticed.'

'They're happy. That's the main thing.' She was almost surprised to find that she meant it.

Barry did not stay for the reception. The rest of the lab group was there, along with some people who turned out to be James' friends from undergraduate days at Liverpool. This meant that the conversation, having dwelt boringly on the weather and dangerously on the general election, went geeky fast. From time to time Colette glanced anxiously at Lydia, but she seemed to be following and even, occasionally, contributing.

At the end of the meal they were herded once more into the anteroom to watch the cutting of the cake, while the tables were cleared and the DJ set up. The first dance would have been a slow waltz, if either James or Giselle had been dancers, to a song that Colette didn't know, but the rest of the evening was devoted to battle-hardened disco classics. Lydia, always more at ease with strangers than with people she expected to see again, alternated between dancing with Colette and getting into assorted conversations with assorted other guests. Colette danced all the way through. She was slightly surprised, several hours later, to discover that she had lasted until the end of the last set. This was a distinct advantage: it was much easier to gather up the bags and shoes and scarves that the two of them had left in various parts of the ballroom once the lights had been turned up.

She hugged James; it was not something that either of them would usually have done, but she had drunk enough and he was happy enough for it not to be awkward. 'Have a lovely honeymoon.'

'Thank you. I'd say, make sure the lab's still there for when I get back, but do you know what? I don't really care. Blow the bloody thing sky-high.' He shook Lydia solemnly by the hand. 'Lovely to see you again. Look after Colette, won't you?'

* * *

141

Lydia was prodding her gently. 'If you're coming to church, you should probably get dressed in the next ten minutes.'

Colette rolled over, groaning. Lydia had said *coming*, not *going*. That meant that it was a St John's week. Yes: because Lydia had gone with her to Wardle Street the previous Sunday. 'I should, shouldn't I?'

'Depends on whether you're going to be sick during the service.'

'That,' she managed, 'depends on the preaching.'

Lydia laughed and chucked a pillow at her. 'If you're not ready by twenty-five past then I won't wait for you.'

Somewhat to her own surprise (and, she thought, Lydia's), Colette got herself out of bed and ready to go with a couple of minutes to spare, and they were at St John's a good five minutes before the service started. And OK, it was a bit loud, but it was just *nice*, she thought, to be able to sit there, without having to explain herself, or, for once, think too hard. Sit there, and occasionally, stand up, and not join in the actions to the songs even though she knew perfectly well what they were, even if Lydia was doing them right next to her.

And if Lydia wasn't performing them quite in her normal enthusiastic way, if she was quieter than usual all round, well, perhaps that was just because her head wasn't entirely clear either.

After dinner, because there was no evening service at St John's, and because Colette wouldn't have felt particularly like going to it even if there had been, and because Lydia's mother had said something to her that she wouldn't repeat to Colette, they went out to the pub.

The Feathers was a recent discovery of Lydia's; she had been there a few times with work colleagues, she said, and sometimes it was nice to go to a place that wasn't full of students.

Colette raised her eyebrows at that.

'Undergraduates,' Lydia clarified.

Which, Colette thought, she could not really argue with.

They approached the bar together. 'What's yours?' Lydia asked.

'Give me a second.' Colette peered at the pumps to see whether there was anything on that she knew she liked, or, failing that, anything on that had a sufficiently silly name for her to overlook the disappointment when it inevitably turned out not to be her thing.

Lydia sighed good-naturedly and said to the barman, 'Gin and tonic, please. And a...?'

Colette said, 'Pint of the Atomic Chicken, please.'

The barman was looking at Lydia as if he had seen her before; but he had not greeted her as a regular. He pulled Colette's pint, poured Lydia's gin, topped off the beer, and opened the tonic water bottle before saying, cautiously, 'Random question. Were you ever in the uni Christian Fellowship?'

Colette restrained herself from correcting that to *Evangelical Christian Fellowship*, and instead concentrated on the first centimetre of her drink. Lydia said, with apparent unconcern, 'I was.' She reached into her bag for her purse, and in the process pushed the sleeve of her sweater up her wrist, exposing a rainbow wristband. It almost looked accidental. 'Were you? I'm afraid I don't remember you.'

He nodded, smiling. 'You came out. Middle of a Fellowship meeting. Middle of my first year.'

'Yup,' Lydia said. 'That was me.'

His smile broadened. 'I always wanted to say thank you. What you said that night... Well, it was something I really needed to hear.'

'You're welcome,' said Lydia, her smile matching his.

'Of all the speakers I ever heard at Fellowship, you were the most impressive.'

Her colour rose. 'Well, thank you.'

'It must have been terrifying.'

Colette had been terrified on Lydia's behalf; she nodded. Lydia said, apologetically, 'It's all a bit of a blur.'

'I was on the sound that night,' he said.

'Oh! So you could have cut me off, and you didn't!'

'That's right.'

'So really I should thank you. I remember thinking at the time that I couldn't believe they were letting me get away with it. Now I know.'

He shook his head, still smiling. 'I think maybe we both did each other a favour.'

Colette wondered whether Lydia was going to offer to pray for him, or if he was going to ask her. She picked up the drinks to take them off to a table and provide a bit of privacy, if desired, but someone else approached the bar, then, and the moment was gone. Lydia said something meaningless and followed her.

'Are you OK?' Colette asked gently when they had sat down.

'Yeah. Thanks.' Lydia sipped at her drink. 'Whew. It's good. I mean, for both of us. It's just, well, when I think, it's all in the past, I'm moving on, something like *that* happens.'

Her eyes were shining. It was not so surprising, Colette thought. Lydia must have spent literal years, and who knew how much emotional energy, keeping herself secret. Now it all flowed outwards. Coming out had, ironically enough, made her a far better Christian. Although this was not really ironic at all, just depressing.

'There were probably about a hundred people in that hall,' Colette said thoughtfully. 'I'd be really surprised if he's the only one it made a difference to.'

'Do you think I'm going to have to have another ninety-nine conversations exactly the same as that?'

'Well, presumably not *exactly* the same. It seems statistically unlikely. But maybe there are still a few more people who needed to question their assumptions, and want to thank you for that.'

'Assumptions. Yes. That's the right word. That insistence on things being a certain way, when they...'

'... Demonstrably aren't that way?'

'Yes. Exactly.' Lydia brooded, chasing a pool of someone else's spilt cola over the table with the edge of a beer mat. 'Idolatry is a terrifying thing,' she said after a while. 'When something can do no wrong, when there isn't room to suggest that they might be right generally but wrong in this particular case, when everything they do *has* to be right because they're the one who's done it...'

'Anyone in particular?' Colette asked, supposing this was something to do with Lydia's parents, or perhaps their church.

'Yes. No. Not just people. Things. Institutions. Principles. *Theories.*'

'I hadn't thought of it like that,' Colette said, 'but yes, you're right.' She thought of Barry's latest exhibition on Twitter, and sighed. 'I don't know why he doesn't *see*.'

'Because he's scared of seeing,' Lydia said, without having to ask who *he* was. 'He's afraid that he won't know what he'll do with himself if he's wrong.' She swirled her drink in its glass and added, 'At a guess.'

Colette shook her head, suspecting that what Lydia guessed was indeed true. 'It's terrible science.'

'It's bad politics. And it's awful theology, too.'

*"He will prick that annual blister/Marriage with deceased wife's sister."* Somehow still topical... #GandS
- @LydiaHawkins
22:52, 26 May 2017

@LydiaHawkins *Are they clinging to their crosses/Where the Breton boat-fleet tosses?*
- @Flissdemeanour
00:13, 27 May 2017

@Flissdemeanour ???
- @LydiaHawkins
08:42, 27 May 2017

@Flissdemeanour *oh, right, looked it up now. Not quite the same thing, but I see what you mean...*
- @LydiaHawkins
09:13, 27 May 2017

'Are you coming up to see Dad in *Iolanthe*?' her mother had asked, and Colette had rolled her eyes a bit at the thought of her father prancing around in knee-breeches and coronet and driven up to Bromsgrove with Lydia.

It was a bit of a scramble for a Friday night, but they were both able to get away early, and most of the traffic was going south. They ate a hasty pub dinner before the performance, crammed onto the end of a long bench at the end of a long table. Colette, taking their empty plates back to the bar to give them some elbow room, was more surprised than she should have been to see Izzy seated a couple of tables away, nursing the end of a Coke and reading the drinks menu apparently out of sheer desperation.

She briefly considered pretending not to have seen her; then told herself off for being chicken. It was too late anyway. Izzy was smiling in a way that suggested she'd recognised her, although it was possible that she had not yet remembered who she actually was. Colette waved.

Izzy came over to their table and loitered awkwardly. 'Hello.'

'Hi,' Colette said.

The woman next to her moved her chair away to make room, which meant that Colette had to add, 'Join us.'

'Oh. Thank you. Jess is coming soon.' She pulled a stool up to the table.

'Congratulations, by the way,' Lydia said. 'Colette told me the news. When's the wedding, again?'

Izzy's face cleared. 'Next July. Thank you. You'll be getting an invitation.'

'Lovely,' Colette said, and tried to mean it.

'So what are you two doing up here?'

'Watching my dad in *Iolanthe*. You know, the Gilbert and Sullivan show?'

'Oh, cool. Does he have a good part?'

Colette had looked up the synopsis the previous night. 'He's one of the lords; he tries to get a shepherdess to marry him, but he doesn't want to fight with his best friend over her. And then he has a song about how the House of Lords never does anything.'

Izzy seemed confused, which Colette had to admit was reasonable. The arrival of Jess allowed her to change the subject. 'Here she is! Jess! Look, it's Colette and Lydia!'

The woman next to them squeezed up further away.

Jess was pleased to pull up a chair, and proud to show off the matching sapphire rings on Izzy's third finger and her own.

'How are the wedding plans?' Lydia asked.

'Coming together, thanks.' Jess did not seem to be tired of the question yet; an expression of catlike satisfaction spread over her face. 'Of course, it's early days, and there's loads we're not even thinking about until we get a bit closer to the date.'

'Do you know where you're doing it?'

Jess glanced at Izzy. 'We've looked at a few places. I don't think we've found *the one* yet.'

Colette, remembering tense mealtimes at Jess's house, the parents not speaking to each other, and Jess brightly chatting to everybody without expecting answers, did her best to play along with the conversation. 'Do you know what you're going to wear? Dresses? Suits? One of each?'

'I have my eye on a red fishtail dress,' Izzy said.

(Jess had taken her mother's side against her father, and her father's side against her mother, and relayed every argument to Colette afterwards. She wished she'd had the courage to break up with her over it.)

Lydia asked, 'What about you, Jess?'

She shook her head and laughed. 'I don't know yet. But apparently the red dress is non-negotiable.'

'Quite right,' said Colette. 'It sounds amazing.'

(The problem, Jess had told her when they were nineteen, in the summer holidays when they almost got back together, was that her parents should never have married each other, should never have stayed married, should never have had children with whom to share the disaster of their marriage, and should never have used the children as a reason to remain married.)

Jess said, 'And Izzy's been looking at readings.'

'There are loads out there!' Izzy said. 'I didn't realise until I started looking. And it's so weird when usually you have the same ones over and over again.'

(Simone de Beauvoir, Colette thought, would probably not be a constructive suggestion, for all that Jess had quoted *The Second Sex* at every opportunity the last term of A-levels.)

'Well, there was one you really liked, wasn't there,' Jess said, 'but it turned out that we wouldn't be able to use it.'

'Really?' Colette said. 'Why not?'

'Oh, it had something about angels in it, and loads of people on the site I looked at said they weren't allowed it because you can't have religious stuff in a civil marriage.'

'Yeah, that's true,' Lydia said. 'What a pity.' Colette tried not to notice the wistfulness on her face.

Jess looked at their empty glasses. 'Do you have time for another drink?'

Colette checked her watch. 'We'd better get on, really,' she said. 'This show starts at quarter to.'

Jess flashed a broad grin. 'Well, it's been great to see you both.'

'You too,' Colette said. 'So I guess we'll see you next July, if not before.'

'Definitely!' Her grin got even broader.

Colette once more wondered who this woman was. 'Good luck with it all,' she said; because really, what else could you say?

'Thanks! Enjoy the show!'

Lydia, who had never previously encountered Gilbert and Sullivan, seemed to find the whole thing bewildering and charming in equal parts.

'Marriage with deceased wife's sister, eh?' she said at the end of the first half.

'What?'

'Just at the end there. The Fairy Queen said she was going to make sure that Strephon got into parliament and then pass all these contentious laws.'

'Oh, is that what was going on? I was too busy worrying whether Dad's coronet was going to fall off to pay attention to the plot.'

'Honestly. Yes, it was. And marriage with deceased wife's sister was one of them.'

'So what about it?' Colette asked.

Lydia's face lit up with earnest enthusiasm. 'It was just really interesting to hear that reference to it. You can tell there's meant to be a laugh there; it must have been a running gag for the Victorians. And of course it was the same-sex marriage of its day.'

'Was it?' Colette had given up trying to get her head around the contemporary references in the Savoy operas after getting hopelessly lost in the receipt for a Heavy Dragoon when her father had first joined the society.

'Oh, yes, the debate went on and on and when it was finally allowed nobody actually cared that much. I only know,' she added, 'because people have been bringing it up all over Twitter as a direct comparison.'

'Maybe we need some fairies to sort it out.'

Lydia snorted. 'They couldn't do a worse job than the current government.'

She dragged her back to their seats well before the end of the interval. Colette grumbled gently, but was happy enough to sit and eat her ice cream.

'Your dad's good,' Lydia said, after she had got rid of the rubbish and finished reading the programme for a second time. 'I suppose a teacher has to be a bit of an exhibitionist, really. You sell the kids on the Mr Russell Show and move them quietly on to the History Show.'

Colette had never really been convinced by either. 'Mr Russell' had been Dad for too long for the show to be convincing, and history was too human, too susceptible to changes in fashion and too liable to misrepresentation for her to feel safe with it. Not that science seemed much more like solid ground, these days.

She began to say, 'It's different, of course, when…'

But the lights were going down.

Lydia clutched her hand. 'Sh!'

And the curtain rose.

'I almost thought your dad and that other lord were going to end up with each other,' Lydia said at the end, 'not two random fairies.'

'They're not random fairies. They're Celia and Leila. Or maybe Fleta.'

'Whatever. Then I remembered that this was written in eighteen eighty-something and that would be a bit daring for a provincial amateur production anyway.' She whistled a couple of bars of the finale. 'Not that it isn't still painfully relevant.'

'Bring on the magic wands?' she said, thinking of the way that Gilbert and Sullivan – well, presumably Gilbert alone – had resolved the central dilemma of the plot by amending a law to reverse its requirement. *Every fairy shall die who marries a mortal.* She made a swish-and-flick gesture with her mobile phone, narrowly avoiding dropping it down the back of the row in front.

'It's weird, isn't it? Waiting. Waiting for the wheels of bureaucracy and justice to finish grinding so that we can get on with our lives.'

'It'll be weirder still when it happens. It'll go from *you must not* to *you must* overnight. Every fairy shall die who *don't* marry a mortal.'

Lydia looked keenly at her. 'And you wouldn't necessarily consider that a happy ending.'

Colette turned away to put her jacket on. 'No,' she said. 'I wouldn't. Not necessarily. Come on, let's get out of here and find Dad.'

They waited for him outside the front of the theatre.

'It's a lovely night,' Lydia said, looking up through the young leaves into a clear sky.

Colette moved to stand a little closer to her. 'I'd suggest going for a walk, except I've no idea whether Dad will be two minutes or twenty.'

They watched the rest of the audience, most of which was at least four decades older than them, disperse, chattering quietly about the show. Colette was not impatient: it was pleasant just to be outside with Lydia on this still May evening, hearing the voices that sounded like home.

Her father appeared from around the side of the building bearing a clutter of coat and score and carrier bags. There was something odd about his face, which when he got close turned out to be a lingering streak of stage make-up. Carefully, Colette moved to hug him. 'Hello, Dad. Well sung.'

'Hello, love. Thanks for waiting. Hello, Lydia. Good to see you.' He waved one of the carrier bags at her.

'What *have* you got in those?' Colette held her hand out to take one of them while her father got his coat on. 'I'm parked across the other side.'

'Marking. I had very good intentions of getting some done when I wasn't on stage.'

'It's the thought that counts,' Colette said. She led the way across the car park.

'Are you still driving Hannah's old car? How's it holding out?'

'It's doing very well,' Colette said, 'considering the fact that I've lulled it into a false sense of security with a supermarket run every other Friday, and then sprung a surprise cross-country adventure on it.'

'Your mother and I are engaged in a battle of wills over whose car is going to be the first to be got rid of.'

She felt in the pocket of her jeans for her car keys. 'Isn't that going to come down to which of you retires first?'

'The current plan is that we'll go together.'

Colette laughed. 'Are you sure that's wise?'

'It's wiser than letting either of us get used to having the run of the house. No, Lydia, I promise you that I can manage quite well in the back. Anyway, how are you? Do I ask about the PhD? Do I ask

153

about the C of E?'

Colette glanced at Lydia, who said, 'The cogs are turning.'

'In which particular sausage machine?'

'Both.' Lydia pushed the front seat back into place with a click.

Colette added, as she put her seatbelt on, 'I also seem to be meant to be constructing the sausage machine, because there's not much there at the moment.'

'Ah,' her father said. He dropped the teasing note. 'I can't say that we've been particularly impressed by what we've seen of your supervisor in the media.'

'Nor am I,' Colette said, 'but there's not much I can do about that.'

'No. Quite. Unless – why don't you ask for a different one?'

Colette turned the key in the ignition. 'I've thought about it; but I can't see any way in which it'll be less hassle than getting on with things.'

'Hmph. Well. Let us know if you want either of us to come down and put a rocket up somebody. Now. Lydia. Assume I know nothing about the Church of England at all, and explain to me what you're currently up to.'

Lydia turned as far around in her seat as possible and began, 'So at the moment I'm talking to the Diocesan Director of Ordinands once a month or so, and she's setting me books to read and things to think about.'

'And what happens when you've both got bored?'

'Well, either we decide that, because we're both bored, ordination isn't for me, or she recommends me to the Bishop.'

'And what's a Bishop?'

'*Dad*,' Colette protested. Rolling her eyes was pointless in the semi-darkness, but she did it anyway.

Lydia just said, 'And if the Bishop agrees with her then he puts me forward for a Bishop's Advisory Panel.'

'What happens when you get there?'

'Three interviews, a written exercise, and a whole load of angst. And if *they* like me then they recommend me back to the Bishop, and then I can start training. Then it's three years at theological college and three more years in a parish.'

'Well,' said Colette's father, 'that sounds perfectly reasonable to me. But then I married a doctor.'

The doctor in question was waiting up for them. 'Well? How was it? What did you think of Dad?' She looked at him with fond, indulgent pride, and Colette was struck by an old sharp memory of Jess saying, incredulous, *Your parents still hold hands?* That, she supposed, had been the first time she'd understood that she couldn't necessarily extrapolate from her parents' relationship to everyone else's; the first time she'd appreciated the hell that Jess had grown up in.

'It was good,' she said, which was close enough to an answer to any of those questions. 'Haven't you seen it?'

'Yes, of course. I went yesterday with Richie.'

'What did Richie make of it?'

'Once he'd got over the hideous embarrassment he seemed to enjoy it.' She turned to Lydia. 'What did you think? You don't have to be diplomatic.'

'Yes, you do,' said Colette's father.

'I don't need to be,' Lydia said. 'I loved it.'

'She did,' said Colette.

He looked delighted. 'Are you a Gilbert and Sullivan fan?'

'No, this was my first one, but it was just really interesting... Well, I suppose from the English Lit point of view. There was so much stuff I knew that it was clearly sending up.'

'And what did you think of Strephon?'

'That's a loaded question,' his wife warned. 'Don't answer it. Or, at least, not until you've had the High School sports hall drama explained to you.'

'Oh, dear,' said Colette. 'Go on.'

Her father sat back in his chair and began, 'Well, you'll remember how Harrison's got the contract in the first place, and that there was some grumbling about that in certain quarters. Then the floor started peeling last summer, and it's getting worse and worse, and there's no money, because there's never any money, and the PTA wouldn't cough up. Or so we thought...'

It took a good half hour to work through all the ins and outs, and they were very glad to go to bed straight afterwards.

Colette woke early: her old bed had become unfamiliar. She left Lydia asleep on the mattress on the floor and went downstairs.

Her mother was already up, sitting at the kitchen table with the *Guardian*. When she saw Colette she laid the newspaper aside and smiled at her.

'Tea? There's some in the pot.'

'Thank you.' She fetched a mug from the cupboard, poured tea, and added milk.

'I saw Jess the other day. Don't look so horrified: it was in the supermarket, not the surgery.'

'I wasn't horrified,' Colette said, 'just surprised. I saw her yesterday, as it happens.'

'So you'll have seen the sapphire ring, then?' There was a note in her mother's voice that suggested that this was not just gossip, but concern as well.

Colette responded first to the gossip. 'Pretty, isn't it?' Then to the concern. 'She texted me when they got engaged.'

'And you're OK with it?'

'Of course I am.' Did her mother think she was still pining after Jess? 'I think Lydia would be a bit worried if I wasn't.'

'Well, no, but I meant, since you and Lydia can't get married yourselves...'

'That's not a reason to take it out on the rest of the world, is it?' Although she feared that her current impatience exposed her hypocrisy there. 'And Lydia and I are fine.'

To her relief, her mother abandoned the subject of Jess. 'I understand that Lydia's... *process* is still ongoing.'

'It's slow,' Colette said. 'They want to be sure. And they want her to be sure.'

'That's not easy for you, though. More uncertainty.'

She sipped her tea. 'Yes, but I think we'd be uncertain anyway. I mean, she wouldn't be planning on staying with the council long-term even if this wasn't on the cards.'

Her mother said, 'She could do worse. If she stayed there for a while, got her feet under the table, she might find herself rising up the ranks more quickly than she thinks. And it's a decent pension, and there's legal protection. Of course everyone's *meant* to comply with the Equality Act, but you do find that the public sector is better, on the whole.'

'She's mostly out at work now. It sounds like it's been OK.' Colette remembered a time when Lydia had not been out to anyone at all. 'I've been invited as her plus one to the wedding of two of her colleagues.'

'That's good. That's very good.'

'Have you been reading up on this?' Colette asked suspiciously.

'What? The Equality Act, you mean? No. Veronica – do you remember Veronica? She was my practice manager before Sharon – was very keen – quite rightly – on equality training. And of course backing her up on that often meant going to it myself. Quite rightly,' she said again.

'As it is,' Colette said, bitterly, 'Lydia's trying to get into the one organisation in the country that's managed to wangle its way out of having to comply with the Equality Act.'

A disapproving tut-tut. 'It really shouldn't be that difficult. What's the wording? *No unreasonable refusal to provide goods or services.*'

'Ha. Refusal to provide services is exactly the problem, isn't it?'

Her mother smiled sympathetically. 'And how are *you*?' she asked.

'I'm all right, thanks. Plodding on.'

'Your dad said you weren't too worried about your supervisor's problems.'

'There isn't really any point in worrying, is there?'

'Mm.' A quick glance up at Colette and back down at the cup. 'Is there a procedure to get you a new one if he quits, or gets sacked, or anything like that?'

'I assume they have to find me somebody.'

'How would you feel about that?'

Colette said, helplessly, 'It would depend who I got instead, I suppose.'

'Would you get any say in that?'

'I wouldn't have thought so.'

'You might want to look up what the procedure is, assuming that one exists at all.' She looked sternly at Colette, who sought refuge in her tea.

'OK.'

'And of course you always have the option of pulling the plug from your end.' Colette did not answer that. After a moment of silence her mother asked, 'Have you thought any more about what you want to do afterwards?'

She imagined a shining railway line leading away from her into some unpictured distance. 'The obvious thing would be a postdoc, which should be feasible if Lydia's going to theological college. And after that I suppose I'd just see what happened.'

'You're thinking you'll stay in academia, then?'

'Oh, yes.' Colette did not want to say that she would not know what else to do with herself. 'Well, you know, I've got this far.' She wondered whether her mother had opinions about things like *ivory towers* and *the real world*. It would make sense if she did. The seven years' labour to earn her title had been a mere prelude to thirty-five years' service.

Her mother only said, 'I found it very helpful, being with your dad, who was going out to work and coming back again at a predictable time, and earning proper money. It made me feel like there was light at the end of the tunnel. I expect you're finding the same thing, with Lydia working.'

'Mm.' Colette poured herself some more tea. 'Not that she earns proper money, but I know what you mean.'

'I don't think anyone your age is earning proper money. It's disgraceful.'

Colette bristled, and then reflected that it was probably meant as a disparagement of society in general rather than her generation in particular. 'So are you say that it's going to be easier if *I* have a real job while Lydia's studying?'

Her mother shrugged her shoulders. 'As you say: finish your PhD and then see what happens.'

That was not, in fact, what Colette had said. But she let it go.

# *June*
*Yaaaaaaaaaaaaaaaaaaaaaaaaaaaaaayyy!!! #pisky*
@LydiaHawkins
17:04, 8 June 2017

'Heard the news?' Lydia was smiling delightedly.
'No – what is it?'
'The Scottish Episcopal Church has voted to allow same-sex marriages!'
'No!'
'Yes!'
Colette sat down on the futon to unbuckle her sandals. 'The Scottish Episcopal Church: are they... I don't want to say, Anglican?'
'Part of the Anglican Communion, yes.' Lydia came to kiss her.
'What does it mean for the Church of England?' Colette asked. She kicked her feet free. 'What, if anything, does it mean for you?'
Lydia kissed her again. 'Goodness knows. Wailing and gnashing of teeth, I expect.'
'For you, or for the Church of England?'
'It depends on how they take it, doesn't it? At least it's good news for the Piskies.'
'*Piskies*?'
'E*pisc*opalians,' Lydia explained.
'Oh. Do you want to move to Scotland now?'
'I don't think I'd make a very good Pisky,' Lydia said. 'They're very High.'
She joked, 'Maybe we should just elope to Gretna Green, then. Do you think there's an Episcopalian church there?'
Lydia sat down next to her and reached for her phone. 'Let's have a look.' She was playing along, but there was a wistfulness in her expression that told Colette not to push things too far. 'So it turns

out there is. All Saints, Gretna.' She sighed. 'I can't, though.'

'I know.'

'I'm sorry.'

Colette shifted closer to her and put an arm around her shoulders. 'Don't be. It isn't your fault, and I...'

Lydia turned to face her. 'And you what?'

Colette drew her closer and kissed her, slowly, deliberately, and rephrased the words that had first come to her. 'I love you whatever.'

Friday was the end of the university term, a fact which Colette would not have noticed had James not pointed it out to her. The undergraduates had finished their exams and had been lounging on the lawns and in the bars for several weeks now, and it made little difference for anybody else. She was as present as ever; so was James, now he was back from honeymoon; Barry, as absent.

She accomplished little and drifted home in a state of antisocial lethargy, to find Lydia home early and ironing her dress.

'Oh,' Colette said, dismayed.

Lydia looked up and waved the iron as if in explanation. 'Jorick and Maddie's wedding.'

'I know.' She did know; she had just been avoiding the thought of it.

'The invitation says seven thirty but I think eight will be fine.'

'Oh, really?' Colette prayed that Lydia would somehow change her mind and decide not to go.

'Do you know what you're going to wear?' *You'd better*, said the subtext.

Colette winced. 'I hadn't thought about it. I suppose the same thing as I wore to James and Giselle's. Except it's got a wine stain on the skirt...'

'I thought I washed it.'

'Yeah, but the stain hasn't come out. And then I just never got round to sorting out anything else.'

'It's been on the calendar for months.'

'I know,' Colette said again, miserably.

Lydia tilted the iron to see how much water was left inside it. 'They're lovely, I promise.'

'I believe you,' Colette said, and knew that it sounded like she didn't. In actual fact it didn't seem relevant.

Lydia looked at her severely. 'You don't want to go, do you?'

Colette could not deny it, and she could not put her finger on *why*, beyond the fact that she didn't know them, that they were representatives of Lydia's life beyond the confines of church and university, that she couldn't face attending another wedding and having to think about why they would never have one themselves. 'Not really,' she admitted.

'Hmm.'

She let herself ask, 'Is it going to cause massive problems if I don't? Like, it's just the evening thing, isn't it? It's not like they're going to have to rewrite the whole table plan or whatever.'

'No.' Lydia added, 'That isn't really the point.'

Colette sighed, too theatrically. 'Well, if you really want me there, I'll go.'

'If you really don't want to be there, I don't want you to drag yourself there.' But Lydia looked hurt.

'It's not that.' It was that. It was the prospect of scores of people she didn't know, knowing that she would be asked about what she did, that she would then have to try to explain her studies to people who weren't really interested, that she wouldn't pitch it right, would get caught up explaining her explanations. Even if she managed to keep them off the subject, there was still the whole thing of learning names that she would immediately forget. Perhaps that wouldn't matter. Lydia *might* only be working there for a few months more;

she might never have to meet any of these people again. Conversely, it might go on for years. This might be only the beginning of a social life that Lydia was going to expect her to share.

She rebuked herself: James' wedding must surely have been as intimidating for Lydia. But Lydia was better at this stuff.

'Mm?' Lydia was looking expectant, tapping a pen against the edge of her hand.

Colette shook herself. 'Sorry.'

'What is it, then?' She could tell by the tone that it wasn't the first time she'd asked.

'I'm sorry. I just don't think I can do it.' She looked sideways at Lydia, trying to read her expression. There was irritation there, which sparked an answering irritation, and sympathy, which only induced guilt.

'Look. You clearly won't enjoy it. So don't go.'

'Will you enjoy it, without me?' She realised too late how that sounded, and added, 'I mean, you'll have loads of people to talk to, won't you? And they won't think it's too weird that I'm not there?'

'I think I'll survive. What will you do if you don't go?'

'Oh,' Colette said, 'I'll survive, too.'

She wasted the evening doing nothing in particular, and must have been asleep by the time Lydia got back; she was woken the next morning with a swift kiss. When she dragged herself out of bed a quarter of an hour later she found Lydia attacking Thursday's washing up.

She went to hug her from behind, but Lydia had turned to face her before she completed the manoeuvre.

'Sorry about yesterday,' Colette said. 'That was pretty pathetic, wasn't it?'

Lydia shrugged her shoulders within the embrace, clearly not wanting to agree, but not able to disagree. 'How are you feeling today?'

Colette thought about it. 'I'm OK, I guess.'

Lydia looked up at her, tilted her head back so that she looked straight into Colette's eyes. 'Up to a trip into town? There's a new café opened up just off Broadway and everyone from Maddie's team was raving about it. Apparently they do really good coffee and fancy ice creams.'

'Town on a Saturday? In summer?'

'We don't have to. I just thought, it'd be better now than after schools break up.'

'No,' Colette said bravely. 'Let's do it.'

They went that afternoon. The café was as good as Lydia's colleagues had promised, and not as crowded as Colette had feared. It took her a while to decide on zabaglione ice cream. Lydia went straight for chocolate.

'Another one?' Lydia asked, when both their dishes were empty.

'I liked the look of the passion fruit sorbet,' she admitted.

'Go for it. I'll have a cup of coffee. Yes,' she said, before Colette could change her mind. 'Really.'

'No, I'll go.'

She stood up before Lydia could argue.

The sorbet was good, a burst of tartness and sweetness after the creamy zabaglione. She ate it thoughtfully, half a teaspoon at a time, letting each chunk melt on the tip of her tongue.

Lydia stifled an exclamation.

'What?'

'Shh!'

Colette lowered her voice. '*What?*'

Lydia muttered, 'It's Tina. She's the one ordering just now. No. *Don't* look round. Wait. No. No, it's too late. She's seen me.' She took a breath, plastered on her church coffee smile, and waved.

Colette laid her spoon down and turned.

The Reverend Tina Audley was a wispy-looking woman in her mid fifties. She had blonde hair, fading to grey, mostly piled up on top of her head. She wore a pink cardigan over a black clerical shirt; it needed, Colette thought, to be a tiny bit more pink to look deliberate.

'Lydia! What a nice surprise!' She seemed faintly flustered: perhaps it was as unsettling to her to run into one of her candidates (was that even the right word?) in the course of her everyday life as it was for them to meet her.

'And you,' Lydia said, answering the spirit rather than the letter of the words. 'Um, this is Colette. Colette, this is Tina.' She opened her mouth, as if to say something else, and then closed it.

Tina's smile appeared to be genuine. 'It's very good to meet you, Colette.'

'And you.' Colette hoped she was half so convincing.

Tina made a careful little gesture with her cup. 'May I join you? Are you in a hurry?'

There were several empty tables, but it was not really the sort of request that one could decline. Lydia clearly thought so: she said, 'No, of course, do sit down.'

Tina sat. She said, brightly, 'Well!'

'Well,' Lydia echoed. 'How's your Saturday?'

'It's been lovely, thank you. I've just been seeing someone at St Peter's and I thought I'd stop in here to see what all the fuss is about.'

'Us too,' Colette said.

Tina turned her attention to her: it was faintly overwhelming. 'And what do you make of it?'

The question seemed to be dripping with hidden meaning. Colette tried to answer it on the most superficial level possible. 'The passion fruit sorbet is gorgeous.'

'I must try that next time!'

'I'd recommend it.'

'And how are you, Lydia?'

Lydia, looking flustered, launched into a lot of extraneous detail about her week at work and last night's party, omitting the part where Colette had failed to go to it.

Tina listened patiently and then said, 'That sounds lovely.' She paused. 'Actually, I'm very glad to have bumped into you two.'

'Yes,' Lydia said, meaninglessly.

Tina sailed on: 'Now, if I was talking to a potential ordination candidate who happened to be married, I'd arrange to meet their spouse. And I've been thinking that, while you two obviously aren't married, it's very clear to me that you're a very important presence in Lydia's life, Colette, and I've been very conscious that ideally I'd have a similar conversation. So I'm wondering if this is that opportunity.'

Lydia darted a helpless, apologetic look at Colette.

Colette, hoping she did not look horrified, said, 'Oh, right. I see.'

Tina smiled. 'It's good to make sure that she's been clear about what the next steps in her journey might mean for her, and that you've got a realistic idea of what the next few years might look like. And that you're, er, prepared to support her through that, and so that we can be confident that if that's what you agree to do then you're making an informed decision.'

'That all makes sense. I mean, I could tell you that she *has* told me all that...'

'But you don't know what you don't know. Of course.' Tina smiled encouragingly. 'Why don't you tell me a little bit about yourself?'

Colette, having been thinking that Tina would be interested in her only as she formed an adjunct to Lydia, was taken aback. 'Me? What would you like to know?'

'Oh, you know, your background, what you do...'

Hadn't Lydia told her all this? But perhaps Tina wanted both sides of the story. 'Well, I'm a PhD student at Stancester University. My subject is nuclear magnetic resonance, and at the moment I'm trying to finish off the research part of it. I'm hoping to start writing up some time in the next few months. I'm twenty-four. I'm originally from Bromsgrove in Shropshire.' She added, to make it sound less like a University Challenge introduction, 'I've got two brothers and two nieces and a nephew.'

Tina nodded. 'And how long have you known Lydia?'

Colette wondered how much of a euphemism *known* was meant to be. 'We met in our second year at university – through some of the Christian student groups.' (Should she have mentioned the faith stuff first? Probably. Oh well: too late now.) 'I'm a Methodist,' she added.

'Ah, yes, Lydia's told me that. It's very good that you share that faith.'

'Yes.'

'It really does make a difference. It isn't necessarily very easy, living with someone else's calling.'

'I'd worked that out,' Colette said drily.

Lydia was pleating a napkin into neat accordion folds. When Tina glanced at her, she put the napkin down and wrapped her two hands around her empty mug.

Tina said, 'I do try to encourage candidates to think what it might mean for the whole of the rest of their lives, particularly if there are, er, long-term partners on the scene. And of course the children of clergy... But you wouldn't need to worry about that...'

Colette found herself struck by a perverse, unprecedented broodiness. Lydia said, 'We hadn't ruled it out. I mean, years down the line, obviously, if at all, maybe adoption or fostering...'

Tina flushed. 'Oh! Well, all I was going to say was that it can be difficult for the children of clergy, because their parents become such prominent figures in the local community that it's a challenge to find their own identity.'

'My mother is a GP,' Colette said.

'Ah, so you'll know what I mean.' Tina glanced at her with a new understanding. Colette wondered whether she had children herself. They would probably be grown up, if so. Perhaps not all of them would be straight. Would they have told her?

Lydia was still looking uncomfortable. 'Colette's parents know what's going on. They've been very supportive, as well.'

'Oh? That's very good to hear.' Tina was looking out of the corner of her eye at Colette as she said, 'Of course, we've discussed *your* parents.'

'Of course,' Lydia said. Colette tried to make her expression concerned but neutral. If this went on much longer, she thought, Tina was going to have to get them all another cup of coffee, and that would push it out of 'chance meeting' territory and into 'semi-formal assessment'.

Tina seemed to have come to the same conclusion. She glanced at her watch and said, 'Well, this has been lovely. Colette, I'm so glad to have met you at last.'

'Oh, yes, you too.'

Tina turned to Lydia. 'We're meeting in a couple of weeks, aren't we?'

Lydia looked distinctly relieved. 'That's right. I should have finished that book by then.'

'Brilliant. I look forward to hearing your thoughts!' Tina picked up her bag. 'Goodbye!'

'Goodbye!' they said.

'Well,' Lydia said, when the café door had closed behind Tina, 'that was more intense than I was expecting for a Saturday afternoon.'

Colette exhaled loudly. 'Yeah.'

'It could have gone a lot worse.'

'Could it?'

Lydia said, 'Of course it could! If it had to happen at all, that was about as good as I could have hoped for. You and Tina had a good conversation; she got to see how supportive you are of me and that I've got that faithful support at home; nobody said anything about Tim Farron; neither of us snapped when she said that thing about kids...'

Colette wondered whether Lydia had been party to an entirely different conversation; except she couldn't remember anything about Tim Farron either. She said, 'You can buy the ice creams next time.'

Lydia touched her lightly on the upper arm. 'I'm not dumped, then?'

'Of course not. At least, not if I'm not, for standing you up last night.'

A quiet laugh. 'Let's call it quits.'

'To be honest,' Colette said slowly, 'it's a bit of a relief, having met her. It makes me feel a bit less like your dirty little secret, and a bit more like I have some sort of significance in this whole process.'

'Ouch.' Lydia bit her lip. 'I'm sorry. The thing that she's been trying to establish all along is, am I up to the training, and, beyond that, am I up to ministry? And if I'm in a relationship with you, then it affects you too, and she wants to find out if you're going to be supporting me or just gritting your teeth and going along with it. And it isn't Tina's fault that the rules are so stupid.'

'I suppose it isn't,' Colette said, grudgingly. 'Come on, let's go home.'

They stopped on the way for the ingredients for dinner. Lydia shook off her discomfiture and was singing to herself as she cooked pasta and prawns in chilli sauce. Colette smiled and let her get on with it, and went to deal with the pile of laundry that Lydia, prioritising her dress for the wedding, had not got around to sorting. She felt faintly troubled. She had told the truth: it was a relief to have come face to face with a representative of the discernment process. Even so, there was something more to it than that.

She pulled at one leg of a pair of jeans. Lydia's. Up to now, she thought, it had been easy – no, *possible* – to pretend that there was nothing going on.

A lilac T-shirt, rather faded. She folded it and added it to her own pile. No, it was more that if there was something going on, she had been able to tell herself that it had nothing to do with her, that it was Lydia's business to work out in her own good time.

Several black socks, which were Lydia's work ones. Colette folded them into pairs. It was true, too, that she had been being as supportive as she knew how; but that did not mean that she was being as supportive as she could be.

Another pair of jeans. Her own. Colette folded them carefully. It was time, she concluded, that she started taking this seriously.

Lydia appeared in the doorway. Colette waved a pair of underwear at her. 'Are these yours?'

'No, they're yours. You think I'd get into those?'

She added them to her own pile. 'I don't remember ever having seen them.'

'That's because I bought them for you – do you remember, back in October or so when we went to stay with Georgia?'

'Of course. You're right. Five pairs and a packet of paracetamol. How did these get into the laundry now? I've never worn them.'

'I knocked some stuff into the basket by mistake when I was

looking for my blue bra. I thought I'd put it all back, but clearly not.'

'Mystery solved.'

'*We bought these knickers!*' Lydia sang. '*We bought these knickers in Marks and Sparks!*' She broke off and added, 'Dinner's ready, by the way.'

Lydia did not seem disposed to talk any more about their unexpected meeting with Tina; and indeed, Colette thought, what was there to talk about? (Except the obvious, which she was ignoring until it became impossible to ignore.) Instead, they discussed the wedding. Lydia described it by reference to James and Giselle's, and Colette tried hard to match up names to stories Lydia had already told her. Then they played a few rounds of Boggle before Lydia said reluctantly that she probably ought to read some more of *Becoming Reverend*, since they'd mentioned it today and Tina would probably be expecting some sort of reaction to it next time.

Colette finished sorting the laundry, and then took herself off to the study to mess around on the internet. After a while she could hear Lydia moving around the flat: she must have finished the chapter or whatever she'd been aiming for, or just given up on it in favour of the washing up. Then she heard the shower going, and then the particularly intense silence that probably meant that Lydia was praying. Colette realised that she was glad, guiltily so, that she hadn't asked her to join her tonight.

She went to the Church of England website; found the section on vocations; found the page that outlined the nine criteria for selection. *Relationships*. No, there was nothing exceptionable there. She scrolled further down. *Further information... Age... Gender... Sexuality*. That was it. *Issues in Human Sexuality*. This was the guidance that Lydia would have to agree to abide by. She opened it up. (A PDF of a photocopy: that wasn't exactly good practice, she thought.) It started at section five; what, she wondered, did sections one to four contain, and did anyone care about them? Perhaps they only bothered with section five these days, kept it around for use as a weapon.

And section five was teeth-grindingly *wrong* from the first page. It flittered around making apparently reasonable points. It lined up good and convincing arguments and dismissed them out of hand. She rolled her eyes at the section on bisexuality ('*inevitably unfaithful* my arse!') and moved on. 'Not my Church,' she murmured to herself. 'Not my Church.' But that didn't help, because it was Lydia's, and she knew that, for all that this was a statement that dated from before the two of them were born, that itself claimed not to be the last word, that had been assigned far more weight than it could bear, it would be taken to apply to Lydia. Clergy must not be in an *active homophile relationship* (what an expression!) because some laity (some laity twenty-five years ago) would find it difficult. Candidates for ordination were to abide by the same standards.

It was horribly clear.

And then Lydia was standing in the doorway, barefoot, with her flimsy mauve cotton dressing gown barely done up, and Colette couldn't bear it. She shut the browser window in a hurry.

'Ready for bed?' Lydia asked, as if nothing was wrong.

'Just a minute.' She closed all the other programs, and shut everything down. 'I haven't done my teeth or anything.'

'OK.' Smiling in a way that made Colette's heart beat hard, she turned and left the room.

Colette went to the bathroom and brushed her teeth angrily. Apparently they were not going to be able to ignore this. Apparently they were going to have to have this conversation now. Either Lydia was forcing her into it, or, conversely, she was managing to ignore it far better than Colette could. She rinsed and spat. Then she flossed, to give herself more time to think. It didn't help.

When Colette came into the bedroom, Lydia was sitting up

against the headboard, cross-legged, the dressing gown slipping from her right shoulder, the duvet pulled up into her lap. She laid her book down on the bedside table.

Colette pulled her socks off as a token gesture towards getting ready for bed. Taking off anything more would have been too much like giving in; taking off everything and putting on pyjamas would make it look like she was just being deliberately obtuse. At a loss, she sat down on the edge of the bed.

Lydia, who had been waiting with ill-concealed impatience, kicked the duvet away and pulled her in towards her, and Colette could not help turning to face her, could not help responding to her kiss. It occurred to her (Lydia's fingers creeping up under her T-shirt) that perhaps Lydia had found some way around it; then she thought (Lydia's mouth opening to hers) that there wasn't any possible way around it. And she thought furiously that she didn't care.

But she did. She hesitated, broke away, her fingers on the sash of Lydia's dressing gown. 'Should we... not?'

Lydia jerked backwards. 'What?'

'You know.' Her face was hot; she must be bright red. And she was half in and half out of her T-shirt. She tried to shuffle it back down. 'Sex. It's just that... Well, I've been thinking, you're going to have to either commit to celibacy at some point, or decide to stick two fingers up at the whole thing. And, well, here we are.'

'This is really not the point at which I contemplated making that decision.' Lydia smoothed her dressing gown down around her hips. 'For the record, it's "stick two fingers up at the whole thing", and I'd actually made my peace with that about six months ago.'

'Oh,' Colette said weakly. Unwilling to conduct this conversation with her T-shirt rucked around the top of her chest, she pulled it over her head.

Lydia raised her eyebrows. 'And I'd have told you that at the time, if you'd asked.'

'I didn't know there was anything *to* ask.'

'There always has been. Ever since all this started.' Lydia managed to laugh. 'What a moment to bring it up.'

'It seemed, I don't know, appropriate.'

'You're a better person than I am. If I'd seriously thought that it was going to be the last time, I'd have waited until afterwards.'

Colette reflected ruefully that it seemed unlikely there would be an *afterwards*, tonight, at least. But then it seemed that it was not going to be *the last time*. 'I don't know what I thought. I... It just seemed very important, in the moment, that we actually talk about it.'

Lydia sighed. 'OK, so let's talk about it. What's the problem?'

'I've just *said*. You're not meant to be doing this.

She looked defiant. 'No one's ever said that in so many words.'

'*Homosexual genital acts*, it sounded pretty clear to me.'

'Yes, but if you read the rest of it, the genitals they're really worried about aren't the sort that we have.'

It was not like Lydia to obey the letter of the law and not the spirit. Colette said, 'Are you trying to embarrass them into submission, or what?'

Lydia chuckled. 'Why not? It works on you.'

Colette undid her jeans and removed them as if to prove something. 'Seriously.'

'Seriously. Do you think I haven't thought about that?'

Colette shrugged her shoulders. 'I don't know. *What* have you thought about it, then? Why are you carrying on as if it wouldn't make any difference to, you know, *your entire future?*'

'Because,' Lydia said, gathering the duvet up around her shoulders like a mantle, 'what became very obvious when I started thinking about it was that, wherever we stopped, it was never going to be enough. You know. Where you stopped, just now, would have been far too far for some people. Even if we keep all our clothes on at all times, there are still going to be people who think we shouldn't be kissing. If we stop kissing, there will still be people who won't be satisfied until we stop holding hands. And even if we never so much as look at each other then it still won't be enough if we're living together, because some people are just going to make the assumption anyway.'

'I know they are,' Colette said miserably. *Issues in Human Sexuality* had wrung its hands over that very point. 'I just thought... I had to ask.' Swiftly, efficiently, she dispensed with her underwear and put her pyjamas on.

Lydia watched her with an ironic expression on her face. 'If I keep trying to please other people's consciences, then I'm going to end up so far from my own then I don't think I'll know who I am any more. So the question then becomes: can I make any sense of the arbitrary line that the Church of England draws in the sand? And I just can't. I feel very strongly that it's not fair on you. Marriage is one thing, because I know it doesn't bother you nearly so much as it bothers me, but this – *you* don't believe that we shouldn't be doing this, do you?'

'You know I don't. At least – not when it's between you and me.' And when had she invited the Church of England into her bed?

Lydia shook her head vigorously. 'And nor do I. Maybe, if we'd got together after all this kicked off, then I'd think differently. But even then, maybe not. Maybe I'd pull the plug on the whole process if I'd started it single and then met you.'

'You wouldn't,' Colette said, shocked.

'Maybe not. Anyway, that's not where we are. So far as I'm concerned, you were in my life first; I don't think I'd even have got to this point if you weren't; and I don't think that giving you up is a good way of expressing faithfulness.'

Colette got into bed. 'You wouldn't have to give me up. That's what I'm saying.'

Lydia snuggled up against her, tentatively at first, and then, when Colette put an arm around her shoulders, with more confidence. 'Giving up a significant part, maybe one of the holiest parts, of what we have together, then. That's what *I'm* saying. And OK, maybe we'd get used to it, maybe it's even true that by the time we hit the age of forty we wouldn't care any more anyway, but I'm not sure that's relevant.'

'No,' Colette said. 'We're not forty yet.'

She kissed Lydia, hard, but the mood was comprehensively ruined, for that night, at least, and Lydia turned the light out, and Colette's pyjamas stayed on.

# *July*

*The first ever Stancester Pride!*
*Saturday 22 July*
*Parade starts 12 noon outside the Guildhall*
*Stage and stalls in the Meadow*

'So,' Lydia said, 'are we doing Pride?'
Colette raised her eyebrows. 'Pride? Is that today?'
'It is.'
'Ah. I wasn't planning on it.'
'Oh.'
'Oh?' she echoed.
'I was assuming we would.' Lydia's attempt to sound breezy fell some way short.

Colette sighed. 'How long ago should we have left?'
'About ten minutes, because I wanted to get a card for Abby and Paul and the new baby. There's a service of blessing at All Saints at half ten, and then we walk down to join the parade, and then it ends up at the Meadows, which is where all the stalls are.'

'OK, then.'
'You could sound a little more enthusiastic.'
Colette was not sure that she could. 'I know we ought to.'
'You don't have to. It's a free country. That's the point of it, really.'

'I know.' Again she heard her own snappishness, her lack of enthusiasm, and felt guilty for it. The prospect of not going to Pride had much the same quality as the prospect of not going to church – on a St John's Sunday, at least – and for much the same reason. There was another element in there as well, though: a suspicion of ungratefulness. Someone had put a huge amount of time and effort into this, and she was seriously considering not even bothering to turn up. (Which, she supposed, applied to church, as well.) 'You want to go?'

Lydia looked almost hurt. 'Of course I do.'

Of course she did. 'You could go without me.'

'I *could.*'

'Why do you need me to be there?'

'I don't *need* you to be there. I just think it would be nice if you came, that's all.'

'Oh,' Colette said once more.

'I'm getting the impression that you don't really want to.'

'I can't, really. I've got so much to do in the lab.'

'But it's Saturday. You never go to the lab on a Saturday.'

'I do today.'

It did not have to be a lie. She went to the lab.

James was not there, and Colette was relieved. James might have noticed it was Pride, and asked awkward questions.

Barry was there. He was in a suspiciously helpful mood, very interested in what Colette was up to, very keen to see her findings, and very ready to advise her which avenues to explore next. She tried to feel vindicated, but all the rest of the morning she was thinking about Pride, wondering what Lydia was up to, whether she'd found other people to hang around with...

She went down to the Students' Union café for lunch; she was the only person there, apart from the bored girl behind the bar. Perhaps, she thought, she could wander down into town after all. But she'd have to text Lydia to see where she was, and maybe she'd be in the middle of something... Colette walked back up to her office, and tried organising her report the way that Barry had suggested. It made sense. It made a lot of sense. The afternoon stretched out, long and hot, and she settled down into focus...

Some time later, her phone buzzed. She pressed the button on the side to make the notifications show, and glanced at the screen. A text from Lydia: *hi we're going on to the feathers see you there maybe? Love you xxxxx*

She sighed, and let the screen fade back to black. There was a headache gathering at the front of her skull. She got up from her chair and went to make a cup of tea.

She brought it back to her desk, turned back to her report, turned to Google to check the spelling of *homogeneous*, was distracted by *homogonous* (*pertaining to flowers that do not differ in the length of stamens and pistils*), and was lost.

She knew that she really ought to shut down and go and find Lydia.

At the Feathers there would be the barman who had once been a Christian Fellowship member and had not turned the sound off when Lydia came out; there would be whoever she was going there with; there would be other people who Colette might or might not know, and she would have to think of something constructive to say to them, and then explain to them why she had not gone to Pride when Lydia had.

*I had things to do in the lab* might have been an excuse. But then she would have to explain what it was that she did in the lab.

What *was* she doing in the lab? Barry had gone hours ago, muttering something about a phone call about a documentary. Even the woman in the Synthetic Chemistry team who was widely reputed to sleep under her desk must have gone: the lights were out across the corridor. Uncomfortably aware that in fact she had achieved nothing of note in the last two hours, Colette shut her computer down and set off home. From the top of the hill she could hear the pile-driving bass reverberating up from the Meadows. Somewhere down there, she thought, people were having fun. Somewhere down there was Lydia. No. She knew exactly where

Lydia was. At least… She squinted, trying to place the Feathers from up here, in the still, colourless, evening light. Start from the cathedral. That was easy. And tonight the Meadows were bright with the lights from Pride, and those pale blotches were surely marquees. The dark band of the river was crossed in places with strings of lights: bridges. The big one was Exeter Road. So one to the left would put you opposite the council offices, which meant the Feathers was just this side, surely. But perhaps it was one to the right…

Abandoning the attempt, she headed on down the hill. It didn't matter. She wasn't going to go there. She was going home. Sooner or later Lydia would turn up, and would forgive her (yet again) for being an antisocial disaster.

The flat was uncomfortably stuffy. Colette opened all the windows and chucked a dead fly out. She washed her hands and then raided the fridge. Finding the remains of the previous day's pasta bake, she ate it, cold, out of the serving dish, followed it with a dutiful apple, and left the washing up in the sink to soak. She relocated herself to the futon with the intention of reading something, but fell into a doze before she had got more than three pages into *The Watchmaker of Filigree Street*.

She woke, hours later, in a blaze of electric light. She blinked, and observed her own mind as if from a distance as it curated the new items of evidence. The room was bright. The window was dark. She was not alone.

'I'm sorry,' Lydia was saying. 'I didn't realise you were asleep.'

'I didn't mean to be.' Colette was annoyed both with herself for having succumbed to fatigue, and with Lydia for waking her. She sat up straight and unfolded her right arm – it was not quite numb, yet – and stretched it out along the top edge of the sofa.

Lydia took that as an invitation to come and sit down next to her.

She was warm, and smelled slightly of cigarette smoke and beer. 'I did text you a couple of times. I guess you didn't see?'

'I saw one,' Colette said guiltily. 'I didn't know what I was going to do, so I couldn't work out how to reply. So I didn't.'

Lydia just said, 'Mm,' and arranged herself closer under Colette's arm. She seemed impermeably cheerful. Colette resented that for a moment, reminded herself that she had only herself to blame, and resented it a little more. But she let her arm slip off the back of the sofa and come to rest round Lydia's shoulders.

'So you had fun.'

'Mm? Oh, yes. It was good. We started out with a service at All Saints –'

'*Not* your usual style,' Colette couldn't resist putting in.

Lydia took it as a mere statement of fact. 'Yes, but not theirs, either. It was lovely, actually. I was sorry you weren't there.'

'It didn't occur to me that I could have done church and not the rest of it.' It seemed safe to admit it, with Lydia in this generous mood.

'Oh. Was that the matter?'

Colette nodded. 'I couldn't face the thought of all those people. I really did have stuff to do, but it wouldn't have had to take all day.' And there had been no good reason to spend most of the evening up there; she could just as well have gone into town to find Lydia once the crowds had dispersed. 'Anyway, tell me about it.'

'All Saints? It was quite simple, by their standards. They had *Just As I Am*, which I wouldn't have expected to work at all, but actually it did, and *Bringing In The Sheaves*, which made me cry.' She sang, half under her breath, '*When our weeping's over, He will bid us welcome. We will come rejoicing, bringing in the sheaves.*'

'Not their usual style at all,' Colette agreed. 'I wonder who picked the hymns?'

'I don't know. But the choir did do something – I think from the

Song of Solomon. And the reading was 1 Samuel 20 – you know, David and Jonathan.'

'I know.' (She had not known, but she thought a little crossly that she would have been able to work it out from context.) 'And then what?'

'A blessing. Well, actually the second hymn, but I said it out of order.' Lydia tipped her head back to see Colette's face. 'And *then* the blessing. And then we went out and did the parade. I walked with the Christians for a bit, and then I got a bit too far ahead, but I found Trevor, so I walked with all the unions as far as the Meadows. Then I ran into Rowan and we wandered round the stalls, and I ended up in the Feathers with the work lot. Oh, and Gabe. Do you remember Gabe? Muso. Friend of Georgia's. He had the room next to me in Richmond in my second year.'

'No.'

Lydia looked up at her. 'You probably would if you saw him. Anyway, he sings with the Stancester Gay Men's Chorus.'

'Along with half of All Saints' choir, no doubt.'

Lydia laughed and resettled herself against Colette, her hair soft against her bare arm. 'I wish,' she said, 'that I'd known all this existed when I first came to Stancester. I wish someone had said that St John's was wall-to-wall lesbians. I wish that Peter had told me in words of one syllable that when Father Steven talked about Jesus "coming out" he knew exactly what he was doing and that it was for the benefit of the whole, extremely queer, congregation. I wish I'd known about whatever the equivalent is in Hastings, if it even exists. I wish I'd known there was such a huge safety net there before I had to jump.'

'And instead,' Colette said, with some bitterness, 'all you knew about was me.'

Lydia sat up slightly and turned back to face her, contrite. 'And you were wonderful. You always have been. I just – I don't know. I just imagine that it might have been easier, those first few months, if I'd known about someone who was like me who I wasn't already falling for. I might have treated you better.'

That was an old regret, and Colette did not want to give it house room. 'Aren't we past that?' she murmured fiercely. '*Can't* we be past that? Can't you believe it's forgiven?' Then, feeling herself to have been ungracious, she added, 'I wish someone had told you, too. But only because you deserve to have had people loving you and respecting you and letting you be who you are all through your life.'

Lydia buried her face in Colette's shoulder. 'But the important thing,' she said, muffled, 'is that now I've got it. And I want you to have it, too.'

'I just couldn't face it, OK? I'm very glad that you had a good time, but I'm still not sure that I would have done.'

'Yes. OK. I don't think that was what I really meant to say. Perhaps I should just stop talking.' She leaned back, smiling sleepily, and Colette felt affection flood in.

'Next year,' she said, 'I definitely won't be in the lab.'

And Lydia laughed, and pulled her down to her.

*We're delighted to announce the birth of baby Keren-Happuch on Wednesday morning. I'm sore, and exhausted, but very, very happy.*
Invisible, Bisexual, Bloggable
23 July 2017

Lydia had not quite drawn the curtains all the way across the previous night, and Colette was woken by the sunlight falling across her face. She blinked, frowned, and turned onto her side. Lydia was still fast asleep, flat on her front with her face turned towards Colette. The light caught in her hair and made her shoulder glow. There was still a smudge of glitter on her left cheekbone.

Colette looked at her for a moment, awed and a little regretful. 'I'm sorry,' she said, making almost no sound. 'I should have come with you.'

Lydia did not stir, and Colette leaned across to kiss her shoulder. Then, closing her eyes, she rolled onto her back.

The sudden shrilling of Lydia's phone destroyed the idyll. Colette rolled over as Lydia mumbled something incomprehensible and groped to pick up the phone.

'*Dad?*' She wriggled up into a seated position and pulled the duvet up with her, over her bare shoulders. Then she said, 'Oh, no. When?'

Colette lay dead still.

Lydia asked urgently, 'But will she be OK?'

She gripped Colette's hand. Colette gripped hers in return.

'So where is she now? Where are you?'

Colette looked up at her inverted face, distorted by worry.

Lydia said, 'Well, I'll come down.' The answer angered her. She said, fiercely, 'No, I *do* want to.'

She shook her head, then nodded.

'Thanks Dad. Thanks for letting me know.'

She let the phone drop onto the bed, but stayed sitting bolt upright with the duvet pulled up to her throat. Colette got out of bed, and found her own dressing gown, and Lydia's. 'Was that what I thought it was?' she asked.

Lydia nodded slowly. 'Mum's in hospital. Heart attack, they think.'

Colette sat down next to her. 'How bad?'

'Dad doesn't know.' The duvet slipped, and she pulled it up again. 'I should be there.'

Colette did not quite trust herself with words. 'Mm?'

Lydia seemed to have been expecting her to try to talk her out of it; she said, 'I have to. It's my mum.'

Colette thought of the long drive to the Sussex coast; of how Barry had been unexpectedly present, and unexpectedly helpful, the day before. 'I'll check the oil and water in the car.'

Lydia looked aghast. 'No. You don't have to.'

'No, but I want to.' It was not quite the truth, and not quite a lie. She could quite happily have gone the rest of her life having nothing to do with Lydia's parents, but if Lydia was going to insist on seeing them, she would make sure that she was on the spot to mop up afterwards. 'Do you think Peter's parents will put us up? Or should we get a B and B?' She wasn't sure they could afford one.

Lydia blinked a little. 'I'll try Molly,' she said.

Colette squeezed her shoulder, dressed quickly, and went out to see to the car. When she came back, picking up yesterday's discarded clothes on the way, she found that Lydia had dragged a holdall out from under the bed and gathered together a bundle of underwear and T-shirts.

'Molly says it's fine,' she reported. 'We can stay as long as we want. Peter's there at the moment. So is Natalie.'

'Oh, right. Well, it will be nice to see them, if nothing else.' Colette dumped the armful of clothes in the laundry basket, and went off to get her suitcase and her laptop from the study.

It was a long, hot drive. Lydia sat hunched in her seat, tense with anxiety, saying little beyond calling out the directions from her phone. Colette, virtuous and cowardly, kept her mind on the road.

They went straight to the hospital. Colette waited as long as she dared at the drop-off point while Lydia went in to see if she could see her mother. An open-ended wait, with no way to tell how long it might go on: when it became clear that Lydia would not be coming back soon, Colette drove off to find a parking spot on a nearby residential street. She scrolled through Twitter, then the news, then Twitter again. When the battery threatened to go flat she put her phone back in her pocket. She drove around the block, then back to the drop-off point, and sat reading a commentary on John's gospel that Lydia must have left in the car.

Lydia emerged about fifteen minutes later, her face blank.

'Did you see her?' Colette asked.

'Yes,' Lydia said bleakly. She slid into the passenger seat and fastened her seatbelt.

'And?'

'She's alive. Asleep.'

'Your dad?'

'He was there. I didn't know what to say. Nor did he.'

'What do we do next?'

Lydia bit her lip. 'I think we stay here until she wakes up. Not *here* here. In the area. Until we know she's going to get better.'

Colette heard the unspoken *or until she doesn't*. Not knowing how to answer it, she turned the key in the ignition. 'OK. Let's get to Tonbridge.'

One or other of the Nathans had been looking out for them: Colette was only just beginning to reverse onto the drive when the front door opened and Peter and his mother appeared.

Colette shut her door and found that she had nothing to say.

'Welcome,' Molly said, 'both of you.'

Lydia said, 'Thank you.'

Peter said, 'Bags?'

That at least was something practical. Colette opened the boot and got out her suitcase and Lydia's holdall.

'You're in Delphine's room, you two. Colette, it's where you were before: up to the top of the stairs and to the right. We only have so many bedrooms in this house,' Molly added, not looking at anybody in particular, 'and I have already evicted Delphine from one of them onto the sofa. Therefore those of you who are couples are going to have to share rooms.'

'You know I don't mind,' Natalie said, and Colette was fleetingly aware of the remnants of an argument hanging in the air like the smell of burning.

'I'm sorry to be such a pain,' Lydia said. Colette glanced at her: she looked exhausted.

'You're not.' Molly touched her shoulder. 'Not in the slightest.'

She nodded gratefully. 'One day I'll manage to show up here for something that isn't a horrific family crisis.'

'Speaking of which,' Peter said, 'how is your mum?'

The invocation of someone else's, more serious, trouble went some way to dampen the tension. They all turned to look at Lydia.

'She's OK. Not great. *Stable*, they said.'

'That's good,' Molly said. 'That means she's not getting worse. *That* means they can work on making her better. Colette and Lydia, I'm going to ask Peter to carry your bags upstairs, and I want all of you down for dinner at seven.'

*If you're someone who prays, please pray for my aunt. She's not well at all.*
Invisible, Bisexual, Bloggable
25 July 2017

Colette phoned Barry first thing on Monday morning, and explained where she was, and why. He was sympathetic, but seemed at a loss as to what, if anything, to do about it.

'You can work remotely in these circumstances, of course,' he said, as if conferring a great favour.

'Of course.' If he hadn't noticed that she had already logged on, then she wasn't going to tell him.

'And make sure you drop a line to the, um, er, the support people, just so they know what's going on.'

She was fairly sure that he was meant to be the one to do that. She decided that she would settle for copying him in on the email.

'I tell you what,' he said at last, 'I'll ask James to email you with some things you could be getting on with.'

Colette bit her tongue on the retort that she knew what she should be getting on with; the difficulty was *how*. Then she thought that this was not really fair on James, but she could not face arguing with Barry over it.

'That's fine,' she said. 'And I'll email you if I run into any problems, shall I?'

For all that they had left in haste and arrived with no semblance of organisation, a routine emerged remarkably quickly. Lydia took the train down to Hastings every morning to arrive at the hospital for the start of visiting hours. Meanwhile, in Tonbridge, Colette attempted to do some work across the network. She tried to keep out of the Nathans' way; she felt very conscious of the fact that she and Lydia had invited themselves. Andrew and Molly, both teachers, deserved to enjoy their summer holidays. Peter's sister

Delphine was out at work or with friends almost all the daylight hours. Colette feared that this was at least partly to do with the fact that her house had been invaded by her brother's girlfriend and friends. Peter himself was writing up a report on his placement in a hospice chaplaincy. Natalie seemed to spend the time either reading or singing.

Monday, Tuesday, Wednesday, passed: a holiday that was not a holiday; a change that was not really a rest. Colette began to run out of things to write. Perhaps, she thought, if Lydia's mother continued to improve, they would be able to go home, and she would be able to get back into the lab.

On Thursday she couldn't settle to work, and went to help Peter, who was dealing with the laundry. He declined her offer of assistance with a rather shocked, 'You're the guest!'

'Then at least let me make you a cup of tea.'

'Go on, then.'

She made them a cup each and took hers to the kitchen table.

'How's it going?' she asked. 'College, I mean.'

He made a thoughtful kind of noise. 'Yeah, it's OK. I'm still not sure whether or not it's what I thought it would be.' He folded two satin pillowcases.

'Is *anything* really what you think it's going to be?' She was aware that this was a bit of a cop-out.

He chuckled. 'Well, I suppose not, if only because you're that little bit older and more experienced when you get to it than you were when you were thinking about it.'

An eerie *hee-hoo-hee-hoo* drifted through: Natalie, practising.

'And – did you ever read *The Towers of Trebizond*?'

Colette shook her head. 'Lydia read it by mistake, a couple of months ago. She liked it, though.'

Peter seemed rather charmed. 'How on earth do you read *The*

*Towers of Trebizond* by mistake?'

'She's been reading children's books all year. She thought it was a school story.'

'Hmm. Well, I know it's an Anglo-Catholic classic and all that, but my granddad was a bus conductor.'

'What's that got to do with anything?'

Peter shook his head. 'Spoilers.'

'Oh,' she said, feeling lost. 'So what was the point you were originally trying to make?'

He laughed. 'I've forgotten! Oh. About things not being like what you think they're going to be like. I suppose, that there are assumptions that people make about you, and you spend a lot of time unravelling them. And they assume either that you're just like them, or else that you're not like them at all.'

'In what way?'

Peter spread a shirt out on the ironing board. 'Oh – right – like back in May, I got into a really stupid argument about Roman Catholics with one of those people who not-so-secretly wants to be one himself, and he assumed that so did I. And he was almost offended when I said that actually my grandparents had left the Roman Catholic Church for what were quite good reasons, at the time, and I was OK with that.'

'Well, you wouldn't exist if they hadn't,' said Colette, who knew the story.

'Oh, I don't know: my parents might have met just by living in the same bit of London. It's not as if Dad never set foot outside Grandpa's church.'

'True.'

'But anyway, then the same afternoon I was telling somebody else about you and Lydia, and he was really surprised that I had friends who were gay. Um, and bi. Despite the fact that he knows I know he's gay himself.'

'Hmm.'

He shrugged his shoulders. 'Yeah. And clearly I don't want to start making assumptions myself but I do wonder if he'd have been *quite* so surprised about it if I were white.'

'Why were you telling him about us?'

'Something about Stancester. Oh, yes, because I was saying I'd meant to go to Mass at the cathedral the morning after Lydia's party but hadn't made it. Which reminds me. I don't think I ever asked how the Easter Vigil went, and the confirmation.'

'I enjoyed it.' The word seemed inappropriate once it was out of her mouth, but she left it. 'As for the confirmation, you should probably ask Lydia.'

'Are we going to church tomorrow?' Lydia asked Peter on Saturday night.

'Yes, if you'd like to – I mean, yes, we all will be, except Delphine – she's working – and you two would be very welcome to join us.'

'I would like to,' Lydia said seriously.

'It won't be what you're used to,' he said, his expression a little worried. 'Colette, *you* know, you've been before...'

'I can guess,' Colette said, 'but I haven't.'

'Didn't you come when you stayed back in 2012 or whenever it was?'

She shook her head. 'No. I think maybe I arrived on a Sunday and went on a Saturday. I'd remember going to church with you.'

'Compared to All Saints...?' Lydia suggested.

'Oh, not nearly as much so. That's true. You have survived All Saints.'

'Once,' Lydia said. 'Not counting the Pride service.'

The next morning, it did not occur to anybody until it was too late that they were not all going to fit in the same car.

'If the choir had been singing,' Peter said, 'Dad and I would have gone early.'

'I'm happy to drive,' Colette said.

'I could walk,' Lydia offered.

'You couldn't really,' Peter said. 'I mean, you *could*, but it's not a nice road and you'd have to have started half an hour ago.' He added, 'This is where you get to give the Nathan family a lecture on the evils of church-shopping.'

'It's not as if I go to my parish church,' Lydia said. 'In fact, I'm not sure I've *ever* gone to my parish church regularly. Which is a bit ironic, because what I said when Tina asked me what it was that made the Church of England distinctive was that it has a presence in every town and village.'

'Well, quite,' Peter said. 'Everybody needs a church they don't go to.'

'I'm not sure,' Andrew said, delicately, 'that I'd encourage you to go to the church in *this* parish, unless you've done some research. We go outside the parish, but I'm happier that the preaching will be, you know...'

Peter looked worried. 'I know it won't really be your style, Lydia. Either of your styles, in fact.'

Lydia said, 'Honestly, don't worry.'

Andrew cleared his throat. 'We won't be getting anywhere unless we get a move on. Colette, may I take you up on that very kind offer? It's not too difficult to find.'

'Look for the spire, right? Or is it a tower?'

'Yes, it's a spire,' said Peter. 'Come on, this is us. Head for the spikiest thing you can see.'

Andrew was scrawling a map on a piece of scrap paper. 'Here you go. You should be able to follow us, but just in case... I'd give you the postcode, but for some reason the sat nav can't cope with it at all.'

Peter said, 'Wouldn't it be easier if one of us just went with you?'

'That,' said his father, 'is a reasonable point, but it probably needs to be somebody other than you, because you're serving, and you need to leave now.'

'Am I?' Peter looked horrified. 'Did I know?'

'I *told* you...'

Peter held his hand out for the car keys. 'Fine, good, let's go. Anyone who's ready, come with me. Anyone who isn't, go with Colette.'

Molly appeared in the doorway. 'What on earth are you all doing? Peter, you need to go, you're serving.'

'I know,' he said through clenched teeth. 'Dad just told me. I assume you're ready, Mum?'

Colette glanced at Andrew's map, then at Andrew himself, and raised her eyebrows. He smiled slightly.

'Nat?' Peter jangled the keys.

'Give me a minute.' Natalie swallowed the last of her coffee, and choked on it. Andrew thumped her on the back. Lydia went on quietly eating her toast. Colette decided that she was finished, and stacked her mug on her plate, ready to take the lot to the dishwasher when the others had got out of the way.

The church was easy enough to find, and the parking was reasonable, a bare hundred metres from the lychgate. At the north door a sidesman handed them a service booklet each and apologised for the fact that there wasn't much of a congregation. 'Everyone's on holiday, you see.'

They slid into a pew next to Molly and Natalie.

Peter laid one hand on her shoulder, and one on Lydia's. They turned their heads to look at him.

'Would you two be able to take the elements up?'

Colette knew she was looking blank. 'The what?'

'The bread and the wine. At the offertory. Unless –' he was looking worried – 'you'd rather not do alcoholic wine...'

'Don't be ridiculous.' She was hardly going to develop temperance principles just because she'd stepped into an Anglican church. 'Tell me what we need to do.'

He looked relieved. 'OK. Third hymn. When the collection gets taken. You take the paten and the chalice from the little table at the back, one each, obviously, and carry them up the aisle to the front, where they'll be taken from you. Then you go back to your seats.'

Colette glanced at Lydia. 'You OK with that?'

'It's fine by me,' Lydia said. 'I can cite it as evidence of exploring different Anglican traditions.'

'Awesome. You're legends, the pair of you.' And he was off.

On the other side of Lydia, Natalie said nothing, very pointedly.

The service held few surprises for Colette, who was used to Peter's preferences for long white robes and a lot of kneeling. She had formed the impression, somewhere along the six years she had known him, that he was rather more into that side of things than either of his parents; now she wondered if she was wrong. Molly had been crossing herself at various points in the service; it was impossible to tell what Andrew was doing, up in the organ loft. It was more formal than any service that Colette usually attended, and she found the structure soothing.

When the introduction to the third hymn sounded, Molly gave her a little push. Colette nodded to Lydia, and they slid out of the pew and walked quietly to the back, where the flask and the plate stood on a little white-clothed table.

At her side, Lydia was tense as a piano string. Silently, she gestured for Colette to make her choice. With some vague idea of *not worrying Peter*, Colette picked up the silver plate on which the bread lay.

They proceeded down the aisle, Colette shortening her steps to match Lydia's. She was very conscious of the plate in her hands and the broad, round, wafer upon it. It did not weigh nearly as much as she had expected, the silver hammered thin and the bread light as a breath.

At the front, two white-robed servers were waiting for them, or for what they carried. They made awkward little bows, just out of synch with each other, and turned back to process back up the aisle. She just caught Peter's smile as they went.

Knowing how important the Eucharist was to Peter, Colette aimed for particular reverence in his church, but found the choreography unfamiliar and disconcerting, and got into a misunderstanding with the chalice minister. She returned to her seat flushed with embarrassment. Natalie had done everything perfectly, probably. Lydia probably hadn't, but she wouldn't be letting it get to her.

Colette stared miserably at her service sheet. *Communion hymn.* She glanced at the hymn board and looked up the number. 475. *Immortal love, forever full*. Some people were singing; some weren't. Natalie was, of course, sweet and full; so was Molly, gentle and breathy. Lydia clearly didn't know it, but was picking it up fast. Feeling contrary, Colette did not join in, but followed the words with her eyes.

*The healing of his seamless dress*
*is by our beds of pain.*

Only Colette heard Lydia's quiet, quick, indrawn breath.

*We touch it in life's throng and press*
*and we are whole again.*

Colette's gaze drifted down to the foot of the page. *John Greenleaf Whittier (1807-1892)*. The name sparked a memory so vivid it made her gasp. Becky and Will, arguing... not over this one, though. No.

*Dear Lord and Father of mankind.* 'John Greenleaf Whittier was a Quaker,' she remembered Becky saying, eyes glowing and accent even more Lancashire than usual. (Or was that a trick of the memory?) 'This whole poem is about the importance of silent worship! *Let us, like them, without a word, rise up and follow thee.* It takes a particular kind of Anglican public school arrogance to turn that into a *hymn.*'

She couldn't remember what Will had said in return. He'd been caught between two fronts, Colette seemed to remember, tempted to defend the tradition he came from while admitting that it had never done much for him. Becky had come out on top, but then she usually did.

Around her, they were singing:

*the last low whispers of our dead*
*are burdened with his name.*

She absolutely could *not* start thinking about Becky, she told herself far too late. The last thing that Lydia needed was for her to break down.

*Alone, O Love ineffable,*
*thy saving name is given.*
*To turn aside from thee is hell;*
*to walk with thee is heaven.*

She closed the book with a soft thud that was drowned out by the end of the hymn, and concentrated very hard on the post-communion prayer.

They escaped the after-service coffee with the excuse that Lydia wanted to get down to the hospital. Colette was relieved: there had been too much in that service, somehow, and she wasn't sure that she trusted herself to talk to strangers without embarrassing herself.

Lydia was quiet on the way down. 'I can get the train back if you like,' she said before she shut the car door and waved Colette off. 'I don't like to think of you losing the whole afternoon ferrying me around.'

'Don't worry,' Colette said. She didn't have anything better to do with the afternoon. She thought about just driving off by herself, but a vague, oppressive sense of obligation urged her back to Tonbridge.

A Sunday afternoon peace had descended upon the house. She could hear quiet conversation from upstairs: Andrew and Molly. She put her head round the sitting room door, to see if there was anyone in there.

'Come in,' Peter said. He had been sprawling on the sofa, his feet up on Delphine's pillows, but he sat up straight. 'Talk to me.'

Colette was not sure that talking was a good idea, but she came in.

'How was the hospital?' Peter asked.

'I didn't go in.'

'Mm?'

'Came back to do some work.' From this distance, she wondered why she had thought this might be a viable proposition.

'It's Sunday. Day of rest. Unless you have a deadline tomorrow, of course.'

'No,' Colette said. 'No, I don't.' The deadline was huge and terrifying, but it was also a long way away. She thought that she would have appreciated there being one tomorrow; it might have spurred her to actually do something.

'How's it all going, anyway, your PhD? We haven't really talked about it.'

'Slowly,' she said. 'The trouble with being down here is that I can't do very much but I can't stop thinking about it either, and all the time I'm feeling guilty because for goodness' sake what's my PhD worth when Lydia's been this close to losing her mum?'

'Which is a particularly complicated situation in itself.'

'Yes, exactly, and so I need to be here for her, and not all wrapped up with my own stuff which I probably wouldn't even be working on if I was still in Stancester...' Furious with herself, she found herself weeping. Peter, looking embarrassed (he's going to have to get over that, some detached part of her thought), handed her a clump of tissues and patted her awkwardly on the shoulder.

'Colette,' he said, 'you honestly don't need to be this hard on yourself. It isn't easy. I can see that.'

'I'm sorry,' she sobbed. 'I'm sorry...'

'Hush. You're allowed to fall apart...'

'But Lydia...'

'Needs you to be there for the long run, not just for as long as you can pretend to hold it together.' He put an arm around her shoulders, and she turned her face against his chest and sobbed.

'I'm sorry,' she managed to say once again.

'You don't need to be. Honestly. We're here for both of you, and just because Lydia gets all the drama doesn't mean it's not hard for you as well.' He put his other arm around her, closing the circle.

'I don't usually cry...' At least, she thought, not in front of other people.

'I know you don't.'

She sobbed and sobbed, gasped and hiccupped and sobbed, until her head ached and her eyes stung, and Peter held her all the while. At last, when she fell silent and moved a little way away from him, he put one hand on each of her shoulders and looked her intently in the eye. 'Better?'

She met his gaze, saw the troubled compassion in his dark eyes, quelled the impulse to apologise for worrying him. 'Yes. Thank you.'

He was beginning to say, 'You're welcome,' but the sound of the door opening made him look up. His expression changed: perhaps it was only that he was startled, but it looked like hostility.

'Oh, sorry,' Natalie said; but she didn't sound sorry.

Peter let his hands fall, almost guiltily, and Colette turned round.

Seeing her, Natalie said, 'Sorry,' again, in a kinder tone.

Colette nodded, grabbed a soggy tissue from the mass in her lap, and blew her nose inelegantly. Peter looked between the two of them for an awkward long moment, then, without touching Colette, got up and went to Natalie.

Left alone, Colette indulged herself in a half-hearted howl into the sofa cushion; but Peter and Natalie had only got as far as the hall, and their incomplete absence was inhibiting. It came as something of a relief to notice that it was getting on for three, and early enough to decently leave for the hospital: she sidled past them and went straight for her car.

Colette was quiet on the drive back, but so was Lydia, who seemed to be too preoccupied to notice. And nobody mentioned the incident during the evening: there were the usual enquiries about Lydia's mother over dinner, and then Andrew insisted that anyone who was watching *The Guns of Navarone* do so in complete silence, which suited Colette. Natalie and Peter were sitting close on the sofa, but not holding hands or cuddling or showing any other particular sign of accord. Colette contemplated the whole situation for a moment, and then thrust it aside in despair and attempted to distract herself by wondering whether anyone had ever seen David Niven without a moustache.

She updated Lydia in a whisper as they undressed for bed: 'I got a bit upset earlier and Peter gave me a hug, and Natalie saw it and I think she got the wrong end of the stick. And I swear he was just being nice, I swear it, but one of us has misread something and I'm almost certain it's her. I don't know, maybe I'm just overdramatising...'

Lydia seemed more concerned about Colette. 'Upset how?'

Colette mumbled, 'Oh. You know. Crying.'

She froze in the act of folding her jeans. 'I didn't realise it was getting you down so much. I'm sorry.'

'*I'm* sorry.' She shook her head angrily. 'I'm being stupid.'

Lydia sighed. 'You're not. I've dragged you down here when you've got work to do, and then abandoned you so that I can spend time with my mother, who would probably rather you didn't exist. I wouldn't blame you for being upset.'

Colette grabbed the opportunity to move the conversation on. 'How is she?'

'Mum? Much the same as yesterday.' She sat down on the edge of the bed, pulled her pyjama top over her head, and continued, 'The nurse said she's definitely doing better, but I'm having to take his word on that. She's sleeping a lot. Saying some very weird stuff when she's awake. Apparently that's the medication.'

Colette switched the overhead light off and got into bed. 'Well, I'm glad things are moving in the right direction.'

Lydia attempted to scoot under the duvet in a manoeuvre that was far more complicated and less effective than simply getting up and turning it back would have been. Colette laughed and, when Lydia had finally settled in, pulled her into an embrace.

They lay there, kissing quietly, for a little while, and Colette felt sleep beginning to wash over her. Lydia seemed tired, too; she was just pulling her arm out from under Colette when they heard a low, but clearly audible, voice through the wall:

'Are you going to say anything, then?'

It was Natalie. Colette rolled onto her back and held her breath.

Peter, sulky and petulant: 'What about?' He sounded guilty, Colette thought; which was usually a sign of the opposite. When he knew himself to be in the wrong he tended to affect a kind of self-conscious bravado which he carried off far better than he did genuine innocence.

'Colette.' Natalie's voice was contemptuous: of whom, Colette was not sure.

Lydia gripped her hand. 'Want me to do something?' she whispered.

'Like what?' Colette whispered back.

'Pretend to have a screaming nightmare?'

Before Colette could respond, they heard Peter say, 'There's nothing to say. She was upset. I gave her a hug.'

Lydia let go of Colette's hand and, rolling over, reached for her phone.

'What are you doing?' Colette hissed.

Natalie again: 'Oh, come on. What's she got to be upset about?'

Colette shut her eyes against the blue-white glare when Lydia held her phone in the air, and was genuinely startled when it emitted a piercing jingle.

Lydia let it continue for several seconds, and managed a very convincing, 'Mm... What? Oh, *go away.*' She shut it off again, looking – Colette saw when she opened her eyes again – rather pleased with herself.

On the other side of the wall, the voices were silent. Colette said, at a normal volume, 'What was that?'

Lydia said, 'Nothing important. Come here.'

'I think we should go home soon,' Lydia said the next morning.

'Yes,' Colette said, with feeling. 'But what about your mum?'

'She's doing OK. She isn't about to die or anything. And really, am I doing anything useful down here?'

'More than I am. It probably is time I went back to the lab.' The thought of it flapped around in her mind, and then settled, menacingly, somewhere near the front. She sighed; but the prospect of remaining here was no more enticing. 'And I was trying so hard to like her,' she said.

Lydia poked her hard in the ribs. 'It's difficult to like someone you've never met,' she said in a particularly carrying tone.

'Oh. Yeah. Good point.' Colette got out of bed. 'So I'll give you a lift to the hospital today. Breakfast?'

Lydia was more keen than usual to get to the hospital, and they arrived almost before visiting hours had properly started. Colette dropped her at the main entrance and drove off to find somewhere cheaper to park. She went down into the town and, with no particular idea in her mind, all the way to the seafront. There she found a space in the car park and got out to wander along the esplanade.

It was bright but not hot, with the intensity stripped from the sunshine by a lively breeze. She bought a bag of chips, because there was a chip shop that was open, and ate them angrily, too fast, so that she was left with a hot choking sensation in her throat. Then she went down onto the beach, cursing quietly as bits of the reddish shingle found their way into her shoes.

She did not have the capacity for things to be complicated with Peter. The infuriating thing was that up until now they had not been. And they had never been complicated in this particular way. Peter had never been anything other than supportive of her relationship with Lydia. Before that, there had been that two-month thing he'd had with Sophie in the summer term of Colette's first year, and yes, she'd been regretfully conscious of having missed the boat there, but she'd never breathed a word about it. *She* hadn't made it awkward. And she'd always got on well with Sophie, before and afterwards. Before that there had been that time in her very first term, when he'd asked her out, and that had been flattering and also completely the wrong time, but crying over it in the kitchenette in Markham Hall had led to her meeting Becky, so that had worked out far better than it might have done.

She missed Becky horribly. There was nobody quite like her for seeing that something needed to be done, and doing it. Becky would have sorted this one out, she thought.

*So what's her problem?* she imagined Becky asking. *Why is she being like this?*

'Because when we're on the spot she can't help remembering that we were there first,' she said, out loud. 'We knew him before she did. And logic and common decency mean she can't resent Lydia, particularly at a time like this, so I'm getting the lot.'

It made sense, and Colette, having articulated it to herself, found that she rather felt for Natalie. She went on, 'So either they break up, in which case I guess the problem solves itself, or they don't, and the longer they're together the less insecure she'll feel about me having been around longer than she has, because it'll become proportionately less significant.'

She picked up a stone and tossed it into the water, where it made no visible splash amid the churn of the breaking wave. 'It's her problem, anyway.'

Becky would have made that sound more convincing.

She stood watching the sea until her phone buzzed against her leg.

*When Keren-Happuch has been asleep, or breastfeeding, I've been reading* The Return of the Prodigal Son *by Henri Nouwen, and, my goodness, is it striking a chord. He invites you to think about which of the characters in the parable (and Rembrandt's painting) you identify with, and for me it's the older brother all the way. I'm an only child, but I've spent all my life following the rules, being a good girl, and, as they say, nobody thanks you. When do I get a party? When do I get a parade? Ticker tape? Seventy-six trombones?*

*(But then I go and take a look at my new baby and am overwhelmed by love for her, can't imagine what would be enough to make me turn her away from me, and I see where the Father is coming from...)*
Invisible, Bisexual, Bloggable
31 July 2017

*Can you come down to the hospital a bit earlier?* Lydia's text read. *Lunchtime?*

Colette thought that lunchtime was quite a lot earlier, really, but she made some allowances for circumstances, and at least she hadn't left Hastings.

*I'll be in the canteen,* Lydia had said.

Colette set off to look for her, and found her talking to a young Asian woman with a teal cotton dress, staff badge, and hair in a long plait down her back.

'Priya, this is Colette,' Lydia said. She sounded a little apologetic. 'My girlfriend. Colette, Priya. We were at school together.'

Colette slid into the seat next to Lydia's, and saw Priya's eyes widen ever so slightly in surprise. 'Nice to meet you,' she said. She had to raise her voice a little against the clatter and buzz of the canteen.

'You too,' Priya said, and then, to Lydia, 'I'm so sorry. I didn't realise. Everybody thought it was your sister who –'

'Was gay?' Lydia suggested helpfully.

'Yes, and ran away.'

'No, both of those were me.'

Priya leaned forward, eyes wide. 'But your sister just disappeared. Straight after the last GCSE exam, I think. According to

Jaz, Mr Graham was furious, because she got the best grades of the whole year and they couldn't get her picture for the paper.'

Lydia grinned. 'Oh, yes, I remember. I'd forgotten your sister was in Rae's year. No, it was all planned. She went to live with my cousin in Bristol. Still lives there, in fact.'

'And she's OK?' Priya asked. '*You're* OK? I would have thought... Well, you were the religious one.'

'I still am,' Lydia admitted cheerfully. 'But Colette is, too, so it all works out.'

Colette bristled, and felt that she was unreasonable to bristle. 'So do you work here, Priya?' she asked, though the blue pass holder and lanyard rendered the answer obvious.

'I do. I'm an audiologist.'

She was not a GP's daughter for nothing. 'Hearing aids?'

'Basically. Hearing aids, or else telling people that we can't do anything until they get rid of their earwax build-up.'

'Lovely.'

'Isn't it?' She chuckled, and kept eating her risotto in neat right-handed forkfuls.

'So you ended up back here,' Lydia observed.

'I know. I never meant to.' Priya launched into an involved explanation and Colette let her mind wander. *Why* had Lydia summoned her here? She had assumed that it was for an early getaway, but the reverse seemed to be true. And Lydia was very slightly on edge, apparently enjoying Priya's company and interested in the news she had to share (they were talking about someone called Tilly, now), but always keeping an eye on the big clock on the far wall.

'I'd better get back,' Priya said at last. 'Lydia, it's been lovely to see you, and I'm really glad you're OK.' Her gaze flickered between the two of them, and she added, 'Colette, it's great to meet you, too.'

'And you,' Colette said.

Priya stuffed her purse into her bag, and, with an awkward little wave, got up from the table. They watched her go.

Lydia turned to Colette. 'Have you eaten?'

'An hour or so ago.'

'Good.'

'Priya seems nice,' Colette said, and meant it as a compliment.

'She is. She always was.' Lydia sighed. She lowered her voice. 'I had such a crush on her, back in the day.'

'No! Does she know?'

'I hope not.' Lydia looked suddenly mischievous. 'You needn't worry. I met her boyfriend just before you turned up. He works in ENT.'

'I wasn't worried,' Colette said, more defensively than she'd meant to. Lydia had been nicer about the Peter thing than was strictly necessary. 'It's interesting to...'

'Compare and contrast?'

'Something like that.'

Lydia laughed. 'I think the common factor with all my crushes is that they were impossible. You're the only one I ever had a chance with.'

'The only one you *knew* you had a chance with,' Colette corrected her.

'Mm. I suppose. But Priya would have been even more impossible than anyone else when I was fourteen, even if she hadn't been straight. Falling for a Christian girl when I was twenty was difficult enough.' She thought for a moment, and added, 'I'm pretty sure Priya's straight.'

'So, why me, then?'

'You were impossible because you were possible.' Her tone changed. 'Which is why we're here, now.'

'Oh?' Colette said, not following.

'It's Mum,' Lydia said, as if her mother were not the entire reason for their being here at all. 'She wants to meet you.'

'She wants to *meet me*?'

'Yes.' Lydia's voice was urgent.

'Did she bring the subject up?'

Lydia frowned. 'Sort of. She's still pretty out of it. She was fretting about not being at home to feed me and put clean sheets on the beds, so I said it was fine, I was staying with Peter and his family. She was quite pleased about that, because she's always liked Peter. And then she asked if I'd taken the train, so I said no, you'd driven us down. And then she asked if you were still around, if you were staying with Peter too, so I said yes, you were. And then she said she wanted to meet you.'

Lydia's face was a mixture of hope and fear that made Colette's heart twist. 'Do you think it's a good idea?'

'I honestly can't tell. I can't work out whether it's something she really wants deep down, or whether going along with it is just indulging myself.'

'That wasn't exactly what I meant.' Colette did not say that it was not what she had asked, either. 'What I meant was, will it upset her?'

'Will she start screaming at you for corrupting her daughter, do you mean?' There was a suggestion of inverted commas around the phrase. 'I don't think so. I think she's forgotten that there's any reason for her not to like you.'

'But she'll remember again, sooner or later.'

'I have to hope so, don't I?' Lydia's voice was bitter, and Colette couldn't blame her. 'But Colette – please – just once. She's my mum.'

What else could she say? 'OK, then. Now?'

Lydia led the way through the hospital with an assurance that Colette found dizzying; she would herself have been hopelessly confused by the maze of identical corridors and staircases.

'Nearly there,' Lydia was saying, when they came face to face with a stocky, balding man in his late fifties.

Her reaction – an involuntary step backwards; an impulsive grab at her hand, swiftly suppressed; a sharp breath – told Colette who he was.

'Dad.' Lydia affected a businesslike tone, and Colette was not sure whether he would see through it. 'I've brought Colette to see Mum. She asked me to, when I was here earlier.'

He frowned, disapproving, and Colette saw Lydia flinch, but he nodded. 'She's asleep.'

Lydia said, 'We'll be quiet, then.'

He nodded once more, and then turned away. He did not acknowledge Colette, and she was glad of it.

Lydia remained still for a few seconds. She took a breath and released it, and then strode forward as if their visit had become infinitely more urgent. Colette matched her pace. The room came sooner than she had expected, and she continued a few steps past the door before she realised that Lydia had paused, her hand on the finger plate. Colette caught her eye. Lydia raised her eyebrows and smiled, which made her feel awful. Lydia should not have been the one reassuring her.

She nodded. Lydia pushed the door open and led the way across the ward to the bed where her mother lay.

They sat down on a pair of plastic chairs that were just too close to each other, and waited.

The face was slack. Colette searched it for family resemblance, and found it in the sharp nose and honey-coloured hair.

Lydia took Colette's hand, then dropped it again.

Colette was prepared for a long wait, would have been relieved if Mrs Hawkins slept all afternoon. But in fact it was only a few minutes before she stirred, coughed, opened her eyes, closed them again.

'Mum,' Lydia said, 'this is Colette.' She took a breath, harshly audible in the quiet of the room, and said, 'My girlfriend.'

It hung, festering, in the air.

Mrs Hawkins opened her eyes. Then closed them again. Then blinked twice or three times more, then, slowly, looked at Lydia, and then at Colette.

She smiled.

'Colette,' she said. 'It's very good to meet you.'

At her side, Lydia grew utterly still.

'It's, er, very good to meet you, too,' Colette said.

The smile became anxious. 'I wondered what you would be like. I wondered a lot.'

Lydia's lips were tight with unspoken words.

'I thought, do you listen to her, do you look after her, do you pray with her, do you take her to church? I used to do all that, and it didn't work. I don't know what went wrong.'

'*Mum,*' Lydia said.

Mrs Hawkins seemed to be becoming distressed. 'She's so far away. *Both* of them.'

Colette thought, And whose fault is that?

'I'm here, Mum. I'm here. And Rachel sends her love.'

'Where is she? Where's Rachel?'

'She's with Abby, helping her with the new baby.'

That seemed to have been the right thing to say. 'That's good. She'll be all right with Abby.'

'She will,' Lydia agreed.

'So it's just you that I need to worry about.' Her eyes became hazy, unfocussed. 'Don't I?'

'You don't need to worry about me. Look at me. I'm fine.' There was a choke in her voice.

Mrs Hawkins looked at her, then at Colette. 'Look after her, won't you?'

Colette said, 'Of course I will. I do.' She wondered if that was really true.

'She's wonderful,' Lydia said.

'I'm so glad,' said her mother, and it sounded absolutely sincere.

After that they were all quiet for a long time, and when Colette looked up, she saw that Mrs Hawkins was asleep again, and tears were running silently down Lydia's face.

She held out a hand to Lydia, who took it, and stood. Colette let herself be pulled to her feet. She wondered if she was meant to say something. Lydia took a step towards her mother, and then, whatever her idea had been, abandoned it, and led Colette out of the room.

Outside, Colette took Lydia by the elbows and drew her close. She wiped the newest tears away from Lydia's eyes with the flat of her little finger and tried to hug her.

Lydia shook her head. 'Not here.' It was a valid point: goodness knew where her father was.

'Right,' Colette said. 'Coffee.'

She led the way back towards the stairs.

But the café was crowded, and the canteen felt too big and exposed. In the end Colette bought drinks in takeaway cups and they went back to the car, and sat there in its hot plasticky smell while Lydia wept and wept and wept.

'It wasn't so bad,' Colette said. 'Was it?'

Lydia shook her head vigorously. 'No. It was wonderful. And awful. I used to dream that it would be like this, that she'd say something half so lovely. But I didn't imagine it being – like *this*.'

## *August*

*About five years ago, I asked my cousin to be godmother to baby Jemima. She'd recently come out as gay, and she declined on the ground that she didn't want to cause a family row. Looking back from where we are now, that was probably a wise decision. But I'm so glad that she's agreed to be Keren-Happuch's godmother instead. Now we just need to find a weekend that she can do...*
Invisible, Bisexual, Bloggable
1 August 2017


The next day Lydia returned to the hospital, alone, one last time before they went home. Colette did the packing and talked about inconsequential things with Peter and, when Natalie claimed his attention, Molly.

Lydia arrived back at the Nathans' just after they had finished lunch, just as Colette had started wondering where she had got to and whether they ought to start thinking about leaving. She helped with the washing up in a desultory fashion, glancing first at Colette and then at Andrew in a way that betrayed a desire to talk in private.

'Let's go out into the garden,' Colette suggested at the first possible opportunity. 'You could probably do with some fresh air.'

She led the way outside and sat down at the little iron table on the patio, and, when Lydia also sat down, took her hand. It trembled, very slightly, in her own.

Lydia said, 'I'm glad you didn't come today.'

'Oh?'

'Yes.' Lydia shifted in her chair, and opened her mouth, and then said nothing.

'So it wasn't good.' Colette managed not to make it sound like a question, not to disclose her curiosity. She squeezed Lydia's hand.

'It wasn't anything, really.' She bit her lip. 'I was expecting... Hoping... After yesterday... But they were both there. If it had just been Mum, then maybe...' She fell silent, and then continued, 'No, I don't think I could have done it, unless she'd brought it up. Brought *you* up.'

Like a cat puking, Colette thought. She did not say it.

'Maybe even if *Dad* had said something. I don't know, I might have been able to have the fight again. Except, no, not again, not in front of Mum, not while she's ill.'

'So nobody said anything?'

'No.' Lydia moved closer to her. 'I couldn't risk dropping Mum in it, that was the thing. I mean, what if she doesn't even remember? It wouldn't be fair.'

Colette could not help showing her surprise. Lydia had always, if speaking of her parents at all, implied that they were an indivisible unit, had certainly never alluded to any possible conflict between them. 'It's not very fair on *you*,' she pointed out.

'Yeah, but I'm a long way away and –' her voice cracked – 'I can take it.'

Colette put her arm around her shoulders, a gesture that felt inadequate in every way. 'You shouldn't have to,' she said, knowing that it was true, knowing that it was irrelevant.

Lydia pulled herself together with an effort that Colette could almost feel in the flesh, and said, 'We'd better get going, hadn't we?'

'Well,' Molly said. 'Well. It's been lovely having you to stay.'

'Thank you so much,' Lydia said. 'It's made everything so much easier, I can't tell you.'

Natalie managed a smile and a wave; they returned them equally awkwardly. Peter had been standing next to her in the doorway, but he strode forwards and caught first Lydia and then Colette in a hug.

'Do look after each other, won't you,' he said as he let them go. 'And it's been lovely to see you both and I only hope that next time it's under less worrying circumstances.'

'Amen to *that*,' said Lydia.

The moment stretched. Just before it became excruciating Colette remembered that she held the power to end it. She pulled the car keys from her pocket, tossed them a couple of inches into the air and caught them again. 'Goodbye,' she said, 'and thank you so much.'

Inside the car the air was stale. Colette concentrated on the road, doing her best to ignore the haze of disquiet that seemed to have followed them.

'That *was* a fun holiday,' Lydia said after a little while.

'Yeah. Oh, well.'

'I'm sorry it's all been so horrible.'

'I don't think any of it was your fault.'

'Still.'

'They say a change is as good as a rest.' Colette thought wistfully of that morning on the beach, and wished she'd spent more time there.

'They do.' Lydia started to say something else, and then stopped herself.

'What?'

'Oh, nothing. It was going to be something about Mum.' She paused. 'And Dad.'

Colette chuckled. 'Yes, so at least I've met your parents now.'

'True.' Lydia shifted slightly to look out of the window. Colette wondered if she had been hoping that the meeting would change something, perhaps that they might think of her as a human now, and not the enemy. She thought wryly that she would not have that confidence in her own personality, herself. Lydia had hinted at a break in the ranks: might they come around separately, if not together? She doubted it.

After a little while, she said, 'Let's go somewhere else, next year.'

'What, like a proper holiday?'

'Why not?'

'Well, because if I'm about to start training I won't have any money to spare.'

Colette did not point out that she might not get selected. 'Well, if we win the lottery, then.'

'One of us would have to start playing it.'

'Use your imagination.'

'Oh, I don't know.' Lydia was quiet for a little, and then said, 'I've always wanted to see India.'

'Any particular part?'

'All of it. Or as much as I could in a month or six weeks, just travelling around.'

'Sounds fun. Hot, though.'

'In terms of actually realistic ideas, I'd quite like to go to Scotland.'

'Ah, right.' Colette did her best to sound encouraging. 'Edinburgh?'

'We could start there. And then go into the mountains and go walking.'

'I've never been there.'

'Edinburgh?'

'Anywhere in Scotland.'

'Let's do it.'

Colette liked the idea of visiting a place that belonged to neither of them. 'Yes,' she said. But really, anywhere would do.

The road signs and the trees and the semi-detached houses flicked into view and out of it again, past the windscreen, through the wing mirror. Afternoon wore on into evening. They debated stopping to eat, and decided that they had come far enough to make it easier to keep pushing on westwards.

Colette sighed – a long, self-indulgent exhalation.

'What?'

'Oh. I don't know. I think I was thinking how green it all is.'

'Rains more,' Lydia said knowledgeably.

'I know.' She thought how much more generous the landscape seemed here. The south-east coast had felt sparse and worn, with its dried-out tangles of grass or scrub clinging onto dusty chalk. Here the hills were rounded and friendly, upholstered in rich, comfortable green.

'Not long now.' Lydia patted Colette's knee in a chaste gesture clearly intended not to distract. 'Thank you.'

'You're welcome,' Colette said, and she was almost sure that she meant it.

*Bit of a rant today, sorry. But I keep seeing people talking about 'equal marriage' as if we've already got it, and sorry, we haven't. We have same-sex marriage. And no, they're not the same thing.*

*Every time I'm tempted to think that we've got equal marriage, I do a little thought experiment. Let's imagine that, instead of meeting and falling for the man who eventually became my husband, I met and fell for a woman.*

*Would I be able to have the same wedding? Because that's what 'equal' means, isn't it? Access to the same thing.*

*No. Because the Church of England has managed to get it written into law that it can't perform same-sex marriages. Not just that it doesn't have to. That it can't.*

*Bring on disestablishment, I say.*
Invisible, Bisexual, Bloggable
3 August 2017

Back in Stancester, little seemed to have changed. Campus was almost deserted. In the Sciences Block, Colette moved between the office (uncomfortably hot) and the lab (uncomfortably cold) and tried to make the work she'd done in Hastings match up with the work she had left behind her.

Halfway through the morning, Barry called her into his office. 'Colette. I'm glad you're back.'

He was superficially and clumsily sympathetic about Lydia's mother (to be fair, Colette thought, the whole situation was an obstacle course) and then moved on to his real purpose. 'There's a conference in Cambridge coming up in the autumn.' He half-scowled at her. 'I think it would be worth your while to go, but you will need to pull something together sooner than perhaps you might have been imagining.'

Colette flinched at the sarcasm. 'Something?'

'A poster.' He made it sound like a primary school assignment.

'Oh,' Colette said doubtfully.

The scowl became more pronounced. 'Give me a moment, won't you?' He hunted through a jumble of papers on his desk and turned up a glossy A4 pamphlet which he thrust into her hand. 'There. Take it away. Read it. Ask me if you have any questions.'

Colette resolved not to have any questions.

'Barry's in a foul mood today,' she observed to James over lunchtime baked potatoes in the Union bar.

'Yeah.' He glanced around. 'I take it you haven't heard why?'

Colette shook her head. 'Did I miss something?'

James leaned forward across the table and lowered his voice. 'This is what Mariam told me, and she said she heard it from Vince, and I don't know whether there's any truth in it at all, though I admit it's certainly tempting to think so –'

'Any truth in *what*?'

'A rumour that Barry's next TV series has been canned.'

'*Oh*.'

He looked broodingly at his beer. 'Like I said, there might be nothing to it. But as you said yourself, he's not a very happy bunny today. And television is a fickle god, and I do get the feeling that dear Barry is not such hot property all of a sudden...'

Colette felt embarrassingly naïve. 'You don't think it's me, then?' she couldn't help asking.

'Oh, he's been horrible to everyone. Don't take it personally. We'll probably get back and find him being exquisitely sarcastic to his coffee cup because it happened to look at him the wrong way.'

Colette laughed at the idea, but did not much fancy the idea of facing the reality just yet. 'Another drink?'

'I shouldn't,' James said. 'Ah, what the hell. It's not like anyone's going to be doing anything useful this afternoon. At least, not until his lordship clears out.'

The house phone rang while Lydia was cooking dinner. Colette picked it up, recognised the Hastings dialling code on the screen, and wished she hadn't. 'Hello?'

'Good evening.' A man's voice, curt, gruff. 'Can I speak to Lydia?'
She said, politely, 'Of course,' and called, 'Lydia!'

Her hand was shaking when she passed the phone over: she felt ashamed of it. Lydia, meanwhile, was speaking with the distant politeness that she usually reserved for double glazing sales and PPI scams, but Colette knew that it was not a stranger.

She remained within earshot while Lydia continued the conversation, aware that this was new ground. Lydia's responses were short – not curt, exactly, but no more detailed than they needed to be.

'I see. I see. Thank you for calling.'

Colette put a hand out, but did not touch her.

'I'll call again on Sunday as usual. Yes. Give her my love. No, I... Yes. Goodbye.' Lydia put the phone down and stood for a moment with her hand pressing down on the receiver. 'Well,' she said, '*that* was grim.'

'It *was* your dad?'

'Yes.' For the first time, Lydia's voice betrayed some loss of composure. 'He... He thinks it's my fault that Mum had the heart attack. That I – that I shouldn't have brought you to see her. And that she'd have got better quicker if I hadn't been there.'

'That's ridiculous,' Colette said stoutly.

'I know that really. But I can't help thinking, *what if he's right?*'

'It's still ridiculous. He phoned you to tell you she was ill. She said she wanted to meet me. They can't have it both ways.'

'I think that's the trouble.' Lydia smiled sadly. 'They want it both ways. They want me to be the good daughter and show up, but they don't like me showing up with a girlfriend.' She squeezed Colette's hand. '*Thank you.* I couldn't, shouldn't have asked that of you, and it means more than you'll ever know.'

'What else was I meant to do?' Colette asked, flustered. 'Anyway, how is she?'

223

Lydia smiled. 'Didn't I say? They've let her go home.'
'Well, that's good news, at least,' Colette said, and tried to mean it.

They went to St John's on Sunday morning. Lydia fidgeted through the service, and seemed faintly put out that someone else was doing the reading when it had been her name on the rota.

'They didn't know that you'd be back by today,' Colette pointed out as they walked home.

'I *know*.'

Colette did not pursue that line of conversation, or any line of conversation.

'Sometimes I think,' Lydia said, after a while, 'that I could just keep on doing what I'm doing, that what I already do in church, coupled with being a witness in a secular work environment, should be enough. And then there are days like today, when I think, *Benjy, what are you doing? I could give a better talk than this in my sleep*.'

'Mm,' said Colette, who hadn't thought much of the preaching either.

'I suppose I'll just have to save my brilliant insights for the house group,' Lydia said, rather overdoing the sarcasm. 'Yes, yes, I know, pride, being puffed up, all of that.'

'Do you think that it really would make a difference to who you are, being ordained?'

Lydia said, 'I feel like it shouldn't, but it would. And I do believe in the priesthood of all believers, and I'm not really worried about apostolic succession and all sorts of other things that would give Peter the vapours. And yet.'

'And yet this is who you're meant to be and that's what you're meant to be doing.'

'Yes. And then sometimes I think, well, if God's put me at the council then maybe He wants me at the council.'

'I hate to say it, but Bellairs Employment Limited isn't actually God.'

'Yes, but God can work through Bellairs, and you know it,' Lydia said severely.

And she still made the Sunday phone call. Colette went off and did the washing up while Lydia took the phone to the far end of the sitting room. She ran water into the bowl, boiled the kettle, tried to make enough noise to stop herself eavesdropping: she had heard enough variations on one side of a conversation to last a lifetime. All the same, there seemed to be a different note in there tonight. Lydia seemed to be trying to persuade someone (her mother, surely?) of something.

At the end, Lydia padded back into the kitchen and, sighing, laid her face against Colette's back. Colette turned around to fold her into her arms.

'Well,' Lydia said, and didn't say anything else.

Colette moved backwards and raised her eyebrows sympathetically.

'Same old, same old.'

She tried to look disappointed. She had always thought a miracle too much to hope for. 'What did you talk about?'

'How she was. What it was like, being back at home. All the church people who have and haven't been to see her.' She paused. 'Dad.'

'Mm?'

Lydia said, cautiously, 'I said that if ever she wanted to get away, she was very welcome to come and stay with us for as long as she wanted.' She looked up at Colette, brows furrowed. 'I'm sorry. I know we've never discussed anything like that.'

'What did she say?' Colette tried to suppress her horror at the idea, her guilty hope that the answer would be *no, thank you*.

'She said she'd think about it.'

'Do you think she will?'

'Probably not.' Lydia looked agonised. 'You can't solve other people's problems for them, can you? Not unless they want you to, and even then they have to do most of it themselves. And I don't know where I'd even begin with Mum.'

'Do you think she remembers, you know, what she said at the hospital?' Colette asked, and immediately wished that she had not.

'She was off her face, wasn't she? I honestly can't tell whether she doesn't remember saying it, or whether she does and is pretending that she didn't, she couldn't possibly have said something like that. Because, you know...'

Colette searched for some kind of plausible comfort. 'Does it help to think that, well, maybe that's what she really thinks underneath?'

'A bit, I suppose. What it proves is that, whatever she really thinks, I can't rely on her. But then I always knew that.'

August wore away. More than once Colette thought of suggesting a real holiday, but funds were limited. Besides, Lydia was reluctant to leave her team short-handed for any longer than she had already, and Colette felt obliged to make the most of Barry's increased presence in the lab for as long as it lasted. The bank holiday weekend might have had possibilities, if only she had managed to organise something. But she hadn't, and, the Monday before it, Lydia called her over. 'Are we busy on Saturday?'

'I'm not. I can't answer for your church commitments.'

'For once I don't have anything. So, Peter messaged me – well, both of us, but I assume you haven't seen it – to say are we around, because he's going to Salisbury Plain on a Routemaster bus, and has had the offer of a lift to Stancester afterwards.'

'That's a very Peter sort of thing to do,' Colette acknowledged. 'Well, it sounds good to me. Does he want a bed?'

'I'll ask him. It's a bit far to do it in a day, I'd have thought.'
'And is he bringing Natalie?'
Lydia frowned. 'He didn't say.'
'Hmm.'
'Should I ask? I don't want to put my foot in it.'
'I know.' Colette thought about it. 'It's a reasonable question, though. Just drop it in when you're asking if he wants a bed.'
'That makes sense.' Lydia tapped at her phone, and, after a little while, reported, 'He says, *Yes please, and no, just me.*'
'No more detail than that?'
'No. Do you think there's something up?'
'Goodness knows. On the one hand, it's the holidays, so maybe she's seeing her family or something. On the other, she seemed like the sort of person who'd be quite happy to go along with Peter's weird bus thing, so I'm raising my eyebrows a bit.'
'And they did have that row, when we were there.'
'Yeah,' Colette said. 'They did.'

The first thing that James said when Colette walked into the office on Wednesday morning was, 'Don't answer the phone.'
'Why?'
It rang then. 'Fuck,' James said. He picked it up. 'Spectrometry Group?'
Colette perched on the edge of her desk to listen.
'No, I'm not Barry Parnell... No, he's not here...' He made a V sign at the receiver with his free hand. 'No. No comment. Goodbye.' He slammed the receiver down.
Colette drew the obvious conclusion. 'Reporters?' She was genuinely impressed. Barry's relationship with the media had not thus far extended to journalists phoning their office. Usually the people who wanted to get hold of him already had his mobile number.

'That was the third this morning. Mariam said that she's had a couple too.'

'What are they after?'

'They're hoping to get Barry to expand on his reaction to having been dropped like a hot potato.'

'Really? Is there nothing else for them to report on?'

'Not much. It's the silly season, isn't it?' He glared at her. 'But I particularly don't want them getting hold of you. So far, nobody's caught on that Barry's got another female PhD student, and my guess would be that your life is going to be easier if it stays that way.'

Colette thought this a little chauvinistic, but had no desire to defend Barry to the national press. 'I don't think I've got anything worth suppressing,' she said gloomily. She walked over to James' desk, picked up the telephone receiver, and set it down to lie on its back, turtle style, next to the body.

'There,' she said. 'Solved your problem.'

Peter turned up at half past eight on Saturday evening, bearing a miniature rose bush in a pot and a bottle of red wine.

'You didn't need to,' Colette said.

He grinned. 'Oh well, I did anyway.' He put the plant down to hug first her and then Lydia, who had followed from the kitchen.

'Come on through,' Lydia said, 'and tell us about your day on the buses.'

'Just give us the highlights,' Colette added hastily.

He laughed. 'We came. We saw. We conquered. We do it all again next year.'

'*It* being?'

'Ride Routemasters to a deserted village on Salisbury Plain. It's a bit creepy, actually, all those empty buildings. Like time stopped at some point in the seventies.'

'It sounds like it.' Colette could not imagine that a convoy of scarlet double-decker buses would make it any less creepy.

He smiled. 'Fun, though. I mean, it's always nice to get out on the buses. They sound good. They like being out on the open road.'

Lydia, who was always suspicious of any attempt to anthropomorphise inanimate objects, said, 'Are you ready for dinner now? It'll keep if you aren't.'

'Let me wash my hands,' said Peter. He disappeared off to the bathroom; Colette put the plant pot on a saucer in the middle of the dining table and tidied a clutter of papers into the far corner. Lydia, meanwhile, had got out wine glasses and was rinsing the rice in boiling water.

'It smells delicious,' Peter said when he returned. It did, and it was: a rich, complicated chilli con carne.

Colette poured the wine. 'Cheers!'

'Cheers!' Lydia echoed.

'Cheers! And thank you,' Peter said.

'Ah, any time. At least, any time you're passing through because of some ridiculous heritage transport event.'

'It'll make a nice *what I did on my holidays* conversation starter, anyway,' Colette said. '"I went on a magical mystery tour."'

Lydia shook her head. 'Summer holiday.'

'No,' Peter said. 'The bus in *Summer Holiday* is an RT, not an RM.'

Colette looked at Lydia and raised her eyebrows; they both burst out laughing. 'Will your fellow ordinands know that?' Lydia asked. 'Or care?'

Peter was laughing too. 'I shouldn't be at all surprised if they did. Though most people there are into trains, not buses.'

'Really?'

'Really. Well, quite a lot of them. More than you'd get in an average sample of the population.' He grinned. 'So, we had had this lecture on personal safety and lone working and all that sort of thing. And the speaker said that he'd heard of a Church conference of some sort where a thief managed to get in and pick up a whole load of wallets and credit cards.'

'I don't see the connection,' said Lydia.

'I'm getting to it. The point was, not only did they all learn a valuable lesson about keeping their eyes open, but it also turned out, when he emptied their bank accounts, that a whole load of them used one of two PIN codes.'

'I assume you're still getting to the connection?' Colette said.

'Yes. So one of them was 1662, obviously.'

'*Obviously*,' Lydia echoed.

'I don't get it,' Colette said, because she didn't, and in case Lydia hadn't either and it was something she'd need to know.

'Book of Common Prayer, sixteen sixty-two,' Peter explained. 'And the other was 4472.'

Colette shook her head; Lydia, too, looked blank.

'Flying Scotsman. The locomotive, not the service. Ah, go to York and take a look at her sometime. She's a lovely thing.' He added, 'Though of course I still prefer buses.'

'Of course,' Lydia said drily.

To prevent things sliding further into transport geekery, Colette asked, 'Are you back in Cambridge yet?'

'No, not for another couple of weeks.' He added, 'Natalie's there already,' in a way that made Colette reluctant to enquire further.

'Barry's talking about sending me to a conference up there in the autumn.'

'Oh? Let me know if that materialises, and we can meet up for a drink. I'll show you around.' He glanced at Lydia, then back to Colette. 'You can see what you think of the place.'

'You can report back to me,' Lydia said.

'I'll take you round college, if you like,' Peter said, 'though I suspect it's of limited relevance.'

Lydia laughed. 'Do you know anyone at Ridley?'

Peter looked slightly uncomfortable. 'A few.'

'Nobody you'd be prepared to ask to show your female friend's female partner around?' Lydia guessed.

'Not without some delicate conversations first. If it's any help, I do know someone who's training in Durham who's in a civil partnership and lives with his spouse in a house somewhere in the city.'

'What, at Cranmer?' Lydia sounded surprised.

'Where else? I do have some Evangelical friends, you know.'

Lydia shot him a filthy look. 'Well, yes, there's me, for a start.'

'What does the spouse do?' Colette asked.

'I want to say he does software development, but I might be making that up.'

'Something in the real world, anyway?'

'You could say that.'

Colette had liked Durham when she had visited an undergraduate open day, seven years before, in another life. 'Then maybe Durham's an option for us,' she said.

'Of course,' Peter said, 'you need to be quite careful, because in most places single ordinands have to live in college. Not that you two are *single*, I mean.' He tried to disentangle himself. 'Legally single. You know. Not married. Not straight-married. Not civil partnered.'

'Mm,' Colette managed, and hoped that perhaps she'd given the impression that she'd known all along. Lydia was looking – *guilty*, she decided. And definitely as if *she'd* known all along. Colette resolved to ask her about it later, and concentrated very hard on stacking the plates and taking them round into the kitchen.

'You know why they didn't let me in the first time?' Peter was saying when she returned to the table. 'It was because of all the

Fellowship shit – sorry, the Fellowship mess. I'd got myself so hung up on it all that I'd completely lost touch with the idea of the Church universal and I was disgracefully out of charity with my fellow Christians.'

'Is that what they said?' Lydia asked.

'They didn't *quite* write that on the report,' Peter said, 'but if you read between the lines...'

'Well, I've got no hope, in that case,' said Lydia. 'If you were hung up on it, I was right in the middle of it.'

'Yes, but you couldn't help that,' Colette objected. She sat down and topped up all the glasses. 'It was...' She had been about to say *Becky's fault,* which was true – Becky had, by getting the Students' Union involved, brought the whole horrible situation to a head – but felt treacherous.

'Circumstances, I know,' said Lydia. 'All the same, it's shaped who I am as a Christian for better or for worse, and if it turns out they don't like that...'

Peter's was looking remorseful. 'That was why they turned *me* down,' he said. 'I don't think it would have anything to say to anyone else. And remember, I managed to get hung up on it from the other side of the country. You were right there and it wasn't your fault.'

'I suppose,' said Lydia, but she didn't look happy.

And Colette had the words *single ordinands* buzzing around her mind.

Peter said, 'So, have you heard from Georgia recently? Or Will?'

'Not for a while,' Colette said, and the awkward moment was deferred, at least until bedtime.

'I'm sorry,' Lydia said, the moment they were in the bedroom together. She held her hands out, palm upwards.

Colette did not need to ask what she was sorry for. She sat down on the bed and said, very quietly, 'How long have you known?'

Lydia came and stood facing her, suppliant. 'I haven't managed to ask Tina to clarify yet.'

'You might,' Colette suggested, 'have told me that it was a possibility, even if not a probability.'

'I know.' Her expression was now a mixture of guilt and devastation. 'But I didn't want you to have to worry about something that might not even happen.'

'But which probably will.'

Lydia said, in a very small voice, 'I don't know what I'd do without you.'

'You'd cope,' Colette said brutally. 'It'd just be like being back in halls, wouldn't it?'

'Yes, and I couldn't wait to get out of halls, because I had to spend all the time I was there pretending you didn't exist!'

'So I suppose I'd have to find somewhere to live on my own, not too far from wherever you were...'

'Three years,' Lydia said, bleakly.

Colette pictured a chilly bedsit, a narrow bed, long evenings without Lydia. She said, with artificial cheerfulness, 'And a job...'

'Most of the colleges are in university cities.'

That was something. Colette thought again of Durham. 'What would happen after that?'

'Another three years, in a parish. That should be easier, because it should be possible to find one that will just take us as we are.'

'Us.'

Lydia looked a little reproachful. 'Yes, us. You don't have to do the whole vicar's wife thing, but I do want us to be somewhere that makes you feel welcome, too.'

Colette, feeling contrite, said, 'What, a scandalous non-conformist like me?'

'There are plenty of clergy spouses who don't go to church at all.'

It was not the moment to quibble about the term *spouses*. 'I suppose it would make a difference. In a positive way.'

'You could always run off to the Methodists when you'd had enough of my preaching,' Lydia said. But she still looked unhappy.

'Anything else you need to tell me?'

'No.'

'Are you sure? You don't exactly seem at peace with the world.'

Lydia shook her head angrily. 'There is something,' she said, 'that just rubs me up the wrong way about having to settle for a civil partnership.'

'Settle?' She made inverted commas with her fingers.

'Yeah. Obviously, if it was the only way that I could train and still live with you, then I'd do it. But it isn't the same thing as marriage, is it?'

'I'd say that depends on what you think marriage is,' Colette said, feeling perverse for no good reason.

'Oh, don't *you* start.'

'No, seriously. If the best that we can hope for is *two people in love and living together in a relationship recognised by the state*, what's the difference?' She reached out for Lydia's helpless hands and drew her closer.

'According to the Church of England,' Lydia said, 'people in civil partnerships don't have sex, and people in marriages do.'

'We both know that's not true.'

'Yes.'

'So what's the difference?'

'I don't know,' Lydia said, 'but there is one.'

The loose thread of illogic was too tempting not to pounce on. 'So what *is* marriage? Morally speaking, I mean. Can you swap gold rings with someone else and call it marriage? Do there have to be witnesses? Clearly there doesn't *have* to be a religious element – or are we discounting every wedding we've been to in the last two years, and, if so, why did we go to them?'

'I'm sure we've had this conversation before.'

They had. Colette recalled the conclusions that Lydia had come to then – *witnesses, blessing, intention* – and found them too intimidating to consider. She said, 'Isn't there some theology involved?'

Visibly at a loss, Lydia said, 'All I can remember at the moment is that there's an argument over whether or not it's a sacrament.'

'How can it be, if anybody can do it?'

'Well, not all marriages are the same.'

'But Peter says that the ministers of a marriage are the couple themselves.' She remembered that much. 'So it shouldn't matter. But you know it does.'

'Peter also believes it's a sacrament,' Lydia said. She had a worried, dissolving, look on her face. Colette knew that she should not push her too much further on this. She left it, but she felt irritated by her own decision to do so.

'Come on,' she said. 'Let's go to bed.'

## *September*

"*Can you all hear me?*"
"*More to the point, can you all see me?*"
*(slight pause)*
"*It's a shame our Labels Sunday was last week, because I have a label to go along with my name. Yesterday was Bisexual Visibility Day, and well, here I am, wearing my brightest pink jacket and my little stripy badge...*
"*If you're curious and want to know more about what that means for me as a Christian, come and find me at coffee... and be prepared for a very boring answer.*"

*It's not a bad speech, is it? But I didn't make it. Didn't have the guts. I sat there all the way through the service, perfecting it, psyching myself up, praying for strength, and then when it came to the notices I just couldn't do it.*

*I always say that I have nothing to lose – I'm married to a man, I don't work for the church – but discovered that I was worried about losing my friends, my reputation, my standing. What would our minister think? What if Jemima's friends' parents stopped letting them play with her? Would I be asked to stop helping with Youth Church? And a thousand other fears.*

*I couldn't do it. I knew that I was being called to, but I just couldn't. I sat there berating myself for my cowardice and my pride, until, in the brief pause before the last song, I remembered to say, 'I'm sorry, God,' and suddenly I felt settled, at peace, certain that God loves me anyway.*

*(I did keep my badge visible all through coffee, but nobody asked me about it. They were much more interested in the baby. Maybe next year...)*

Invisible, Bisexual, Bloggable
24 September 2017

Campus was cluttered with new undergraduates, and with people trying to recruit the new undergraduates to societies and sports teams. Colette decided that on the whole she preferred this to the wilderness of the vacations, but that she would like it still better once Induction Week was over and there were fewer people in ridiculous outfits trying to give her flyers. She turned down the rowing society, SciSoc (of which she was in fact already a member, not that she'd been to any of their events for years), and LARP on the way up the hill on Wednesday morning.

James did not arrive until after lunch, and didn't come in then. He hovered at the door. 'Colette,' he said, 'let's get a coffee. I need to tell you something.'

There was something about the way he was standing, shoulders hunched and hands in pockets, that told her it was going to be bad news. Still, she followed him out of the office, down the stairs and across the courtyard to the café, let him buy coffees for both of them, and waited until they were both seated at the counter before she asked, 'What is it, then?'

'I'm quitting.' The sound was soft as a sandbag to the head.

'Oh,' she said, equally softly. Then, 'Like, for good?'

'That's what quitting usually means. Otherwise I'd have said, taking a break.'

She flinched. 'Yeah. Sorry.'

'No. *I'm* sorry.'

She couldn't believe it, didn't want to believe it. 'It really is that bad, then?'

He nodded. 'I can't do it any more.'

'I thought it was just the wedding stress.'

An ironic smile bloomed on his face. 'So did I, until the wedding was over and the stress was still there.'

'What does Giselle think?' What she meant was, *was it Giselle's idea?*

The ironic smile widened. 'She's been very understanding.'

That probably meant that it wasn't. 'What will you do instead?' She seemed to have nothing but questions.

'I've got a few job interviews lined up. I was going to wait until I'd got an offer, but I... I couldn't.'

It must have cost him something to admit that; although presumably not as much as it had cost him to decide to quit. 'Have you told Barry yet?'

'I've sent him an email. I don't know whether he's read it yet. He certainly hasn't replied.'

'Wow,' Colette said. 'He really is something.'

James shrugged his shoulders, magnanimous in his new freedom. 'Give him the benefit of the doubt. He might not have seen it.'

'When did you send it?'

'Friday.'

'So even if he wasn't the kind of person who checks his emails twice a minute, which we know he is, he'll have had plenty of time.' She was a little shocked by her own cattiness: had this made her heir to James' cynicism?

'Yeah. I was going to wait until he'd got back to me before I told you, but it was getting to the point where I thought it just wasn't fair.' He fidgeted with his hands. 'I mean, even less fair than doing this to you at all.'

Colette wanted to be angry, but it was difficult when she understood perfectly. She looked from him to her cup and back again, and thought that she wasn't going to get anything done today. 'Shall we go to the pub?'

She got home, only slightly wobbly, just after half past five: the Students' Union bar had become increasingly rowdy and clogged with people in unlikely costumes throughout the afternoon ('You know,' James said, having been pennied by a stranger in a grass skirt, 'I can't say that I'm going to *miss* academia,') and they'd decided to call it a day at four forty-five.

'Oh. Hello.' Lydia seemed surprised to see her.

'Hi.'

'Is everything all right?'

'James quit.' She felt herself blushing as she said it, ashamed to admit to the misfortune that had visited her. She wondered now if it was her fault, and had to tell herself not to be absurd.

'Oh, no! Why?'

Colette shrugged her shoulders miserably. 'He's had enough. I can't blame him.'

'Had enough of...?'

'Barry, I suppose, and never getting enough support.' Should she have supported him more? How? She was only just managing to cling on herself – no; she mustn't think like that; she was just going to have to keep on clinging on, with or without him.

'Well, that sucks. Is it going to affect you? I mean, beyond his being your friend and not being around any more?'

'It shouldn't,' she said, and didn't bother adding, *But it will.*

Lydia moved to hug her, 'I'm so sorry,' she said.

Unable to bear much more talking about it, Colette asked, 'How about you? Good day?'

'It was fine, thanks.' But there was an odd note in her voice, and Colette, despite her preoccupation, hugged her back.

'What's up?'

'Nothing, really.' She paused. 'I had a text from Rae, and I was thinking, shouldn't I be at home – in Hastings, I mean – with Mum?'

'You shouldn't,' Colette said, with all the decisiveness that Lydia had lacked.

'I just worry about her.'

'You worry about her, you worry about Rachel...'

'I worry about you,' Lydia said, with a distinct air of relief, 'Weren't you going to AngthMURC?'

'Oh.' Colette tried to sound casual; best not to show the roiling, shameful mess of fear that had sent her home from campus with her arms braced across her chest to keep herself together. 'No, I decided not to.'

'Any particular reason? Because of James?'

Colette hoped that her attempt at nonchalance had been more successful than Lydia's; she suspected not. 'No. Well, not really. Just, you know, didn't feel like it.'

'Oh?'

'I didn't really fancy socialising.' She added, 'We went to the Union, and I'm feeling a bit old for the whole society thing.'

'Don't be silly,' Lydia said. 'This is AngthMURC. You know as well as I do that it's for postgrads too.'

'Yeah, but this week it'll all be Freshers.'

'That depends how good the publicity's been,' Lydia pointed out. 'It might equally just be the committee.'

'I just don't feel like it, OK?' she flashed, and felt immediately ashamed.

'OK,' Lydia said.

'Besides, it's the woman from that organisation for persecuted Christians. I've heard it before.'

She felt Lydia laugh into her shoulder, and for the first time that day felt that something was in the right place.

# *October*

*LGBTX West Country*
*Speaker: Rev Aaron Coverley-Symes, author of 'Faithfully Me'*
*Saturday 14 October, 3-6pm*
*St John the Evangelist, Stancester*
*Refreshments available from 2.30pm*

'Are you coming?' Lydia had asked, that morning.

Colette told herself that it was pathetic not to go, given the fact that the thing was in Stancester for once and Lydia's church friends thought she was stand-offish at the best of times. 'I'll go,' she said. 'You might have to prod me.'

In fact she had rallied after an hour or so of gloom, and had managed a sort of brunch of satsumas and a ham sandwich in between reading her emails and getting very gradually dressed, and by the time Lydia came back in with a huge box of teabags and six assorted packets of biscuits she was feeling almost human.

'I need some fresh air anyway,' she said, and Lydia laughed and squeezed her arm with the hand that didn't have the shopping bag.

'So how do these meetings go?' Colette asked. 'Or services, sorry, or whatever they are?'

'They start with worship. A few songs, a few prayers. Then the speaker and the questions. More songs; more prayers. Finally, coffee and awkward chitchat.'

'Do people hug you?' She did not feel up to hugging anyone.

'They might hug *me*, but only if they're people who know me.'

Colette nodded. 'How many people am I likely to know?'

Lydia slid the handle of the carrier bag up her wrist to leave both hands free to check names off with her fingers. 'Rowan. The St John's crowd, obviously – Felicity and Eve; Claire and Ida. Steph. Some people from All Saints. Um. There's someone from Cathsoc but I don't know if they're out apart from this so I'm not going to say who they are if they're not there. Leah from the chapel choir. And Josh, that barman from the Feathers, has been a couple of times.'

'And when you say worship...?'

'Well, it wouldn't be Peter's scene, but it's fairly staid. A bit quieter than what you'd usually get at St John's, if anything.' She added, smiling, 'You might see the odd hand in the air.'

'I'm sure I can cope with that.'

'And the prayers aren't anything alarming... Oh, you'll see.'

Colette asked, 'Do you know anything about the speaker?'

'Not much. He's a vicar. *Was* a vicar, rather. He's written a book.'

'I take it you haven't read it?'

She shook her head. 'I'm waiting to see if I like his style. If I do, I'll buy a copy today and get him to sign it. But I've got a nasty feeling I'll have heard it all before.'

The Reverend Aaron Coverley-Symes was a tall man in his mid forties, with attractively crinkled eyes, pepper-and-salt hair and a ringing voice with which to tell his story. It must, Colette supposed, be one that was common enough in the ranks of Church of England clergy.

Opening his talk, he said as much. 'I'm going to tell you about something that happens all the time, about a dilemma that has to be dealt with by everyone who's gay and has a vocation to ordained ministry – at least in the Church of England. I'm going to tell you what happened to me, and I both hope and fear that it will have some resonance for you. Hope, because I know that there will be people in this hall who need to know that they are not alone. Fear, because this isn't easy, and nobody should have to go through what I went through.

'Let's start at the beginning. I knew that I was gay from a very young age. I also knew that I couldn't ever tell anyone about it. Nobody at home. Nobody at school. *Definitely* nobody at church. So I didn't.

'I met the man who is now my husband at theological college. I didn't tell anybody there that I was gay, either. My husband tells me that he'd worked it out by the end of week one, but he's got no proof of that so I don't believe him.

A nervous giggle broke and swelled through the hall; he smiled encouragingly at it. 'Of course everybody knew that *he* was gay, and so lots of us were a bit funny with him. A bit funny *about* him. And I regret to say that included me. I think now of the amazing gift of love that I've been given, and I am so ashamed when I remember my attitude to it back when I was in the closet. But what could I expect? I couldn't love anybody then, because I couldn't admit the existence of one of the most significant forms of love in my life – so how could I have *been* loved?

'I got through training. *He* didn't. And we didn't keep in touch, after he left.

'I got ordained deacon. Took up my curacy. Got ordained priest. I spent three wonderful years in that parish. But all the time, I knew that something wasn't right. And I knew what it was.

'I'm not proud of what I did then.' He paused. 'I did exactly what I was meant to do. The whole heterosexual thing.

'Yeah.

'I did OK at it. I even got engaged to a young woman, but the longer things went on, the more I realised things weren't right.

'Don't get me wrong. I really tried to make it work. My fiancée was beautiful and funny and godly, and you know, I couldn't work out what was going wrong. Because I wouldn't *let myself realise* what was going wrong until I just couldn't deny it any longer.

'I think that in the end she was relieved that it wasn't her fault. Relieved that she wasn't the one who wasn't normal.

'I went back to the loneliness, to the empty house. Then I got my first post-curacy job and moved on to an empty vicarage.

'I was pretty happy, those first few years in my parish. After the disaster that was my engagement, I'd decided against getting into anything emotionally complicated. I'd recommitted myself to celibacy and thrown all my energy into my ministry.

'It worked. Up to a point. And that point was at about a quarter past ten every night, when I'd got home from a PCC meeting, or finished my sermon, or dealt with some pastoral emergency. It was when I tried to pray, and remembered that I'd been lying to people all day. It was when I had to face the reality of that empty vicarage.

'But, you know, I was usually pretty tired by that point, so for a while it was OK, because I could just go to bed – alone – and by the time I'd woken up – alone – there was a whole new day's worth of ministry to get stuck into, and put off dealing with the question.

'You'll be thinking: surely that's not a sustainable way of life. Or, I don't know, maybe you expect your ministers to be superhuman.' Some rather guilty laughter. 'And for me it wasn't sustainable. But remember there are hundreds, maybe even thousands of clergy who are still putting themselves through that torture they call a way of life, refusing to admit who they really are, *maybe* telling themselves that they're bisexual as a kind of halfway house that they never move on from.'

Colette shifted in her chair. Lydia became attentive in a different way.

'Jesus said, *Deny yourself. Take up your cross.* What he never said was, *Lie about who you are.* But that's what the Church asks thousands of its members to do. And thousands of those members comply with that request.

'But I couldn't keep on going like that, and I think that was something I knew even before this wonderful, amazing man walked back into my life. Or maybe I should say, *fell*. Because he tripped over right at my feet.

'I'd gone up to London on my day off to see an exhibition. And so had he. Not the same exhibition, but the same gallery. So I was going upstairs, and he was going downstairs, and just as I got to this little landing he tripped down the last couple of steps: so we ended up there at the same time. I stepped forward to help him get up, obviously, and it was then that we recognised each other and did the whole "Funny seeing *you* here" thing.

'I don't remember which of us suggested going for a drink to catch up. I do remember thinking that it was probably a bad idea if I wanted to keep this whole closeted ministry thing going, and doing it anyway.

'At first we just talked about people we knew. "Have you heard from so-and-so?" "How is whatshisname doing?" And then he said, "But what about *you*? How are you finding parish ministry?"

'I said that it was great, that it was hard work, that it was rewarding, that it was very busy, that I liked it that way. I thought, *He's going to see through this*, and he did.

'And he said, "It's difficult, isn't it?", and I forgot that he didn't know, that nobody was meant to know, and I said, "Yeah. It is."

'Nothing happened that day.

'It was just that my whole world had been opened up.

'We agreed to keep in touch, and over the next couple of years we started seeing more of each other. Just as friends. Until it came to the point where he couldn't see me as just a friend any more. And when he told me that I said, "Yeah. Me neither."

'I don't want to pretend that things were easy, because they weren't. Sometimes it was really difficult. There were some people in my parish who couldn't cope with the idea at all. In the end I resigned from that post. It was easier to start afresh in a new parish where they knew what they were getting.

'What they were getting was a couple. And I was open about that.

It made the application process frustrating, but it was worth it in the long run. We found a parish that suited us – yes, *us*, because one of the great joys in my life at that time was the fact that my partner was rediscovering his Christian faith – a parish that *wanted* us. It was wonderful.

'Three years ago something happened which I could never have imagined when I was that sad, scared, kid in the closet. Gay couples got the right to marry.

'But not in the Church of England. Particularly not if they were ordained ministers in the Church of England.'

Colette took Lydia's hand.

'We talked it over for a long time. We prayed about it a lot. We knew that it could easily be the end of my career. But ultimately we agreed that if we had an opportunity to show the world that our relationship was as faithful, as loving, as committed, as any straight couple's, then we should take it up. We wouldn't be able to get married in church, so we would have to bear witness in other ways, while being legally married.

'Some people have called us cynical. Some have called us naïve. All I know is, we did the only thing we could, knowing what it would probably mean for us, praying that it wouldn't.

'Our wedding day was joyful and sad at the same time. We would have loved to have been married in church, and we couldn't even have a blessing there.

'Well, I got a stern talking-to from the Archdeacon, who, to be fair to her, didn't like doing it any more than I liked hearing it. Then the next level, with the Bishop. There was a lot about *unity* and *obedience* and *what it looked like to the outside world*, which I found hypocritical in the extreme.

'After that, nothing much happened. My parishioners were very supportive – well, most of them were. A few faces disappeared from the pews. But there were plenty of new faces to replace them.

'It was when my husband's company closed the office that he worked in that things got tricky.

'Now, not a word against my husband's employer. They bent over backwards to accommodate the staff there. Those that wouldn't or couldn't transfer got very generous redundancy packages. And my husband thought about taking one, but I said, No. That's not fair. You love your job, I said, and there's nothing similar within fifty miles. Meanwhile, everywhere needs a vicar. So he went to his boss – who had been very patient about the whole thing – and said that he was willing to transfer – and I started looking for jobs in the same area as his new office.

'And there were plenty of them. And plenty that would have suited me. Places where – for example – the vicarage was right on a busy road and completely unsuitable for children. But guess what? As soon as the powers that be clocked that we were married – bang – not interested.

'What did we do? What *could* we do? It became obvious that we were looking at a choice between my vocation and my husband's job. And I don't think it's unfair to say that by this point his job was no less of a vocation to him than mine was to me. And maybe you'll be horrified to hear that this was a consideration, but it paid quite a bit better. And you know what? His employer had treated him much better than mine had me. It wasn't an easy decision, but we made it. I left.

'So this is me. Ex-vicar, still an ordained minister, part-time speaker, part-time library volunteer. Hey, I'd done a lot of reading during my training. It made sense to put it to some use.'

There was some nervous laughter. He grinned encouragingly at it. 'So, what can I say to you all? How can I give you some hope? Why am I even here, if I'm just going to depress you all? Well, for a start, I feel very strongly that I'm called to tell the truth about what's happened to me, to put my head above the parapet, and say that *this happens and it is not OK.*

'But I also believe that this is not the whole story. Because the whole story is bigger than me or you or anything that I've just told you. The whole story is the one in which Christ died for me and in which God reaches out and tells me, *Aaron, I love you.*

'The whole story is this: God loves me. Just as I am. And God loves you, too.'

He took a single step back from the lectern.

Several hands were waving. The compère selected one near the front. 'George.'

George was a sandy-haired man about the same age as the speaker himself. He took the microphone and glanced around him before he spoke.

'Aaron, thank you for sharing your story with us. I'm sure I'm not the only person here who's shocked and horrified by the treatment you've received.' There was a murmur of assent. 'I wanted to ask: do you have any regrets about coming out? What do you think you'd be by now if you'd stayed in the closet?'

The speaker smiled. 'That's a good question. I suppose I don't like to think about *regrets*. More, *wonderings*. I guess that's what you're asking about really. And it depends what you mean by *what*. Do you mean, *where* would I be? Or do you mean, *who* would I be?' He left a brief pause, not long enough for George to reply. 'Where would I be? Some people have told me they thought I was going to go all the way to the top.' He smiled modestly. 'Obviously I don't know. As for *who* I'd be, that's a very different question. Who would I be? I'd be scared. I'd be small. I'd be knowing all the time that I was lying about who I was. I would be hurting myself and the people I loved, whether that was through letting them believe that we had a future, or telling them that we couldn't. I wouldn't be the person who God wanted me to be. I mean,' he added, 'I'm not that person now, none of us is, but I'm closer. And I'm loved, the way I am. If I'd stayed in the closet I don't think I'd ever have known that.'

George still had the microphone. 'So what would you say to someone who was gay and in the closet, or even who was in a gay relationship, and who wanted to be ordained?'

Colette felt the sudden tension in Lydia's arm.

'I'd say, good luck.' There was a ripple of laughter. 'No, I mean it. There's so much that gay people have to offer the Church, and it's such a tragedy that only a fraction of those gifts are used to their full potential. So I really would say, go for it and good luck. But I would also mean, *good luck with that*, because it's going to be hard. You know that.

'You live in this world as yourself, whether you're in or out of the closet; you're familiar with the dilemma of whether or not to tell someone the truth, knowing that if they then reject you they'll be rejecting your true self. You'll have to make the choice, and it won't be an easy one. You probably won't get as far as you deserve. There are probably people in this church today who should be bishops some day. And there are people in the House of Bishops who could be in this church.' He waited for the murmur of shock to dissipate before saying, 'It's an open secret. There are several bishops who are gay – well, technically I should say bisexual, since a lot of them go as far as getting married to women in their quest to fit in, and I can only trust that they keep their marriage vows – and who, having got to where they are, have effectively pulled the ladder up after them.'

Colette drew in a breath. Told herself he didn't mean it like that. It stung anyway, and she thought that *not meaning it like that* wasn't necessarily a good excuse.

The microphone had gone to someone else. 'Thank you. I was going to ask, so do you see sexual identity as a fluid thing, then? Or do you think it's something that people are stuck with?'

He nodded a couple of times. 'That's a good question, thank you. I don't think I'd like to say *stuck with*, because I prefer to see it as an amazing gift from God, but I know what you mean. In the secular world, people often come out as bisexual before they can commit to their full gay identity. In the Church, it's the other way round. They go into the closet when ordination becomes a possibility. They might have the honesty to admit to their gay past, but they act like that's been overwritten by their straight present.'

Colette put her hand up without really knowing what she was going to say. Somebody had to challenge that in some way, surely. But she couldn't rely on anyone else doing it.

Next to her, Lydia looked startled, but she patted her knee encouragingly. Glancing sideways, Colette saw that Eve had her hand up too. But the compère once again selected someone near the front.

This was a woman in her sixties with cropped, greying hair. 'Aaron. You said you weren't loved until you came out. Is that really what you believe?'

He looked horrified. 'No! I apologise. I didn't mean to say that at all. I *didn't know* I was loved until I came out. Of course I believe that God has loved me all the way through my journey – my journey towards being who I really am.'

'One more question, and that's really going to have to be the last...' The compère scanned the rows, passing over Eve's upraised hand, and Colette's, and settled on someone in the back. 'Harry, yes?'

Harry grinned round at the audience before replying, which Colette found unreasonably irritating. 'Thanks. So, how would you interpret the clobber texts in the light of what you've just said? I mean, Corinthians, for example...'

Eve was already halfway out of the hall, heels clicking indignantly on the parquet. With a vague idea of making sure that she was all right, Colette scrambled over ankles and rucksacks and jackets and wished that she too had chosen to sit at the end of a row.

Reaching the aisle at last, she headed in the same direction as Eve, out of the door, but found the lobby empty. The front door was swinging shut. Colette caught it as it swung and went outside. Somebody was just catching her up: a tubby, blond man in his early thirties.

They saw Eve at the same time, standing at the corner of the building and searching frantically through her handbag. The man reached into the pocket of his jeans and held out a packet of cigarettes.

'Thanks,' Eve said, and took one.

He smiled. 'You're welcome,' he said, and proffered the packet to Colette.

She shook her head. 'I don't. Thanks, though. I almost wish I did.'

Eve had managed to find her lighter. 'Well,' she said as she lit up, 'that was a thing that happened, as the kids say.'

'You know,' the man said in a quiet, furious, staccato, 'I could have been at home with my wife, on whom I've never cheated with anybody of any gender. I didn't have to fucking well come out – in any sense – to be written off as my non-existent post-gay respectable phase.' He held out his free hand to Eve. 'Tommy, by the way.'

'Eve.'

'Colette.' She shook his hand in turn. 'Speaking as a Methodist, I'm mostly offended at being lumped in with the bishops.'

'And not just any bishops,' said Tommy. 'The hypocritical secretly gay bishops who throw the rest of us under the bus.' He paused a moment, and added, 'Oh, sorry. That was a joke. I just realised.'

'It was certainly sarcasm,' Colette allowed.

Eve was puffing away angrily. She said, 'It's not just me, is it? That really was pretty fucking offensive.'

'I don't think it was meant to be,' Colette said, 'but it really was.'

'Any sufficiently advanced incompetence is indistinguishable from malice,' Eve said. 'He just didn't see us, did he?'

'It didn't occur to him that there was anyone to look for.'

Tommy snorted. 'Because obviously we're all at home in our smug respectable relationships, polishing our mitres.'

The door swished open once more. They looked round.

'Am I too late to join the whingeing party?' asked Rowan.

'Walk right up,' said Eve.

'I'm sorry,' Lydia said, rather later, at home.

'It's not your fault,' Colette told her, knowing it was true and not really believing it.

She still looked mortified. 'I know that. But I'm sorry that you heard that particularly offensive hot take, particularly after I'd talked you into coming in the first place.'

'I appreciate the fact that the man has been treated very badly. I couldn't help thinking of the parallels with your situation. I just resented – the rest of it.'

'I promise it isn't usually like that.'

'Is that because usually nobody mentions bisexuality at all?'

She could not help laughing at the consternation that gathered in Lydia's face.

'I always assume they mean you, too,' she said after a little while. 'I mean, it's the being attracted to women, being in a relationship with me, that gets you on the list, isn't it? When the homophobes talk about *same-sex attraction*, they mean you, too.'

'Same-sex attraction,' Colette repeated. 'It's a pity the other side came up with that one: it could have been such a useful phrase, for people like Tommy, or your cousin Abby. You know. People who wouldn't act on their feelings for people of their own gender, but refuse to be ashamed of them.'

'Only in the same way that they'd never act on their feelings for anyone of another gender, surely. On account of taking their marriage vows seriously.'

'Yes, that's what I mean. And there's a world of difference between Tommy coming out to this because he's still queer, never mind who he's married to, or Abby agonising all the time about whether she should tell all the people who assume she's straight because they're too lazy to think of the other possibilities, and the bloody bishops sitting there letting everyone believe they're straight and stopping people marrying who they want to marry. And I bet some of them *are* just plain gay.'

'Maybe your lot were right all along,' Lydia said in a transparent attempt to lighten the mood. 'Maybe bishops are a mistake.'

'You're only saying that because you've got to go and see one next week,' Colette teased her.

Lydia groaned. 'I know.'

Colette said, thoughtfully, 'Rowan said that theirs are all celibate. That might solve the problem.'

'I don't think it has. I'm so sorry,' Lydia said once more. 'And I was so excited about your coming, too. Next time I'll do some more research.'

'Next time I might just go straight to the pub with Eve and Rowan.'

'Do I look OK?' Lydia asked, anxiously. She was wearing a variation on her normal work clothes: black trousers; grass-green blouse; a V-neck sweater in a black-and-white houndstooth knit.

'You look fine.'

'It's not too loud?'

'It's smart. It's you.'

'Are you sure I shouldn't wear a skirt?'

Colette thought about it, then shook her head. 'No. That would look like you're trying too hard.' She paused a moment, and said, 'Sure you don't want to wear the purple shirt?'

Lydia stuck her tongue out at her. 'Absolutely sure. Thank you.' She laughed, but she still looked worried.

'He's basically just rubber-stamping Tina's recommendation. Isn't he?'

'I expect it will feel like that if he does put me through. But he could still veto me. It wouldn't be unusual.'

'He's a fool if he does.'

'Peter thinks he *is* a fool.'

'Because he's an Evangelical?'

'Because he took Fellowship's side when they got kicked out of the Students' Union,' Lydia reminded her.

'That was years ago. He's probably forgotten.'

Lydia picked a speck of fluff from her sleeve. 'Yes, but there's still a bit of me that's worried that he's going to put two and two together and realise that I was the one who made the scene.'

'Does he even know there was a scene? It all died down after that, really, didn't it? It had to.'

'You're right. He probably doesn't. But *I* know.'

Colette had to admit that this was true, and that it made a difference. She took a step closer to Lydia to turn her collar down where it had got folded over at the back of her neck; and, when she had done that, caught hold of her hands. 'I suppose the only thing that I can say to that,' she said, 'is that the whole horrible mess is part of what made you who you are, and you and Tina and Marcus have spent the last two years working out that the person you are is someone who should go forward for this.'

Lydia's hands tightened around hers. 'You're right. I suppose.'

Colette hoped very much that she was. 'Come on. Let's go.' She drew Lydia closer and kissed her; then, remembering that it would hardly do to make an exhibition of themselves outside the diocesan offices, kissed her again.

After dropping Lydia as close to the cathedral green as she could get, Colette drove up to campus and spent a distracted few hours reordering her findings thus far. She had tried to tell herself that she was glad of the extra space in their office – *her* office – but the truth was that it felt all wrong without James. He had been a fixture ever since she began her PhD; he was an approachable, if cynical, guide to the tortuous world of postgraduate academia. Almost a month had passed since he had left, and she was coming to understand at a level deeper than the mere intellectual that he would not be coming back.

Barry was in the building, but tied up with meetings. Mariam told her this with a slight frown. Colette wondered about the meetings, but did not ask more. She would have liked to speak to him about the structure for her thesis, but she admitted reluctantly that perhaps today wasn't the best day for it. She knew that she was jumpy and preoccupied. She had not yet introduced the subject of her possible impending life change, and, with approval or dismissal in the Bishop's gift today, it seemed pointless to distract him with something that might never happen.

And so, although she glanced up whenever somebody passed the office on the off-chance that they were Barry, she did not seek him out herself. Anyway, she told herself, she really needed to learn to stand on her own two feet, to live in the real world where she didn't have her hand held all the time.

At ten past five she drove home again, without much to show for her truncated day's work, and without much caring about that. Whatever Lydia's news, it would dwarf anything else.

She had grown used to thinking of this as a slow process, geological both in its ponderousness and in its capacity to reshape their lives and their destinies. Sometimes it seemed almost as if the huge gaps between meetings and outcomes were provided not so much for them to make their decisions, as for them to get their heads around the decisions that had already been made in some cosmic sphere. But today they did not have to wait, and it was dizzying. Lydia was hopping from one foot to the other like an excited child.

'You've heard.'

'Yes.' She was smiling broadly.

'Tell me,' Colette said, though she already knew.

'Well, apparently he likes me. He's recommending me to the BAP, and now all we have to do is see if the BAP recommends me back to him.'

Colette's heart dropped. 'Whew.'

'I know. It's feeling very real.'

'Tell me about it.'

'I just did.' Her smile matured to a sweet, earnest, seriousness, and Colette's heart lurched. She knew, suddenly, that this was indeed Lydia's calling, and that, whatever else happened, she must not stand in her way.

*Thank you for registering to attend the 29th annual Symposium on Nuclear Magnetic Resonance and Spectroscopy at the Weatherhead Centre, Cambridge, 25-28 October 2017. Authors are requested to submit final versions of their research abstracts, papers, and posters by 20 October at the latest.*

A thin red bleeping picked at the edges of her consciousness. Lydia's alarm. There was a shifting that was Lydia rolling first one way to turn it off, and then the other to wrap herself briefly around Colette. It was welcome, but too quick: it took a second or two for Colette to unfurl her mind and limbs, and Lydia was gone. Colette heard her moving around in the kitchen: the clanking of plates, the gentle grumble of the kettle. She told herself that she should get up; that it would be easier now, with Lydia present and awake and making things happen, than it would be later if she had to generate her own energy and start everything from cold. But she lay there, not moving. She was going to have to shower. She was going to have to get dressed. She was going to have to decide what to get dressed in.

Lydia came back in with a cup of tea, not quite as milky as Colette would have made it herself, and put it down on the bedside table. She bent to kiss Colette's forehead before going to the chest of drawers to rummage for socks.

'Awake?'

'I'll get back to you on that one,' Colette mumbled. With an almighty effort, she dragged herself upright.

Lydia glanced at the clock, and then sat down on the edge of the bed next to Colette. 'Are you going to AngthMURC this evening?' she asked, too neutrally.

Colette groaned. 'I know I said I would.'

'Is that a *probably not*?'

'Probably not, yes.'

Still in the same neutral tone, Lydia said, 'You've missed a few weeks, now.' She pulled her right foot up to her left knee to put a sock on.

'I know.'

'You haven't left?'

'Well,' Colette said, thinking that she wasn't awake enough for this, 'not officially.'

With unexpected firmness, Lydia said, 'I don't think you should.'

The headboard felt far more substantial than she was. 'I'm not sure that I have anything to offer them any more.'

'And *it* doesn't have anything to offer *you*, because you've seen it all before.'

'Yes,' Colette said, and then worried that she sounded horrifically arrogant.

'You're wrong, though. You have a lot to offer them. Seven years of experience, for a start.'

'Six years.'

Lydia waved the other sock impatiently. 'Six years, whatever. You've been there all that time; that's important in itself. You know more than anybody else there about being a student. And don't you ever think it isn't important, having someone there just being who they are. And who you are is queer, and a scientist, and... probably loads of other things that people think they can't be at the same time as being a Christian.'

Colette tried to recognise herself in the portrait Lydia had sketched, and failed. She said, more honestly, 'I don't think I can face it. And I don't know why. I just can't.'

'Because you're tired.'

'Yes, and that's not fair, either, because you have to work longer hours than me.'

'And yet somehow you're often home several hours after I am.' Lydia twisted around to kiss her.

In the office, an email was waiting for her from the conference organiser, giving details of accommodation, and explaining the arrangements for the poster display.

'Shit,' Colette said, quietly.

There was nothing particularly intimidating about it, at least, not in itself. It was the unwritten reproach that accompanied it; the knowledge that at this moment she had no poster; that now, weeks later than she could have been, she was going to have to face the blank screen and put something on it.

It was the sort of thing that she would normally have talked over with James, and felt better about after five minutes. Now she was going to have to go straight to Barry with it if she wanted any help at all, and that was more or less unthinkable.

'Don't be stupid,' she told herself, out loud. 'You know how to do a poster.'

But it seemed that she had forgotten. Or perhaps it was just that she knew, deep down, she hadn't found anything worth putting on a poster. All day she sat with the blank page burning white into her eyes, writing a sentence, and deleting it, copying in a paragraph, and cutting it out again, looking for a diagram, and discarding it. When she left to go home, she didn't bother saving anything.

Lydia asked about her day, in words that sounded conventional but covered obvious and genuine concern.

'It's been awful.' She hadn't meant to admit it, but, now she had started, she couldn't stop. 'I'm meant to do this poster for the conference, and I just can't get my head around it. There's far too much to get on there, and every time I make a start I get overwhelmed by everything else that I haven't put down.'

Lydia was smiling gently, perhaps at the concept of having to make a poster, though she had known Colette for long enough to be conversant with modern scientific communication methods; more probably because she had known Colette for long enough to recognise an irrational assessment panic when she saw it. But that was the thing: this one wasn't irrational; this time she genuinely couldn't do it. She wondered absently what she would be like when she had to defend her thesis at the viva, and found the idea too terrifying to contemplate. She turned her attention back to the idea of the poster; it wasn't much better.

Lydia asked, 'What have you tried so far?'

'Oh... Everything! I've tried starting with the hypothesis and I've tried starting with the results and I've tried sticking the diagrams in the middle and going on from there and it's just all too *big*!' She could see that Lydia was about to disguise another helpful suggestion as a question, and she could not face that. To pre-empt it, she asked the question that had been gnawing at her for months now. 'Do you want me to give it up?'

She did not know what she wanted the answer to be.

Lydia paused, her mouth half-open. Eventually she said, 'I don't want to be the one who tells you to.' She shook her head. 'I know you've been working for it for years. I know it's what you've always wanted. And OK, I don't think it's doing you any good – doing *us* any good – but if you were to stop it just because I said so, well, it wouldn't say much for us, would it?'

'Your training isn't going to be any easier than this.' Except it would, because she knew that there was at least supposed to be some sort of structure, with lectures and essays and placements, and besides, Lydia was far better at getting things done and not getting stuck in her own head.

'I know.'

Colette could not resist adding, 'If you get as far as training,' and immediately felt bad about it.

Lydia just said, 'I know,' again.

Feeling ever more remorseful, Colette said, 'You might cope with it better than I have.'

Lydia said, evenly, 'You've had a lot to cope with.'

'We can't assume that you won't.' In fact – she did not add – since part of what Colette had had to cope with had been Lydia's own discernment process, it seemed inevitable that she would. She thought irrelevantly of Peter. But it wasn't irrelevant: he had got to where Lydia was aiming. She thought about James, who had just walked away from it all. Could she ever be that brave? *Yes*, she told herself, *if it came to it*. Came to what, though? That was the question, and all she knew was that so far she had not come to it. Yet.

'No. We can't.' Lydia added, as if to change the subject, 'So Mel tells me that Rory's changed his mind.'

'Oh?'

'He's decided not to go out to Africa.'

'Oh.'

'I think it's probably wise. For the moment, at least.'

'Yes,' said Colette. She really didn't care.

Lydia stood there for a moment, then turned away, sat down at the table, and took out her phone. After a while she said, 'Colette?'

'Mm?'

'When are you in Cambridge?'

'The twenty-fourth to the twenty-eighth. Why?'

'I thought so. I've just seen that one of the college choirs is doing an anthem by Gabe on the twenty-sixth.'

'What, you mean at Evensong?' It was, presumably, quite an achievement. 'That's pretty cool.'

'I know. He sounds really excited about it.'

'So you want me to go and listen, and report back?'

'Well, since you'll be in Cambridge anyway... The only thing is, it's St Mark's.'

Colette frowned, wondering why she was meant to care that it was St Mark's. Then she remembered. 'Oh. Natalie.'

'Yeah. Would that bother you?'

'I don't see why it should,' Colette said quickly. 'Unless she sees me and thinks... Oh, I don't really care what she thinks. It's her business.'

'Maybe you could go in disguise,' Lydia suggested with a wink. 'Dark glasses, floppy hat, false moustache...'

'You know, I really think I have enough to do with making my poster. If you want me to go in disguise, you can get it together for me. And try and find out from Gabe what would be an intelligent reaction to his piece.'

Lydia looked relieved. 'On it.'

*St Mark's College, Cambridge*
*Thursday 26 October 2017*

*Choral Evensong*

*Responses: Radcliffe*
*Psalm: 119 (verses 145-160), Naylor*
*Canticles: Noble in B minor*
*Anthem: Passing Away Saith The World, Hammond*

Cambridge in October was aloof and chilly, its gracious buildings washed in thin gold light. The conference was a bus ride out of town, in an echoing featureless hall with no windows and the heating turned up too high. Colette stood next to her poster and wished that James was there. Barry flitted in and out, always talking to somebody new, and dropping cryptic hints about why he had deleted his Twitter account. The evenings were dark and dank, with a chill that hung in the air and sapped the energy. Colette did her best to join in with the organised socialising on the first night, and to chat with other delegates at coffee breaks. She was not the youngest person there, which was encouraging; the youngest person seemed far more confident, which was not. She missed Lydia. Had it been this bad when she went out to America in the first year of her PhD, she wondered? She thought not. She seemed to have gone backwards. She hadn't known, then, what she knew now: that she had nothing worth saying.

On the second day she skipped the last session (she was by no means the only one to do so) and took the bus back into town to attend Evensong at St Mark's College.

She stood outside the gate for a couple of minutes, trying to work up the nerve to go in. She had been here before eight years ago, for an interview – not St Mark's, but the air of distilled, deep-rooted, learning, was the same. The memory of the rejection did not help her. Nor did the memory of the relief that had followed it.

Cambridge, she had decided, was not for her. (Nor, presumably, was Oxford.) The thought that she was returning in triumph with a hard-won First and most of a doctorate had helped her to bluff her way through the conference, but it was powerless in the face of this concentrated superiority. Standing in the street outside St Mark's with the bicycles whirring past behind her, it was painfully clear that she was unimportant and that she did not belong here.

But she could hardly tell Lydia that she'd wussed out of going to a public service of worship. She shook herself, twitched her scarf into place, and approached the porters' lodge.

She said, hesitantly, 'I wanted to go to Evensong,' and, when the porter waved her through, slunk across the quad and into the chapel.

The chapel was a study in monochrome: black wood, white walls, and grey monuments to the great minds whose heads had bowed within it. Its severity was softened somewhat by a gilded wrought iron screen, and wide, high windows whose stained glass showed nothing tonight but velvety darkness.

Colette had been dragged to enough chapel Evensong services in Stancester to know her way around the format, although she did not think that she recognised any of the music. Her attention wandered in the psalm. The readers both seemed rather incoherent. She tried hard neither to look at Natalie nor to look as if she was avoiding looking at her. She failed, at the first goal at least, and found halfway through the second lesson that Natalie was looking at *her*; suspicious, surprised. It was a most definite relief to turn to face east for the Creed and to be able to stare directly at the tweedy shoulders of the man who sat next to her.

She did her best to listen attentively to Gabe's piece. It was a setting of lines by Christina Rossetti, and Colette felt uncomfortably conscious that Lydia would certainly have drawn her own intelligent conclusions about the text. She consoled herself with the thought that Lydia didn't know much about choral music either.

After the prayers and the Grace, Colette sat tight in her stall and watched the choir file out. She promised herself that she would stay until the end of the organ voluntary, and then leave. She was more than half expecting Natalie to ignore her, but it did not seem impossible that curiosity would win out.

It did. The organist was crunching majestically towards a resolution when Natalie came back, with her gown folded over her arm. She glanced around the chapel before coming over to Colette. 'Hi,' she said warily.

'Hello,' Colette said, unable to ignore her own nerves any more. Without looking down, she scrabbled under her seat for her rucksack.

'What brings you to Cambridge?'

'I'm at a conference.'

'Oh, OK. I'd ask you what it was about, but I expect I wouldn't understand the answer. So you thought you might as well pop along to Evensong while you were here?'

'That's right,' Colette said, ignoring any sarcasm that might have been meant. 'It was a lovely service, I thought.'

'Thanks,' Natalie said, accepting the praise on behalf of the whole choir, perhaps the whole college. 'And...?'

'One of Lydia's friends wrote the anthem.'

'Really? Gabriel Hammond?'

'They used to live next door to each other in halls.'

'Oh, fair enough. It wasn't at all bad,' she allowed.

Colette risked a smile. 'I'm meant to be reporting back to her with intelligent observations. Unfortunately I'm in no way a musician, so I don't know whether I'll be able to do any better than, *it sounded very nice*.'

'Well, she could tell him that the *divisi* in the B flat minor part work much better if the second sopranos have the D rather than the first altos.'

'Can you write that down for me?'

Natalie started to reach for a pencil, then hesitated. 'Would you like to come for a drink?'

'Will they let me into your bar?' Colette asked, surprised.

'Oh, yeah, it'll be fine.'

Feeling distinctly uncomfortable, Colette followed her across the quad and into the bar. This was an odd, L-shaped room panelled in yellowish wood, furnished with leather armchairs and decorated with oars painted with the names of long-dead crews and other antique sporting memorabilia.

'What's yours?' Natalie asked.

'Let me.'

Natalie shook her head, half-smiling. 'I insist.'

'I'll have a red wine, then. Thanks.'

She glanced around the bar while Natalie bought the drinks, studying the sepia faces of the 1929 rugby team as if they would be able to offer her advice.

'Now.' Natalie handed her a glass of wine, sloshing her own drink. 'Let's find somewhere to sit down.'

Colette followed her to a tiny round table in a corner. The chair was disconcertingly squashy. 'Thank you.'

'You're welcome.' Natalie did not look hostile. She was trying, Colette thought, not to look curious. 'So. Tell me everything.'

'Everything?'

'Well for a start, did Peter put you up to this?'

'Peter doesn't know I'm here. I mean,' she added pedantically, 'he knows that I'm in Cambridge; we're meeting up tomorrow; but I didn't tell him that I was going to come to St Mark's, and I didn't know until ten minutes ago that I was going to end up talking to you.'

Natalie narrowed her eyes, and then apparently decided to

believe her. 'How is he?'

'As far as I know, he's OK, but I haven't talked to him properly since late August.'

'When he went on that trip with the buses?'

'Yeah. He came down to stay with us in Stancester afterwards.'

'I know.' She looked wistful. 'That was the end, really. We were meant to be going back to Cambridge together: I'd fixed up to housesit for a friend of one of the Fellows, and he could have stayed with me, but he didn't.

'Right. I did wonder whether everything was all right, but, you know. We didn't like to ask.'

'It was probably a bit silly – we could have had the whole of September to do stuff together – but I had friends coming down that I wanted him to meet, and it stung a bit that he wanted to spend time with *you*, instead.' She added, hurriedly, 'I mean, he had only just seen you, and I realise the circumstances weren't exactly ideal, but...'

'... But we'd already ruined your week with his parents?'

'It hadn't occurred to me that it must have been as awkward for you as it was for me. I mean, I guess Lydia had other things on her mind, but you were just having to hang around.'

'It wasn't much fun, no,' Colette admitted.

Natalie confessed, 'So the thing was, you didn't want to be there, and I didn't want you to be there, but Peter was really glad you were, and I... couldn't help resenting that. Like, we never got time to see each other here, and then we went to see his family and then you popped up.' She followed up that outburst with, 'And his parents really like you.'

'Do they not like you?'

Natalie wrinkled her nose. 'I... guess they do?'

'They like everybody. There's nothing special about me. They're just nice people. When Lydia... left home, they took her in at midnight, never mind the fact that they'd never met her before.'

'You stayed with them before, though, right? And you and Peter were together then?'

Colette shook her head. '*Lydia* and I were together. In fact, there was a time when we were all letting Lydia's mother believe *she* was going out with Peter. I'm not going to pretend that there haven't been times in my life when I'd have liked it to happen, but it hasn't, and really that's for the best.'

Natalie nodded. 'No matter what his parents might or might not think? OK.'

Colette could feel herself going red. 'No, and anyway, it's not the point. It's never happened, it's never going to happen, and I'd hate to think that the two of you had given up on a good thing because of me. I mean, if it wasn't working anyway, then fair enough, none of my business. But I know things were weird over the summer, and if that was because Lydia and I turned up unexpectedly, then I'm sorry.'

'Trust me, it was weird before you got there.'

'We didn't help, though, right?'

'Not really.' She sipped her drink. 'The trouble with Peter,' she said, 'is that he always follows the rules. Even when the rules are completely ridiculous.'

'Should I ask which rules in particular?'

'Your partner is probably going to theological college. I'd imagine you'll be coming up against them yourself.'

*Those* rules. 'Oh, so you heard things were heading in that direction?'

'Peter used to talk about you a *lot*.'

Colette shrugged. 'He used to talk about you a lot, as well. In a good way.' Unexpectedly, she found herself regretting Peter and Natalie's break-up. 'I thought it was good for him to have someone in the real world.'

Natalie laughed. 'Cambridge isn't the real world.'

'You know what I mean, though.'

'Yes,' Natalie said. 'I know what you mean. Well. I don't really know what to say. Just, thank you for saying all of that.'

Colette felt compelled to say, 'I'll be seeing Peter tomorrow.'

'Will you tell him you saw me?'

'I don't have to, but I probably would.'

'I don't mind.'

'Did you want me to say anything – or not say anything – in particular?'

Natalie drained her glass. Then she shook her head. 'No. Thank you. I'll work out if there's anything that needs to be said, and if there is then I'll say it myself.'

Peter had sent her directions to the Free Press because it was close to the bus station, and, he said, there were far too many good pubs in the city for them to have to cram into the Eagle with all the tourists. Having again skipped out of the last conference session early, Colette got to the pub a good half pint before she needed to. Peter (who was in fact only five minutes late) looked rather flustered when he saw her, and nearly dropped the stack of books he had with him. A greetings card, still in its plastic film, fell out of one of them and fluttered to the floor. Colette scrambled for it. *Mrs and Mrs.* Peter saw her looking, and laughed awkwardly.

'I bought it by mistake. Didn't read it properly. I've been using it as a bookmark ever since.'

'It's encouraging that it's now possible to make that mistake,' Colette allowed.

Peter grinned. 'There is that. Natalie said we should save it for you two, but I said that by that point it would be *Dr and Rev.*'

Colette stopped herself saying, *if that point ever comes*. Instead she asked, rhetorically, 'Wasn't that a *Friends* episode? Anyway, it's really not our style.'

'I did tell her that.'

She said, cautiously, 'There's no guarantee of either, of course.'

'I know. I assume you *are* still both aiming at those two titles respectively? No shame if you're not, of course. And please tell me if you'd rather I shut up about it.'

'I will. At the moment we still are.'

'OK. Good.'

Peter had opened the door a crack. Colette pushed it a little further. 'The thing is, what either one of us does affects the other. If I were to quit, then maybe I'd have more energy to support her through it. If she isn't selected, then a whole load of options open back up again, but it'll be miserable.'

'It might be miserable if she is, too,' Peter said, quietly.

'I know.'

'Are you seriously thinking about quitting?'

For the first time, she confessed: 'Sometimes. More, since my research assistant went. I can't, though.'

'Why not?'

'Well – because –' She could not put it into words, the conviction that backing out now would nullify the past four years' worth of effort, the sense of obligation to do something constructive with the results that she had extracted with such trouble.

'What does it feel like, when you think about it?' He said it with a touch too much self-consciousness to seem natural.

She glared at him. 'What am I, a pastoral skills resuscitation dummy?'

'I wasn't going to try giving you the kiss of life.'

Her stomach dropped as if she had missed a step; she said, quickly, 'Disappointed. *Angry.*'

'Angry?'

'Yes,' she said, absurdly surprised. 'Really, really, fucking angry.'

'With...?'

'Myself. And James. And Barry. But mostly myself.'

'Because...?'

'Because I shouldn't have to quit, and if I do, it must be somebody's fault. Probably my own.'

Peter nodded. 'What if you imagine the scenario where Lydia does get selected?'

She considered the question. 'Then it becomes something more like resentment. Because why should she get her thing if I don't get mine? Then I feel guilty because I know that it just puts her where I was three years ago, and she might not do any better than I have. Maybe it's easier.'

'Maybe,' Peter said, tonelessly, and Colette was struck once again by a sense of wrongness.

'But really I feel bad even thinking about that because I know the chances are she won't be selected at all, and we'll both be so angry about that that there won't be room for anything else. Or else she'll fall in with the party line on why she hasn't been, and I'll have to be angry for her.'

He raised an eyebrow. 'Will you?'

'Someone would have to be.'

'Why?'

Surely he knew? 'Because she'd make such a good minister. You know she would. She's patient; she's prayerful; she's forgiving, but she doesn't let me get away with stuff. And people *talk* to her. Even the Fellowship types. Rory and Mel and that lot. You'd have thought that they wouldn't ever have spoken to her again after she came out, but they're always round at ours telling her their problems.'

Peter's smile was quick and fond. 'You know why that is, don't you?'

'Because she's really good at listening?'

'No. I mean, yes, but that's not the main thing. It's because *they don't think of her as being perfect*. They know she'll understand the faith stuff, because she's from that sort of background, but they also know, or maybe they just assume, that she'll understand that there are things you can't admit to when you're talking to your perfect Christian friends, because you're all trying to be perfect. And – I can't think of a way for this to not sound terrible, because it *is* terrible, and I'm being very uncharitable – they find it very easy to think of her as not being perfect. And that makes her a safe person to admit their imperfection to.'

'*I* think she's perfect,' Colette said staunchly.

'That's sweet. And a lie.'

Colette laughed. 'Yeah.'

'But you're right. She is easy to talk to. And she will be good at it.'

'If she gets through.'

Peter acknowledged that with a who-can-say nod. 'Indeed.'

'What's it like?' Colette asked. 'The interview, I mean. What's she going to need from me?'

He flicked thoughtfully at his lower lip with the tip of his thumb. 'What she's going to need from you is to love her either way, whatever happens. Because it gets so deeply inside you, and either it rejects you, or it sends you off to become a completely new person. And I've been through both and I honestly don't know which was the more difficult to get my head around. She'll need continuity.'

Colette nodded. After a little while Peter continued, 'It was awful the first time. The second time felt so much better, but maybe that's because I knew what I was getting myself into then. Even so, it was intense. There's a whole lot of talking, and a whole lot of waiting, and there are very few people who are comfortable with both of those things.'

She nodded, wondering on Lydia's behalf which she would find the easier.

'And of course that's only the beginning. It's only the beginning of the beginning.'

'So what's it like? College?'

'It definitely has its moments. I enjoy the theology. And of course there's all the delightfully random stuff that just wouldn't happen anywhere else.'

'Such as?'

'Cricket. Us versus Ridley.'

'Cricket happens everywhere, though, surely.'

'True. Oh, like the Polari Evensong that there was all that fuss about earlier in the year.'

'Did you go to that?'

He laughed and shook his head. 'It would have been the teeniest bit appropriative, don't you think? But I bet you that in forty years' time it's going to be like Woodstock. If everyone who's going to claim to have been at the Polari Evensong had actually been there, they'd have had to do it in Ely Cathedral.'

'What's not so good?'

'I think,' Peter said slowly, 'that I expected to like living in community more than I in fact do. I hadn't quite realised how much your life ceases to be your own.'

Colette was sceptical. 'We lived with Georgia.'

'It's more than a washing-up rota.' He shook his head. 'Oh, well, at least I know now that becoming a monk is not for me.'

'I could have told you that.' She hesitated, and then added, 'I went to Evensong at St Mark's yesterday.'

'Oh?' Peter looked suspicious.

'They were singing something by Lydia's friend Gabe, so she wanted me to go along and hear it.'

He took the cue with obvious relief. 'Any good?'

'It seemed OK to me, but I'm no expert.' She paused. 'I had a drink with Natalie afterwards.'

The suspicious look returned. 'And?'

'And nothing, really. I just didn't want you to think that I'd been going behind your back, on the off-chance you heard about it somehow.' Although, she supposed, she had.

Peter sighed. 'That's another thing. I mean, I know I couldn't even have met her if I hadn't been here, but it's all been so weird. You can't have a normal relationship like normal people do. Sometimes I wanted to say, let's just dump the whole thing and not have college breathing down our necks all the time. But I never did and now it's too late.'

'Is it?'

He glanced sharply at her. 'Yes.'

She wanted to say, *Natalie said*... But Natalie had said that she would do her own talking.

When she did not speak, he said, 'I wish we'd met each other before, and not here. Maybe, if we had, I would have taken that as a sign not to go for selection again. Maybe she'd have asked me not to. Maybe, if she had, I wouldn't have done.'

Colette considered that. 'But would that have been what you wanted? I don't think it's fair to ask somebody to sacrifice their... their *calling* for somebody else. Apart from anything else, what does it do to the relationship?' She sighed. 'I say that, and I wonder what I'm asking Lydia to do for me.'

'And what she's asking you to do for her.'

She shrugged her shoulders. 'Let's not go there.' She added, 'No. I guess we have this unspoken arrangement that we'll quit if it ever gets too much. But we've never defined *too much*.'

'Some people are worth quitting for,' he said, and an odd expression flickered over his face.

Unsettled, she asked, 'Have *you* ever thought of quitting?'

He looked very slightly surprised. 'Everybody does. But if I don't do this, what do I do? And I know –' he said before Colette could reply – 'if that's my only reason for doing it then I shouldn't be doing it at all, but I find that thinking of it like that doesn't seem to help.'

'You'd find something. I suppose we all would really,' she added quickly, not believing it.

'What's your James up to now?' Peter's tone had changed, but Colette knew that the subject had not.

'He's got a job as a lab technician at Stancester Girls' School.'

'Does he like it?'

'He likes having a nine to five.'

'I've heard of those,' Peter said with deep irony.

'What worries *me* is that we're shutting off options all the way. We're painting ourselves into a corner.'

'I don't think that's true. I can see several possibilities for you. For both of you.'

'OK,' she challenged him. 'Tell me one of them.'

'You're a research assistant at a university in a city with a diverse choice of churches. Lydia's a chaplain at the same university. Or maybe at the hospital. Or at an affirming church in the city.'

It sounded plausible. 'She wouldn't even need to learn to drive.'

'Exactly. And if you don't want to keep on in academia, there'll be other possibilities. Not just being a lab tech like your friend. Look at the Science Park here: it's crawling with people with PhDs. Does Lydia have a Plan B for if she doesn't get through? Or is she just going to see what happens?'

'Lydia's Plan B is to keep on at the council. And that was only ever meant as a stopgap, really.'

'Yeah. I know.'

'She quite likes it, though.'

'Well, that's good.'

'It's just... It's not what she was born to do, is it? She's *meant* to be a minister, isn't she?'

'*I* think so.'

'And so do I, much as I hate admitting it. And so do her minister and the people at her church and apparently so does every random barman in Stancester. And if she misses out on that vocation because of me, I don't know how we're going to get past that.'

'It won't be because of you,' Peter said patiently.

'No, I know, she's always telling me that herself, but it might as well be, mightn't it? I mean, we keep hearing that her being gay isn't a problem. It's her being gay and having a partner who she can't marry and isn't meant to be having sex with.'

He took a gulp of beer. 'She could always marry me, if that would help.'

'*What?*' Colette thought for one seasick moment that they were talking about Natalie again.

He added, 'In name only, of course. I just thought it would solve the problem of...'

'The panel thinking she might be gay? That ship has sailed.' Colette shook her head, bewildered. 'I don't know if she told the Bishop, but everyone else in the process knows.' The Lydia who could conceivably go along with such a harebrained plan was so far from the Lydia of reality that she was finding it difficult to come up with anything to say to the Peter who had suggested it.

'There's a long and honourable tradition of marriage of convenience.'

There was, she realised now, the glint of a grin in his eye. Had it been a joke? Anger was pushing its way up through her throat. 'In the nineteenth century, maybe. No. Seriously. What the fuck. What makes you think that could possibly work?'

He said, defensively, 'Well, we're friends, aren't we? All three of us?'

Fuck. It *had* been a joke. Taking it seriously herself, she'd forced him to do the same, and she couldn't see a way back now. But it wasn't funny. 'At the moment,' Colette said, 'yes.'

He was looking increasingly embarrassed. 'No. You're right. I'm sorry: it was a stupid thing to say. Forget I said anything.'

'I'll try.'

He said, presumably because it was the only possible thing left to say, 'Another drink?'

And when he came back from the bar they talked about Stancester, and about the new building that was going up for Business & Accounting, but all the time she was conscious that the ground had shifted under them, and she did not like it at all.

*dep Cambridge 1517*
*arr Kings X 1605*
*Circle/Met/H & City W*
*dep Paddington 1639*
*arr Stancester 1832*

Lydia met her at the station, and Colette felt at once pleased and relieved to see her, and guilty for putting her out.

'It's not putting me out,' Lydia said. 'I just did an extra hour at work and got the 3 instead of the 53.'

'If you say so.'

'I do.'

Lydia took the canvas bag into which Colette had stuffed three magazines, a book, and a jumper she hadn't needed. 'Tell me about the conference.'

'It was OK. Too many people, too much coffee, not enough daylight.'

'And you said you made it to Evensong at St Mark's.'

She resettled her rucksack. 'Yes. I even had a drink with Natalie afterwards.' Then she remembered that Lydia's main interest in Evensong was the anthem, and added, 'She said that Gabe could move the division round, or something. She wrote it down for me to pass on.'

'Oh. Fair enough.' It didn't seem to mean anything to Lydia either. 'But you liked it?'

'I've certainly heard worse,' Colette acknowledged with a grin.

They turned out of the station car park and started up the hill towards home.

'How was Peter?'

She had to laugh at that. 'Oh, goodness. Where do I begin?'

'Not good, then?'

Colette hesitated. 'He was in a very weird mood.'

'Weird in what way?'

She prayed that Lydia would not start looking for hidden meanings. 'He isn't enjoying college.'

'Did he say why?'

'Part of it is not being able to have a proper relationship when you've got the whole hierarchy looking over your shoulder.'

Lydia whistled. 'Did Peter tell you that?'

'Sort of. But Natalie told me in so many words.'

'How was Natalie?'

'Actually, she was OK. Enjoying her course, enjoying her singing. Very keen to make sure that I knew that she didn't think the break-up was in any way my fault.'

'Oh, really? That's a bit of a change of tune.'

'Isn't it just?'

'Did Peter say anything about it?'

'He blamed college, mostly,' Colette said uncomfortably.

'Mostly? What else did you talk about?'

'Oh. Well. It all came back to that, one way or another. The Process, and you, and me.'

Lydia looked wary. 'In what sense?'

'You know. What happens next, and what to expect. And then –' she laughed – 'And then he suggested a marriage of convenience.'

'*No*,' Lydia said immediately. Then, 'Wow, you weren't kidding about his being in a weird mood.' Then, 'Which of us?'

'You. And he was joking. Still no?'

'Double no.' Lydia raised her eyebrows. 'I suppose *you* could if you really wanted to.'

'You just wouldn't want to be with me any more if I did. Right. I don't want to, anyway.'

'I don't think it would be very convenient for *him*,' Lydia mused.

Colette sighed. 'Well, yes, it sounds like absolute hell.'

'I can't see how it solves anything. Wouldn't it be the worst-case scenario for all three of us?'

'Maybe he's thinking it would be like Alma Road, mark two. But no, it couldn't be, because if we were all living together then someone would notice and freak out. To be honest, *I* was too busy freaking out to ask about the details.'

'Well, I wish he'd just have the guts to drop out on his own behalf,' Lydia snapped, 'not drag us into his angst until someone notices and kicks him out.'

Colette took a long breath, giving the revelation time to land. 'You think that's what he's trying to do?'

'That's what it sounds like. He wants someone to make the decision for him.'

'It's not easy, pushing the self-destruct button.'

'He can stop any time he likes, same as any of us. Click those ruby shoes together, Dorothy.'

'I'd have thought you'd be sympathetic.'

'So would I. Funny, isn't it?'

They walked on in silence. It *was* the steepest part of the hill, Colette told herself; she was a little out of breath; but she was conscious of a sort of cowardice. She'd come to a decision on the train: was failing to speak it the same thing as backing out of it? At last she said, 'Look, I've been thinking. About you and college.'

'Oh?' Lydia looked worried.

'Living in, I mean.'

'But we talked about that.'

'We didn't. Not really.'

'So what do you think?'

'I know it would be horrible,' Colette said, 'but we could do it. If it's only for three years, if we were in the same city, if I could see you every day or almost every day… I mean, people put up with worse.' The doubt that kept niggling away under the surface thrust its head up again. *If Peter couldn't hack it…* But Peter's situation was different in all sorts of ways, she told herself. 'Don't they?'

283

'They do,' Lydia admitted cautiously. 'Are you sure?'

'If it's the way to make it work. Like I said. I don't want to hold you back.'

'Would you ever remember to eat dinner if you lived on your own?'

'It's probably about time I learned how to do that anyway. Learned how to stop being a complete disaster.' Privately, she was terrified by the idea.

'You're *not* a complete disaster.'

Colette disproved her point by bursting suddenly and humiliatingly into tears.

Lydia stopped, and made her take off her rucksack, and found her a tissue, and waved away a concerned passer-by. 'One thing I've noticed about you,' she said, very gently, 'is that when you start talking like that, like you think you're the worst person in the world, it's often when you're very, very, tired.'

Colette thought that both things could be true. 'So?'

'So I'm not going to argue with you about it until you've had some sleep.'

Lydia was considerably more irritating when she was deliberately not arguing. And sometimes that would needle Colette so much that she would force the argument out into the open, but tonight... Lydia was right about one thing, at least: she was very tired. 'You're too nice to me.'

Lydia smiled, apparently not willing to argue about that, either. 'Come on,' she said. 'Let's go home.'

## November

*Happy birthday Colette! Quarter of a century!*
*Lots of love from*
*Mum and Dad xxx*

Left to herself, Colette would probably not have done anything to mark her birthday at all. And Lydia had other things to be worrying about. So it was probably just as well that Chris and Hannah and the children charged into Stancester for a grand family lunch.

'That big pub out on the retail park,' Lydia had said, when consulted on the matter. 'With the ball pit.'

Which was why Colette was now sitting at a table covered in half-finished plates of chips and beans, watching her nieces and nephew work off some of the energy they had just taken in. Olivia was flailing around in the ball pit, rather solemnly, as if she knew that this was what she was *meant* to be doing but still wasn't convinced. Ben and Maisie were taking it in turns to pile balls into Lydia's cradled arms; she was kneeling up against the fence and emptying the balls back into the pit every time they both turned their backs. Chris sat cross-legged on the floor at the edge of the play area, occasionally calling out some encouragement to Olivia. The twins didn't need it. Colette feared that she was poor company, not speaking much during the meal, and not joining in the shenanigans now.

Hannah was finishing up Ben's abandoned chips. 'Well,' she said, 'don't we take you to all the classy places?'

Colette laughed. 'Better a dinner of chips with friends...'

'Well, it's very nice to see you.'

'You too, and the kids. And I suppose my brother would sulk if I didn't say, him too.'

'He's all right, is your brother.' She smiled. 'So. Twenty-five.'

'I know. It doesn't feel like anything special.' Maybe it would break upon her with a fanfare of trumpets on Monday morning. It didn't seem likely.

She looked thoughtfully at Colette for a moment before saying, 'If it's any consolation, I don't remember mine at all.'

Colette couldn't remember how old Hannah was. 'So that was, what, four years ago?'

'Nearer six.' Another pause. 'It would have been about two months after Olivia was born. I wasn't in a good place. That whole year is a grey fuzzy blur in my memory.'

'Oh goodness. I'm sorry.' Had she known? She'd been excited about becoming an aunt, but somewhat out of the loop, down in Stancester. She wouldn't have known. She hadn't ever thought to ask.

Hannah shook her head. 'Don't worry. I've been OK since then, thankfully. Just as well, with two to deal with the second time round.' Again she looked at Colette, narrowing her eyes. 'Actually, I think things do tend to get easier as you get older. I wouldn't go back to my twenties if you paid me.' She watched the scene in the ball pit for a moment. 'If I don't get round to telling Lydia she's brilliant before we have to go, will you tell her from me?'

She glowed. 'Of course.'

Hannah turned almost all the way back around to face her. 'So I understand this is crunch time for her? This is the big interview?'

'Starting on Thursday, yes.'

Maisie had made a break for it, clambering up onto a chair and planting her hand on a dirty plate. Now she reached her arms as far as they would go around Hannah's waist. 'Oh, sweetie, *no*. Look – Give me your hands. Both hands.' Hannah wiped her down and asked Colette, 'And you're waiting on the result to see if you're allowed to get married?'

She had heard the same sentiment in almost exactly the same

wording from her mother earlier in the day. 'I wouldn't put it *quite* like that,' she said, for the second time. 'I mean, if she gets through then we definitely can't get married, but that doesn't necessarily mean that if she doesn't we'll run straight down to City Hall.'

Hannah was dabbing at a tomato sauce mark on her jumper, but she was listening. 'Because she might go for it again, you mean...? What's that, Maisie? A red ball? Lovely. Why don't you take it back to Auntie Lydia? Good girl.'

'Well, there's that, and...'

'And you don't have to just because your mum thinks you should.'

Colette smiled despite herself. 'Something like that.'

'It's all bullshit, really.'

'What is?' Colette asked, startled.

'Marriage. Oh, God, I shouldn't say it to you, probably, being religious and all. I really shouldn't say it to you. Sorry.'

'No, go on.' Colette was intrigued. She hadn't been paying much attention when Chris and Hannah got engaged; she'd been a bridesmaid at their wedding, which had been quite fun, in its way. Jess hadn't been on the scene, or maybe it had been very early days, before anyone else knew. It had just seemed like the normal progression of life, back then: your big brother found a girlfriend; he proposed; they got married. Now she wondered what it had looked like from Hannah's point of view.

Hannah shook her head. 'Like, the hearts and flowers stuff doesn't last, everyone knows that. And that's a good thing, because if someone doesn't love you once the hearts and flowers have fallen off, then what's the point?'

'Go on,' Colette said, again.

'Marriage is just a cover story, really. I meet someone for the first time, they want to know about me; I say, married, three kids. And then they think they know everything about me, but really it doesn't say anything, and the two of you can just quietly get on with being your own people.'

'OK.'

'Yeah. But the questions keep coming. They ask you when you're going to get married. Then you get married and they ask when you're going to have kids. Then you have one kid and they ask when you're going to have another one.'

'And now?' Colette glanced at the twins, who both now seemed to be lying giggling in the ball pit.

'Now I can't hear anything over the sound of screaming.'

Colette laughed.

'Seriously, though. There's nothing magic about it. At its best, it's two grown-ups trying to do *their* best, and that can be amazing, of course it can. But it doesn't turn someone awful into someone decent. And at its worst, if they are awful, then you're stuck with them; it makes it that much harder to get away.'

'Chris isn't awful,' Colette protested, and then realised that she might not know. 'Is he?'

'Oh, no, Chris is lovely.' She frowned, and Colette was unsettlingly aware of other stories, of a circle of acquaintance that overlapped only marginally with her own, of griefs and trials that she would never know about. 'I wasn't talking about Chris.'

He heard that, and looked round. 'Why not?'

Hannah called back, 'Because we've both known you long enough to have more interesting topics of conversation. Come and talk to your sister.' She stood up. 'Sorry,' she said. 'I've just been wittering at you.'

'It's fine,' Colette said. 'Honestly.' Although she wasn't sure what to do with any of it.

On Monday morning she walked up to campus, feeling the weight of another year lying heavy on her. Another year gone, and the thing still not done. A year to go, and the thesis not even begun. Another year gone, and nothing really interesting to put *in* the thesis.

She arrived in the Sciences Block even more despondent than when she had left home.

'Happy birthday!' Mariam said, as she passed, and Colette did her best to smile, and thanked her, and then reflected that there had probably been a reminder on Facebook. She resisted the urge to *look* at Facebook. Instead, she dug up the results that she had been working on before she went to Cambridge, and hadn't had the chance to look at properly. She had lost two weeks to this conference, at least. Not that it was probably –

'Oh,' Colette said. '*Oh.*' She spun round, and remembering too late that James wasn't there any more, said, 'Look at this.'

The words died to nothingness in the empty office.

She turned back to look at the screen. It could be a blip, she told herself. Probably was a blip. It fell within normal variation, just about. She might have been careless. She probably had been careless.

Oh, but if it was real...

She told herself that it didn't matter either way: even if it was only negative evidence, the ten thousandth way that *didn't* work, she had enough to write up and present as a useful contribution. She might end up as a footnote to the PhD of the person who solved the problem properly.

But this could be exciting. This could be the one way that *did* work.

She felt a stirring of long-dormant interest, the lovely sense of flow, of things coming together. But there was too much that needed checking, too many things that she might have got wrong, too much risk of this being a wild-goose chase, like everything else, for it to be worth risking getting carried away.

She wrote an email to Barry. It was surprisingly difficult to get the tone right: to convey her excitement without sounding hysterical; to request advice without sounding needy. The facts alone seemed increasingly unpersuasive.

With the excitement already beginning to dissipate, she sent it, and wondered what to do next.

'Having a good birthday?' Lydia asked.

'Oh,' Colette said, smiling quietly, 'it's all right, so far. You know. Normal day. Nothing special.'

'Really? Well, you seem to be in a good mood about it.'

'Well, I did find something. I just don't know whether I'm going to have time to do anything with it.'

'Will I understand it?'

'I don't know whether I can even explain it, yet.' She didn't add, *or whether there's anything there at all*.

Lydia looked expectant; Colette felt a superstitious dread that putting the thing into words might make it crumble away into nothing. She looked at her phone, instead.

*Jess Barker updated her status: Soooooooooo exciting! Just put the deposit down on our wedding venue. I was really worried we wouldn't find anywhere, but it is going to be \*perfect\*.*

'Well, bully for you,' Colette said out loud.

'What?'

'Oh, nothing,' Colette said, already aware that she had been bitchy, and feeling guilty about it. 'Just another wedding update from Jess.'

'Oh?'

She flopped into a chair. 'They've booked the venue. It all seems to be coming together *beautifully*.'

'Well, that's good.'

'It's not. It's sickening. You're far too nice to live.'

Lydia laughed. 'I'm not. I'm wildly jealous. But it's not as if my being jealous of other people will make things work out the way I want them, so what's the point in wishing them ill?'

It was a fair point. 'You're assuming that I think that their being married is a good thing.'

'Don't you?' Lydia's tone was dangerously calm.

She had surprised herself with that. 'Apparently not.'

'Why's that?'

Colette saw the trap she had been just about to blunder into. 'Oh, goodness. Not like that. I...' She examined her feelings, and found that she didn't have any. 'I don't think I actually care. Mild irritation presenting as disproportionate bitchiness.'

'Interesting,' Lydia said sceptically.

'I don't get it.' Colette thought as she spoke that perhaps it wasn't a good idea to say this out loud. 'It's not like I would ever want to get back together with her. Why can't I just be happy for her?'

'Something about your not being able to marry me, perhaps?' Lydia suggested.

'*Yes*,' Colette said, and then stopped to think about it. 'But that doesn't make any sense, because I honestly don't want to get married.'

Lydia raised her eyebrows. She repeated, in a very neutral tone, '*Honestly don't want to get married.*'

Colette opened her mouth, and shut it again. She wanted to say, *Not like that*, but she was not sure that it would have been true this time.

Lydia said, very calmly, 'Tell me more about that?'

'I didn't mean...'

'I don't want to have another argument. I just want to understand.'

Now that Lydia had named it, the new argument loomed menacingly in the corner of Colette's eye. She tried to ignore it. 'I suppose it makes sense, really. It's all the things I *should be* feeling. I should be feeling happy for Jess, because I'm a grown-up who can be on good terms with my ex. But I should also be jealous of her, because she's got something that we can't have. And I don't feel either of those things, so I just feel like a horrible person. I'm sorry,' she added inadequately.

Lydia said, slowly, 'I see. So the sense of having the wrong feeling gets transferred to not being happy about Jess.'

'Yes, because that's the one that people would understand.' She hid her face in her hands. She did not dare to look at Lydia: she must surely have hurt her badly.

Now Lydia was kneeling at her side, a gentle hand on her knee. 'Why didn't you tell me you were feeling like this? No, sorry, that's a stupid question, you've only just worked it out. Why did you think you weren't allowed to feel like this?'

'Because it's what everyone wants, isn't it? And if you don't want it you can't say so, because other people have fought so hard for it that you just look ungrateful.'

Lydia laughed. 'I think you can say so. Pip did, back in the spring, when we were talking about sacraments. She's proper old school: smash the patriarchy, destroy the institution of marriage.'

'That sounds like a lot of effort.' She added, miserably, 'I don't care what other people do.' Was that true? She didn't know.

'Do you know why *you* don't want it?'

Colette kept her hands over her face. She thought of what she had said to Peter. At last she said, 'I want you to be able to leave me behind if you need to. I don't want to be a millstone.'

'Colette, you're not. I would never leave you behind.'

'And that's the problem. You'd sabotage your whole life to keep me on course, and I'm not worth it.'

A swift, hurt expression crossed Lydia's face, but, rather than directly contradicting her, she said, 'Your parents. So far as I can see, they have a really good marriage.'

Colette nodded. 'I think so, yes.'

'But you're worried that we wouldn't.'

'I think that over the past couple of years I've come to realise how very unusual a good marriage is.'

'I see.'

'They've both got really strong personalities. Like, I can't imagine my mum being anything other than the person she is no matter who she was married to, or if she was married to nobody at all. My dad, too. But I didn't realise they were the exception rather than the rule. And then on the other side of the equation I see all these people who have had their personalities warped, their horizons narrowed, by being with people they really shouldn't be with, and can't stop being with. So, Jess's parents before they got divorced. Rory and Mel, maybe.'

'My parents,' Lydia said flatly.

Colette wondered if she wanted her to argue. She didn't argue. She couldn't have argued, couldn't have turned back the surging tide of grievances. 'And then there's James and Giselle – they had a really strong relationship before they got engaged, and the whole getting married process almost broke them up. It's like this huge force, this pressure, crushing people and crushing relationships. And I don't want any part of that, no matter how confident I might be that we could escape the pressure and be ourselves.'

'Then we don't get married.' Lydia was smiling as if it was the simplest thing in the world.

Colette drew an astonished breath. 'It would solve your immediate problem,' she conceded, 'but is that really what you want?'

Lydia thought about it. 'I think,' she said at last, 'that so far as I'm concerned we *are* married, or at least as married as we need to be, from a moral point of view.' She looked worriedly at Colette. 'All the tax and pensions stuff, that's not what you're worried about, is it?'

'I know I should be.'

Lydia waved that away. 'You're not worried about that. Here's what worries me: I feel married. You don't.'

'I feel like a stereotype,' Colette said. 'Commitmentphobic, unreliable, can't make my mind up...'

'The only reason you would get married is that you think you ought to get married,' Lydia observed. 'I'm not doing that.'

'I would do it if you wanted to.'

'There are two things at the moment that I really, really want, and they're incompatible. I can't have them both, at least, not until something changes that's far beyond my control. I've been praying for a sign about which of them I should give up. This might be it.'

'But I don't want you to give things up for me,' Colette said wearily. 'That's the whole problem. I want you to be free to make your own choices.'

'That's what you've done. You've set me free.' Lydia was glowing. 'When I thought that I was going to have to balance your happiness against the hypothetical people I might be called to serve, it was impossible. But if your happiness moves over to the other side of the scale, it becomes obvious.'

It couldn't be that easy, Colette thought. 'What if they do end up changing the rules? What if they decide that you have to get married?'

Lydia bit her lip. 'Then we return to this exact spot, don't we? Then we take a decision on whether I leave ministry or we get married. Or –'

'Or we break up.'

'Yes. And if we aren't married we'll have the freedom to do that.'

Colette thought that she detected the tiniest, unwillingly sarcastic, stress on *freedom*. She did not mind: it was proof that Lydia had understood. 'It can't be that easy.'

Lydia got to her feet, grinning delightedly. 'Oh, it won't be *easy*.'

She held both hands out to Colette, who took them and let Lydia pull her to her feet, feeling a smile spread across her own face. She said, 'Good God, you actually sound like a minister.' Laughing, she put a hand either side of Lydia's face, and kissed her. The giddiness drained away; she let her hands drop to Lydia's waist, and stood there looking into her lovely, loving face.

Lydia seemed to feel the same seriousness; she gazed back, eyes wide, lips slightly parted. 'You're sure?' she said after a few seconds.

'Very.'

'No, about the rest of it. About me doing this. About this thing being in our lives.'

Colette was tempted to say, *Are you?* But she knew that would not be fair: if Lydia had been on her own, she would already have made her decision. (If Lydia had been on her own, something inside her head pointed out, she would probably not yet have admitted to being who she was, let alone started exploring what she was meant to be.) 'I reckon I owe you one for the PhD,' she joked feebly.

Lydia answered it earnestly. 'A PhD's four years. This is the rest of my life.'

'Whatever I say, it will always be in our lives. Yes, I'm sure. If this is what you're meant for, then of course you have to do it, and I'll deal with your having to do it.'

Lydia smiled. 'You've been saying that all the way through, haven't you?'

Colette shrugged her shoulders. 'What else could I do?'

She half-expected Lydia to say that this was what marriage meant, but she only kissed her, gently, deeply.

Breathless, Colette made herself ask, 'How does it all work? What about living together? Could they make us get a civil partnership?'

'I'll ask,' Lydia said. Her face became grave. 'If I get through selection.'

'If,' Colette repeated, and wished she hadn't. She tried to make it better by saying, 'That's the thing,' and realised that she had made it worse.

Lydia said, 'We'll just have to wait and see, won't we?' and did not sound optimistic.

'You must be sick of saying that.'

'Sick of thinking it, too.' Lydia had been quietly arming herself for battle, or perhaps stripping herself bare for it, for months now. 'We'll know soon, for better or worse.'

'It should be for better. Either way.' Again she reproached herself for her clumsiness.

'What, you mean *God doesn't give you what you want, he gives you what you need?*'

'What? No! My feeling is, if you get turned down, God will have had very little to do with it.' Judging by Lydia's face, it seemed that she could still scandalise her. 'You must think it's what God wants for you, or you wouldn't have come this far.'

'Well, yes,' Lydia said, gravely, 'but you'll remember that I've been wrong about what God wants for me before. I'm trying not to let myself think that way. If I'm going to be turned down, I want it to be because I'm not called – not called to ordained ministry, I mean,' she put in quickly.

Colette had not, in fact, been about to wheel out the platitude about everyone being called to *something*. 'Mm.'

'I want it to be because I'm not called to ordained ministry, not because I'm gay.'

'Not because the panel is homophobic, you mean,' Colette said. She said to an imaginary Peter, *You see?* Out loud, she said, 'And what I meant was, if that's how it works you're better off out.'

*From: tina.audley@stancester-diocese.org.uk*
*To: lydiahawkins2@yourmail.com*
*Date: 13/11/17*

Hi Lydia,
Just a line to make sure you're clear on the timetable for this weekend. You need to arrive in Ely by 5pm on Thursday and you can expect to be done by 4pm on Saturday. It's perfectly possible to walk from the station to Bishop Woodford House, but you might prefer to take a taxi if your luggage is heavy.
   I know I've told you this before, but just to reiterate: there is a lot of waiting around, above and beyond what you'll need to work on your pastoral exercise, so you might want to bring a book – of course you can also visit the cathedral, explore the city, etc.
   Apologies again that I had to cancel our last meeting. You can be assured that I will be praying for you through this weekend and afterwards.
With very best wishes,
Tina


Colette spent Thursday and Friday in the lab as if they had been any other days; except that now she was wondering all the time what was happening in Ely, how the interviews were going, and overlaying everything with a layer of impotent prayer. Barry had not been seen in Stancester. There was a rumour going around that he was suing Tessa Carhart-Johnson. Colette hoped that this was not true, for everyone's sake. Nor had he replied to her email. She supposed that it wasn't as if it mattered; she probably hadn't been onto anything important, after all. She couldn't really bring herself to care, not with her future hanging on the outcome of the next few days, and nothing that she could do to influence it. She did not like coming home to an empty flat, and she tried to push away the knowledge that if Lydia had got through selection – if she was getting through selection, right at this moment – this would be what their lives would be like.

   She went up to campus on Saturday, too, and stayed until the porters started asking her politely if she hadn't finished yet.

   Then she walked back down to the flat, picked up the car, and drove straight to the station.

'I'm tired,' Lydia said. 'I have never been so tired in my life.'

She looked it, Colette thought: there were deep shadows under her eyes, and her posture was oddly hunched, as if she were having to make a conscious effort to hold herself up. Her hair was flattened on one side (perhaps she had fallen asleep on the train) and rumpled on the other.

'Have you eaten?'

Lydia shook her head. 'I wasn't hungry by the time I got to Paddington. They gave us a huge lunch and a huge tea.'

'About five hours ago, presumably?' It felt odd, being the one fussing over food.

'Yeah.'

'Let's get pizza. We can order it now.'

Lydia yawned. 'Good idea.'

'Got to keep your strength up.' She gestured at the station entrance. 'The car's just in the drop-off bit.'

'You brought the car. You are lovely. I –' She broke off.

Colette picked up Lydia's suitcase. 'You what?'

'I was going to say, I must see about driving lessons, but let's wait and see.'

'It's a useful skill, whatever happens.'

'That's true, but I don't know whether I'll be in the mood.'

'You could book them this week, before you know.'

'No,' Lydia said, 'I couldn't.'

Colette put her free arm around Lydia's shoulders. 'Fair enough,' she said. 'Let's go home.'

'So,' Colette said once they were back at the flat, 'how was it?'

'Horrible. Like being chopped up into bits and then having each bit prodded to see what it was made of.'

'Your pastoral...'

'Pastoral exercise. That was the easiest bit, actually, once I'd stopped panicking. Because, you know, it's a written assignment. Read the question, examine the evidence, write your response. And it turned out to be – something I knew at least something about. So that's something.' She laughed wearily. 'I'm sorry; apparently I can't talk any more. No, it was the rest of it that was grim. Waiting. And then interviews. And then more waiting. And then another interview. And this one guy who seemed to think it was a competition. And knowing that even then I was probably doing more to sabotage my chances than he was...' She fell silent.

Colette, feeling inadequate, said, 'Mm?', but Lydia shook her head.

'Not tonight. I can't do any more tonight.'

Colette fell back on the other supportive gesture in her repertoire. 'Cup of coffee?'

'Tea, please. Better not be coffee, this late.'

Privately, Colette thought it would be unlikely to make much difference – Lydia seemed exhausted – but the prospect of having her exhausted, miserable, and too wired to sleep, was not enticing. She kissed the top of Lydia's head and went to put the kettle on, asking as she did so, 'What happens now?'

'Now,' Lydia said, with a feeble attempt at a cartoon Eastern European accent, 'we wait.'

The buzzer sounded.

'Not for pizza, though,' Colette said, and left the kettle chuntering away to itself while she went downstairs to accept the delivery. When she came back, she found that Lydia had stretched her legs out on the futon and was apparently dozing off, one trouser leg rucked up, hair flopping forward over her eyes. Colette felt a sudden, shocking, surge of love and concern. *What if she hasn't got through?* Followed, immediately, by *What if she has?*

The kettle clicked off. Lydia, startled, opened her eyes, and relaxed. Colette placed the pizza box carefully in her lap. 'Tea's coming,' she said.

Lydia smiled fuzzily at her. 'Thank you.'

Colette made tea for both of them and came to sit next to Lydia, who swung her legs off the seat to make room for her. 'Pizza.'

'Yes.'

They ate in silence until Colette asked, 'What are we waiting for now? When will you find out?'

Lydia sighed. 'I did say.'

She almost certainly had, but Colette could not dredge up any memory of it. 'I'm sorry.'

'They'll be deciding now. They're not allowed to go home until they have.'

'Really? Wow. And then what? Will they email? Phone?'

'No, they write. They write to the bishop, and then the bishop writes to me; or his PA does. Because apparently we're the last diocese to join the internet age.'

'So there's no point waiting up.'

'Goodness, no. It'll be at least a week, anyway.'

'Then let's go to bed.' Colette stood up, sending a shower of pizza crumbs onto the carpet. (She would deal with them in the morning, she promised herself.) She held out a hand to Lydia, who glanced at what remained in her mug, frowned, and stood to join her.

The first thing that Lydia said the next morning was, 'I haven't got through.'

She said it with such certainty that Colette, who was still mostly asleep, thought for a moment that she had heard for definite. She made a sympathetic noise.

'I can't have got through.'

Colette sat up. 'What makes you say that? Just a horrible feeling?'

'I've thought of something I should have said, and didn't.'

'What?'

Lying flat on her back, Lydia shook her head. 'It doesn't matter now.'

Colette wriggled back down under the covers and put her arms around her. 'You must have done as well as you could in the moment.'

Lydia rolled over to face her. 'Yes, but... I don't think what I said was what they wanted to hear.'

'Peter said to me, ages ago, that they aren't necessarily looking for the right answers, they're looking at who you are as you answer the questions.'

Lydia sighed, a deep shudder that seemed to resonate down the length of her body. 'Right now, I'm not sure that helps.'

Remembering that it was Sunday, and hoping that it might be helpful, Colette asked, 'Do you want to go to church?'

'Yes.' Then, 'But Wardle Street, if that's OK with you?'

'Of course it's OK with me.'

And it was a relief for both of them to go to a service where nobody knew that anyone was waiting for anything.

They filled the uncertainty with the reliable padding of routine. Lydia went to work, and if this was her last stint of a nine-to-five job nobody there would have known it. Colette went to the lab, and was about as productive as she had been in the days before their whole future stood on a knife-edge.

Ten days later, on the last day of November, it came.

It was waiting in their mailbox when Colette came home: an A5 envelope franked with the diocesan logo, with the letter inside a little off-centre so that half of Lydia's name was obscured. She made a little stack of the rest of the post (takeaway curry menu; water bill; postcard from Georgia) and held it in the other hand to take it upstairs; then she had to put the whole lot down on the doormat to get her key into the lock and the door open. She put Lydia's letter in the middle of the table, looked at the washing up, sighed, and went back to the hall to take her shoes off.

She was frettingly aware of the letter's presence while she dealt with the rest of the post and the washing up, and while she sat on the futon and fidgeted with her phone, unable to settle to anything she could classify as useful. In the end she went and had a shower, but she kept thinking she heard the sound of the door opening or Lydia's tread on the stairs, and was out again in five minutes.

How best to support Lydia when she opened it? Colette had not anticipated being the first one to the mailbox on the day it arrived. Perhaps she should have left the letter there for Lydia to find herself; perhaps she should sneak it back down now. But what if Lydia caught her on the stairs? No: it had better stay where it was.

Would Lydia want her in the room while she read it? That, Colette thought, would depend on the news it contained. If it was good, it wouldn't matter; if bad, Lydia might well want the chance to compose herself. But she might equally want to have someone on the spot.

She remembered her saying, about something else entirely, 'I don't mind them knowing. I just hate telling them.' That was that, then. Colette dressed quickly in clean jeans and a green shirt, and combed her wet hair out to dry in its own time. Using the hair-dryer, she felt rather obscurely, would look selfish and unfeeling; more practically, it might well drown out the sound of the opening door.

For something to do, she returned to the drying up, and was therefore looking more virtuous than she deserved or had intended, when Lydia came in at last.

'Any post?'

'On the table.' Colette uncrumpled the tea towel and hung it on the cupboard door handle. She left the cutlery in the drainer, and remained facing the sink, running her fingers through a splashed pool of water, while she listened.

The tearing of the envelope; the rustle of the unfolding paper; and a change in the quality of Lydia's breathing – a stillness –

– Colette stepped to the kitchen doorway –

– knowing already that Lydia would have said something, if it had been easy to say –

– and found herself halfway across the room, arms tentatively extended –

– waiting for Lydia to put the letter down again –

– holding her, while she took long, controlled, deliberate breaths, and was rigidly calm in her arms.

'Go on,' Lydia said through gritted teeth. 'Ask me.'

'What's the news?' Colette asked with obedient jollity.

'They don't want me. Not now. Maybe never.' She forced out each word with a jerk and then was very still. Then she ripped herself clear and strode off to the bedroom.

After ten minutes Colette followed. Lydia was lying face down on the bed, her shoulders shaking. Colette sat down next her, and laid a hand on her back as if to feel her heartbeat.

Lydia rolled over and sat up. 'Sorry.'

'You don't need to be. Do I need to kill somebody?'

'I don't know who. Probably better not.'

Colette found Lydia's hand. 'Scapegoat,' she said.

'What?'

'The painting. You – did you ever see it? In real life?' She had remembered, with unexpected, intense vividness. A school trip, the class piling into a coach for a day in Birmingham. Traipsing around the botanic gardens. Sandwiches. The art gallery, and there, in amongst the moody knights and drooping ladies, that desert with its intense, alien, luminosity; the doomed, innocent animal. The only painting there, Colette thought, that had retained its power to shock through a century and a half.

'No. Why?'

Colette shook her head: it would have been difficult to explain.

'Scapegoat,' Lydia repeated. 'No. There was only one scapegoat at a time.'

'The worst of it is,' Lydia said, reading the report through a little later, 'is that they're right. And they're wrong. And I'm right and I'm wrong, and it's the right thing but the wrong time, and I'm also the right person but the wrong person.'

'I have no idea what you're talking about.'

Lydia covered a quarter of the page with her hand. 'It's not happening now because between the two of us we have far too much going on.'

'Too much going on?'

'Personal stuff. Family. They thought I was being protective of my parents and being protective of you.'

Colette whistled. 'They think I'm the same as your parents... *You* think I'm the same as your parents...?'

It was not fair to ask that question of Lydia; it was not fair at all to equate years of support and validation with years of rejection and wilful ignorance. And yet Colette could not help thinking that the panel had a point. Lydia had surely spent too much time and energy this last year cajoling and humouring her through the disaster that her PhD – her whole *life* – had become, had probably always been; and in return Colette had offered her only doubt and stupid scruples over the one thing that she had to give her; not that *that* was worth anything.

'You're nothing like my parents,' Lydia growled. 'What I could possibly have said to make them think you were in any way comparable...' She shook her head, anger replaced by doubt. 'I must have downplayed how important you are to me. Internalised homophobia? Or worrying about externalised homophobia from them?'

'I think,' Colette said bleakly, 'that they heard what you didn't tell them. That you've been putting a whole lot into keeping me going, and you don't get much back. I've ruined it for you. I'm sorry.'

'No! Colette, no, that's not true...'

It only took Lydia's touch to release the tears that Colette had been trying to suppress. But Lydia was weeping too; they clung to each other and sobbed.

Lydia blew her nose and said, 'The thing is, it *might* still be the homophobic thing. If I can scrape through on eight headings out of nine, and fail the test on relationships, and also happen to be gay, well, I can't help wondering...'

'Which do you think it is?'

'I can't answer that,' Lydia said at once.

Colette said, with a sense that winning this point would be a Pyrrhic victory, 'Then it could be either, and you believe that it could be either.'

She had never made Lydia cry before today, she thought.

'Yes,' Lydia said after a little while. 'I suppose you're right. Oh, but Colette, not like *that*.'

'But it is true, isn't it? You've spent the last year propping me up.'

'The propping's mutual.'

'But it's mostly you. You earn the money, you cook the food, you talk to me when my bloody useless supervisor won't...'

'That's a point,' Lydia said, with an air of surprise. 'I'm starving.'

'Oh,' Colette said, remorsefully. 'And it's my night.'

'Sandwich?' Lydia suggested, and Colette was furious with herself for making her have to think about it.

'Stay there,' she said. 'Cheese or ham?'

'Whichever.'

The worst of it, Colette thought as she buttered the bread, was that there wasn't space to be shocked or appalled, because it wasn't really a surprise. She'd always known that the Church was quite capable of screwing Lydia over if it seemed expedient to it to do so; and it seemed that it had. Outrage felt like self-indulgence. *You knew*, something told her in the back of her mind. *You knew. Don't you dare make a fuss about it. Don't you dare pretend you're surprised.*

But she was still angry about it; more angry, she thought, than Lydia was letting herself be, and she could not let her see. She'd said to Peter... But she couldn't involve Peter now; he stood on the far side of a divide. He'd been where Lydia was now; but she might never get to where he was; and Colette could heartily wish herself to be a long way away from either standpoint; if it was not for the fact that she was hardly going to abandon either of them now.

'Not that I'm much use,' she said out loud. She had done neither good nor harm to Peter's vocation, she thought; she had probably ruined Lydia's.

*She knows. She chose this.*

Lydia had said so over and over again.

And had she known what she was letting herself in for when she chose? No. But, Colette thought, who could ever know that?

## *December*

From: *n.r.russell@stan.ac.uk*
To: *b.d.parnell@stan.ac.uk*
Date: *01/12/2017*

*Hi Barry,*
*Just checking that you received my email of the 13<sup>th</sup>. I'd really welcome the opportunity to discuss these results and see whether you think there's any value in pursuing them.*
*Many thanks,*
*Colette*

He didn't reply to any of her emails, but he was in his office that first Monday of December, so Colette went to see him.

He looked up when she tapped on the glass panel of his half-open door; raised his eyebrows and beckoned her in. 'Colette. What can I do for you?' Then, before she could reply, he said, 'No, wait. It's that set you emailed me about, isn't it? Sit down.'

Surprised, she sat down on the low, padded armchair. 'That's right.'

He made a little show of searching through his emails; she made a point of looking away. After a minute or so he said, 'Here we are.'

'Mm.'

'Yes,' he said, opening the file. 'Yes,' he said, glancing through it. 'Yes.'

He swung his chair round to face her, put his glasses on, and, when he met her hopeful eye, took them off again.

She wanted to say, *well?* She didn't, just tilted her head interrogatively to one side.

'What did you think?' He gestured for her to draw the chair closer. It snagged on the edge of a tile. She stood up instead, so that she could point at the screen.

'I thought,' she said, 'that these first three sets didn't show

307

anything particularly interesting, but this fourth one had potential, because look, *here*, that's like nothing else, and I wondered whether that was worth following up.'

'Hmm,' he said, and he sounded, if not encouraging, then at least sympathetic. 'I think I agree.'

She wished he could have said so before, back when she stood a chance of being remotely enthusiastic about it. 'Oh. Good.'

His eyes flicked over the screen; he became withdrawn, absorbed. Colette began to feel almost as if she was intruding on a private moment.

At length he nodded, and pushed at the edge of his desk so that his chair rolled a little way backwards. He twisted a quarter turn clockwise to face Colette, and brought his right ankle up to cross over his left knee.

'Well,' he said, 'I'd want to double check all of this, of course.'

'Of course.'

'But if it's what it looks like, it's certainly worth looking into further.' He, too, seemed less keen than the situation warranted: his expression passed from interest through enthusiasm to regret. 'Tell me, Colette, what are you planning to do now that I've said it's worth following up?'

It had all the marks of a trap. 'Follow it up, I suppose,' she said, and hoped that she would sound funny if nothing else.

'Right. But *are* you planning to do that?'

'Well, I mean, I should. Shouldn't I?'

'No. I mean: how long do you have left?'

He was meant to *know* this, Colette thought. 'A year. Eighteen months, at a stretch.'

'You're including writing up time in that?'

She nodded. 'But not the viva.'

'Oh, well, who knows when that'll happen?' He flashed a conspiratorial grin. 'But seriously, my point is: it'll be tight, and you need to think about that.'

'Are you saying I should leave it? Just concentrate on what I've got?'

'What you've got,' he said, 'is fine. It's solid. It's not spectacular, but then science very rarely is.'

Colette wondered why that felt like a shock, when she knew it perfectly well. Then she realised: Barry had never seemed to believe it. 'What would you do, if you were me?'

'If I were you...' He shook his head. 'What are you planning on doing afterwards?'

She couldn't imagine an *afterwards*. 'I was assuming I'd look for a postdoc somewhere. But I've been having second thoughts, since... Well, since James left, I suppose.'

'James,' he repeated, and it took Colette a moment to identify the expression on his face as one of hurt.

'And things are up in the air anyway. My partner... Well, her plans have become more open, so we're both doing some rethinking.'

Already she was despising herself for using Lydia's agony to soothe Barry's feelings. She was half relieved, half resentful that he did not pursue the subject, saying instead, 'I know it's been difficult, with, er, with her mother. You seem to have coped very well with that: but if you, er, needed an extension on mental health grounds, we could see about that.'

It was a bit late for that, Colette thought; and she was not sure that she was coping at all. She said, 'It's just one of those things,' and prayed he'd leave it.

He did. 'It's such a shame about James. He could have gone a long way, you know. And I do understand why he left. I do feel responsible.'

Colette tried not to let her surprise show. 'I think he stayed as long as he could.'

Barry's brow furrowed. 'It does feel a bit like a betrayal. Another betrayal. But I do understand,' he repeated. He turned away from her to gaze out of the window, or at something beyond the window. Then he swung back round to face her. 'And that's why you need to think about your next steps. I don't want to talk about rats leaving a sinking ship, because I do believe in James in spite of everything, but it's only fair to tell you that you won't be such hot property as you might have been a year ago.' He looked blank, bewildered; then his eyes narrowed. 'You'll find that your diary isn't as full as it should have been. You'll find that meetings with the powers that be are suddenly full of insultingly inappropriate questions. You'll find that your career will stop dead, stagnate; you'll find yourself looking down the barrel of day after day, week after week, of utter boredom, and you'll have no hope of things ever changing. You'll have to accept that this – this is your life now. You'll find that nobody's interested in you, when they find out you were my student.'

'Not *that* student,' Colette ventured, doubtful of the wisdom of saying so.

A humourless smile cracked his face. 'Not that student. Indeed. And believe me, I'm grateful. I can't see that attacking me has done *her* much good, but I suppose the poor woman must have thought she had her reasons.'

Colette could think of nothing at all to say to that.

'And you *are* a student. After this, you won't be. You'll be on your own. You need to think about that, too.' He turned once more to look out of the window: an angle, Colette thought, that nobody ever saw in a TV documentary. They seemed to have got a long way away from the question of whether to follow up her intriguing results; in the last half hour, she thought, she'd learned more about Barry than about anything else. It helped, of course, that he was here, no longer an absence. And no longer a TV personality, no longer a vindictive Twitter troll, no longer the unpredictable mentor-power whose whims must be indulged before one could request one's due. In this moment, with his hands laid on the arms of his chair, with the fabric of his jeans wearing thin at the knees, with his gaze turned softly on nothing in particular, he was simply a human being.

And perhaps it was not reasonable to expect him to have the answers. So she said, 'So how about you double check my results? And meanwhile I'll think about whether to take them forwards?'

He looked back at her and raised his eyebrows. 'Don't you think it should be the other way around? There's no point in my checking something if you're not going to use it.'

'I suppose not,' Colette said, though she didn't see why someone else couldn't.

'Well,' he said, 'let me know what you decide. As I say, it's completely up to you.'

She supposed he meant that to be reassuring.

*From: peternathan@yourmail.co.uk*
*To: n.r.russell@stan.ac.uk*
*Date: 08/12/2017*

*Dear Colette,*
*Just a quick (and belated!) email to say how lovely it was to see you the other week. I wanted to apologise for anything I said that might have made things weird. Please forget it. I am trying to, without much success. You're too good a friend for me to want to spoil that.*

*Lydia let me know about the result of her BAP. Part of me is very angry on her behalf, and part of me thinks she's dodged a bullet. I'll email her separately, but in the meantime please give her my love and let her know I'm continuing to pray for both of you.*
*Peter*

'What on earth is he on about?' Colette said, out loud.

'Who?'

'Peter.'

Lydia came and looked over her shoulder, then, seeing that it was an email, said, 'Oh, sorry,' and moved away again.

'No, it's OK. If you can make any sense of this I'd be grateful.'

Lydia sat down next to her and held her hands out for the laptop.

'It reads to me,' she said after a little while, 'as if he'd asked you out and has only just realised that he was the one who made it awkward.'

'Yes. That's what I thought. He didn't, though. At least, if he did I didn't notice. And you'd think I'd be able to recognise the signs by now.'

'Well, if he hasn't done it for a while...' Lydia shook her head. 'You said he suggested a marriage of convenience. That sounds awkward.'

'Yes, but it was such a ridiculous suggestion that it clearly wasn't serious. Anyway, it was awkward at the time and he apologised at the time. And if he doesn't want to make it weird, why is he making it weird?'

'Maybe he's relived the horror somehow – you know what, I bet he's been to confession – and thought you needed to as well.'

Colette shook her head. 'No. It just doesn't feel like the same thing.' She frowned, trying to recall that strange evening in Cambridge. Because it *had* been strange, and Peter *had* been in a weird mood, saying odd things. There had been the comment about resuscitation dummies; but she had been the one who started that. But there had been something else: something that had felt wrong in an otherwise sensible part of the conversation...

'Quitting,' she said.

'What?'

'He said that some people are worth quitting for. I thought he meant you, of course: that if it came down to a choice between being with me and following your vocation then you'd be justified in choosing me. But if he meant that he'd be prepared to dump the whole lot if it meant I'd agree to go out with him...'

'That *would* be awkward.'

Colette was horrified. 'But he wouldn't, would he? He knows you and I are together; he knows I wouldn't do anything like...'

'Which is why he's apologising.' Lydia read the email once more, with an irate flush rising up her cheeks and her eyebrows flattening into an ominous straight line. 'He's got the idea of you mixed up with the idea of quitting, as things he wants to do – er, not like that – but knows he shouldn't, and he knows that because you're not going to mess me around you're a safe fantasy to play with.'

'*Really?*'

'Not that sort of fantasy. But if you look at this and the marriage of convenience thing, they both involve him having to stop training without it really being his decision. He'd jump off that particular cliff if you told him to.'

'I wouldn't, though. You of all people should know that.'

Lydia's face shed the anger that had been gathering, and became frighteningly vulnerable. 'I do. I'm not sure if Peter's noticed. And if on the even less likely chance I did marry him on your behalf it would be bound to collapse and we'd both be kicked out. Oh, it's such a *mess.*'

Understanding burst in. 'He's got what you want, and is trying to lose it.'

'He needs to talk to someone about it. Someone who isn't either of us.'

'Are you going to tell him that?'

'I was thinking I'd send an anonymous letter to the college principal,' Lydia said, with heavy sarcasm.

'It had better be Georgia. She won't be tactful, though. He'll hate it.'

'Tough shit. Somebody needs to say something straight.'

'Oh, so *that's* why it can't be either of us?'

Mercifully, Lydia laughed. 'Do you want me to get Georgia on the case?'

'I should do it, really.' She sighed. 'Can you help me write something?'

'To her, or to him?'

'Oh, goodness. Both.'

'I can try.' Lydia looked at Colette for a moment, an odd expression on her face. 'Mind you, he's right about one thing.'

'What?'

Lydia's expression resolved into a smile. 'You. You are worth quitting for.'

Colette did not believe it coming from Lydia, either. She wrote a sorry draft of an email while Lydia cooked pasta and stirred pesto through it, and then Lydia redrafted it while Colette did the washing up. After this Colette sent it, and then spent three hours aimlessly following links on Wikipedia in one tab and chatting to Rowan over Messenger in another until Lydia appeared in pyjamas and suggested that she come to bed. Colette then lost a further forty minutes to the internet before she noticed that her feet were freezing and her arm was cramping up.

Lydia had, sensibly, given up on her; she had fallen asleep with a book in her hand and the bedside light on. Colette rescued the book, changed, shivering, into pyjamas, clambered into bed and reached across Lydia to turn the light off. Lydia groaned but did not wake, and Colette lay staring into darkness for a long time.

*Some things are worth quitting for,* Peter had said. *You are worth quitting for,* Lydia had said. And Barry had said, *It's worth following up.* But he hadn't said it as if he'd believed it, hadn't spoken with anything like the conviction of either of the other two. He hadn't said it as if he believed that she was the best person to follow it up. It wasn't exactly an overwhelming vote of confidence.

But, she thought, Peter had meant quitting his own studies, not hers. What had Lydia been thinking of? She didn't have anything left to quit, except a temporary job. Did she mean that she, too, would have walked out of the vocations process if Colette had asked her to? Did she think that Colette was glad that she had been rejected? Was that true? It might be true. That was the awful thing. It might be true.

She woke in the light when Lydia got out of bed, was fleetingly aware of warm lips pressed to her forehead, rolled over, and slept again.

The next time she woke, Lydia was gone; her pillow was cold, and her pyjamas were folded neatly under it. So much Colette could tell without getting out of bed. She listened intently for any sounds of activity, but the flat seemed to be empty apart from her. There was a faint hiss of music coming from upstairs, and people were talking down in the courtyard. Men's voices. Not Lydia.

Colette looked at her phone. There were no messages, and she was alarmed to see that it was already half past ten. Then of course

Lydia had gone to work – but of course she hadn't, not on a Saturday. Perhaps she had gone out... To get milk. It was a plausible hypothesis. She couldn't be bothered to test it. She told herself sternly to get up and get dressed. This had no noticeable effect. She rolled onto her side and curled up. She read the news on her phone, and wished she hadn't. All of it was gloomy, and there wasn't anything she could do about any of it, except pray, she supposed, and her prayers hadn't been going anywhere for months.

If I'd been better at praying, she thought, Lydia would have got through. She rejected the thought immediately: she knew, she was surely a sufficiently mature Christian to know, that prayer didn't work like that.

Half an hour had passed, somehow. If Lydia had indeed gone for milk then she ought to have been back by now. And she had not texted... An awful, irrational, fear got Colette out of bed.

She wrote a text (try not to look paranoid): *Sorry, just woken up. Are you OK?*

In the interest of honesty, she replaced *woken* with *got*, then deleted the word altogether, and sent the message. Holding the phone in her hand lest she fail to hear it, she stalked around the flat, looking for clues. Lydia's bag was on the futon; but her keys were not on the hook. Her waterproof was gone. So were her walking boots.

She had found a plausible hypothesis by the time Lydia texted back, confirming it: *Yes, fine. Out for a walk. Do you want me to get anything on the way back?*

Colette sent, *Lunch, maybe?* and then reflected that, knowing Lydia, she could be halfway to Glastonbury and not planning to be back for lunch. She added, *Or dinner, whatever.*

The reply was *Dinner!* and a laughing face, and Colette felt a little better.

Lydia reappeared at sunset with her trousers splashed with mud and her rucksack heavy with vegetables. 'Stew,' she said. 'I got some yellow-stickered beef from the Co-op.'

'That works for me.' Colette realised with a jolt that she had not eaten, other than a slice of toast at eleven o'clock or so. 'Do you want me to peel anything?'

'Nah, don't worry.'

She winced at the unspoken *it'll be quicker if I do it*. It was probably true. Lydia peeled and chopped and sealed and stirred with more energy and commitment than Colette had mustered all day. She seemed to have walked herself out of her fury, into some kind of peace. Colette leaned against the door frame to watch. 'How far did you go?'

'Ten, twelve miles? Up as far as the Beacon and back again. I had lunch at the Fox.'

'Sounds good.'

Lydia turned to look at her, her face illuminated by a smile. 'It was. I think I could just about see the sea from the top of the Beacon. I mean, I might have been wrong, it was just a bluish smudge on the horizon, but it was lovely, whatever it was. And then, coming home, the light was glorious, all golden, but the air was so clear and still, and I heard a chaffinch.' She placed a lid on the pan and wiped her hands on a tea towel. 'There. Done. I'm going to have a bath while that cooks.'

Colette told herself that she could at least wash up the chopping board and knives, and did so. Lydia emerged half an hour later, pink and damp, her wet hair springing into curls.

Before she could change her mind, Colette spoke the words that had been niggling at her all day. 'So I guess we could get married now, if you wanted,' she said.

Lydia rolled her eyes. 'You could sound more enthusiastic about it.'

'Sorry,' Colette said, and tried again. 'We could get married now, if you wanted.'

'No. Because you're going to have to do better than that if you're going to persuade me that *you* want to, particularly after everything you've said.'

Colette said, 'But I thought the reason we couldn't was that the Church of England wouldn't like it, and since they've now...'

'Resigned their interest in the question?' Lydia said it with an ironic smile. She came over to Colette and put her arms around her. 'Please don't do this to yourself,' she said.

'Do what?'

She tipped her face upwards to look Colette in the eye. 'Please don't pretend that you... I don't know, that you don't exist, or that you don't have any preferences, or that if you do then they don't matter?'

But what was the point, Colette thought, when her preferences were *wrong*? 'I thought you wanted to...'

Lydia gave her a quick, frustrated, hug. 'And I know you didn't. What do you think I am? How can you think that I'd want this if you didn't?'

'Why shouldn't I say exactly the same thing?'

'Well, for a start, this is the status quo. And I'm happy with it, and you're not happy with changing it. So.'

Colette didn't say that she wasn't happy anyway. She knew that she had no right to.

When she didn't answer, Lydia said, with sweet seriousness, 'Colette. One of the most important things I've learned since I came out is that wanting things, or not wanting things, isn't *wrong*.'

Colette shook her head.

'And the fact that you don't want to do something isn't necessarily a sign that God *does* want you to do it.'

'Yes, but...' She wanted to say that Lydia had not always been enthusiastic about the idea of ordained ministry, but had set her hand to the plough and had not turned back. But they had reached the end of that furrow.

Lydia took both Colette's hands in hers. There was passion in her voice when she said, 'You've said over and over again that you don't want to hold me back, that if being married to you stopped me reaching my full potential for whatever reason then you wouldn't want to do it. Why is it different for me?'

Because she couldn't blame this one on the Church of England. She did not say that. 'Because it's important to you. And I can see that and respect that even if I can't understand it.' And because Lydia's positive inclination seemed to outweigh her generalised, suffocating, sense of negativity.

'But if we can't share that it's basically meaningless. That's not what marriage is, surely.'

'Oh, I don't know,' Colette said, trying to *sound* humorous at least. 'Sometimes it seems like that's exactly what it is.'

'For example?'

'For example... Oh, Rory and Mel and their kids-or-mission dilemma. They can't both have what they want, because what he wants is incompatible with what she wants.'

'Or it looks as if it is.'

Had Lydia thought of a way around it, or did she just think it was possible that one might exist? Colette didn't really care. 'So they're compromising and they're miserable.'

'I see.'

'Do you?'

Lydia nodded. 'I've been thinking, since Mum had her heart attack, of all the things she could have done and been, and hasn't, of everything that she'd never admit to regretting, if she even lets herself regret it, and I wonder how much of that was Dad and Proverbs 31. I can promise you: it wouldn't be like that for me. But if it's like that for either of us then I don't want to do it either.'

'What *would* it be like for you?' Colette asked slowly.

'For me,' Lydia said, 'it would be what we have now: living together, looking after each other, each of us trying to help the other be what she was created to be, however imperfectly, however often we turned out to be wrong about what that was. And it would be... a crown on that. It would be a choice. It would give us space to make us more fully ourselves. Do you know, Colette, how often I look at you and think how glad I am to be with you, how many bullets I've dodged?'

Colette made an unhappy little noise. She could not think herself much of a prize.

'Really. When I think of other choices I could have made, and been convinced that I was doing the right thing, and how terribly they would have turned out...'

'Like what?' Colette asked, and wondered whether, asking that, she was fishing for compliments or genuinely curious.

'Like going out with any Christian man who might have asked me. Like marrying one of them. Like spending a lifetime convincing myself that this was how things were meant to be, kidding myself that I was happy, telling myself that even if I wasn't it was the promise I'd made and I'd have to stick with it.'

'*Did* any ask you?' Colette knew it was curiosity this time. Lydia's first year at Stancester remained unknown territory: she rarely talked about it on any level beyond the superficial.

Lydia looked sheepish. 'Not really. I went to the Freshers' Ball with a guy called Rob, but it was all a bit weird, and afterwards I pretended we'd only ever been going as friends. And that was it.'

'Well, I suppose we already do the "for better, for worse" bit.' She thought about adding, *and the "in sickness and in health" bit, too*, but stamped hard on the impulse. She could not let herself start thinking like that; it was an insult to people with real sicknesses.

Lydia laughed gently. 'We do that. Are you going to ask, what's the point of getting a piece of paper to say so?'

'I suppose I could,' Colette said, 'but I wasn't going to.' For the first time, she thought that she began to understand; but she had always known that the piece of paper was not the point.

*Today we light the second candle on our Advent wreath and think of the prophets who looked forward to the coming of a Messiah. Good news might feel like it's a very long way away. But in fact it's just around the corner.*
Benjy's Bulletin, 10 December 2017

Eve had written a new song. Colette had to admit that it wasn't at all bad. It began with an excited verse in a marching rhythm, sticking close to one particular note:

*Fill your lamps, our Saviour-King is coming;*
*Fill your lamps, the bridegroom's on his way;*
*Fill your lamps, we eagerly await him;*
*Fill your lamps, for this might be the day.*

Then it opened out into a lyrical, expansive, chorus, climbing up through the scale a few steps at a time:

*Then wait in hope, and be faithful in the darkness:*
*the darkest hour comes just before the dawn,*
*Until from the tower you hear the watchman calling,*
*"The morning breaks! Our Saviour-King is born!"*

The verse was repeated (*Light your lamps*), followed by the chorus. By the third time (*Guard your lamps*) the congregation had got the hang of it and was singing with gusto. It ended with one final rendition of the chorus, with the last line sung twice. *Our Saviour-King is born*. Peter would have tut-tutted, Colette thought: they weren't quite there yet. But then the talk on *waiting expectantly* seemed unfairly mistimed. They *had* waited. They had waited, and now there was nothing.

That wasn't true. That was the sin of despair. But it felt true.

Then Lydia had to endure the sympathy of the congregation. And sympathy and coffee took them all the way through to lunchtime, and the afternoon fizzled out into darkness without anything much having happened.

Lydia had not called her parents since before she went to Ely, and she did not today. She had said, 'They can call me, if they want to know.'

Today, it seemed for a moment that they did. But it was Colette's phone, for once not on silent, that was ringing. It shrilled out and buzzed against the table where she'd left it on her way to the bathroom.

'It's Georgia,' Lydia called.

'Pick up,' Colette said, hurrying back over. She peered over Lydia's shoulder. Georgia's face filled the screen, grainy and yellowish in an unfamiliar light, but smiling.

'Oh, it's both of you. Excellent!' She sounded breathless, excited.

'How are things?' Colette asked.

'Things are good. Colette, all I can see is your chin. Yes, that's better.'

Colette thought, *they're engaged*. Then she thought, *Please, no, don't let them be engaged*. Then she thought what a horrible person she was.

'What's going on?' Lydia asked.

'I thought we should catch up before Christmas! Your card's in the post, by the way. What's going on is, I've been working with Natalie and I think we've got something that's got a whole load of potential!'

'Peter's Natalie?'

'Of course Peter's Natalie – who else?'

'Well,' said Colette, inadequately.

Georgia continued regardless. 'You know what we were talking about... Ooh, way back at Easter? Or was it even Lydia's birthday party? About how you just can't find music to suit actual real world choirs because it's all written for trebles and men in 1862 or whatever?'

'I remember,' Colette said, very confused.

'We're going to crowdfund for an anthology of flexible anthems. But not naff ones. Keep the melody line under an E so as not to frighten off the people who aren't really sopranos but can only sing the tune. Have an interesting alto line that can also work up the octave as a descant. Make the bass line optional. You know, get things written for the people that are actually, physically, there in the stalls. And maybe follow it up with one of canticles and mass settings if this takes off.'

'Wow, really?' Lydia seemed to be genuinely enthusiastic about this. Colette thought it very gracious of her.

'Natalie knows all these networks of women composers. And I talked to Gabe and he's really keen. And then I thought, oh, I'd better tell Lydia before he does!'

Lydia laughed at that.

'So, you know, if you have any texts you think we should set...'

'I will let you know,' Lydia promised.

Georgia asked, 'How are you two?'

'Surviving,' Lydia said. 'You know about the result of my...'

'Yeah,' Georgia said. 'I'm sorry about that.'

'Oh, well. It is what it is.'

'There'll be something else. Something better.' Georgia said it as if she was going to arrange it personally, and Colette almost smiled. 'How about you, Colette?'

'Also surviving. I thought I'd had a breakthrough, but I... I think it's going to take too long to look into.'

'Oh, shame,' Georgia said. 'But you don't need a breakthrough, do you? You've already done loads.'

'Well,' Colette said, 'I suppose I've found out how much I don't know.'

'I wish my Year Tens would,' said Georgia. Her tone changed. 'Oh, and Peter's going on retreat.'

Lydia said, 'That's probably a very good idea.' Colette was too relieved to say anything.

'At least, he hasn't booked it yet, but he's worked the dates out. I'll check back in a week or so to make sure he has booked, of course.'

Lydia smiled. 'Of course.'

'If he doesn't do it before Christmas, he'll forget about it. You know he will.'

He wouldn't *forget* about it, Colette thought, but something else would take priority. She knew the feeling herself. 'I know.'

They passed a few more conventional remarks between them ('Give our love to Will!'), and then Georgia rang off, saying she had lesson plans to finish. ('It's not *quite* close enough to the end of term to just stick a DVD on!')

Colette took the phone back and put it into the pocket of her jeans. She took a deep breath. 'I'm going up Vic Street.'

Lydia looked at her. 'OK.'

She took a coat, because she knew that Lydia would worry if she didn't, and shoved her trainers onto her feet without bothering to unfasten or fasten the laces. The tongues folded over themselves and rubbed. She walked fast, so that the raw air caught at her throat and her chest burned.

She had to stop when she reached the brow of the hill, and sat down on the wall outside the Baptist church. She was, she supposed, irrationally upset by all this. It was because she couldn't talk to Peter about it any more. More particularly, it was because she couldn't talk to Becky about this, or about anything.

What would she say to Becky, if she could? She hadn't needed to, until –

'Georgia phoned,' she said, out loud.

*Georgia phoned. I thought she was going to say that she and Will were engaged. That wasn't it. I suppose you know. If you know anything.* She did not like that thought. *You'd think it was hilarious, wouldn't you? I bet they will, though, sooner or later. But you'd be pleased if they did, wouldn't you? You didn't have to die for that to happen, you know. If you'd just kept shouting at them – well, shouting at Will – they'd have worked it out.*

She slid her hands into the opposite cuffs and clasped her forearms, feeling the chilly imprint of her fingers. *And this thing with me and Lydia getting married. If you were here you'd probably have pointed out that we could do it if we were Quakers and we'd have had an argument over whether or not you'd been obnoxious about it. Probably about ministry, too, which is why we can't do it in the first place. I don't know why she wants to do that. Peter's hating it.*

She laughed. *Adam would have been really obnoxious about it. You know I never really liked him. Maybe he was better once you got to know him. Does he talk to you? I suppose he talks to the version of you that he knew. It's the same thing. Would you two have got married? I always assumed you were going to, but maybe I'm wrong. You always did your own thing.*

She gazed out over the twilit city, the pinpoints of street lamps struggling through the fog. *It isn't fair. You shouldn't have died. You were too young and you had so much more that you were going to do.*

*I can't say,* it isn't fair, can I? *Life isn't fair. It happened. Human fallibility? Definitely the driver; maybe you, too. Will said they were too soft on her. You weren't there to defend yourself. Georgia did her best for you. And then everybody said that it wouldn't have brought you back. I knew that. I wanted to punch them all. I suppose you'd say that if they needed to say that for themselves then so be it.* She wondered whether that was, in fact, the sort of thing that Becky would have said, or whether she had picked it up from somebody else in the intervening years, and didn't like that thought, either. *I miss you. I miss you so much.*

She had her eyes shut, and so did not see Lydia approach until she opened them at the sound of her footsteps.

'Hello,' she said.

'Hi.' Lydia raised her eyebrows.

There was plenty of room on the wall, but Colette shuffled along, to make it obvious.

Lydia sat down. 'My mum phoned after you went out.'

'Oh?'

'I suppose it is Sunday.'

'It is.' Colette moved up closer to her.

'I don't know if Dad was out, or what.'

'What did you talk about?'

'Nothing much, really. Except. Well. The BAP. She phoned to see what happened, because I hadn't told her. She was...' Lydia sounded surprised. 'She was really nice about it.'

'Oh.'

'I don't think she would have been if I'd got through. And of course I didn't say why I didn't get through. Just let her think... I don't know what she thinks. I suppose this stops her having to think too hard about it. We're back to the status quo. Except of course we never will be...'

Colette wanted to ask, *Did she say anything about me?* But she didn't. Instead, she said, 'What do you think of this scheme of Georgia's?'

Lydia laughed. 'It's very Georgia, isn't it?'

'Changing the world through sheer force of will. Yes. She might even do it.'

'Single-handedly reform the English choral tradition?'

'Well, Natalie's in on it too,' Colette reminded her.

'True. I suppose that doubles their odds.' Lydia sighed. 'Maybe it's possible, to change it from the inside, to change it *enough*. And good luck to them. But at the moment, I just want to burn the whole thing down.'

'The choral tradition?'

That made Lydia laugh. 'Call that collateral damage.'

It was Colette's turn to cook, so she made a diversion to the Co-op while Lydia went home to put the kettle on. After some thought, she selected a packet of sausages and a bag of carrots, and got another pint of milk in case she felt up to making the sausages into toad-in-the-hole. On a whim, she got a bag of porridge oats as well. Flapjacks would be easy, and comforting. Perhaps she was over-reaching herself. Did she really trust herself with melted sugar? Well, it wasn't as if buying the stuff committed her to anything. She refused a carrier bag, knowing that she would regret it; but it really wasn't worth it for four items, however awkward they were... She set off towards home.

In fact, she managed to make both flapjacks and toad-in-the-hole, and in spite of everything it became a quiet, companionable evening of stodge and pyjamas and not going to the evening service and getting used to the way things were, now.

After they had eaten, she put the pans in the washing-up bowl to soak. She stretched up to the top shelf of the cupboard to put the syrup away – and, twisting back again, caught something with her elbow. It fell over with a dull clunk. To her dismay, Colette saw that it was the bottle of olive oil; it had come open and oil was spilling out across the worktop, dripping onto the floor around her feet. She grabbed at the bottle, and it slipped out of her hands and onto the floor.

Her howl of despair brought Lydia from the study.

'Don't move,' she said, when she saw what had happened. She tore off handfuls of kitchen roll; righted the bottle and then picked it up and stood it in the sink; laid paper down to soak up the oil.

Colette watched her, feeling utterly pathetic.

'That may be the end of those pyjamas.' Lydia had dropped to her knees and was working closer and closer to Colette; when she reached her, she picked up her right foot, and, with a fresh sheet of paper, wiped the oil away with a tenderness that Colette knew she did not deserve.

She wanted to say, 'You don't need to do that,' but she knew that trying to do anything herself would only result in more chaos; and now Lydia had moved on to her left foot.

'There.'

'I'm sorry I'm such a liability at the moment.'

'These things happen,' Lydia said cheerfully.

'Mostly to me.' She did not add, *And you end up dealing with the fallout.*

'Maybe you need an early night.'

Colette felt a stab of panic. Lydia wasn't prepared to go along with the pretence that nothing was wrong. When her phone rang yet again, she was partly grateful for the respite, and partly irrationally afraid that it was going to be one more thing that she would turn out not to have done.

Lydia looked up.

'Mine,' Colette said.

'Where is it?'

'On the table.'

Carefully, Lydia shuffled a little way backwards, away from the oily patch, before getting to her feet. She darted out of the kitchen as the phone kept ringing.

'It's your mum.'

Colette sighed. 'OK.'

Lydia accepted the call before it could ring off and handed the phone to Colette; then she started scrabbling in the cupboard under the sink.

'Hi, Mum!' She sounded far too bright.

'Hello, darling! How are things?'

'A bit fraught.' She described the oil incident.

Her mother laughed. 'Oh, dear. I can call back in ten minutes if that helps.'

'Lydia doesn't want me to move until she's cleaned it up,' Colette said, 'so I might as well talk to you while she does.'

'Well, that works for me. How *is* Lydia?'

Colette looked down at her; she was now using neat washing-up liquid on an old sponge to get the oil off the floor. 'She's doing OK. Thinking about her options. Deciding what to do next.'

(Lydia sat back on her heels and looked up on her, smiling: a wary smile, though.)

'So is she back at the council?'

'Yes, but she always would have been. They like her there.' Who wouldn't, she thought, who but the bloody Church of England? And yet she knew that given half a chance the Church of England would have taken her on; it was Colette they'd seen through, not Lydia; or, rather, they'd seen through Lydia's redundant effort to protect her, to conceal what a disaster she was, to clean up after her.

(Lydia was filling the washing-up bowl with water and lowering it to the floor.)

Her mother was asking, 'And how about you? What's the latest in the supervisor saga?'

'Gone very quiet. I mean, the saga has, and so has he. I thought I'd got somewhere, but he doesn't think it's worth pursuing.' For a moment, she felt a cold flicker of the excitement she had known all those weeks ago, when she'd thought she had something that might make a coherent whole, not just meaningless unconnected points of data.

'Oh, that's annoying.'

'Yeah.' (Lydia had laid newspaper down, and fetched a soft towel; she was drying Colette's feet with it, very gently.)

'Could you write that up anyway?'

'Not really. Maybe. I don't know.'

'I do think that it's time you spoke to somebody else in your department, because you're clearly not getting the support that you need in this.'

There had been a voice in Colette's head that had been saying the same thing to her for months, but admitting it was hard, and doing anything about it was impossible. 'Mum, I'm so *tired...*'

'Perhaps you need a break.' Her mother's voice was firm, but kind. 'I think you should talk to somebody. Are you registered with the medical centre on campus?'

'Yes. But I really do want to get this finished.' She knew that she was saying it because she knew that she ought to say it; was afraid that if she let go of the anchor of duty she would just go drifting off into procrastination.

'Sometimes, when I was training; in fact, once a month or so, I just used to say, *Fuck it! I quit!*'

Colette was irritated. 'You never did, though, did you?'

'No, but I didn't know that at the time, and anyway that wasn't really the point. The point was that I could quit if I wanted to. And knowing that I could walk away meant that I never had to.'

'I can't, though,' Colette protested.

Her mother's voice changed, grew grave. 'Colette. As a doctor and as your mother, I think I need to remind you that you can and possibly you should. Your wellbeing is far more important.'

It was, Colette thought, easy for her to say. 'I don't even know where to start with all that.'

There was a humorous edge to her mother's sternness when she replied: 'I'll write you a note if you like.'

'Maybe,' Colette said, and tried not to notice that she was close to tears. 'Maybe.'

Perhaps her mother had noticed. 'You look after yourself, OK?

Both of you. You *and* Lydia. It isn't worth all this.'

'OK, Mum.'

Prescription issued, her mother said her goodbyes. ('And let me know when you've decided when you're coming up at Christmas!') Colette pressed the *end call* button with a distinct sense of anticlimax.

Lydia looked up from the floor. 'How is she?'

'She wants me to quit,' Colette reported. She knew that it was not quite what her mother had said, but it had hardly been difficult to read between the lines.

'Mm?' Lydia's neutral expression was far too deliberate to be true. She held out a hand; automatically, Colette took it so that Lydia could pull herself up to a standing position.

'Well, I can't quit.'

Lydia led her gently out of the kitchen, into the living room. 'No?'

Perhaps it wasn't a question. Perhaps it was an admission. Colette said it again. 'I can't quit. I've got to finish it. What's the point of the last three years otherwise?' In her mind, she heard the obvious response: *sunk costs fallacy,* and did not know whether she was more grateful to or irritated with Lydia for not making it. 'I mean, I've come this far. Don't I deserve some proof of it?'

'There's the MPhil,' Lydia said gently.

'That doesn't count.'

'Well, I'd be impressed by it.'

Colette suppressed several unforgivable retorts, and said, 'It was what I wanted when I got it. Now it's not nearly enough.'

'And it's not enough that you've done the work?' Lydia was trying to let no emotion into her voice.

'Not really, no.' She heard the bitterness and couldn't do anything to curb it. 'I dare say it's petty, but I want the floppy hat and the gender-neutral title.' Too late she remembered that Lydia would not be getting her own gender-neutral title any time soon.

Too late, she remembered her own part in Lydia's rejection.

'That's reasonable enough.'

'Is it?'

'Yes. As you say, you've worked for it.'

'I –' she began, and could not continue. Everything she could possibly say led back to that indisputable fact, that Lydia's vocation had been torn up and flung back at her, and that it was beyond selfish of her to be indulging herself in this trivial angst while her own purpose still remained within her grasp.

'Say it,' Lydia suggested.

'I can't –' *Tell you*. 'I don't know –' *Who I am*. 'If I don't –'

Wave after wave, of guilt, fear, shame, battered her, left her choking, spluttering, knowing that she must not ask for help, for she had already dragged Lydia down with her once.

But Lydia had her arms around her, was holding her regardless, and Colette couldn't summon the strength of will to push her away.

I'll disappear, Colette thought, I'll shrink down to nothing and she'll let go and find she isn't holding anything at all. The idea was oddly comforting, but a sob burst from her, and suddenly she was crying, great ugly, gasping clots of tears, and still Lydia held her.

'Your top –'

'It doesn't matter.'

'I'm sorry...'

'You don't need to be sorry.'

It was not true. It could not possibly be true. 'I'm sorry. I'm awful.'

'You're not.'

'I'm useless. I shouldn't be dumping all this on you. *I* should be taking care of *you*.'

Lydia insisted, 'You *do* take care of me. You made flapjack.'

'And a giant mess that you had to clear up.'

'Fine. What about when I came back from the BAP?'

'What, getting pizza? It wasn't exactly...' Colette hesitated, searching for words that would not sound terrible. It had been the obvious thing to do. It was a practical response to a practical need. She sniffed, and settled for, 'I can't help feeling that real love would have looked more like a casserole ready waiting for you.'

Lydia waved that away. 'You came and picked me up when I was really exhausted. And pizza was perfect, honestly.'

'Yes, but I didn't know that.'

'Do you think you have to know?' Lydia asked with what seemed to be disinterested curiosity.

'Well, yes, I think so,' Colette said, surprised for a moment out of her tears. 'Otherwise it's just me being lazy, isn't it?'

'I really don't think you're lazy.'

But that, Colette thought, was not very relevant, because *she* knew she was. 'I just go through the motions of being a decent human being,' she said, disgusted with herself.

'You drove me to Hastings.'

'And I give money to charity and I phone my parents and I recycle, but it's all just because I know I'm meant to.'

'That makes you no different from anyone else, at least some of the time.'

'It's all I ever do. There's no actual feeling behind it; it's just the guilt. The what-kind-of-awful-person-am-I if I don't.'

Lydia came over to Colette and put her arms around her in a tight, unexpected hug. 'That's not true.'

But how, Colette thought, could she know? 'Don't. I'm not worth it.'

Lydia loosened her hold, but kept Colette's hand in hers. 'Even if that were actually the case,' she said, 'it wouldn't be relevant. As it is, all I can do is tell you that you're clever and kind and conscientious and honest and –'

The words rattled around Colette's head like pebbles in a plastic bucket. 'Don't,' she begged. 'I'm not, I'm really not.'

Lydia laughed sadly. 'Fine. I'd still love you even if you were the pathetic puddle of goo you seem to think you are.' And she did not let go of Colette's hand.

Colette did not have the energy to argue any more; she sank exhausted onto the futon. Still Lydia did not leave her: she came and sat next her and drew her in with warm, comforting arms, and Colette let herself hide her face in her shoulder and close her eyes. And they sat like that for a long, long time.

Colette woke, and immediately closed her eyes against a harsh spear of sunlight. Something was wrong: but it was only that she was not in bed, but curled on the futon with the duvet from their bed tucked around her.

She sat up, and found that she had kicked Lydia in the face. 'Ugh. Sorry.'

Lydia smiled up at her from where she was lying on a roll mat on the floor. 'Don't worry. That was more or less the idea.'

'Why are we in here?'

'I didn't want to wake you up, and I didn't want you to be alone.'

Colette felt hugely, overwhelmingly, undeserving. 'You didn't need to.'

Lydia let that one pass. 'How are you feeling?'

Like a desert, Colette thought. Arid, shrivelled, barren. She settled for, 'Headachey.'

Lydia nodded, unwound the sleeping bag and rug from around herself, and was off to the kitchen before Colette could point out that she was capable of getting herself a couple of paracetamol tablets and a glass of water. But the very thought of it was exhausting. When Lydia returned, she took the pills from her without protest, and swallowed them with a gulp of the water. Lydia sat down next to her, close, but not touching, and took the glass of water from her.

Colette wished she were closer; she longed for the warmth and the comforting solidity of her. Lydia leant back against the cushion, apparently quite content to remain there all day.

'Shouldn't you be getting dressed?' Colette asked after a while.

'I decided to take some leave,' Lydia said. 'Texted my manager. Don't worry. It's all fine.'

'Oh.' Yesterday, last night, rolled back into her mind, and she shuddered. Lydia passed the glass to her again. She took it distrustfully. It tasted cold and bright, and there was not nearly enough of it.

'Would you like some more?' Lydia asked, but Colette shook her head. She did not want her to leave her side.

'You're here.'

'I am,' Lydia agreed, as if it wasn't a miracle.

Daring, Colette shifted an inch closer to Lydia, so that they just touched at the elbows. Lydia responded, seemingly relieved, by putting an arm around her. Colette exhaled, letting herself relax into Lydia's side.

'I need to think.'

'Do you want me here?'

Colette shrugged her shoulders helplessly: she did want Lydia to be there, very much, but even acquiescing to her suggestion felt like an imposition. And she was not sure that she was actually capable of thinking; at least, not the measured, deliberate, thinking that would justify asking her to remain. She needed something to *offer*, she thought, not this morass of overwhelm and despair.

But Lydia seemed to be staying. She retrieved the duvet from the floor and wrapped it around both of them, and for some minutes Colette managed to convince herself that not everything was awful.

'We can't stay here all day,' she said after a little while.

'We could.' Lydia seemed to mean it.

'You must be getting bored. *I'm* getting bored.'

Lydia laughed, cautiously. 'Well, we don't have to if you don't want to.'

'We need some more olive oil. And ketchup. And probably washing-up liquid, now.'

'Shall we go into town, then?' Lydia asked, watching her face.

She shuddered at the thought of the noise and all the people in whose way she would get. 'I don't think I can face it.'

'We could just go for a walk.'

The idea felt unconscionably frivolous, with errands to be run, but Lydia seemed perfectly at ease with it. Colette looked at her sideways: she was waiting, patiently, to be told. Colette wished she would make the call herself. 'We could,' she managed. If it was something that Lydia wanted to do, then it probably wasn't selfish to go along with it.

Lydia nodded and, tucking the duvet in around Colette's shoulders, got up and bustled around. Colette stopped herself from calling out when she went out of sight (what was she, a baby?) but was more relieved than she would have liked to admit when Lydia reappeared. She had an armful of Colette's clothes, which she deposited next to her. 'Feel free to substitute anything, obviously; I just thought it might help to have a starting point.

'It does. It helps a lot.' She picked up a sock and looked at it. It was, she supposed, a perfectly good sock. Lydia watched as she put it on and then, apparently satisfied, went off to the kitchen.

She had managed to put on the other sock, a bra, a T-shirt, and her glasses by the time Lydia came back.

'Breakfast,' Lydia said. She had poured cornflakes into two bowls and made one cup of tea and one of coffee, but she handed the milk to Colette to sort out for herself.

'What time is it?' she asked.

'Getting on for eleven.'

'Oh. Sorry.'

'No need to be.'

Colette thought about the possibility of that actually being true, and ate her cereal.

'More?' Lydia asked when she was done.

She shook her head. 'No, thank you.'

Lydia took the bowls and spoons away. Colette could hear her rinsing them in the sink. She called, 'How's the floor?'

'Fine, this morning. It's dried off nicely. No harm done.'

'Oh, good. Thank you.'

Lydia came back around to her, drying her hands on her jeans. 'Let me know when you want to go out.'

She didn't, really. 'Let's do it now.' She wriggled out of her pyjama bottoms and into knickers and jeans while Lydia gathered together coats and scarves.

'Do you want to go anywhere in particular?' Lydia didn't seem surprised when Colette shook her head. 'Then let's head up Thorn Hill, and if we feel like it we can go on to Stanbridge for lunch, and if we don't we can come down again.'

'OK.' It sounded as good a plan as any.

She walked beside Lydia, her legs leaden, and every step demanding a conscious effort. Down the stairs, out of the building, out of the courtyard; out of the estate; over the main road and up the hill on the other side. Her shoelace came loose; she upbraided herself for not having fastened it properly in the first place, and trudged on. It had rained overnight, and the morning sun shone in the remains of puddles, glinted on windows, illuminated bare trees. The further they went up the hill, the larger the gardens became; it would be nice, Colette thought, to have a garden, one day, but she wouldn't trust herself to keep it under control. Her shoelace trailed behind her; occasionally she caught it with her other foot, and just managed to not fall over it.

Lydia said nothing, and seemed to be happy saying nothing; she just walked. Perhaps this was what she always did when she walked alone.

'I'm sorry,' Colette said at last, when they were very close to the top of the hill, 'I'm going to have to stop and sort this out. It's driving me up the wall.'

'That's fine,' Lydia said, with the faintest note of surprise in her voice. 'This bench?'

She sat down on it and watched while Colette raised her foot to the armrest and examined the shoelace. It was flattened and soggy, and the knot had worked itself too tight to loosen easily. She took off her gloves and tried with bare fingers, wishing she hadn't bitten her thumbnail down.

'Could you take the shoe off?' Lydia suggested.

Colette tried, but it was fastened too tight around her ankle to come off easily. 'Not really.'

'Oh, well. Do you want me to have a go?'

'All it needs,' Colette said, her eyes on the shoe, 'is a little bit of wiggle room.' And as she said it she felt a tiny slackening in the knot between her fingertips. She worked the nail of her forefinger in between the strands, turning it first one way and then the other, until the loop shifted and loosened. '*There.*' She unthreaded it from itself, drawing it through its own coils. It dangled from the hole like a dead snake. She felt a disproportionate thrill of satisfaction.

'Well done.' There was a teasing note in Lydia's voice, but a warm caress of affection, too.

'Are you OK? Not getting cold?'

'I'm fine. Come and sit by me.'

'I'm happy to move on, honestly.'

'Actually,' said Lydia, 'I was looking at the view.'

Colette refastened her shoelace, making a symmetrical bow and knotting the loops into each other for good measure. 'OK.' She went to sit next to her, glancing at her face. Lydia was gazing out into the far distance, calm, thoughtful. Colette wondered at her serenity.

'How long until you can go for selection again?' she asked.

If Lydia was surprised, she did not show it. 'Two years.'

Two years was a long time, Colette thought. Long enough for the PhD to be done, long enough for her to have found a job with set hours and measurable outcomes, perhaps even long enough for something to have shifted in the Church of England.

Lydia added, 'If I can bear doing all that again.'

'You said before that you couldn't see yourself doing it twice.'

'I might be wrong about that.' Her tone was almost apologetic. 'Or I might not. I don't feel like it's quite finished with me.' She shook her head fiercely. 'But if I do it again it'll be on my terms. I have to be able to say no, or it can't be a meaningful yes. That's what they've given me, turning me down. That's what I didn't have before. But if they can say no, then so can I, and even if all of us are wrong God will still work around us or through us or with us.'

'Well, you'll have two years to think about it.' Colette nodded to herself. 'That gives me time, too.'

'Time?' She sounded wary.

'Time for me to finish, if I'm going to, and then get things sorted out.'

'Which things in particular?'

'I'm not sure yet. I need to think.'

'Please,' Lydia said, 'please give me some idea.' Her control had slipped very slightly, enough for Colette to catch a mortifying glimpse of her worry, and to be stung once more with guilt.

'I'm sorry. I didn't mean anything about us.'

'No, I'm sorry. You don't need to tell me if you don't want to.'

But she did. 'I think,' Colette said slowly, 'that I want to finish my PhD.'

Blessedly, Lydia did not remind her that she had already said this. 'Yes?'

'Perhaps not straight away. Mum pointed out that I could ask for a break.' She stopped, overwhelmed once more.

'That sounds like quite a good idea.'

'Yeah.' It sounded flat even to herself.

'What's up? Do you not want to?'

'I'd need to go to the doctor. Get a sick note or whatever.' This felt impossible.

'Wouldn't it be the student welfare services? I could come with you,' Lydia offered.

'I couldn't ask you to.'

'You wouldn't need to.' Lydia hugged her fiercely. 'It's fine: I know how it all works. We went before, didn't we? After Becky?'

That was true. It wasn't unknown territory after all. Something in Colette's head tried to tell her that Becky's death had been a real problem, not like this pathetic blockage in her own mind.

But Lydia urged, 'Go on.'

'I think just a month or two would help.' *Just*. It seemed an eternity. 'And if I had a month or two without having to think about it at all, maybe I'd have the perspective to decide whether to follow up this new thing or just write up what I've got already.'

'And then, when you'd finished it?'

Colette appreciated the assumption that she *would* finish it. She said, as steadily as she could manage, 'I don't know.' To her surprise, the admission made her future seem no more blank than it had looked before.

'Not the postdoc?'

The very idea of it was terrifying: a monolith of a task, with no obvious approach. 'I *really* don't know. I don't think I want to rule it out. But maybe not the postdoc.' She didn't want to rule anything out: the postdoc, or leaving academia; finishing – or not finishing.

'Well, it's not as if you have to decide now.'

'I hate not knowing what happens next,' Colette said. She heard herself, and added, 'But I haven't known for ages, really.' A breeze lifted the ends of her hair.

Lydia let her arm rest around her shoulders, reassuringly close, but gentle. 'Join the club.' Her voice was rueful but contented, as if she'd found after all that it was not a bad club to belong to.

'You wanted to burn everything down.'

'Perhaps I don't need to. Perhaps I already have.'

Colette squeezed her hand. She said, very carefully, 'How do you feel about it?'

Lydia gazed out over the city. 'About not knowing what comes next?'

'Yes.'

'Remember when you said that you didn't want to get married?'

Colette did. 'Oh, no. I'm sorry.'

She chuckled quietly. 'No. Don't be. But it does feel a bit like that. It's freedom. It's whole worlds of possibilities I hadn't even thought of.'

Colette said, 'I used to think there were four possibilities.'

'How do you work that out?'

Her theory was already out of date. 'I finish and you get through; I don't finish but you get through; I finish but you don't get through…'

'Or it's a no for both of us.'

'Then, if you throw in marriage, it doubles the options. Except it doesn't, because it kills some of them straight away. But that's not really the point, because it's more than that, isn't it?'

Lydia nodded eagerly. 'It's much more. Being here, now, not knowing what comes next – it's not what I thought I wanted. I don't think I can even say that it's better or worse than what I wanted. It's in a completely different dimension.'

And Colette, whose field of view had been narrowing and narrowing for so long that she had forgotten what it was like to choose anything except the thing that was in front of her, over and over until she had forgotten that there was anything to choose at all, found that in that moment she could trust in the existence of this huge new perspective that Lydia seemed to have discovered. 'There's always more,' she said, letting her words shape, inadequately, her understanding. 'More to find out. More to know. More than we can see.'

Lydia smiled, perhaps at all of it. 'Thank God.'

Colette said, 'Amen.'

Then they were silent for a long time, sitting there together in the brave December sun, side by side, and they looked out across the city, its spires and towers; the grey-brown smudges of parks, the neat rows of houses, the egg-box concrete of the university and the glint of plate glass from the offices and the shops; the sinuous shining lines that were the roads and the river and the railway, snaking into the city, and through it, and out again until they narrowed into invisibility, lost in the gentle curves of the hills beyond.

## Also in the Stancester series

## Speak Its Name

A new year at the University of Stancester, and Lydia Hawkins is trying to balance the demands of her studies with her responsibilities as an officer for the Christian Fellowship. Her mission: to make sure all the Christians in her hall stay on the straight and narrow, and to convert the remaining residents if possible. To pass her second year. And to ensure a certain secret stays very secret indeed.

When she encounters the eccentric, ecumenical student household at 27 Alma Road, Lydia is forced to expand her assumptions about who's a Christian to include radical Quaker activist Becky, bells-and-smells bus-spotter Peter, and out (bisexual) and proud (Methodist) Colette. As the year unfolds, Lydia discovers that there are more ways to be Christian – and more ways to be herself – than she had ever imagined.

Then a disgruntled member of the Catholic Society starts asking whether the Christian Fellowship is really as Christian as it claims to be, and Lydia finds herself at the centre of a row that will reach far beyond the campus. *Speak Its Name* explores what happens when faith, love and politics mix and explode.

*Winner of a Betty Trask Award 2017*

*Finalist, North Street Book Prize 2016*

## Also by Kathleen Jowitt

## A Spoke In The Wheel

*The first thing I saw was the wheelchair.*

*The first thing she saw was the doper.*

Ben Goddard is an embarrassment – as a cyclist, as an athlete, as a human being. And he knows it.

Now that he's been exposed by a positive drugs test, his race wins and his work with disabled children mean nothing. He quits professional cycling in a hurry, sticks a pin in a map, and sets out to build a new life in a town where nobody knows who he is or what he's done.

But when the first person he meets turns out to be a cycling fan, he finds out that it's not going to be quite as easy as that.

Besides, Polly's not just a cycling fan, she's a former medical student with a chronic illness and strong opinions. Particularly when it comes to Ben Goddard…

*Shortlisted for the Exeter Novel Award 2018*

*Shortlisted for the Selfies Award 2019*

*Finalist, North Street Book Prize 2018*